THE COLLECTED WORKS OF
G. K. CHESTERTON

XII

D0869824

THE COLLECTED WORKS OF
G. K. CHESTERTON

XII

THE FATHER BROWN STORIES: PART I

THE INNOCENCE OF FATHER BROWN

THE WISDOM OF FATHER BROWN

THE DONNINGTON AFFAIR

With Introduction and Notes by
John Peterson

IGNATIUS PRESS   SAN FRANCISCO

CONTENTS

GENERAL EDITORS' INTRODUCTION

When the first collection of Chesterton's mysteries, *The Innocence of Father Brown*, was published in July 1911, a reviewer in *The Nation* proclaimed: "Mr. Chesterton has adopted a new form—ingenious, clever, and satisfying—for the exhibition of his brilliant ideas.... They are so rich in spontaneous gaiety, in psychological force, in original philosophy, in fecund criticism of human nature that they compare happily with Stevenson's stories of Prince Florizel."

This volume of *The Collected Works* includes the twenty-five Father Brown stories published before the beginning of the Great War in 1914. Chesterton returned to his detective-priest after a hiatus of nine years and Volume XIII comprises the twenty-six stories he wrote between 1923 and his death in 1936.

The final story in the present volume, "The Donnington Affair", is unique in conception and requires an explanation. Chesterton explained it a follows:

> The magazine method to which I refer consisted in publishing a detective story written by a new collaboration which rather resembled conflict. One writer was to invent the mystery and the other writer the solution. It was understood as a point of honour, I think, that even from the stand-point of the mystery-maker there should really be a solution. I remember that I myself had the honour of solving, or pretending to solve, a riddle of crime propounded by Mr. Max Pemberton. He undertook by a certain date to deliver a fresh, attractive corpse, and I undertook by a certain date to tell him where he had got it from.

Pemberton's presentation of the crime appeared in the October 1914 issue of *Premier* magazine. Chesterton's solution followed in the November issue.

The distinguished Chestertonian, John Peterson, of Barrington, Illinois, introduces Chesterton's Father Brown mysteries. Mr. Peterson, a founder and officer of the American Chesterton Society, is an editor and frequent contributor to *Gilbert Magazine*.

George J. Marlin
Richard P. Rabatin
General Editors

Dale Ahlquist
Patricia Azar
Joe Mysak
Associate Editors

A NOTE ON THE NOTES

Chesterton sprinkled his stories with literary and historical allusions many of which will be unfamiliar to today's readers. However, lest the annotations overwhelm the stories, the Father Brown volumes in *The Collected Works* include footnotes for only those allusions a reader must understand in order to follow the thread of the story and where the context does not provide sufficient information for a satisfactory guess.

EDITOR'S NOTE ON THE TEXTS

The texts for the two Father Brown volumes of *The Collected Works* are based, primarily, on the first British and first American editions of the original five Father Brown books: *The Innocence of Father Brown* (1911), *The Wisdom of Father Brown* (1914), *The Incredulity of Father Brown* (1926), *The Secret of Father Brown* (1927), and *The Scandal of Father Brown* (1935). I used the American version only when it offered extra material or when it was the obvious choice for clarity. I subsequently studied the differences between these texts and the original magazine versions of each story. Most of the differences were a matter of differing styles of spelling and punctuation in the two countries. Other differences, if significant, are referenced in the footnotes. My comparisons of texts were undertaken at the Marion E. Wade Center at Wheaton College in Wheaton, Illinois, which boasts a comprehensive Chesterton collection. The Center generously awarded me its 1996 Clyde S. Kilby Research Grant for this purpose and for which I wish to express my gratitude.

— John Peterson

Anthem Detection Club Dinner
1932

INTRODUCTION

The Father Brown stories appeared initially in English and American popular magazines beginning in 1910. They were collected in a series of five books beginning with *The Innocence of Father Brown* in 1911 and ending with *The Scandal of Father Brown* in 1935. The stories were then, as they are now, the most widely read of all of Chesterton's writings. Aside from the excellence of the stories themselves, these works have the advantage of appealing to two audiences. Both the avid reader of detective fiction and the avid reader of Chesterton will eventually decide to sample Father Brown, and many will stay to become his loyal fans.

Today and for some decades past, the standard length for detective fiction has been that of the short novel. This was not true when Chesterton turned his talents to the genre, for he followed the short-story format developed in the nineteenth century for readers of the new mass-circulation magazines.

In America in the 1830s, George R. Graham created *Graham's Magazine* by purchasing and merging two successful periodicals, *The Casket* and *Burton's Gentleman's Magazine*. The new enterprise offered its readers a variety of short features: fiction, essays, and poetry. Edgar Allen Poe served for a time as *Graham's* literary editor. Importantly, Poe contributed three detective stories—the first such stories ever written—beginning with "The Murders in the Rue Morgue" in 1841.

The detective-story plot formula is easily summarized. A mystifying crime is discovered and a convincing explanation proves elusive. The mystery deepens until the eccentric but brainy sleuth (not a member of the official police), studies the evidence in his own way, deduces the truth, and reveals the surprising solution at the story's conclusion. The sleuth then reappears in subsequent magazine stories to solve other puzzling crimes.

The first novel-length detective stories also appeared in magazines, with successive issues carrying the narratives in installments. Arthur

Conan Doyle's first two Sherlock Holmes stories, *A Study in Scarlet* and *The Sign of the Four*, were novels and were not a major success. As the first respected literary critic to write extensively on the genre, Chesterton argued that there are inherent weaknesses for murder mysteries spun out to the length of a novel. He noted that the authors often pad their stories by having the detectives chase the wrong suspects and follow false leads or by digressing into lengthy expositions of the setting in which the crime takes place, such as a hospital or a bank. But his foremost objection was this:

> The chief difficulty is that the detective story is, after all, a drama of masks and not of faces. It depends on men's false characters rather than their real characters. The author cannot tell us until the last chapter any of the most interesting things about the most interesting people. It is a masquerade ball in which everybody is disguised as somebody else, and there is no true personal interest until the clock strikes twelve. That is, as I have said, we cannot really get at the psychology and philosophy, the morals and the religion, of the thing until we have read the last chapter. Therefore, I think it is best of all when the first chapter is also the last chapter. The length of a short story is about the legitimate length for this particular drama of the mere misunderstanding of fact.[1]

Graham's Magazine remained number one in America until it was overtaken by *Harper's Weekly* in the 1850s. By the 1890s, *Harper's* and similar American magazines were selling so well in England that publisher George Newnes decided to start a British version. Aimed at the middle class, *The Strand* was down-to-earth, readable, and half the price of London's highbrow literary magazines. It was an instant success. One key point is that Newnes wanted each issue to be self-contained—there would be no serialized novels. Conan Doyle was a *Strand* contributor, and the July 1891 issue carried the first Sherlock Holmes short story, "The Red-headed League". It was immediately apparent that the short-story format was the perfect vehicle for Holmes.

[1] *Illustrated London News* (hereafter *ILN*), August 19, 1922, *Collected Works of G. K. Chesterton* (hereafter *CW*), 32:432.

The *Strand's* circulation soared and Conan Doyle and his detective became household words.

Although Poe was first to author a series of short detective stories linked together by a continuing central character, Conan Doyle saw in this idea the way to merge the novel-in-installments with the self-contained short story. He explained in his autobiography:

> Considering the various journals with their disconnected stories, it had struck me that a single character running through a series, if it only engaged the attention of the reader, would bind that reader to that particular magazine. On the other hand, it had long seemed to me that the ordinary serial might be an impediment rather than a help to a magazine, since sooner or later, one missed one number and afterwards lost all interest. Clearly the ideal compromise was a character which carried through, and yet installments which were complete in themselves, so that the purchaser was always sure he could relish the whole contents of the magazine. I believe that I was the first to realize this and 'The Strand Magazine' the first to put it into practice.[2]

Conan Doyle's triumph was not lost on *The Strand's* competitors. Soon there was a host of Holmes-like sleuths: Martin Hewitt, Dick Donovan, Dr. Thorndyke, Florence Cusack, The Man in the Corner, and many others. Unfortunately, none of these had the Sherlock Holmes magic, and today their stories seem artificial and contrived.

Chesterton said as much at the time. Of course he was a great admirer of Holmes and wrote, in 1922, "There have never been better detective stories", and, "I do not think that Sir Arthur Conan Doyle has ever been thanked enough for them."[3] But he was less happy with Conan Doyle's imitators. He deplored unlikely endings that introduce at the last minute the identical twin brother from America, or the secret society of Tibetan assassins, or the freshly invented poison that leaves no trace. He said that when, in the typical puzzler, a curate is quickly cleared of suspicion because he was barred from the scene by a high fence, we will probably learn on the last page that the curate had once been a pole-vaulting champion. "It always makes

² Arthur Conan Doyle, *Memories and Adventures* (London: John Murray, 1930), 113–14.
³ *ILN*, August 19, 1922, *CW*, 32:432.

me feel", he wrote, "that the last page is the worst, when the last page should be the best of all." [4]

He disliked the concentration on the mechanics of crime and detection and wanted more of the human aspects emphasized—motives and emotions, innocence and guilt:

> The only thrill, even of a common thriller, is concerned somehow with the conscience and the will; it involves finding out that men are worse or better than they seem, and that by their own choice. [5]

He wanted the authors of these stories to focus on domestic crimes enacted in familiar settings, with the action restricted to a short span of time, located in a confined place, and involving a small cast of characters or suspects. He conceived of the stories as a kind of literary game and demanded that the writers play fair by showing their readers all the clues and evidence known to the sleuth.

Chesterton argued that the stories should never take place in a den of thieves or in the midst of a gang of thugs. He recommended popular resorts and suburban homes, with the murders and robberies committed by neighbors or next of kin. The stories must have surprising resolutions, he believed, but with resolutions that might be guessed from clues and hints the author has both revealed and disguised. And, in his view, the focal point of the stories must not center on someone's ability to identify a telltale cigar ash or to interpret a peculiar footprint. At their heart must be human motives: greed, jealousy, pride, hatred, and fear; and he offered the example of the great Victorian novelists who had dabbled in the detective story form—Charles Dickens, Robert Louis Stevenson, and Wilkie Collins. Finally, Chesterton insisted that however complex the mystery might be made to appear, its eventual solution had to be simple enough to be explained in a single shout from the rooftops. His illustrative example was, "The Archdeacon is Bloody Bill!" [6]

---

[4] *ILN*, July 28, 1934, *CW*, 36 [forthcoming]. Collected in *As I Was Saying* (1936) as "About Shockers".

[5] Ibid.

[6] *ILN*, August 19, 1922, *CW*, 32:431. Collected in *Generally Speaking* (1929) as "On Detective Novels".

Chesterton did not claim a literary superiority for the detective story compared with the novels critics and academicians take more seriously. But he did claim that detective stories present a more accurate portrayal of life, packed as they must be with dangers and surprises. He pointed out that life itself is packed with dangers and surprises. He saw detective stories as a series of contests between individual free wills rather than as the conflict of impersonal forces. In his view, modern novels of psychological urges or social pressures are inferior in representing life because their outcomes are made to seem inevitable.

Chesterton's ideas captured the attention of the leading mystery writers of his day, ushering in the Golden Age of detective fiction and setting the tone and direction of the genre for a generation. It is indicative that when Anthony Berkeley founded London's Detection Club in 1929 one of its avowed purposes was to promote Chesterton's precepts. This small and select group included such detective-story luminaries as Dorothy L. Sayers, Agatha Christie, Baroness Orczy, Hugh Walpole, and Freeman Wills Crofts. Chesterton, of course, was duly installed as the club's first president, a position he held until his death in 1936.

Chesterton's own first attempt at writing mysteries came in 1904 when he published a series of stories in *The Idler* about a most unlikely sleuth, a reclusive former judge named Basil Grant. The stories are still in print in the collection titled *The Club of Queer Trades*, which has been included in volume VI of the *Collected Works*. The premise was that Basil's brother Rupert was a Holmes-struck amateur detective. Rupert investigated crimes and chased villains when actually, as Basil would invariably prove, there had been no crimes and there were no villains. Spoofing Sherlock Holmes was nothing new, but Judge Grant's approach was new. He used the moral wisdom he had learned from his years on the bench.

"Facts," murmured Basil, like one mentioning some strange, far-off animals, "how facts obscure the truth. I may be silly—in fact I'm off my head—but I never could believe in that man—what's his name, in those capital stories?—Sherlock Holmes. Every detail points to

something, certainly; but generally to the wrong thing. Facts point
in all directions, it seems to me, like the thousands of twigs on a
tree."[7]

Grant succeeded by ignoring the facts in favor of what he called "the
atmospheres". It was the seed of an idea that would blossom when
Chesterton's critical theories were put to the test with the Father Brown
stories.

Father Brown debuted in *The Saturday Evening Post* in July of 1910.
In a critical essay for *The Listener*, Chesterton's friend Monsignor Ron-
ald Knox repeated something he had heard about the origin of "The
Blue Cross":

> I believe it is true that Chesterton walked into the office of his agent
> and asked if there was any book the publishers wanted. "Nothing in
> your line, I'm afraid. The last thing we heard of was *The Saturday Eve-
> ning Post* wanting detective stories." "Oh, well, I don't know," he said,
> and sitting down there and then wrote the first of the Father Brown
> stories.[8]

The inspiration for making his detective a priest was provided by
another of Chesterton's friends, Fr. John O'Connor, the Roman Catholic pastor of St. Cuthbert's in Bradford. We have the story on Chesterton's authority as recorded in his *Autobiography* and as later confirmed
by O'Connor in his own memoirs.[9] It is a tale often repeated. The
two had spent some hours walking on Ilkley Moor discussing a variety of subjects when Fr. O'Connor disagreed with some of Chesterton's kindly views on begging and beggars. The priest was obliged to
inform his friend about some practices of professional beggars so
depraved and cruel that Chesterton was profoundly shocked. Not then
a Roman Catholic himself, Chesterton had assumed that priests were
less acquainted with such "glimpses of hell" than someone like himself, a Fleet-Street journalist and well-read man of letters. However,

---

[7] *CW*, 6:67.

[8] "G. K. Chesterton: The Man and His Work", June 18, 1941; as reprinted in D. J.
Conlon, *A Half Century of Views* (Oxford: Oxford University Press, 1987), 47.

[9] Chesterton, Chap. XVI, "The God with the Golden Key", *CW*, 16:312–31;
O'Connor, Chap. VII, *Father Brown on Chesterton* (London: Muller, 1937), 38–46.

as Father Brown would remark in the first of the stories, "a man who does next to nothing but hear men's real sins is not likely to be wholly unaware of human evil".

Shortly after their walk, Chesterton and O'Connor sat with two Cambridge undergraduates and chatted with them about art and music. When the priest left the room, the two young men remarked, with worldly condescension, on Fr. O'Connor and the cloistered innocence of priests. Chesterton's reaction bears repeating.

> To me, still almost shivering with the appallingly practical facts of which the priest had warned me, this comment came with such a colossal and crushing irony, that I nearly burst into a loud harsh laugh in the drawing-room. For I knew perfectly well that, as regards all the solid Satanism which the priest knew and warred against with all his life, these two Cambridge gentlemen (luckily for them) knew about as much of real evil as two babies in the same perambulator.[10]

Father Brown, the unassuming parish priest who understood evil, was born out of that conversation.

Chesterton made his priest's appearance as commonplace and conventional as possible. Father Brown was a short little man with a moon face and blinking, owlish eyes. He wore a black cassock, a clerical shovel hat, and carried a large, shabby black umbrella. As Chesterton explained,

> [I]t was his chief feature to be featureless. The point of him was to appear pointless; and one might say his conspicuous quality was not being conspicuous. His commonplace exterior was meant to contrast with his unsuspected vigilance and intelligence; and that being so, of course, I made his appearance shabby and shapeless, his face round and expressionless, his manners clumsy, and so on.[11]

Chesterton claimed that he took the vigilance and intelligence from his clerical friend but not the externals of Father Brown's appearance or manners. Fr. O'Connor admitted more than this: Father Brown's "flat hat is true to life", he wrote in his memoirs; and "the large

---

[10] *Autobiography, CW*, 16:318.
[11] Ibid., 314.

cheap umbrella was my defense against wearing an overcoat"; and as to the brown paper parcels in "The Blue Cross" with which Father Brown was burdened, "I carried them whenever I could, having no sense of style or deportment." [12]

Viewed in retrospect, the idea of a fictional priest-sleuth makes perfect sense. Part of the allure of the Golden Age formula derives from the contrast between the murderer and the detective—between the brutality of the one and the gentility of the other. The classical Great Detective is refined and fastidious (we need only think of Holmes, Miss Marple, Wimsey, and Poirot); he traffics in vulgar atrocities but is not touched by them, as are the detectives of the Hardboiled School of crime fiction. The detective who is also a clergyman might, in theory, press this contrast even further by offering saintly goodness rather than fastidiousness in opposition to the depravity of the criminals and crimes. Thus Father Brown.

As to the other characters in the stories, it is important to note that Chesterton remembered casual acquaintances not by their faces but by their ideas:

> Personally I am in a curious position; it is neither their names, addresses, nor details of physique that I can remember. I always remember people by their opinions. I remember what the man said to me in some far-off argument in the middle of Ludgate-circus. Therefore, if he says to me with a sort of beaming cunning (as he almost always does), "Now you don't know who I am, you know," then I can truthfully assure him that I do know his most secret thoughts, his central pillar of conviction, and the very backbone of his soul. The trifling fact that I have not the faintest notion of his name, or what he is, or where I met him, the mere fact that in this popular phrase I do not know him from Adam (except for the costume), is in no sense an invalidation of my claim that I know him spiritually, as he would be known in Heaven." [13]

His secretary, Dorothy Collins confirmed this. "He always remembered what he had seen and those with whom he had talked," she

[12] O'Connor, *Father Brown on Chesterton*, 39.

[13] "The Queer Memory", *The Daily News*, November 21, 1908, as reprinted in *The Chesterton Review*, May 1991, 148.

recalled after his death, "not so much by their faces as by their minds—for that is how he saw people." [14]

Chesterton's characters are invariably people with ideas. This is not to suggest that they are no more than masks for ideologies, as if Doctor Harris (of "The Wrong Shape") were nothing but a mouthpiece for Social Darwinism or as if Inspector Valentin (of "The Secret Garden") were Anti-Clericalism personified. Chesterton had a natural gift for creating lively characters who act on their convictions.

In 1904, for example, Chesterton began a highly original series for *The Fortnightly Review* in the form of a drama or script of the table talk of three politicians: a Laborite, a Tory, and an Irish Nationalist. Professor Denis J. Conlon, who edited these papers for *The Collected Works*, believes the work is crucial for anyone searching for the essence of Chesterton, and Professor Conlon is surely right. The title, echoing Hamlet, was *Times Abstract and Brief Chronicle*, and as the discussions unfolded the three men came to life not only as theoretical advocates but as flesh and blood human beings.

> THE COLONEL: You, my good Desmond, must have drunk somewhere about four large lagers in the course of this evening. But I would willingly see you drink four more rather than produce from your pocket the minutest particle of opium.
> MR. DESMOND: You are very kind. I don't mind if I do. Waiter, four more large lagers. Put them down to Colonel Bartram.[15]

George Bernard Shaw, following the series and noting Chesterton's mastery of dialogue and character, demanded that the younger man drop his other work and immediately author a drama for the London stage. For the Father Brown stories, the important point is that, as in *Times Abstract and Brief Chronicle*, each of the people who present themselves in the stories is a well-rounded character whose physical appearance, mannerisms, thoughts, and moral fiber are as original and real as any ever presented in detective fiction. Hence both Dr. Harris and

---

[14] "The Man at Work and Play", The *Tablet*, May 18, 1974, 477–79. Father O'Connor said much the same thing (op. cit., 37): "He remembered people less by name, face, dress, than by what they talked about. There he had them by heart."

[15] *CW*, 11:95–96.

Valentin act on their ideologies; but Harris, who fancies himself a dispassionate scientist, is betrayed by his very unscientific feelings of remorse; and Valentin's cold analytical mind gives way in the end to a fanaticism that crosses over into madness.

That the villains of the stories are heretics is the cornerstone of the Father Brown stories, and the relationship between heresy and sin, or belief and behavior, preoccupied Father Brown. It also preoccupied Chesterton, as evidenced by this famous passage from *Heretics*:

> [T]here are some people, nevertheless—and I am one of them—who think that the most practical and important thing about a man is still his view of the universe. We think that for a landlady considering a lodger, it is important to know his income, but still more important to know his philosophy. We think that for a general about to fight an enemy, it is important to know the enemy's numbers, but still more important to know the enemy's philosophy. We think the question is not whether the theory of the cosmos affects matters, but whether, in the long run, anything else affects them.[16]

The passage brings to mind Chesterton's recollection of comments he made to a reckless libertine whom he knew in his school days:

> "I have come, rightly or wrongly, after stretching my brain till it bursts, to the old belief that heresy is worse even than sin. An error is more menacing than a crime, for an error begets crimes."[17]

Father Brown was in full agreement with this. In the following passage, he delivers a mild rebuke to an Oxford don who had quoted with approval Alexander Pope's: "His [faith] can't be wrong whose life is in the right."

> How can his life be in the right, if his whole view of life is wrong? That's a modern muddle that arose because people didn't know how much views of life can differ. Baptists and Methodists knew they didn't differ very much in morality; but then they didn't differ very much in

[16] "Introductory Remarks on the Importance of Orthodoxy", *Heretics* (London: John Lane; Bodley Head, 1905); *CW*, 1:41.

[17] *The Daily News*, November 9, 1907. Collected in *Tremendous Trifles* (1909) as "The Diabolist".

religion or philosophy. It's quite different when you pass from the Baptists to the Anabaptists; or from the Theosophists to the Thugs. Heresy always does affect morality, if it's heretical enough.

This closely echoes Chesterton's,

> As a matter of historical fact, of course, conduct and character do definitely vary in relation to creed. The conduct of a person serving Moloch is not the same as the conduct of a person serving Buddha. The character that is modelled upon Thor is not the same as the character modelled upon Christ.[18]

Father Brown explains how this principle applies in practice as he exposes the criminal in "The Crime of the Communist":

> Do you recall what you were all saying in the Common Room, about life being only a scramble, and nature demanding the survival of the fittest, and how it doesn't matter whether the poor are paid justly or not? Why that is the heresy you have grown accustomed to, my friends; and it's every bit as much a heresy as Communism. That's the anti-Christian morality or immorality that you take quite naturally. And that's the immorality that has made a man a murderer today.

As the stories progress, Father Brown confronts error after error, and these are the very ideas Chesterton warred against in his journalism.

The correspondence with his journalism is often striking. In "The Actor and the Alibi", for example, Father Brown condemns the ideology that led to the crime in words that echo the remarks Chesterton had made in a column some months earlier in commenting on the Leopold and Loeb murder case in Chicago.[19] So also in "The Curse of the Golden Cross", written while Egyptology and King Tut were in vogue, Father Brown condemns the popular fascination with pagan artifacts by using the arguments Chesterton was employing at

___

[18] *ILN*, March 10, 1928, *CW*, 488. Chesterton concluded his argument with, "But the statement that we need not bother about the creed, because we bother about the character, is infernal nonsense and there is nothing more to be said of it."

[19] *ILN*, September 20, 1924, *CW*, 33:408–11.

about the same time in another of his columns.[20] Examples could be cited almost endlessly, because of the multiple villainies in the stories.

Furthermore, the legal criminal often uses the intellectual error of the story to hide his guilt or to cover his tracks. In "The Queer Feet" a thief uses the conventional and unconscious assumptions of both diners and waiters to pass unnoticed through an exclusive restaurant. So great is the gulf between the aristocratic diners and the working class waiters that their similarity of dress is never noticed (i.e., both wear formal evening clothes):

> "Oh, hang it all!" said the young man, "a gentleman never looks like a waiter."

In "The Ghost of Gideon Wise", a murderous coal-mining tycoon hides his conspiracy behind a popular misconception about the nature of Capitalism. Father Brown explains:

> There is undoubtedly a Bolshevist movement in the modern world, but what nobody notices is that there is another movement equally modern and equally moving: the great movement towards monopoly or the turning of all trades into trusts. That also is a revolution. That also produces what all revolutions produce. Men will kill for that and against that, as they do for and against Bolshevism.

Father Brown's strength as a crime solver in these cases is his vaunted incredulity when faced with false assumptions that hide the truth about the crime and the culprit; and the lessons of this sort of story have as much to do with the failings of the spectators as with the faults of the criminal.

Father Brown's moral point of view is consistent and implacable. It is a frontal assault on the most cherished doctrines of modernist thought. Neither the Progressive Leftists with their moral relativism and social engineering nor the Patrician Rightists with their moral bullying and economic greed escape Father Brown's reproach. The only characters the reader may safely eliminate from suspicion are reformed criminals and self-confessed failures; these everyday sinners are safe from Father

---

[20] *ILN*, February 17, 1923, *CW*, 33:44–46. Collected in *Generally Speaking* (1929) as "On Egyptian Influence".

Brown. He spends his energies confronting heretics whose foolish and pernicious ideas are the true villainies of the stories. Indeed, this approach has befuddled many a critic whose own philosophy may resemble that of one of Father Brown's heretics.

When the actor and biographer Hesketh Pearson was introduced to Chesterton for the second time, he expressed the fear that the older man had forgotten him.

"I remember you well", Chesterton assured him. "In fact you appear in one of my Father Brown stories." Chesterton declined to say which story. "It is a detective story", he said. "The least you can do is detect yourself." [21]

John Peterson

---

[21] *Nothing to Repent: The Life of Hesketh Pearson* (London: Hamish Hamilton, 1987), 95.

THE INNOCENCE OF FATHER BROWN

1911

To
WALDO AND MILDRED D'AVIGDOR

THE BLUE CROSS

Between the silver ribbon of morning and the green glittering ribbon of sea, the boat touched Harwich and let loose a swarm of folk like flies, among whom the man we must follow was by no means conspicuous—nor wished to be. There was nothing notable about him, except a slight contrast between the holiday gaiety of his clothes and the official gravity of his face. His clothes included a slight, pale grey jacket, a white waistcoat, and a silver straw hat with a grey-blue ribbon. His lean face was dark by contrast, and ended in a curt black beard that looked Spanish and suggested an Elizabethan ruff. He was smoking a cigarette with the seriousness of an idler. There was nothing about him to indicate the fact that the grey jacket covered a loaded revolver, that the white waistcoat covered a police card, or that the straw hat covered one of the most powerful intellects in Europe. For this was Valentin himself, the head of the Paris police and the most famous investigator of the world; and he was coming from Brussels to London to make the greatest arrest of the century.

Flambeau was in England. The police of three countries had tracked the great criminal at last from Ghent to Brussels, from Brussels to the Hook of Holland; and it was conjectured that he would take some advantage of the unfamiliarity and confusion of the Eucharistic Congress, then taking place in London. Probably he would travel as some minor clerk or secretary connected with it; but, of course, Valentin could not be certain; nobody could be certain about Flambeau.

It is many years now since this colossus of crime suddenly ceased keeping the world in a turmoil; and when he ceased, as they said after the death of Roland, there was a great quiet upon the earth. But in his best days (I mean, of course, his worst) Flambeau was a figure as statuesque and international as the Kaiser. Almost every morning the daily paper announced that he had escaped the consequences of one extraordinary crime by committing another. He was a Gascon of gigantic stature and bodily daring; and the wildest tales were told of his outbursts of athletic humour; how he turned the *juge d'instruction* upside down and stood him on his head, "to clear his mind"; how he ran down the Rue de Rivoli a policeman under each arm. It is due to him to say that his fantastic physical strength was generally employed in such bloodless though undignified scenes; his real crimes were chiefly those of ingenious and wholesale robbery. But each of his thefts was almost a new sin, and would make a story by itself. It was he who ran the great Tyrolean Dairy Company in London, with no dairies, no cows, no carts, no milk, but with some thousand subscribers. These he served by the simple operation of moving the little milk-cans outside people's doors to the doors of his own customers. It was he who had kept up an unaccountable and close correspondence with a young lady whose whole letter-bag was intercepted, by the extraordinary trick of photographing his messages infinitesimally small upon the slides of a microscope. A sweeping simplicity, however, marked many of his experiments. It is said he once repainted all the numbers in a street in the dead of night merely to divert one traveller into a trap. It is quite certain that he invented a portable pillar-box, which he put up at corners in quiet suburbs on the chance of strangers dropping postal orders into it. Lastly, he was known to be a startling acrobat; despite his huge figure, he could leap like a grasshopper and melt into the treetops like a monkey. Hence the great Valentin, when he set out to find Flambeau, was perfectly well aware that his adventures would not end when he had found him.

But how was he to find him? On this the great Valentin's ideas were still in process of settlement.

There was one thing which Flambeau, with all his dexterity of disguise, could not cover, and that was his singular height. If Valentin's quick eye had caught a tall apple-woman, a tall grenadier, or even a tolerably tall duchess, he might have arrested them on the spot. But all along his train there was nobody that could be a disguised Flambeau, any more than a cat could be a disguised giraffe. About the people on the boat he had already satisfied himself; and the people picked up at Harwich or on the journey limited themselves with certainty to six. There was a short railway official travelling up to the terminus, three fairly short market gardeners picked up two stations afterwards, one very short widow lady going up from a small Essex town, and a very short Roman Catholic priest going up from a small

Essex village. When it came to the last case, Valentin gave it up and almost laughed. The little priest was so much the essence of those Eastern flats; he had a face as round and dull as a Norfolk dumpling; he had eyes as empty as the North Sea; he had several brown-paper parcels which he was quite incapable of collecting. The Eucharistic Congress had doubtless sucked out of their local stagnation many such creatures, blind and helpless, like moles disinterred. Valentin was a sceptic in the severe style of France, and could have no love for priests. But he could have pity for them, and this one might have provoked pity in anybody. He had a large, shabby umbrella, which constantly fell on the floor. He did not seem to know which was the right end of his return ticket. He explained with a moon-calf simplicity to everybody in the carriage that he had to be careful, because he had something made of real silver "with blue stones" in one of his brown-paper parcels. His quaint blending of Essex flatness with saintly simplicity continuously amused the Frenchman till the priest arrived (somehow) at Stratford with all his parcels, and came back for his umbrella.[1] When he did the last, Valentin even had the good nature to warn him not to take care of the silver by telling everybody about it. But to whomever he talked, Valentin kept his eye open for someone else; he looked out steadily for anyone, rich or poor, male or female, who was well up to six feet; for Flambeau was four inches above it.

He alighted at Liverpool Street, however, quite conscientiously secure that he had not missed the criminal so far. He then went to Scotland Yard to regularise his position and arrange for help in case of need; he then lit another cigarette and went for a long stroll in the streets of London. As he was walking in the streets and squares beyond Victoria, he paused suddenly and stood. It was a quaint, quiet square, very typical of London, full of an accidental stillness. The tall, flat houses round looked at once prosperous and uninhabited; the square of shrubbery in the centre looked as deserted as a green Pacific islet. One of

[1] The priest's stop is given as Tottenham in American editions, perhaps because the editors thought American readers might confuse London's Stratford station with Stratford-upon-Avon.

the four sides was much higher than the rest, like a dais; and the line of this side was broken by one of London's admirable accidents—a restaurant that looked as if it had strayed from Soho. It was an unreasonably attractive object, with dwarf plants in pots and long, striped blinds of lemon yellow and white. It stood specially high above the street, and in the usual patchwork way of London, a flight of steps from the street ran up to meet the front door almost as a fire-escape might run up to a first-floor window. Valentin stood and smoked in front of the yellow-white bonds and considered them long.

The most incredible thing about miracles is that they happen. A few clouds in heaven do come together into the staring shape of one human eye. A tree does stand up in the landscape of a doubtful journey in the exact and elaborate shape of a note of interrogation. I have seen both these things myself within the last few days. Nelson does die in the instant of victory; and a man named Williams does quite accidentally murder a man named Williamson; it sounds like a sort of infanticide.[2]

In short, there is in life an element of elfin coincidence which people reckoning on the prosaic may perpetually miss. As it has been well expressed in the paradox of Poe, wisdom should reckon on the unforeseen.

Aristide Valentin was unfathomably French; and the French intelligence is intelligence specially and solely. He was not "a thinking machine"[3]; for that is a brainless phrase of modern fatalism and materialism. A machine only *is* a machine because it cannot think. But he was a thinking man, and a plain man at the same time. All his wonderful successes, that looked like conjuring, had been gained by plodding logic, by clear and commonplace French thought. The French electrify the world not by starting any paradox, they electrify it by carrying out a truism. They carry a truism so far—as in the French Revolution. But exactly because Valentin understood

[2] The reference is to the sensational and brutal Ratcliffe Highway murders of 1811, committed by a burglar named John Williams, whose victims included an elderly tavern keeper named Williamson.

[3] Chesterton refers to the American writer Jacques Futrelle's hyper-logical Professor Van Dusen, the fictional detective in the 1907 short-story collection *The Thinking Machine*.

reason, he understood the limits of reason. Only a man who knows nothing of motors talks of motoring without petrol; only a man who knows nothing of reason talks of reasoning without strong, undisputed first principles. Here he had no strong first principles. Flambeau had been missed at Harwich; and if he was in London at all, he might be anything from a tall tramp on Wimbledon Common to a tall toastmaster at the Hôtel Métropole. In such a naked state of nescience, Valentin had a view and a method of his own.

In such cases he reckoned on the unforeseen. In such cases, when he could not follow the train of the reasonable, he coldly and carefully followed the train of the unreasonable. Instead of going to the right places—banks, police stations, rendezvous—he systematically went to the wrong places; knocked at every empty house, turned down every *cul de sac*, went up every lane blocked with rubbish, went round every crescent that led him uselessly out of the way. He defended this crazy course quite logically. He said that if one had a clue this was the worst way; but if one had no clue at all it was the best, because there was just the chance that any oddity that caught the eye of the pursuer might be the same that had caught the eye of the pursued. Somewhere a man must begin, and it had better be just where another man might stop. Something about that flight of steps up to the shop, something about the quietude and quaintness of the restaurant, roused all the detective's rare romantic fancy and made him resolve to strike at random. He went up the steps, and sitting down at a table by the window, asked for a cup of black coffee.

It was half-way through the morning, and he had not breakfasted; the slight litter of other breakfasts stood about on the table to remind him of his hunger; and adding a poached egg to his order, he proceeded musingly to shake some white sugar into his coffee, thinking all the time about Flambeau. He remembered how Flambeau had escaped, once by a pair of nail scissors, and once by a house on fire; once by having to pay for an unstamped letter; and once by getting people to look through a telescope at a comet that might destroy the world. He thought his detective brain as good as the criminal's, which was true. But he fully realised the disadvantage. "The criminal is the creative artist; the detective only the critic," he said with a sour smile, and lifted his coffee cup to his lips slowly, and put it down very quickly. He had put salt in it.

He looked at the vessel from which the silvery powder had come; it was certainly a sugar-basin; as unmistakably meant for sugar as a champagne-bottle for champagne. He wondered why they should keep salt in it. He looked to see if there were any more orthodox vessels. Yes; there were two salt-cellars quite full. Perhaps there was some speciality in the condiment in the salt-cellars. He tasted it; it was sugar. Then he looked round at the restaurant with a refreshed air of interest, to see if there were any traces of that singular artistic taste which puts the sugar in the salt-cellars and the salt in the sugar-basin. Except for an odd splash of some dark fluid on one of the white-papered walls, the whole place appeared neat, cheerful and ordinary. He rang the bell for the waiter.

When that official hurried up, fuzzy-haired and somewhat bleary-eyed at that early hour, the detective (who was not without an appreciation of the simpler forms of humour) asked him to taste the sugar and see if it was up to the high reputation of the hotel. The result was that the waiter yawned suddenly and woke up.

"Do you play this delicate joke on your customers every morning?" inquired Valentin. "Does changing the salt and sugar never pall on you as a jest?"

The waiter, when this irony grew clearer, stammeringly assured him that the establishment had certainly no such intention; it must be a most curious mistake. He picked up the sugar-basin and looked at it; he picked up the salt-cellar and looked at that, his face growing more and more bewildered. At last he abruptly excused himself, and hurrying away, returned in a few seconds with the proprietor. The proprietor also examined the sugar-basin and then the salt-cellar; the proprietor also looked bewildered.

Suddenly the waiter seemed to grow inarticulate with a rush of words.

"I zink," he stuttered eagerly, "I zink it is those two clergymen."

"What two clergymen?"

"The two clergymen," said the waiter, "that threw soup at the wall."

"Threw soup at the wall?" repeated Valentin, feeling sure this must be some singular Italian metaphor.

"Yes, yes," said the attendant excitedly, and pointing at the dark splash on the white paper; "threw it over there on the wall."

Valentin looked his query at the proprietor, who came to his rescue with fuller reports.

"Yes, sir," he said, "it's quite true, though I don't suppose it has anything to do with the sugar and salt. Two clergymen came in and drank soup here very early, as soon as the shutters were taken down. They were both very quiet, respectable people; one of them paid the bill and went out; the other, who seemed a slower coach altogether, was some minutes longer getting his things together. But he went at last. Only, the instant before he stepped into the street he deliberately picked up his cup, which he had only half emptied, and threw the soup slap on the wall. I was in the back room myself, and so was the waiter; so I could only rush out in time to find the wall splashed and the shop empty. It didn't do any particular damage, but it was confounded cheek; and I tried to catch the men in the street. They were too far off though; I only noticed they went round the next corner into Carstairs Street."

The detective was on his feet, hat settled and stick in hand. He had already decided that in the universal darkness of his mind he could only follow the first odd finger that pointed; and this finger was odd enough. Paying his bill and clashing the glass doors behind him, he was soon swinging round into the other street.

It was fortunate that even in such fevered moments his eye was cool and quick. Something in a shop-front went by him like a mere flash; yet he went back to look at it. The shop was a popular greengrocer and fruiterer's, an array of goods set out in the open air and plainly ticketed with their names and prices. In the two most prominent compartments were two heaps, of oranges and of nuts respectively. On the heap of nuts lay a scrap of cardboard, on which was written in bold, blue chalk, "Best tangerine oranges, two a penny." On the oranges was the equally clear and exact description, "Finest Brazil nuts, 4d. a lb." M. Valentin looked at these two placards and fancied he had met this highly subtle form of humour before, and that somewhat recently. He drew the attention of the red-faced fruiterer, who was looking rather sullenly up and down the street, to this inaccuracy in his advertisements. The fruiterer said nothing, but sharply put each card into its proper place. The detective, leaning elegantly on his walking-cane, continued to scrutinise the shop. At last he said, "Pray excuse my apparent irrelevance, my good sir, but I should like to ask you a question in experimental psychology and the association of ideas."

The red-faced shopman regarded him with an eye of menace; but he continued gaily, swinging his cane. "Why," he pursued, "why are two tickets wrongly placed in a greengrocer's shop like a shovel hat that has come to London for a holiday? Or, in case I do not make myself clear, what is the mystical association which connects the idea of nuts marked as oranges with the idea of two clergymen, one tall and the other short?"

The eyes of the tradesman stood out of his head like a snail's; he really seemed for an instant likely to fling himself upon the stranger. At last he stammered angrily, "I don't know what you 'ave to do with it, but if you're one of their friends, you can tell 'em from me that I'll knock their silly 'eads off, parsons or no parsons, if they upset my apples again."

"Indeed?" asked the detective, with great sympathy. "Did they upset your apples?"

"One of 'em did," said the heated shopman; "rolled 'em all over the street. I'd 'ave caught the fool but for havin' to pick 'em up."

"Which way did these parsons go?" asked Valentin.

"Up that second road on the left-hand side, and then across the square," said the other promptly.

"Thanks," said Valentin, and vanished like a fairy. On the other side of the second square he found a policeman, and said, "This is urgent, constable; have you seen two clergymen in shovel hats?"

The policeman began to chuckle heavily. "I 'ave, sir; and if you arst me, one of 'em was drunk. He stood in the middle of the road that bewildered that —"

"Which way did they go?" snapped Valentin.

"They took one of them yellow buses over there," answered the man; "them that go to Hampstead."

Valentin produced his official card and said very rapidly, "Call up two of your men to come with me in pursuit," and crossed the road with such contagious energy that the ponderous policeman was moved to almost agile obedience. In a minute and a half the French detective was joined on the opposite pavement by an inspector and a man in plain clothes.

"Well, sir," began the former, with smiling importance, "and what may —?"

Valentin pointed suddenly with his cane. "I'll tell you on the top of that omnibus," he said, and was darting and dodging across the tangle of the traffic. When all three sank panting on the top seats of the yellow vehicle, the inspector said, "We could go four times as quick in a taxi."

"Quite true," replied their leader placidly, "if we only had an idea of where we were going."

"Well, where *are* you going?" asked the other, staring.

Valentin smoked frowningly for a few seconds; then, removing his cigarette, he said, "If you *know* what a man's doing, get in front of him; but if you want to guess what he's doing, keep behind him. Stray when he strays; stop when he stops; travel as slowly as he. Then you may see what he saw and may act as he acted. All we can do is to keep our eyes skinned for a queer thing."

"What sort of a queer thing do you mean?" asked the inspector.

"Any sort of queer thing," answered Valentin, and relapsed into obstinate silence.

The yellow omnibus crawled up the northern roads for what seemed like hours on end; the great detective would not explain further, and perhaps his assistants felt a silent and growing doubt of his errand. Perhaps, also, they felt a silent and growing desire for lunch, for the hours crept long past the normal luncheon hour, and the long roads of the North London suburbs seemed to shoot out into length after length like an infernal telescope. It was one of those journeys on which a man perpetually feels that now at last he must have come to the end of the universe, and then finds he has only come to the beginning of Tufnell Park. London died away in draggled taverns and dreary scrubs, and then was unaccountably born again in blazing high streets and blatant hotels. It was like passing through thirteen separate vulgar cities all just touching each other. But though the winter twilight was already threatening the road ahead of them, the Parisian detective still sat silent and watchful, eyeing the frontage of the streets that slid by on either side. By the time they had left Camden Town behind, the policemen were nearly asleep; at least, they gave something like a jump as Valentin leapt erect, struck a hand on each man's shoulder, and shouted to the driver to stop.

They tumbled down the steps into the road without realising why they had been dislodged; when they looked round for enlightenment they found Valentin triumphantly pointing his finger towards a window on the left side of the road. It was a large window, forming part of the long façade of a gilt and palatial public-house; it was the part reserved for respectable dining, and labelled "Restaurant." This window, like all the rest along the frontage of the hotel, was of frosted and figured glass; but in the middle of it was a big, black smash, like a star in the ice.

"Our cue at last," cried Valentin, waving his stick; "the place with the broken window."

"What window? What cue?" asked his principal assistant. "Why, what proof is there that this has anything to do with them?"

Valentin almost broke his bamboo stick with rage.

"Proof!" he cried. "Good God! the man is looking for proof! Why, of course, the chances are twenty to one that it has *nothing* to do with them. But what else can we do? Don't you see we must either follow one wild possibility or else go home to bed?" He banged his way into the restaurant, followed by his companions, and they were soon seated at a late luncheon at a little table, and looking at the star of smashed glass from the inside. Not that it was very informative to them even then.

"Got your window broken, I see," said Valentin to the waiter, as he paid his bill.

"Yes, sir," answered the attendant, bending busily over the change, to which Valentin silently added an enormous tip. The waiter straightened himself with mild but unmistakable animation.

"Ah, yes, sir," he said. "Very odd thing, that, sir."

"Indeed? Tell us about it," said the detective with careless curiosity.

"Well, two gents in black came in," said the waiter; "two of those foreign parsons that are running about. They had a cheap and quiet little lunch, and one of them paid for it and went out. The other was just going out to join him when I looked at my change again and found he'd paid me more than three times too much. 'Here,' I says to the chap who was nearly out of the door, you've paid too much.' 'Oh,' he says, very cool, 'have we?' 'Yes,' I says, and picks up the bill to show him. Well, that was a knock-out."

"What do you mean?" asked his interlocutor.

"Well, I'd have sworn on seven Bibles that I'd put 4s. on that bill. But now I saw I'd put 14s., as plain as paint."

"Well?" cried Valentin, moving slowly, but with burning eyes, "and then?"

"The parson at the door he says, all serene, 'Sorry to confuse your accounts, but it will pay for the window.' 'What window?' I says. 'The one I'm going to break,' he says, and smashed that blessed pane with his umbrella."

All the inquirers made an exclamation; and the inspector said under breath, "Are we after escaped lunatics?" The waiter went on with some relish for the ridiculous story:

"I was so knocked silly for a second, I couldn't do anything. The man marched out of the place and joined his friend just round the corner. Then they went so quick up Bullock Street that I couldn't catch them, though I ran round the bars to do it."

"Bullock Street," said the detective, and shot up that thoroughfare as quickly as the strange couple he pursued.

Their journey now took them through bare brick ways like tunnels; streets with few lights and even with few windows; streets that seemed built out of the blank backs of everything and everywhere. Dusk was deepening, and it was not easy even for the London policemen to guess in what exact direction they were treading. The inspector, however, was pretty certain that they would eventually strike some part of Hampstead Heath. Abruptly one bulging and gas-lit window broke the blue twilight like a bull's-eye lantern; and Valentin stopped an instant before a little garish sweetstuff shop. After an instant's hesitation he went in; he stood amid the gaudy colours of the confectionery with entire gravity and bought thirteen chocolate cigars with a certain care. He was clearly preparing an opening; but he did not need one.

An angular, elderly, young woman in the shop had regarded his elegant appearance with a merely automatic inquiry; but when she saw the door behind him blocked with the blue uniform of the inspector, her eyes seemed to wake up.

"Oh," she said, "if you've come about that parcel, I've sent it off already."

"Parcel!" repeated Valentin; and it was his turn to look inquiring.

"I mean the parcel the gentleman left—the clergyman gentleman."

"For goodness' sake," said Valentin, leaning forward with his first real confession of eagerness, "for Heaven's sake tell us what happened exactly."

"Well," said the woman, a little doubtfully, "the clergymen came in about half an hour ago and bought some peppermints and talked a bit, and then went off towards the Heath. But a second after, one of them runs back into the shop and says, 'Have I left a parcel?' Well, I looked everywhere and couldn't see one; so he says, 'Never mind; but if it should turn up, please post it to this address,' and he left me the address and a shilling for my trouble. And sure enough, though I thought I'd looked everywhere, I found he'd left a brown-paper parcel, so I posted it to the place he said. I can't remember the address now; it was somewhere in Westminster. But as the thing seemed so important, I thought perhaps the police had come about it."

"So they have," said Valentin shortly. "Is Hampstead Heath near here?"

"Straight on for fifteen minutes," said the woman, "and you'll come right out on the open." Valentin sprang out of the shop and began to run. The other detectives followed him at a reluctant trot.

The street they threaded was so narrow and shut in by shadows that when they came out unexpectedly into the void common and vast sky they were startled to find the evening still so light and clear. A perfect dome of peacock-green sank into gold amid the blackening trees and the dark violet distances. The glowing green tint was just deep enough to pick out in points of crystal one or two stars. All that was left of the daylight lay in a golden glitter across the edge of Hampstead and that popular hollow which is called the Vale of Health. The holiday makers who roam this region had not wholly dispersed: a few couples sat shapelessly on benches; and here and there a distant girl still shrieked in one of the swings. The glory of heaven deepened and darkened around the sublime vulgarity of man; and standing on the slope and looking across the valley, Valentin beheld the thing which he sought.

Among the black and breaking groups in that distance was one especially black which did not break—a group of two figures clerically clad. Though they seemed as small as insects, Valentin could see that one of them was much smaller than the other. Though the other had a student's stoop and an inconspicuous manner, he could see that the man was well over six feet high. He shut his teeth and went forward, whirling his stick impatiently. By the time he had substantially diminished the distance and magnified the two black figures as in a vast microscope, he had perceived something else; something which startled him, and yet which he had somehow expected. Whoever was the tall priest, there could be no doubt about the identity of the short one. It was his friend of the Harwich train, the stumpy little *curé* of Essex whom he had warned about his brown-paper parcels.

Now, so far as this went, everything fitted in finally and rationally enough. Valentin had learned by his inquiries that morning that a Father Brown from Essex was bringing up a silver cross with sapphires, a relic of considerable value, to show some of the foreign priests at the congress. This undoubtedly was the "silver with blue stones"; and Father Brown undoubtedly was the little greenhorn in the train. Now there was nothing wonderful about the fact that what Valentin had found out Flambeau had also found out; Flambeau found out everything. Also there was nothing wonderful in the fact that when Flambeau heard of a sapphire cross he should try to steal it; that was the most natural thing in all natural history. And most certainly there was nothing wonderful about the fact that Flambeau should have it all his own way with such a silly sheep as the man with the umbrella and the parcels. He was the sort of man whom anybody could lead on a string to the North Pole; it was not surprising that an actor like Flambeau, dressed as another priest, could lead him to Hampstead Heath. So far the crime seemed clear enough; and while the detective pitied the priest for his helplessness, he almost despised Flambeau for condescending to so gullible a victim. But when Valentin thought of all that had happened in between, of all that had led him to his triumph, he racked his brains for the smallest rhyme or reason in it. What had the stealing of a blue-and-silver cross from a priest from Essex to do with chucking soup at wallpapers? What had it to do with calling nuts oranges, or with paying for windows first and breaking them afterwards? He had come to the end of his chase; yet somehow he had missed the middle of it. When he failed (which was seldom), he had usually grasped the clue, but nevertheless missed the criminal. Here he had grasped the criminal, but still he could not grasp the clue.

The two figures that they followed were crawling like black flies across the huge green contour of a hill. They were evidently sunk in conversation, and perhaps did not notice where they were going; but they were certainly going to the wilder and more silent heights of the Heath. As their pursuers gained on them, the latter had to use the undignified attitudes of the deer-stalker, to crouch behind clumps of trees and even to crawl prostrate in deep grass. By these ungainly ingenuities the hunters even came close enough to the quarry to hear the murmur of the discussion, but no word could be distinguished except the word "reason" recurring frequently in a high and almost childish voice. Once over an abrupt dip of land and a dense tangle of thickets, the detectives actually lost the two figures they were following. They did not find the trail again for an agonising ten minutes, and then it led round the brow of a great dome of hill overlooking an amphitheatre of rich and desolate sunset scenery. Under a tree in this commanding yet neglected spot was an old ramshackle wooden seat. On this seat sat the two priests still in serious speech together. The gorgeous green and gold still clung to the darkening horizon; but the dome above was turning slowly from peacock-green to peacock-blue, and the stars detached themselves more and more like solid jewels. Mutely motioning to his followers, Valentin contrived to creep up behind the big branching tree, and, standing there in deathly silence, heard the words of the strange priests for the first time.

After he had listened for a minute and a half, he was gripped by a devilish doubt. Perhaps he had dragged the two English policemen to the wastes of a nocturnal heath on an errand no saner than seeking figs on its thistles. For the two priests were talking exactly like priests, piously, with learning and leisure, about the most aerial enigmas of theology. The little Essex priest spoke the more simply, with his round face turned to the strengthening stars; the other talked with his head bowed, as if he were not even worthy to look at them. But no more innocently clerical conversation could have been heard in any white Italian cloister or black Spanish cathedral.

The first he heard was the tail of one of Father Brown's sentences, which ended, "... what they really meant in the Middle Ages by the heavens being incorruptible."

The taller priest nodded his bowed head and said:

"Ah, yes, these modern infidels appeal to their reason; but who can look at those millions of worlds and not feel that there may well be wonderful Universes above us where reason is utterly unreasonable?"

"No," said the other priest; "reason is always reasonable, even in the last limbo, in the lost borderland of things. I know that people charge the Church with lowering reason, but it is just the other way. Alone on earth, the Church makes reason really supreme. Alone on earth, the Church affirms that God Himself is bound by reason."

The other priest raised his austere face to the spangled sky and said:

"Yet who knows if in that infinite universe —?"

"Only infinite physically," said the little priest, turning sharply in his seat, "not infinite in the sense of escaping from the laws of truth."

Valentin behind his tree was tearing his fingernails with silent fury. He seemed almost to hear the sniggers of the English detectives whom he had brought so far on a fantastic guess only to listen to the metaphysical gossip of two mild old parsons. In his impatience he lost the equally elaborate answer of the tall cleric, and when he listened again it was again Father Brown who was speaking:

"Reason and justice grip the remotest and the loneliest star. Look at those stars. Don't they look as if they were single diamonds and

sapphires? Well, you can imagine any mad botany or geology you
please. Think of forests of adamant with leaves of brilliants. Think the
moon is a blue moon, a single elephantine sapphire. But don't fancy
that all that frantic astronomy would make the smallest difference to
the reason and justice of conduct. On plains of opal, under cliffs cut
out of pearl, you would still find a notice-board, 'Thou shalt not
steal.' "

Valentin was just in the act of rising from his rigid and crouching
attitude and creeping away as softly as might be, felled by the one
great folly of his life. But something in the very silence of the tall
priest made him stop until the latter spoke. When at last he did speak,
he said simply, his head bowed and his hands on his knees:

"Well, I still think that other worlds may perhaps rise higher than
our reason. The mystery of heaven is unfathomable, and I for one can
only bow my head."

Then, with brow yet bent and without changing by the faintest
shade his attitude or voice, he added:

"Just hand over that sapphire cross of yours, will you? We're all
alone and I could pull you to pieces like a straw doll."

The utterly unaltered voice and attitude added a strange violence
to that shocking change of speech. But the guarder of the relic only
seemed to turn his head by the smallest section of the compass. He
seemed still to have a somewhat foolish face turned to the stars. Perhaps he had not understood. Or, perhaps, he had understood and sat
rigid with terror.

"Yes," said the tall priest, in the same low voice and in the same
still posture, "yes, I am Flambeau."

Then, after a pause, he said:

"Come, will you give me that cross?"

"No," said the other, and the monosyllable had an odd sound.

Flambeau suddenly flung off all his pontifical pretensions. The great
robber leaned back in his seat and laughed low but long.

"No," he cried; "you won't give it me, you proud prelate. You
won't give it me, you little celibate simpleton. Shall I tell you why
you won't give it me? Because I've got it already in my own
breast-pocket."

The small man from Essex turned what seemed to be a dazed face in the dusk, and said, with the timid eagerness of "The Private Secretary":[4]

"Are—are you sure?"

Flambeau yelled with delight.

"Really, you're as good as a three-act farce," he cried. "Yes, you turnip, I am quite sure. I had the sense to make a duplicate of the right parcel, and now, my friend, you've got the duplicate, and I've got the jewels. An old dodge, Father Brown—a very old dodge."

"Yes," said Father Brown, and passed his hand through his hair with the same strange vagueness of manner. "Yes, I've heard of it before."

The colossus of crime leaned over to the little rustic priest with a sort of sudden interest.

"*You* have heard of it?" he asked. "Where have *you* heard of it?"

"Well, I mustn't tell you his name, of course," said the little man simply. "He was a penitent, you know. He had lived prosperously for about twenty years entirely on duplicate brown-paper parcels. And so, you see, when I began to suspect you, I thought of this poor chap's way of doing it at once."

"Began to suspect me?" repeated the outlaw with increased intensity. "Did you really have the gumption to suspect me just because I brought you up to this bare part of the heath?"

"No, no," said Brown with an air of apology. "You see, I suspected you when we first met. It's that little bulge up the sleeve where you people have the spiked bracelet."

"How in Tartarus," cried Flambeau, "did you ever hear of the spiked bracelet?"

"Oh, one's little flock, you know!" said Father Brown, arching his eyebrows rather blankly. "When I was a curate in Hartlepool, there were three of them with spiked bracelets. So, as I suspected you from the first, don't you see, I made sure that the cross should go safe, anyhow. I'm afraid I watched you, you know. So at last I saw you

---

[4] *The Private Secretary* (1884) was a frequently revived Victorian farce in which the title character was the extreme of timid eagerness.

change the parcels. Then, don't you see, I changed them back again. And then I left the right one behind."

"Left it behind?" repeated Flambeau, and for the first time there was another note in his voice beside his triumph.

"Well, it was like this," said the little priest, speaking in the same unaffected way. "I went back to that sweet-shop and asked if I'd left a parcel, and gave them a particular address if it turned up. Well, I knew I hadn't; but when I went away again I did. So, instead of running after me with that valuable parcel, they have sent it flying to a friend of mine in Westminster." Then he added rather sadly, "I learnt that, too, from a poor fellow in Hartlepool. He used to do it with hand-bags he stole at railway stations, but he's in a monastery now. Oh, one gets to know, you know," he added, rubbing his head again with the same sort of a desperate apology. "We can't help being priests. People come and tell us these things."

Flambeau tore a brown-paper parcel out of his inner pocket and rent it in pieces. There was nothing but paper and sticks of lead inside it. He sprang to his feet with a gigantic gesture, and cried:

"I don't believe you. I don't believe a bumpkin like you could manage all that. I believe you've still got the stuff on you, and if you don't give it up—why, we're all alone, and I'll take it by force!"

"No," said Father Brown simply, and stood up also, "you won't take it by force. First, because I really haven't still got it. And, second, because we are not alone."

Flambeau stopped in his stride forward.

"Behind that tree," said Father Brown, pointing, "are two strong policemen and the greatest detective alive. How did they come here, do you ask? Why, I brought them, of course! How did I do it? Why, I'll tell you if you like! Lord bless you, we have to know twenty such things when we work among the criminal classes! Well, I wasn't sure you were a thief, and it would never do to make a scandal against one of our own clergy. So I just tested you to see if anything would make you show yourself. A man generally makes a small scene if he finds salt in his coffee; if he doesn't, he has some reason for keeping quiet. I changed the salt and sugar, and *you* kept quiet. A man generally objects if his bill is three times too big. If he pays it, he has some motive for passing unnoticed. I altered your bill, and *you* paid it."

The world seemed waiting for Flambeau to leap like a tiger. But he was held back as by a spell; he was stunned with the utmost curiosity.

"Well," went on Father Brown, with lumbering lucidity, "as you wouldn't leave any tracks for the police, of course somebody had to. At every place we went to, I took care to do something that would get us talked about for the rest of the day. I didn't do much harm—a splashed wall, spilt apples, a broken window; but I saved the cross, as the cross will always be saved. It is at Westminster by now. I rather wonder you didn't stop it with the Donkey's Whistle."

"With the what?" asked Flambeau.

"I'm glad you've never heard of it," said the priest, making a face. "It's a foul thing. I'm sure you're too good a man for a Whistler. I couldn't have countered it even with the Spots myself; I'm not strong enough in the legs."

"What on earth are you talking about?" asked the other.

"Well, I did think you'd know the Spots," said Father Brown, agreeably surprised. "Oh, you can't have gone so very wrong yet!"

"How in blazes do you know all these horrors?" cried Flambeau.

The shadow of a smile crossed the round, simple face of his clerical opponent.

"Oh, by being a celibate simpleton, I suppose," he said. "Has it never struck you that a man who does next to nothing but hear men's real sins is not likely to be wholly unaware of human evil? But, as a matter of fact, another part of my trade, too, made me sure you weren't a priest."

"What?" asked the thief, almost gaping.

"You attacked reason," said Father Brown. "It's bad theology."

And even as he turned away to collect his property, the three policemen came out from under the twilight trees. Flambeau was an artist and a sportsman. He stepped back and swept Valentin a great bow.

"Do not bow to me, *mon ami*," said Valentin, with silver clearness. "Let us both bow to our master."

And they both stood an instant uncovered, while the little Essex priest blinked about for his umbrella.

THE SECRET GARDEN

Aristide Valentin, Chief of the Paris Police, was late for his dinner, and some of his guests began to arrive before him. These were, however, reassured by his confidential servant, Ivan, the old man with a scar, and a face almost as grey as his moustaches, who always sat at a table in the entrance hall—a hall hung with weapons. Valentin's house was perhaps as peculiar and celebrated as its master. It was an old house, with high walls and tall poplars almost overhanging the Seine; but the oddity—and perhaps the police value—of its architecture was this: that there was no ultimate exit at all except through this front door, which was guarded by Ivan and the armoury. The garden was large and elaborate, and there were many exits from the house into the garden. But there was no exit from the garden into the world outside; all round it ran a tall, smooth, unscalable wall with special spikes at the top; no bad garden, perhaps, for a man to reflect in whom some hundred criminals had sworn to kill.

As Ivan explained to the guests, their host had telephoned that he was detained for ten minutes. He was, in truth, making some last arrangements about executions and such ugly things; and though these duties were rootedly repulsive to him, he always performed them with precision. Ruthless in the pursuit of criminals, he was very mild about their punishment. Since he had been supreme over French—and largely over European—policial methods, his great influence had been honourably used for the mitigation of sentences and the purification of prisons. He was one of the great humanitarian French freethinkers; and the only thing wrong with them is that they make mercy even colder than justice.

When Valentin arrived he was already dressed in black clothes and the red rosette—an elegant figure, his dark beard already streaked with grey. He went straight through his house to his study, which opened on the grounds behind. The garden door of it was open, and after he had carefully locked his box in its official place, he stood for a few seconds at the open door looking out upon the garden. A sharp moon was fighting with the flying rags and tatters of a storm, and Valentin regarded it with a wistfulness unusual in such scientific natures as his. Perhaps such scientific natures have some psychic prevision of the most tremendous problem of their lives. From any such occult mood, at least, he quickly recovered, for he knew he was late, and that his guests had already begun to arrive. A glance at his drawing-room when he entered it was enough to make certain that his principal guest was not there, at any rate. He saw all the other pillars of the little party: he saw Lord Galloway, the English Ambassador—a choleric old man with a russet face like an apple, wearing the blue ribbon of the Garter. He saw Lady Galloway, slim and threadlike, with silver hair and a face sensitive and superior. He saw her daughter, Lady Margaret Graham, a pale and pretty girl with an elfish face and copper-coloured hair. He saw the Duchess of Mont St. Michel, black-eyed and opulent, and with her her two daughters, black-eyed and opulent also. He saw Dr. Simon, a typical French scientist, with glasses, a pointed brown beard, and a forehead barred with those parallel wrinkles which are the penalty of superciliousness, since they come through constantly elevating the eyebrows. He saw Father Brown, of Cobhole, in Essex, whom he had recently met in England. He saw— perhaps with more interest than any of these—a tall man in uniform, who had bowed to the Galloways without receiving any very hearty acknowledgment, and who now advanced alone to pay his respects to his host. This was Commandant O'Brien, of the French Foreign Legion. He was a slim yet somewhat swaggering figure, clean-shaven, dark-haired, and blue-eyed, and, as seemed natural in an officer of that famous regiment of victorious failures and successful suicides, he had an air at once dashing and melancholy. He was by birth an Irish gentleman, and in boyhood had known the Galloways—especially Margaret Graham. He had left his country after some crash of debts, and now expressed his complete freedom from British etiquette by swinging about in uniform, sabre and spurs. When he bowed to the Ambassador's family, Lord and Lady Galloway bent stiffly, and Lady Margaret looked away.

But for whatever old causes such people might be interested in each other, their distinguished host was not specially interested in them. No one of them at least was in his eyes the guest of the evening. Valentin was expecting, for special reasons, a man of world-wide fame, whose friendship he had secured during some of his great detective tours and triumphs in the United States. He was expecting Julius K. Brayne, that multimillionaire whose colossal and even crushing endowments of small religions have occasioned so much easy sport and easier solemnity for the American and English papers. Nobody could quite make out whether Mr. Brayne was an atheist or a Mormon or a Christian Scientist; but he was ready to pour money into any intellectual vessel, so long as it was an untried vessel. One of his hobbies was to wait for the American Shakespeare—a hobby more patient than angling. He admired Walt Whitman, but thought that Luke P. Tanner, of Paris, Pa., was more "progressive" than Whitman any day. He liked anything that he thought "progressive." He thought Valentin "progressive," thereby doing him a grave injustice.

The solid appearance of Julius K. Brayne in the room was as decisive as a dinner bell. He had this great quality, which very few of us can claim, that his presence was as big as his absence. He was a huge fellow, as fat as he was tall, clad in complete evening black, without so much relief as a watch-chain or a ring. His hair was white and well brushed back like a German's; his face was red, fierce and cherubic, with one dark tuft under the lower lip that threw up that otherwise infantile visage with an effect theatrical and even Mephistophelean. Not long, however, did that *salon* merely stare at the celebrated American; his lateness had already become a domestic problem, and he was sent with all speed into the dining-room with Lady Galloway upon his arm.

Except on one point the Galloways were genial and casual enough. So long as Lady Margaret did not take the arm of that adventurer O'Brien, her father was quite satisfied; and she had not done so, she had decorously gone in with Dr. Simon. Nevertheless, old Lord Galloway was restless and almost rude. He was diplomatic enough during dinner, but when, over the cigars, three of the younger men—Simon the doctor, Brown the priest, and the detrimental O'Brien, the exile in a foreign uniform—all melted away to mix with the ladies or smoke in the conservatory, then the English diplomatist grew very undiplomatic indeed. He was stung every sixty seconds with the thought that the scamp O'Brien might be signalling to Margaret somehow; he did not attempt to imagine how. He was left over the coffee with Brayne, the hoary Yankee who believed in all religions, and Valentin, the grizzled Frenchman who believed in none. They could argue with each other, but neither could appeal to him. After a time this "progressive" logomarchy had reached a crisis of tedium; Lord Galloway got up also and sought the drawing-room. He lost his way in long passages for some six or eight minutes: till he heard the high-pitched, didactic voice of the doctor, and then the dull voice of the priest, followed by general laughter. They also, he thought with a curse, were probably arguing about "science and religion." But the instant he opened the *salon* door he saw only one thing—he saw what was not there. He saw that Commandant O'Brien was absent, and that Lady Margaret was absent, too.

Rising impatiently from the drawing-room, as he had from the dining-room, he stamped along the passage once more. His notion of protecting his daughter from the Irish-Algerian ne'er-do-weel had become something central and even mad in his mind. As he went towards the back of the house, where was Valentin's study, he was surprised to meet his daughter, who swept past with a white, scornful face, which was a second enigma. If she had been with O'Brien, where was O'Brien? If she had not been with O'Brien, where had she been? With a sort of senile and passionate suspicion he groped his way to the dark back parts of the mansion, and eventually found a servants' entrance that opened on to the garden. The moon with her scimitar had now ripped up and rolled away all the storm-wrack. The argent light lit up all four corners of the garden. A tall figure in blue was striding across the lawn towards the study door; a glint of moonlit silver on his facings picked him out as Commandant O'Brien.

He vanished through the french windows into the house, leaving Lord Galloway in an indescribable temper, at once virulent and vague. The blue-and-silver garden, like a scene in a theatre, seemed to taunt him with all that tyrannic tenderness against which his worldly authority was at war. The length and grace of the Irishman's stride enraged him as if he were a rival instead of a father; the moonlight maddened him. He was trapped as if by magic into a garden of troubadours, a

Watteau fairyland;[1] and, willing to shake off such amorous imbecili-
ties by speech, he stepped briskly after his enemy. As he did so he
tripped over some tree or stone in the grass; looked down at it first
with irritation and then a second time with curiosity. The next instant
the moon and the tall poplars looked at an unusual sight—an elderly
English diplomatist running hard and crying or bellowing as he ran.

His hoarse shouts brought a pale face to the study door, the beaming glasses and worried brow of Dr. Simon, who heard the nobleman's first clear words. Lord Galloway was crying, "A corpse in the
grass—a bloodstained corpse." O'Brien at last had gone utterly from
his mind.

"We must tell Valentin at once," said the doctor, when the other
had brokenly described all that he had dared to examine. "It is fortunate that he is here"; and even as he spoke the great detective
entered the study, attracted by the cry. It was almost amusing to
note his typical transformation; he had come with the common concern of a host and a gentleman, fearing that some guest or servant
was ill. When he was told the gory fact, he turned with all his
gravity instantly bright and business-like; for this, however abrupt
and awful, was his business.

"Strange, gentlemen," he said, as they hurried out into the garden,
"that I should have hunted mysteries all over the earth, and now one
comes and settles in my own back-yard. But where is the place?"
They crossed the lawn less easily, as a slight mist had begun to rise
from the river; but under the guidance of the shaken Galloway they
found the body sunken in deep grass—the body of a very tall and
broad-shouldered man. He lay face downwards, so they could only
see that his big shoulders were clad in black cloth, and that his big
head was bald, except for a wisp or two of brown hair that clung to
his skull like wet seaweed. A scarlet serpent of blood crawled from
under his fallen face.

"At least," said Simon, with a deep and singular intonation, "he is
none of our party."

---

[1] The reference is to French artist Jean Antoin Watteau (1684–1721), famous for his
sensuous images and his enchanted and delicate landscapes.

"Examine him, doctor," cried Valentin rather sharply. "He may not be dead."

The doctor bent down. "He is not quite cold, but I am afraid he is dead enough," he answered. "Just help me to lift him up."

They lifted him carefully an inch from the ground, and all doubts as to his being really dead were settled at once and frightfully. The head fell away. It had been entirely sundered from the body; whoever had cut his throat had managed to sever the neck as well. Even Valentin was slightly shocked. "He must have been as strong as a gorilla," he muttered.

Not without a shiver, though he was used to anatomical abortions, Dr. Simon lifted the head. It was slightly slashed about the neck and jaw, but the face was substantially unhurt. It was a ponderous, yellow face, at once sunken and swollen, with a hawk-like nose and heavy lids—the face of a wicked Roman emperor, with, perhaps, a distant touch of a Chinese emperor. All present seemed to look at it with the coldest eye of ignorance. Nothing else could be noted about the man except that, as they had lifted his body, they had seen underneath it the white gleam of a shirtfront defaced with a red gleam of blood. As Dr. Simon said, the man had never been of their party. But he might very well have been trying to join it, for he had come dressed for such an occasion.

Valentin went down on his hands and knees and examined with his closest professional attention the grass and ground for some twenty yards round the body, in which he was assisted less skillfully by the doctor, and quite vaguely by the English lord. Nothing rewarded their grovellings except a few twigs, snapped or chopped into very small lengths, which Valentin lifted for an instant's examination, and then tossed away.

"Twigs," he said gravely; "twigs, and a total stranger with his head cut off; that is all there is on this lawn."

There was an almost creepy stillness, and then the unnerved Galloway called out sharply:

"Who's that? Who's that over there by the garden wall?"

A small figure with a foolishly large head drew waveringly near them in the moonlit haze; looked for an instant like a goblin, but turned out to be the harmless little priest whom they had left in the drawing-room.

"I say," he said meekly, "there are no gates to this garden, do you know."

Valentin's black brows had come together somewhat crossly, as they did on principle at the sight of the cassock. But he was far too just a man to deny the relevance of the remark. "You are right," he said. "Before we find out how he came to be killed, we may have to find out how he came to be here. Now listen to me, gentlemen. If it can be done without prejudice to my position and duty, we shall all agree that certain distinguished names might well be kept out of this. There are ladies, gentlemen, and there is a foreign ambassador. If we must mark it down as a crime, then it must be followed up as a crime. But till then I can use my own discretion. I am the head of the police; I am so public that I can afford to be private. Please Heaven, I will clear every one of my own guests before I call in my men to look for anybody else. Gentlemen, upon your honour, you will none of you leave the house till to-morrow at noon; there are bedrooms for all. Simon, I think you know where to find my man, Ivan, in the front hall; he is a confidential man. Tell him to leave another servant on guard and come to me at once. Lord Galloway, you are certainly the best person to tell the ladies what has happened, and prevent a panic. They also must stay. Father Brown and I will remain with the body."

When this spirit of the captain spoke in Valentin he was obeyed like a bugle. Dr. Simon went through to the armoury and routed out Ivan, the public detective's private detective. Galloway went to the drawing-room and told the terrible news tactfully enough, so that by the time the company assembled there the ladies were already startled and already soothed. Meanwhile the good priest and the good atheist stood at the head and foot of the dead man motionless in the moonlight, like symbolic statues of their two philosophies of death.

Ivan, the confidential man with the scar and the moustaches, came out of the house like a cannon ball, and came racing across the lawn to Valentin like a dog to his master. His livid face was quite lively with the glow of this domestic detective story, and it was with almost unpleasant eagerness that he asked his master's permission to examine the remains.

"Yes; look, if you like, Ivan," said Valentin, "but don't be long. We must go in and thrash this out in the house."

Ivan lifted the head, and then almost let it drop.

"Why," he gasped, "it's—no, it isn't; it can't be. Do you know this man, sir?"

"No," said Valentin indifferently; "we had better go inside."

Between them they carried the corpse to a sofa in the study, and then all made their way to the drawing-room.

The detective sat down at a desk quietly, and even with hesitation; but his eye was the iron eye of a judge at assize. He made a few rapid notes upon paper in front of him, and then said shortly, "Is everybody here?"

"Not Mr. Brayne," said the Duchess of Mont St. Michel, looking round.

"No," said Lord Galloway, in a hoarse, harsh voice. "And not Mr. Neil O'Brien, I fancy. I saw that gentleman walking in the garden when the corpse was still warm."

"Ivan," said the detective, "go and fetch Commandant O'Brien and Mr. Brayne. Mr. Brayne, I know, is finishing a cigar in the dining-room; Commandant O'Brien, I think, is walking up and down the conservatory. I am not sure."

The faithful attendant flashed from the room, and before anyone could stir or speak Valentin went on with the same soldierly swiftness of exposition.

"Everyone here knows that a dead man has been found in the garden, his head cut clean from his body. Dr. Simon, you have examined it. Do you think that to cut a man's throat like that would need great force? Or, perhaps, only a very sharp knife?"

"I should say that it could not be done with a knife at all," said the pale doctor.

"Have you any thought," resumed Valentin, "of a tool with which it could be done?"

"Speaking within modern probabilities, I really haven't," said the doctor, arching his painful brows. "It's not easy to hack a neck through even clumsily, and this was a very clean cut. It could be done with a battle-axe or an old headsman's axe, or an old two-handed sword."

"But, good heavens!" cried the Duchess, almost in hysterics, "there aren't any two-handed swords and battle-axes round here."

Valentin was still busy with the paper in front of him. "Tell me," he said, still writing rapidly, "could it have been done with a long French cavalry sabre?"

A low knocking came at the door, which for some unreasonable reason, curdled everyone's blood like the knocking in *Macbeth*. Amid that frozen silence Dr. Simon managed to say, "A sabre—yes, I suppose it could."

"Thank you," said Valentin. "Come in, Ivan."

The confidential Ivan opened the door and ushered in Commandant Neil O'Brien, whom he had found at last pacing the garden again.

The Irish officer stood disordered and defiant on the threshold. "What do you want with me?" he cried.

"Please sit down," said Valentin in pleasant, level tones. "Why, you aren't wearing your sword! Where is it?"

"I left it on the library table," said O'Brien, his brogue deepening in his disturbed mood. "It was a nuisance, it was getting —"

"Ivan," said Valentin, "please go and get the Commandant's sword from the library." Then, as the servant vanished, "Lord Galloway says he saw you leaving the garden just before he found the corpse. What were you doing in the garden?"

The Commandant flung himself recklessly into a chair. "Oh," he cried in pure Irish; "admirin' the moon. Communing with Nature, me bhoy."

A heavy silence sank and endured, and at the end of it came again that trivial and terrible knocking. Ivan reappeared, carrying an empty steel scabbard. "This is all I can find," he said.

"Put it on the table," said Valentin, without looking up.

There was an inhuman silence in the room, like that sea of inhuman silence round the dock of the condemned murderer. The Duchess's weak exclamations had long ago died away. Lord Galloway's swollen hatred was satisfied and even sobered. The voice that came was quite unexpected.

"I think I can tell you," cried Lady Margaret, in that clear, quivering voice with which a courageous woman speaks publicly. "I can tell you what Mr. O'Brien was doing in the garden, since he is bound to silence. He was asking me to marry him. I refused; I said in my family circumstances I could give him nothing but my respect. He was a little angry at that; he did not seem to think much of my respect. I wonder," she added, with rather a wan smile, "if he will care at all for it now. For I offer it him now. I will swear anywhere that he never did a thing like this."

Lord Galloway had edged up to his daughter, and was intimidating her in what he imagined to be an undertone. "Hold your tongue, Maggie," he said in a thunderous whisper. "Why should you shield the fellow? Where's his sword? Where's his confounded cavalry —"

He stopped because of the singular stare with which his daughter was regarding him, a look that was indeed a lurid magnet for the whole group.

"You old fool!" she said, in a low voice without pretence of piety; "what do you suppose you are trying to prove? I tell you this man was innocent while with me. But if he wasn't innocent, he was still with me. If he murdered a man in the garden, who was it who must have seen—who must at least have known? Do you hate Neil so much as to put your own daughter —"

Lady Galloway screamed. Everyone else sat tingling at the touch of those satanic tragedies that have been between lovers before now. They saw the proud, white face of the Scotch aristocrat and her lover, the Irish adventurer, like old portraits in a dark house. The long silence was full of formless historical memories of murdered husbands and poisonous paramours.

In the centre of this morbid silence an innocent voice said, "Was it a very long cigar?"

The change of thought was so sharp that they had to look round to see who had spoken.

"I mean," said little Father Brown, from the corner of the room. "I mean that cigar Mr. Brayne is finishing. It seems nearly as long as a walking-stick."

Despite the irrelevance there was assent as well as irritation in Valentin's face as he lifted his head.

"Quite right," he remarked sharply. "Ivan, go and see about Mr. Brayne again, and bring him here at once."

The instant the factotum had closed the door, Valentin addressed the girl with an entirely new earnestness.

"Lady Margaret," he said, "we all feel, I am sure, both gratitude and admiration for your act in rising above your lower dignity and explaining the Commandant's conduct. But there is a hiatus still. Lord Galloway, I understand, met you passing from the study to the drawing-room, and it was only some minutes afterwards that he found the garden and the Commandant still walking there."

"You have to remember," replied Margaret, with a faint irony in her voice, "that I had just refused him, so we should scarcely have come back arm in arm. He is a gentleman, anyhow; and he loitered behind—and so got charged with murder."

"In those few moments," said Valentin gravely, "he might really —"

The knock came again, and Ivan put in his scarred face.

"Beg pardon, sir," he said, "but Mr. Brayne has left the house."

"Left!" cried Valentin, and rose for the first time to his feet.

"Gone. Scooted. Evaporated," replied Ivan, in humourous French. "His hat and coat are gone, too; and I'll tell you something to cap it all. I ran outside the house to find any traces of him, and I found one, and a big trace, too."

"What do you mean?" asked Valentin.

"I'll show you," said his servant, and reappeared with a flashing naked cavalry sabre, streaked with blood about the point and edge. Everyone in the room eyed it as if it were a thunderbolt; but the experienced Ivan went on quite quietly:

"I found this," he said, "flung among the bushes fifty yards up the road to Paris. In other words, I found it just where your respectable Mr. Brayne threw it when he ran away."

There was again a silence, but of a new sort. Valentin took the sabre, examined it, reflected with unaffected concentration of thought, and then turned a respectful face to O'Brien. "Commandant," he said, "we trust you will always produce this weapon if it is wanted for police examination. Meanwhile," he added, slapping the steel back in the ringing scabbard, "let me return you your sword."

At the military symbolism of the action the audience could hardly refrain from applause.

For Neil O'Brien, indeed, that gesture was the turning-point of existence. By the time he was wandering in the mysterious garden again in the colours of the morning the tragic futility of his ordinary mien had fallen from him; he was a man with many reasons for happiness. Lord Galloway was a gentleman, and had offered him an apology. Lady Margaret was something better than a lady, a woman at least, and had perhaps given him something better than an apology, as they drifted among the old flower-beds before breakfast. The whole company was more light-hearted and humane, for though the riddle of the death remained, the load of suspicion was lifted off them all, and sent flying off to Paris with the strange millionaire—a man they hardly knew. The devil was cast out of the house—he had cast himself out.

Still, the riddle remained; and when O'Brien threw himself on a garden seat beside Dr. Simon, that keenly scientific person at once resumed it. He did not get much talk out of O'Brien, whose thoughts were on pleasanter things.

"I can't say it interests me much," said the Irishman frankly, "especially as it seems pretty plain now. Apparently Brayne hated this stranger for some reason; lured him into the garden, and killed him with my sword. Then he fled to the city, tossing the sword away as he went. By the way, Ivan tells me the dead man had a Yankee dollar in his pocket. So he was a countryman of Brayne's, and that seems to clinch it. I don't see any difficulties about the business."

"There are five colossal difficulties," said the doctor quietly; "like high walls within walls. Don't mistake me. I don't doubt that Brayne did it; his flight, I fancy, proves that. But as to how he did it. First difficulty: Why should a man kill another man with a great hulking sabre, when he can almost kill him with a pocket knife and put it back in his pocket? Second difficulty: Why was there no noise or outcry? Does a man commonly see another come up waving a scimitar and offer no remarks? Third difficulty: A servant watched the front door all the evening; and a rat cannot get into Valentin's garden any-where. How did the dead man get into the garden? Fourth difficulty: Given the same conditions, how did Brayne get out of the garden?"

"And the fifth," said Neil, with eyes fixed on the English priest, who was coming slowly up the path.

"Is a trifle, I suppose," said the doctor, "but I think an odd one. When I first saw how the head had been slashed, I supposed the assas-sin had struck more than once. But on examination I found many cuts across the truncated section; in other words, they were struck *after* the head was off. Did Brayne hate his foe so fiendishly that he stood sabring his body in the moonlight?"

"Horrible!" said O'Brien, and shuddered.

The little priest, Brown, had arrived while they were talking, and had waited, with characteristic shyness, till they had finished. Then he said awkwardly:

"I say, I'm sorry to interrupt. But I was sent to tell you the news!"

"News?" repeated Simon, and stared at him rather painfully through his glasses.

"Yes, I'm sorry," said Father Brown mildly. "There's been another murder, you know."

Both men on the seat sprang up, leaving it rocking.

"And, what's stranger still," continued the priest, with his dull eye on the rhododendrons, "it's the same disgusting sort; it's another beheading. They found the second head actually bleeding into the river, a few yards along Brayne's road to Paris; so they suppose that he —"

"Great Heaven!" cried O'Brien. "Is Brayne a monomaniac?"

"There are American vendettas," said the priest impassively. Then he added, "They want you to come to the library and see it."

Commandant O'Brien followed the others towards the inquest, feel-ing decidedly sick. As a soldier, he loathed all this secretive carnage; where were these extravagant amputations going to stop? First one head was hacked off, and then another; in this case (he told himself bitterly) it was not true that two heads were better than one. As he crossed the study he almost staggered at a shocking coincidence. Upon Valentin's table lay the coloured picture of yet a third bleeding head;

and it was the head of Valentin himself. A second glance showed him it was only a Nationalist paper, called *The Guillotine*, which every week showed one of its political opponents with rolling eyes and writhing features just after execution; for Valentin was an anti-clerical of some note. But O'Brien was an Irishman, with a kind of chastity even in his sins; and his gorge rose against that great brutality of the intellect which belongs only to France. He felt Paris as a whole, from the grotesques on the Gothic churches to the gross caricatures in the newspapers. He remembered the gigantic jests of the Revolution. He saw the whole city as one ugly energy, from the sanguinary sketch lying on Valentin's table up to where, above a mountain and forest of gargoyles, the great devil grins on Notre Dame.

The library was long, low, and dark; what light entered it shot from under low blinds and had still some of the ruddy tinge of morning. Valentin and his servant Ivan were waiting for them at the upper end of a long, slightly-sloping desk, on which lay the mortal remains, looking enormous in the twilight. The big black figure and yellow face of the man found in the garden confronted them essentially unchanged. The second head, which had been fished from among the river reeds that morning, lay streaming and dripping beside it; Valentin's men were still seeking to recover the rest of this second corpse, which was supposed to be afloat. Father Brown, who did not seem to share O'Brien's sensibilities in the least, went up to the second head and examined it with his blinking care. It was little more than a mop of wet white hair, fringed with silver fire in the red and level morning light; the face, which seemed of an ugly, empurpled and perhaps criminal type, had been much battered against trees or stones as it tossed in the water.

"Good morning, Commandant O'Brien," said Valentin, with quiet cordiality. "You have heard of Brayne's last experiment in butchery, I suppose?"

Father Brown was still bending over the head with white hair, and he said, without looking up:

"I suppose it is quite certain that Brayne cut off this head, too."

"Well, it seems common sense," said Valentin, with his hands in his pockets. "Killed in the same way as the other. Found within a few yards of the other. And sliced by the same weapon which we know he carried away."

"Yes, yes; I know," replied Father Brown, submissively. "Yet, you know, I doubt whether Brayne could have cut off this head."

"Why not?" inquired Dr. Simon, with a rational stare.

"Well, doctor," said the priest, looking up blinking, "can a man cut off his own head? I don't know."

O'Brien felt an insane universe crashing about his ears; but the doctor sprung forward with impetuous practicality and pushed back the wet white hair.

"Oh, there's no doubt it's Brayne," said the priest quietly. "He had exactly that chip in the left ear."

The detective, who had been regarding the priest with steady and glittering eyes, opened his clenched mouth and said sharply, "You seem to know a lot about him, Father Brown."

"I do," said the little man simply. "I've been about with him for some weeks. He was thinking of joining our church."

The star of the fanatic sprang into Valentin's eyes; he strode towards the priest with clenched hands. "And, perhaps," he cried, with a blasting sneer, "perhaps he was also thinking of leaving all his money to your church."

"Perhaps he was," said Brown stolidly; "it is possible."

"In that case," cried Valentin, with a dreadful smile, "you may indeed know a great deal about him. About his life and about his —"

Commandant O'Brien laid a hand on Valentin's arm. "Drop that slanderous rubbish, Valentin," he said, "or there may be more swords yet."

But Valentin (under the steady, humble gaze of the priest) had already recovered himself. "Well," he said shortly, "people's private opinions can wait. You gentlemen are still bound by your promise to stay; you must enforce it on yourselves—and on each other. Ivan here will tell you anything more you want to know; I must get to business and write to the authorities. We can't keep this quiet any longer. I shall be writing in my study if there is any more news."

"Is there any more news, Ivan?" asked Dr. Simon, as the chief of police strode out of the room.

"Only one more thing, I think, sir," said Ivan, wrinkling up his grey old face, "but that's important, too, in its way. There's that old buffer you found on the lawn," and he pointed without pretence of reverence at the big black body with the yellow head. "We've found out who he is, anyhow."

"Indeed!" cried the astonished doctor; "and who is he?"

"His name was Arnold Becker," said the under-detective, "though he went by many aliases. He was a wandering sort of scamp, and is known to have been in America; so that was where Brayne got his knife into him. We didn't have much to do with him ourselves, for he worked mostly in Germany. We've communicated, of course, with the German police. But, oddly enough, there was a twin brother of his, named Louis Becker, whom we had a great deal to do with. In fact, we found it necessary to guillotine him only yesterday. Well, it's a rum thing, gentlemen, but when I saw that fellow flat on the lawn I had the greatest jump of my life. If I hadn't seen Louis Becker guillotined with my own eyes, I'd have sworn it was Louis Becker lying there in the grass. Then, of course, I remembered his twin brother in Germany, and following up the clue —"

The explanatory Ivan stopped, for the excellent reason that nobody was listening to him. The Commandant and the doctor were both staring at Father Brown, who had sprung stiffly to his feet, and was holding his temples tight like a man in sudden and violent pain.

"Stop, stop, stop!" he cried; "stop talking a minute, for I see half. Will God give me strength? Will my brain make the one jump and see all? Heaven help me! I used to be fairly good at thinking. I could paraphrase any page in Aquinas once. Will my head split—or will it see? I see half—I only see half."

He buried his head in his hands, and stood in a sort of rigid torture of thought or prayer, while the other three could only go on staring at this last prodigy of their wild twelve hours.

When Father Brown's hands fell they showed a face quite fresh and serious, like a child's. He heaved a huge sigh, and said, "Let us get this said and done with as quickly as possible. Look here, this will be the quickest way to convince you all of the truth." He turned to the doctor. "Dr. Simon," he said, "you have a strong head-piece, and I heard you this morning asking the five hardest questions about this business. Well, if you will now ask them again, I will answer them."

Simon's pince-nez dropped from his nose in his doubt and wonder, but he answered at once. "Well, the first question, you know, is why a man should kill another with a clumsy sabre at all when a man can kill with a bodkin?"

"A man cannot behead with a bodkin," said Brown, calmly, "and for *this* murder beheading was absolutely necessary."

"Why?" asked O'Brien, with interest.

"And the next question?" asked Father Brown.

"Well, why didn't the man cry out or anything?" asked the doctor; "sabres in gardens are certainly unusual."

"Twigs," said the priest gloomily, and turned to the window which looked on the scene of death. "No one saw the point of the twigs. Why should they lie on that lawn (look at it) so far from any tree? They were not snapped off; they were chopped off. The murderer occupied his enemy with some tricks with the sabre, showing how he could cut a branch in mid-air, or what not. Then, while his enemy bent down to see the result, a silent slash, and the head fell."

"Well," said the doctor slowly, "that seems plausible enough. But my next two questions will stump anyone."

The priest still stood looking critically out of the window and waited.

"You know how all the garden was sealed up like an air-tight chamber," went on the doctor. "Well, how did the strange man get into the garden?"

Without turning round, the little priest answered, "There never was any strange man in the garden."

There was a silence, and then a sudden cackle of almost childish laughter relieved the strain. The absurdity of Brown's remark moved Ivan to open taunts.

"Oh!" he cried; "then we didn't lug a great fat corpse on to a sofa last night? He hadn't got into the garden, I suppose."

"Got into the garden?" repeated Brown reflectively. "No, not entirely."

"Hang it all," cried Simon, "a man gets into a garden, or he doesn't."

"Not necessarily," said the priest, with a faint smile. "What is the next question, doctor?"

"I fancy you're ill," exclaimed Dr. Simon sharply; "but I'll ask the next question if you like. How did Brayne get out of the garden?"

"He didn't get out of the garden," said the priest, still looking out of the window.

"Didn't get out of the garden?" exploded Simon.

"Not completely," said Father Brown.

Simon shook his fists in a frenzy of French logic. "A man gets out of a garden, or he doesn't," he cried.

"Not always," said Father Brown.

Dr. Simon sprang to his feet impatiently. "I have no time to spare on such senseless talk," he cried angrily. "If you can't understand a man being on one side of the wall or the other, I won't trouble you further."

"Doctor," said the cleric very gently, "we have always got on very pleasantly together. If only for the sake of old friendship, stop and tell me your fifth question."

The impatient Simon sank into a chair by the door and said briefly, "The head and shoulders were cut about in a queer way. It seemed to be done after death."

"Yes," said the motionless priest, "it was done so as to make you assume exactly the one simple falsehood that you did assume. It was done to make you take for granted that the head belonged to the body."

The borderland of the brain, where all the monsters are made, moved horribly in the Gaelic O'Brien. He felt the chaotic presence of all the horse-men and fish-women that man's unnatural fancy has begotten. A voice older than his first fathers seemed saying in his ear, "Keep out of the monstrous garden where grows the tree with double fruit. Avoid the evil garden where died the man with two heads." Yet, while these shameful symbolic shapes passed across the ancient mirror of his Irish soul, his Frenchified intellect was quite alert, and was watching the odd priest as closely and incredulously as all the rest.

Father Brown had turned round at last, and stood against the window with his face in dense shadow; but even in that shadow they could see it was pale as ashes. Nevertheless, he spoke quite sensibly, as if there were no Gaelic souls on earth.

"Gentlemen," he said, "you did not find the strange body of Becker in the garden. You did not find any strange body in the garden. In face of Dr. Simon's rationalism, I still affirm that Becker was only partly present. Look here!" (pointing to the black bulk of the mysterious corpse) "you never saw that man in your lives. Did you ever see this man?"

He rapidly rolled away the bald, yellow head of the unknown, and put in its place the white-maned head beside it. And there, complete, unified, unmistakable, lay Julius K. Brayne.

"The murderer," went on Brown quietly, "hacked off his enemy's head and flung the sword far over the wall. But he was too clever to fling the sword only. He flung the *head* over the wall also. Then he had only to clap on another head to the corpse, and (as he insisted on a private inquest) you all imagined a totally new man."

"Clap on another head!" said O'Brien, staring. "What other head? Heads don't grow on garden bushes, do they?"

"No," said Father Brown huskily, and looking at his boots; "there is only one place where they grow. They grow in the basket of the guillotine, beside which the chief of police, Aristide Valentin, was standing not an hour before the murder. Oh, my friends, hear me a minute more before you tear me in pieces. Valentin is an honest man, if being mad for an arguable cause is honesty. But did you never see in that cold, grey eye of his that he is mad? He would do anything, *anything*, to break what he calls the superstition of the Cross. He has fought for it and starved for it, and now he has murdered for it. Brayne's crazy millions had hitherto been scattered among so many sects that they did little to alter the balance of things. But Valentin heard a whisper that Brayne, like so many scatter-brained sceptics, was drifting to us; and that was quite a different thing. Brayne would pour supplies into the impoverished and pugnacious Church of France; he would support six Nationalist newspapers like *The Guillotine*. The battle was already balanced on a point, and the fanatic took flame at the risk. He resolved to destroy the millionaire, and he did it as one would expect the greatest of detectives to commit his only crime. He abstracted the severed head of Becker on some criminological excuse, and took it home in his official box. He had that last argument with Brayne, that Lord Galloway did not hear the end of; that failing, he led him out into the sealed garden, talked about swordsmanship, used twigs and a sabre for illustration, and —"

Ivan of the Scar sprang up. "You lunatic," he yelled; "you'll go to my master now, if I take you by —"

"Why, I was going there," said Brown heavily; "I must ask him to confess, and all that."

Driving the unhappy Brown before them like a hostage or sacrifice, they rushed together into the sudden stillness of Valentin's study.

The great detective sat at his desk apparently too occupied to hear their turbulent entrance. They paused a moment, and then something in the look of that upright and elegant back made the doctor run forward suddenly. A touch and a glance showed him that there was a small box of pills at Valentin's elbow, and that Valentin was dead in his chair; and on the blind face of the suicide was more than the pride of Cato.[2]

[2] The reference is to Cato the Younger (95–46 B.C.), the Roman Stoic and supporter of Pompey, whose pride led him to commit suicide rather than submit to Julius Cæsar.

THE QUEER FEET

If you meet a member of that select club, "The Twelve True Fishermen," entering the Vernon Hotel for the annual club dinner, you will observe, as he takes off his overcoat, that his evening coat is green and not black. If (supposing that you have the star-defying audacity to address such a being) you ask him why, he will probably answer that he does it to avoid being mistaken for a waiter. You will then retire crushed. But you will leave behind you a mystery as yet unsolved and a tale worth telling.

If (to pursue the same vein of improbable conjecture) you were to meet a mild, hard-working little priest, named Father Brown, and were to ask him what he thought was the most singular luck of his life, he would probably reply that upon the whole his best stroke was at the Vernon Hotel, where he had averted a crime and, perhaps, saved a soul, merely by listening to a few footsteps in a passage. He is perhaps a little proud of this wild and wonderful guess of his, and it is possible that he might refer to it. But since it is immeasurably unlikely that you will ever rise high enough in the social world to find "The Twelve True Fishermen," or that you will ever sink low enough among slums and criminals to find Father Brown, I fear you will never hear the story at all unless you hear it from me.

The Vernon Hotel at which The Twelve True Fishermen held their annual dinners was an institution such as can only exist in an oligarchical society which has almost gone mad on good manners. It was that topsy-turvy product—an "exclusive" commercial enterprise. That is, it was a thing which paid not by attracting people, but actually by turning people away. In the heart of a plutocracy tradesmen become cunning enough to be more fastidious than their customers. They positively create difficulties so that their wealthy and weary clients may spend money and diplomacy in overcoming them. If there were a fashionable hotel in London which no man could enter who was under six foot, society would meekly make up parties of six-foot men to dine in it. If there were an expensive restaurant which by a mere caprice of its proprietor was only open on Thursday afternoon, it would be crowded on Thursday afternoon. The Vernon Hotel stood, as if by accident, in the corner of a square in Belgravia. It was a small hotel; and a very inconvenient one. But its very inconveniences were considered as walls protecting a particular class. One inconvenience, in particular, was held to be of vital importance: the fact that practically only twenty-four people could dine in the place at once. The only big dinner table was the celebrated terrace table, which stood open to the air on a sort of veranda overlooking one of the most exquisite old gardens in London. Thus it happened that even the twenty-four seats at this table could only be enjoyed in warm weather; and this making the enjoyment yet more difficult made it yet more desired. The existing owner of the hotel was a Jew named Lever; and he made nearly a million out of it, by making it difficult to get into. Of course he combined with this limitation in the scope of his enterprise the most careful polish in its performance. The wines and cooking were really as good as any in Europe, and the demeanour of the attendants exactly mirrored the fixed mood of the English upper class. The proprietor knew all his waiters like the fingers on his hand; there were only fifteen of them all told. It was much easier to become a Member of Parliament than to become a waiter in that hotel. Each waiter was trained in terrible silence and smoothness, as if he were a gentleman's servant. And, indeed, there was generally at least one waiter to every gentleman who dined.

The club of The Twelve True Fishermen would not have consented to dine anywhere but in such a place, for it insisted on a luxurious privacy; and would have been quite upset by the mere thought that any other club was even dining in the same building. On the occasion of their annual dinner the Fishermen were in the habit of exposing all their treasures, as if they were in a private house, especially the celebrated set of fish knives and forks which were, as it were, the insignia of the society, each being exquisitely wrought in silver in the form of a fish, and each loaded at the hilt with one large pearl. These were always laid out for the fish course, and the fish course was always the most magnificent in that magnificent repast. The society had a vast number of ceremonies and observances, but it had no history and no object; that was where it was so very aristocratic. You did not have to be anything in order to be one of the Twelve Fishers; unless you were already a certain sort of person, you never even heard of them. It had been in existence twelve years. Its president was Mr. Audley. Its vice-president was the Duke of Chester.

If I have in any degree conveyed the atmosphere of this appalling hotel, the reader may feel a natural wonder as to how I came to know anything about it, and may even speculate as to how so ordinary a person as my friend Father Brown came to find himself in that golden galley. As far as that is concerned, my story is simple, or even vulgar. There is in the world a very aged rioter and demagogue who breaks into the most refined retreats with the dreadful information that all men are brothers, and wherever this leveller went on his pale horse it was Father Brown's trade to follow. One of the waiters, an Italian, had been struck down with a paralytic stroke that afternoon; and his Jewish employer, marvelling mildly at such superstitions, had consented to send for the nearest Popish priest. With what the waiter confessed to Father Brown we are not concerned, for the excellent reason that the cleric kept it to himself; but apparently it involved him in writing out a note or statement for the conveying of some message or the righting of some wrong. Father Brown, therefore, with a meek impudence which he would have shown equally in Buckingham Palace, asked to be provided with a room and writing materials. Mr. Lever was torn in two. He was a kind man, and had also that bad imitation of kindness, the dislike of any difficulty or scene. At the same time the presence of one unusual stranger in his hotel that evening was like a speck of dirt on something just cleaned. There was never any borderland or anteroom in the Vernon Hotel, no people waiting in the hall, no customers coming in on chance. There were fifteen waiters. There were twelve guests. It would be as startling to find a new guest in the hotel that night as to find a new brother taking breakfast or tea in one's own family. Moreover, the priest's appearance was second-rate and his clothes muddy; a mere glimpse of him afar off might precipitate a crisis in the club. Mr. Lever at last hit on a plan to cover, since he might not obliterate, the disgrace. When you enter (as you never will) the Vernon Hotel, you pass down a short passage decorated with a few dingy but important pictures, and come to the main vestibule and lounge which opens on your right into passages leading to the public rooms, and on your left to a similar passage pointing to the kitchens and offices of the hotel. Immediately on your left hand is the corner of a glass office, which abuts upon the lounge—a house within a house, so to speak, like the old hotel bar which probably once occupied its place.

In this office sat the representative of the proprietor (nobody in this place ever appeared in person if he could help it), and just beyond the office, on the way to the servants' quarters, was the gentlemen's cloak-room, the last boundary of the gentlemen's domain. But between the office and the cloak-room was a small private room without other outlet, sometimes used by the proprietor for delicate and important matters, such as lending a duke a thousand pounds or declining to lend him sixpence. It is a mark of the magnificent tolerance of Mr. Lever that he permitted this holy place to be for about half an hour profaned by a mere priest, scribbling away on a piece of paper. The story which Father Brown was writing down was very likely a much better story than this one, only it will never be known. I can merely state that it was very nearly as long, and that the last two or three paragraphs of it were the least exciting and absorbing. For it was by the time he had reached these that the priest began a little to allow his thoughts to wander and his animal senses, which were commonly keen, to awaken. The time of darkness and dinner was drawing on; his own forgotten little room was without a light, and perhaps the gathering gloom, as occasionally happens, sharpened the sense of sound. As Father Brown wrote the last and least essential part of his document, he caught himself writing to the rhythm of a recurrent noise outside, just as one sometimes thinks to the tune of a railway train. When he became conscious of the thing he found what it was: only the ordinary patter of feet passing the door, which in a hotel was no very unlikely matter. Nevertheless, he stared at the darkened ceiling, and listened to the sound. After he had listened for a few seconds dreamily, he got to his feet and listened intently, with his head a little on one side. Then he sat down again and buried his brow in his hands, now not merely listening, but listening and thinking also.

The footsteps outside at any given moment were such as one might hear in any hotel; and yet, taken as a whole, there was something very strange about them. There were no other footsteps. It was always a very silent house, for the few familiar guests went at once to their own apartments, and the well-trained waiters were told to be almost invisible until they were wanted. One could not conceive any place where there was less reason to apprehend anything irregular. But these footsteps were so odd that one could not decide to call them regular or irregular. Father Brown followed them with his finger on the edge of the table, like a man trying to learn a tune on the piano.

First, there came a long rush of rapid little steps, such as a light man might make in winning a walking race. At a certain point they stopped and changed to a sort of slow, swinging stamp, numbering not a quarter of the steps, but occupying about the same time. The moment the last echoing stamp had died away would come again the run or ripple of light, hurrying feet, and then again the thud of the heavier walking. It was certainly the same pair of boots, partly because (as has been said) there were no other boots about, and partly because they had a small but unmistakable creak in them. Father Brown had the kind of head that cannot help asking questions; and on this apparently trivial question his head almost split. He had seen men run in order to jump. He had seen men run in order to slide. But why on earth should a man run in order to walk? Or, again, why should he walk in order to run? Yet no other description would cover the antics of this invisible pair of legs. The man was either walking very fast down one-half of the corridor in order to walk very slow down the other half, or he was walking very slow at one end to have the rapture of walking fast at the other. Neither suggestion seemed to make much sense. His brain was growing darker and darker, like his room.

Yet, as be began to think steadily, the very blackness of his cell seemed to make his thoughts more vivid; he began to see as in a kind of vision the fantastic feet capering along the corridor in unnatural or symbolic attitudes. Was it a heathen religious dance? Or some entirely new kind of scientific exercise? Father Brown began to ask himself with more exactness what the steps suggested. Taking the slow step first; it certainly was not the step of the proprietor. Men of his type walk with a rapid waddle, or they sit still. It could not be any servant or messenger waiting for directions. It did not sound like it. The poorer orders (in an oligarchy) sometimes lurch about when they are slightly drunk, but generally, and especially in such gorgeous scenes, they stand or sit in constrained attitudes. No; that heavy yet springy step, with a kind of careless emphasis, not specially noisy, yet not caring what noise it made, belonged to only one of the animals of this earth. It was a gentleman of western Europe, and probably one who had never worked for his living.

Just as he came to this solid certainty, the step changed to the quicker one, and ran past the door as feverishly as a rat. The listener remarked that though this step was much swifter it was also much more noise-less, almost as if the man were walking on tiptoe. Yet it was not asso-ciated in his mind with secrecy, but with something else—something that he could not remember. He was maddened by one of those half-memories that make a man feel half-witted. Surely he had heard that strange, swift walking somewhere. Suddenly he sprang to his feet with a new idea in his head, and walked to the door. His room had no direct outlet on the passage, but let on one side into the glass office, and on the other into the cloak-room beyond. He tried the door into the office, and found it locked. Then he looked at the window, now a square pane full of purple cloud cleft by livid sunset, and for an instant he smelt evil as a dog smells rats.

The rational part of him (whether the wiser or not) regained its supremacy. He remembered that the proprietor had told him that he should lock the door, and would come later to release him. He told himself that twenty things he had not thought of might explain the eccentric sounds outside; he reminded himself that there was just enough light left to finish his own proper work. Bringing his paper to the window so as to catch the last stormy evening light, he resolutely plunged once more into the almost completed record. He had writ-ten for about twenty minutes, bending closer and closer to his paper in the lessening light; then suddenly he sat upright. He had heard the strange feet once more.

This time they had a third oddity. Previously the unknown man had walked, with levity indeed and lightning quickness, but he had walked. This time he ran. One could hear the swift, soft, bounding steps coming along the corridor, like the pads of a fleeing and leaping panther. Whoever was coming was a very strong, active man, in still yet tearing excitement. Yet, when the sound had swept up to the office like a sort of whispering whirlwind, it suddenly changed again to the old slow, swaggering stamp.

Father Brown flung down his paper, and, knowing the office door to be locked, went at once into the cloak-room on the other side. The attendant of this place was temporarily absent, probably because the only guests were at dinner and his office was a sinecure. After groping through a grey forest of overcoats, he found that the dim cloak-room opened on the lighted corridor in the form of a sort of counter or half-door, like most of the counters across which we have all handed umbrellas and received tickets. There was a light immediately above the semi-circular arch of this opening. It threw little illumination on Father Brown himself, who seemed a mere dark outline against the dim sunset window behind him. But it threw an almost theatrical light on the man who stood outside the cloakroom in the corridor.

He was an elegant man in very plain evening dress; tall, but with an air of not taking up much room; one felt that he could have slid along like a shadow where many smaller men would have been obvious and obstructive. His face, now flung back in the lamplight, was swarthy and vivacious, the face of a foreigner. His figure was good, his manners good-humoured and confident; a critic could only say that his black coat was a shade below his figure and manners, and even bulged and bagged in an odd way. The moment he caught sight of Brown's black silhouette against the sunset, he tossed down a scrap of paper with a number and called out with amiable authority, "I want my hat and coat, please; I find I have to go away at once."

Father Brown took the paper without a word, and obediently went to look for the coat; it was not the first menial work he had done in his life. He brought it and laid it on the counter; meanwhile, the strange gentleman who had been feeling in his waistcoat pocket, said, laughing, "I haven't got any silver; you can keep this." And he threw down half a sovereign, and caught up his coat.

Father Brown's figure remained quite dark and still; but in that instant he had lost his head. His head was always most valuable when he had lost it. In such moments he put two and two together and made four million. Often the Catholic Church (which is wedded to common sense) did not approve of it. Often he did not approve of it himself. But it was a real inspiration—important at rare crises—when whosoever shall lose his head the same shall save it.

"I think, sir," he said civilly, "that you have some silver in your pocket."

The tall gentleman stared. "Hang it," he cried, "if I choose to give you gold, why should you complain?"

"Because silver is sometimes more valuable than gold," said the priest mildly; "that is, in large quantities."

The stranger looked at him curiously. Then he looked still more curiously up the passage towards the main entrance. Then he looked back at Brown again, and then he looked very carefully at the window beyond Brown's head, still coloured with the after-glow of the storm. Then he seemed to make up his mind. He put one hand on the counter, vaulted over as easily as an acrobat and towered above the priest, putting one tremendous hand upon his collar.

"Stand still," he said, in a hacking whisper. "I don't want to threaten you, but —"

"I do want to threaten you," said Father Brown, in a voice like a rolling drum. "I want to threaten you with the worm that dieth not, and the fire that is not quenched."

"You're a rum sort of cloak-room clerk," said the other.

"I am a priest, Monsieur Flambeau," said Brown, "and I am ready to hear your confession."

The other stood gasping for a few moments, and then staggered back into a chair.

The first two courses of the dinner of The Twelve True Fishermen had proceeded with placid success. I do not possess a copy of the menu; and if I did it would not convey anything to anybody. It was written in a sort of super-French employed by cooks, but quite unintelligible to Frenchmen. There was a tradition in the club that the *hors d'œuvres* should be various and manifold to the point of madness. They were taken seriously because they were avowedly useless extras, like the whole dinner and the whole club. There was also a tradition that the soup course should be light and unpretending—a sort of simple and austere vigil for the feast of fish that was to come. The talk was that strange, slight talk which governs the British Empire, which governs it in secret, and yet would scarcely enlighten an ordinary Englishman even if he could overhear it. Cabinet Ministers on both sides were alluded to by their Christian names with a sort of bored benignity. The Radical Chancellor of the Exchequer, whom the whole Tory party was supposed to be cursing for his extortions, was praised for his minor poetry, or his saddle in the hunting field. The Tory leader, whom all Liberals were supposed to hate as a tyrant, was discussed and, on the whole, praised—as a Liberal. It seemed somehow that politicians were very important. And yet, anything seemed important about them except their politics. Mr. Audley, the chairman, was an amiable, elderly man who still wore Gladstone collars; he was a kind of symbol of all that phantasmal and yet fixed society. He had never done anything—not even anything wrong. He was not fast; he was not even particularly rich. He was simply in the thing; and there was an end of it. No party could ignore him, and if he had wished to be in the Cabinet he certainly would have been put there. The Duke of Chester, the vice-president, was a young and rising politician. That is to say, he was a pleasant youth, with flat, fair hair and a freckled face, with moderate intelligence and enormous estates. In public his appearances were always successful and his principle was simple enough. When he thought of a joke he made it, and was called brilliant. When he could not think of a joke he said that this was no time for trifling, and was called able. In private, in a club of his own class, he was simply quite pleasantly frank and silly, like a schoolboy. Mr. Audley, never having been in politics, treated them a little more seriously. Sometimes he even embarrassed the company by phrases suggesting that there was some difference between a Liberal and a Conservative. He himself was a Conservative, even in private life. He had a roll of grey hair over the back of his collar, like certain old-fashioned statesmen, and seen from behind he looked like the man the empire wants.

Seen from the front he looked like a mild, self-indulgent bachelor, with rooms in the Albany—which he was.

As has been remarked, there were twenty-four seats at the terrace table, and only twelve members of the club. Thus they could occupy the terrace in the most luxurious style of all, being ranged along the inner side of the table, with no one opposite, commanding an uninterrupted view of the garden, the colours of which were still vivid, though evening was closing in somewhat luridly for the time of year. The chairman sat in the centre of the line, and the vice-president at the right-hand end of it. When the twelve guests first trooped into their seats it was the custom (for some unknown reason) for all the fifteen waiters to stand lining the wall like troops presenting arms to the king, while the fat proprietor stood and bowed to the club with radiant surprise, as if he had never heard of them before. But before the first chink of knife and fork this army of retainers had vanished, only the one or two required to collect and distribute the plates darting about in deathly silence. Mr. Lever, the proprietor, of course had disappeared in convulsions of courtesy long before. It would be exaggerative, indeed irreverent, to say that he ever positively appeared again. But when the important course, the fish course, was being brought on, there was—how shall I put it?—a vivid shadow, a projection of his personality, which told that he was hovering near. The sacred fish course consisted (to the eyes of the vulgar) in a sort of monstrous pudding, about the size and shape of a wedding cake, in which some considerable number of interesting fishes had finally lost the shapes which God had given to them. The Twelve True Fishermen took up their celebrated fish knives and fish forks, and approached it as gravely as if every inch of the pudding cost as much as the silver fork it was eaten with. So it did, for all I know. This course was dealt with in eager and devouring silence; and it was only when his plate was nearly empty that the young duke made the ritual remark, "They can't do this anywhere but here."

"Nowhere," said Mr. Audley, in a deep bass voice, turning to the speaker and nodding his venerable head a number of times. "Nowhere, assuredly, except here. It was represented to me that at the Café Anglais —"

Here he was interrupted and even agitated for a moment by the removal of his plate, but he recaptured the valuable thread of his thoughts. "It was represented to me that the same could be done at the Café Anglais. Nothing like it, sir," he said, shaking his head ruthlessly, like a hanging judge. "Nothing like it."

"Overrated place," said a certain Colonel Pound, speaking (by the look of him) for the first time for some months.

"Oh, I don't know," said the Duke of Chester, who was an optimist, "it's jolly good for some things. You can't beat it at —"

A waiter came swiftly along the room, and then stopped dead. His stoppage was as silent as his tread; but all those vague and kindly gentlemen were so used to the utter smoothness of the unseen machinery which surrounded and supported their lives, that a waiter doing anything unexpected was a start and a jar. They felt as you and I would feel if the inanimate world disobeyed—if a chair ran away from us.

The waiter stood staring a few seconds, while there deepened on every face at table a strange shame which is wholly the product of our time. It is the combination of modern humanitarianism with the horrible modern abyss between the souls of the rich and poor. A genuine historic aristocrat would have thrown things at the waiter, beginning with empty bottles, and very probably ending with money. A genuine democrat would have asked him, with a comrade-like clearness of speech, what the devil he was doing. But these modern plutocrats could not bear a poor man near to them, either as a slave or as a friend. That something had gone wrong with the servants was merely a dull, hot embarrassment. They did not want to be brutal, and they dreaded the need to be benevolent. They wanted the thing, whatever it was, to be over. It was over. The waiter, after standing for some seconds rigid, like a cataleptic, turned round and ran madly out of the room.

When he reappeared in the room, or rather in the doorway, it was in company with another waiter, with whom he whispered and gesticulated with southern fierceness. Then the first waiter went away, leaving the second waiter, and reappeared with a third waiter. By the time a fourth waiter had joined this hurried synod, Mr. Audley felt it necessary to break the silence in the interests of Tact. He used a very loud cough, instead of the presidential hammer, and said, "Splendid work young Moocher's doing in Burmah. Now, no other nation in the world could have—"

A fifth waiter had sped towards him like an arrow, and was whispering in his ear, "So sorry. Important! Might the proprietor speak to you?"

The chairman turned in disorder, and with a dazed stare saw Mr. Lever coming towards them with his lumbering quickness. The gait of the good proprietor was indeed his usual gait, but his face was by no means usual. Generally it was a genial copper-brown; now it was a sickly yellow.

"You will pardon me, Mr. Audley," he said, with asthmatic breathlessness. "I have great apprehensions. Your fish-plates, they are cleared away with the knife and fork on them!"

"Well, I hope so," said the chairman, with some warmth.

"You see him?" panted the excited hotel keeper; "you see the waiter who took them away? You know him?"

"Know the waiter?" answered Mr. Audley indignantly. "Certainly not!"

Mr. Lever opened his hands with a gesture of agony. "I never send him," he said. "I know not when or why he come. I send my waiter to take away the plates, and he find them already away."

Mr. Audley still looked rather too bewildered to be really the man the empire wants; none of the company could say anything except the man of wood—Colonel Pound—who seemed galvanized into an unnatural life. He rose rigidly from his chair, leaving all the rest sitting, screwed his eyeglass into his eye, and spoke in a raucous undertone as if he had half-forgotten how to speak. "Do you mean," he said, "that somebody has stolen our silver fish service?"

The proprietor repeated the open-handed gesture with even greater helplessness; and in a flash all the men at the table were on their feet.

"Are all your waiters here?" demanded the Colonel, in his low, harsh accent.

"Yes; they're all here. I noticed it myself," cried the young duke, pushing his boyish face into the inmost ring. "Always count 'em as I come in; they look so queer standing up against the wall."

"But surely one cannot exactly remember," began Mr. Audley, with heavy hesitation.

"I remember exactly, I tell you," cried the duke excitedly. "There never have been more than fifteen waiters at this place, and there were no more than fifteen tonight, I'll swear; no more and no less." The proprietor turned upon him, quaking in a kind of palsy of surprise. "You say ... you say," he stammered, "that you see all my fifteen waiters?"

"As usual," assented the duke. "What is the matter with that?"

"Nothing," said Lever, with a deepening accent, "only you did not. For one of zem is dead upstairs."

There was a shocking stillness for an instant in that room. It may be (so supernatural is the word death) that each of those idle men looked for a second at his soul, and saw it as a small dried pea. One of them— the duke, I think—even said with the idiotic kindness of wealth, "Is there anything we can do?"

"He has had a priest," said the Jew, not untouched.

Then, as to the clang of doom, they awoke to their own position. For a few weird seconds they had really felt as if the fifteenth waiter might be the ghost of the dead man upstairs. They had been dumb under that oppression, for ghosts were to them an embarrassment, like beggars. But the remembrance of the silver broke the spell of the miraculous; broke it abruptly and with a brutal reaction. The colonel flung over his chair and strode to the door. "If there was a fifteenth man here, friends," he said, "that fifteenth fellow was a thief. Down at once to the front and back doors and secure everything; then we'll talk. The twenty-four pearls of the club are worth recovering."

Mr. Audley seemed at first to hesitate about whether it was gentlemanly to be in such a hurry about anything; but, seeing the duke dash down the stairs with youthful energy, he followed with a more mature motion.

At the same instant a sixth waiter ran into the room, and declared that he had found the pile of fish plates on a sideboard, with no trace of the silver.

The crowd of diners and attendants that tumbled helter-skelter down the passages divided into two groups. Most of the Fishermen followed the proprietor to the front room to demand news of any exit. Colonel Pound, with the Chairman, the vice-president, and one or two others darted down the corridor leading to the servants' quarters, as the more likely line of escape. As they did so they passed the dim alcove or cavern of the cloak-room, and saw a short, black-coated figure, presumably an attendant, standing a little way back in the shadow of it.

"Hallo there!" called out the duke. "Have you seen anyone pass?"

The short figure did not answer the question directly, but merely said, "Perhaps I have got what you are looking for, gentlemen."

They paused, wavering and wondering, while he quietly went to the back of the cloak-room, and came back with both hands full of shining silver, which he laid out on the counter as calmly as a salesman. It took the form of a dozen quaintly shaped forks and knives.

"You—you—" began the colonel, quite thrown off his balance at last. Then he peered into the dim little room and saw two things: first, that the short, black-clad man was dressed like a clergyman; and, second, that the window of the room behind him was burst, as if someone had passed violently through.

"Valuable things to deposit in a cloak-room, aren't they?" remarked the clergyman, with cheerful composure.

"Did—did you steal those things?" stammered Mr. Audley, with staring eyes.

"If I did," said the cleric pleasantly, "at least I am bringing them back again."

"But you didn't," said Colonel Pound, still staring at the broken window.

"To make a clean breast of it, I didn't," said the other, with some humour. And he seated himself quite gravely on a stool.

"But you know who did," said the colonel.

"I don't know his real name," said the priest placidly; "but I know something of his fighting weight, and a great deal about his spiritual difficulties. I formed the physical estimate when he was trying to throttle me, and the moral estimate when he repented."

"Oh, I say—repented!" cried young Chester, with a sort of crow of laughter.

Father Brown got to his feet, putting his hands behind him. "Odd, isn't it," he said, "that a thief and a vagabond should repent, when so many who are rich and secure remain hard and frivolous, and without fruit for God or man? But there, if you will excuse me, you trespass a little upon my province. If you doubt the penitence as a practical fact, there are your knives and forks. You are The Twelve True Fishers, and there are all your silver fish. But He has made me a fisher of men."

"Did you catch this man?" asked the colonel, frowning.

Father Brown looked him full in his frowning face. "Yes," he said, "I caught him, with an unseen hook and an invisible line which is long enough to let him wander to the ends of the world, and still to bring him back with a twitch upon the thread."

There was a long silence. All the other men present drifted away to carry the recovered silver to their comrades, or to consult the proprietor about the queer condition of affairs. But the grim-faced colonel still sat sideways on the counter, swinging his long, lank legs and biting his dark moustache.

At last he said quietly to the priest, "He must have been a clever fellow, but I think I know a cleverer."

"He was a clever fellow," answered the other, "but I am not quite sure of what other you mean."

"I mean you," said the colonel, with a short laugh. "I don't want to get the fellow jailed; make yourself easy about that. But I'd give a good many silver forks to know how exactly how you fell into this affair, and how you got the stuff out of him. I reckon you're the most up-to-date devil of the present company."

Father Brown seemed rather to like the saturnine candour of the soldier. "Well," he said, smiling, "I mustn't tell you anything of the man's identity, or his own story, of course; but there's no particular reason why I shouldn't tell you of the mere outside facts which I found out for myself."

He hopped over the barrier with unexpected activity, and sat beside Colonel Pound, kicking his short legs like a little boy on a gate. He began to tell the story as easily as if he were telling it to an old friend by a Christmas fire.

"You see, colonel," he said, "I was shut up in that small room there doing some writing, when I heard a pair of feet in this passage doing a dance that was as queer as the dance of death.[1]

"First came quick, funny little steps, like a man walking on tiptoe for a wager; then came slow, careless, creaking steps, as of a big man walking about with a cigar. But they were both made by the same feet, I swear, and they came in rotation; first the run and then the walk, and then the run again. I wondered at first idly and then wildly why a man should act these two parts at once. One walk I knew; it was just like yours, colonel. It was the walk of a well-fed gentleman waiting for something, who strolls about rather because he is physically alert than because he is mentally impatient. I knew that I knew the other walk, too, but I could not remember what it was. What wild creature had I met on my travels that tore along on tiptoe in that extraordinary style? Then I heard a clink of plates somewhere; and the answer stood up as plain as St. Peter's. It was the walk of a waiter—that walk with the body slanted forward, the eyes looking down, the ball of the toe spurning away the ground, the coat tails and napkin flying. Then I thought for a minute and a half more. And I believe I saw the manner of the crime, as clearly as if I were going to commit it."

Colonel Pound looked at him keenly, but the speaker's mild grey eyes were fixed upon the ceiling with almost empty wistfulness.

"A crime," he said slowly, "is like any other work of art. Don't look surprised; crimes are by no means the only works of art that come from an infernal workshop. But every work of art, divine or diabolic, has one indispensable mark—I mean, that the centre of it is simple, however much the fulfilment may be complicated. Thus, in *Hamlet*, let us say, the grotesqueness of the grave-digger, the flowers of the mad girl, the fantastic finery of Osric, the pallor of the ghost and the grin of the skull are all oddities in a sort of tangled wreath round one plain tragic figure of a man in black. Well, this also," he

[1] The "dance of death" originated in a fourteenth-century morality play in which Death debates each of his victims in turn, and having defeated them all at the play's conclusion, leads them off stage in a strange capering sort of dance.

said, getting slowly down from his seat with a smile, "this also is the plain tragedy of a man in black. Yes," he went on, seeing the colonel look up in some wonder, "the whole of this tale turns on a black coat. In this, as in *Hamlet*, there are the rococo excrescences— yourselves, let us say. There is the dead waiter, who was there when he could not be there. There is the invisible hand that swept your table clear of silver and melted into air. But every clever crime is founded ultimately on some one quite simple fact—some fact that is not itself mysterious. The mystification comes in covering it up, in leading men's thoughts away from it. This large and subtle and (in the ordinary course) most profitable crime, was built on the plain fact that a gentleman's evening dress is the same as a waiter's. All the rest was acting, and thundering good acting, too."

"Still," said the colonel, getting up and frowning at his boots. "I am not sure that I understand."

"Colonel," said Father Brown, "I tell you that this archangel of impudence who stole your forks walked up and down this passage twenty times in the blaze of all the lamps, in the glare of all the eyes. He did not go and hide in dim corners where suspicion might have searched for him. He kept constantly on the move in the lighted corridors, and everywhere that he went he seemed to be there by right. Don't ask me what he was like; you have seen him yourself six or seven times tonight. You were waiting with all the other grand people in the reception room at the end of the passage there, with the terrace just beyond. Whenever he came among you gentlemen, he came in the lightning style of a waiter, with bent head, flapping napkin and flying feet. He shot out on to the terrace, did something to the table cloth, and shot back again towards the office and the waiters' quarters. By the time he had come under the eye of the office clerk and the waiters he had become another man in every inch of his body, in every instinctive gesture. He strolled among the servants with the absent-minded insolence which they have all seen in their patrons. It was no new thing to them that a swell from the dinner party should pace all parts of the house like an animal at the Zoo; they know that nothing marks the Smart Set more than a habit of walking where one chooses. When he was magnificently weary of walking down that particular passage he would wheel round and pace back past the office; in the shadow of the arch just beyond he was altered as by a blast of magic, and went hurrying forward again among the Twelve Fishermen, an obsequious attendant. Why should the gentlemen look at a chance waiter? Why should the waiters suspect a first-rate walking gentleman? Once or twice he played the coolest tricks. In the proprietor's private quarters he called out breezily for a syphon of soda water, saying he was thirsty. He said genially that he would carry it himself, and he did; he carried it quickly and correctly through the thick of you, a waiter with an obvious errand. Of course, it could not have been kept up long, but it only had to be kept up till the end of the fish course.

"His worst moment was when the waiters stood in a row; but even then he contrived to lean against the wall just around the corner in such a way that for that important instant the waiters thought him a gentleman, while the gentlemen thought him a waiter. The rest went like winking. If any waiter caught him away from the table, that waiter caught a languid aristocrat. He had only to time himself two minutes before the fish was cleared, become a swift servant, and clear it himself. He put the plates down on a sideboard, stuffed the silver in his breast pocket, giving it a bulgy look, and ran like a hare (I heard him coming) till he came to the cloak-room. There he had only to be a plutocrat again—a plutocrat called away suddenly on business. He had only to give his ticket to the cloak-room attendant, and go out again elegantly as he had come in. Only—only I happened to be the cloak-room attendant."

"What did you do to him?" cried the colonel, with unusual intensity. "What did he tell you?"

"I beg your pardon," said the priest immovably, "that is where the story ends."

"And the interesting story begins," muttered Pound. "I think I understand his professional trick. But I don't seem to have got hold of yours."

"I must be going," said Father Brown.

They walked together along the passage to the entrance hall, where they saw the fresh, freckled-face of the Duke of Chester, who was bounding buoyantly along towards them.

"Come along, Pound," he cried breathlessly. "I've been looking for you everywhere. The dinner's going again in spanking style, and old Audley has got to make a speech in honour of the forks being saved. We want to start some new ceremony, don't you know, to commemorate the occasion. I say, you really got the goods back, what do you suggest?"

"Why," said the colonel, eyeing him with a certain sardonic approval. "I should suggest that henceforward we wear green coats instead of black. One never knows what mistakes may arise when one looks so like a waiter."

"Oh, hang it all!" said the young man, "a gentleman never looks like a waiter."

"Nor a waiter like a gentleman, I suppose," said Colonel Pound, with the same lowering laughter on his face. "Reverend sir, your friend must have been very smart to act the gentleman."

Father Brown buttoned up his commonplace overcoat to the neck, for the night was stormy, and took his commonplace umbrella from the stand.

"Yes," he said; "it must be very hard work to be a gentleman; but, do you know, I have sometimes thought that it may be almost as laborious to be a waiter."

And saying "Good evening," he pushed open the heavy doors of that palace of pleasures. The golden gates closed behind him, and he went at a brisk walk through the damp, dark streets in search of a penny omnibus.

THE FLYING STARS

"The most beautiful crime I ever committed," Flambeau would say in his highly moral old age, "was also, by a singular coincidence, my last. It was committed at Christmas. As an artist I had always attempted to provide crimes suitable to the special season or landscapes in which I found myself, choosing this or that terrace or garden for a catastrophe, as if for a statuary group. Thus squires should be swindled in long rooms panelled with oak; while Jews, on the other hand, should rather find themselves unexpectedly penniless among the light and screens of the Café Riche.[1] Thus, in England, if I wished to relieve a dean of his riches (which is not so easy as you might suppose), I wished to frame him, if I make myself clear, in the green lawns and grey towers of some cathedral town. Similarly, in France, when I had got money out of a rich and wicked peasant (which is almost impossible), it gratified me to get his indignant head relieved against a grey line of clipped poplars, and those solemn plains of Gaul over which broods the mighty spirit of Millet.[2]

"Well, my last crime was a Christmas crime, a cheery, cosy, English middle-class crime; a crime of Charles Dickens. I did it in a good old middle-class house near Putney, a house with a crescent of carriage drive, a house with a stable by the side of it, a house with the name on the two outer gates, a house with a monkey tree. Enough, you know the species. I really think my imitation of Dickens's style was dexterous and literary. It seems almost a pity I repented the same evening."

Flambeau would then proceed to tell the story from the inside; and even from the inside it was odd. Seen from the outside it was perfectly incomprehensible, and it is from the outside that the stranger must study it. From this standpoint the drama may be said to have begun when the front doors of the house with the stable opened on the garden with the monkey tree, and a young girl came out with

[1] In the early years of the twentieth century, the Café Riche in Cairo was a celebrated restaurant-theater and gathering place for the wealthy.

[2] Flambeau is referring to Jean Francois Millet (1814–1875), a painter celebrated for his rural scenes and peasant subjects.

bread to feed the birds on the afternoon of Boxing Day. She had a
pretty face, with brave brown eyes; but her figure was beyond conjecture, for she was so wrapped up in brown furs that it was hard to
say which was hair and which was fur. But for the attractive face she
might have been a small toddling bear.

The winter afternoon was reddening towards evening, and already
a ruby light was rolled over the bloomless beds, filling them, as it
were, with the ghosts of the dead roses. On one side of the house
stood the stable, on the other an alley or cloister of laurels led to the
larger garden behind. The young lady, having scattered bread for the
birds (for the fourth or fifth time that day, because the dog ate it),
passed unobtrusively down the lane of laurels and into a glimmering
plantation of evergreens behind. Here she gave an exclamation of wonder, real or ritual, and looking up at the high garden wall above her,
beheld it fantastically bestridden by a somewhat fantastic figure.

"Oh, don't jump, Mr. Crook," she called out in some alarm; "it's
much too high."

The individual riding the party wall like an aerial horse was a tall,
angular young man, with dark hair sticking up like a hair brush, intelligent and even distinguished lineaments, but a sallow and almost alien
complexion. This showed the more plainly because he wore an aggressive red tie, the only part of his costume of which he seemed to take
any care. Perhaps it was a symbol. He took no notice of the girl's
alarmed adjuration, but leapt like a grasshopper to the ground beside
her, where he might very well have broken his legs.

"I think I was meant to be a burglar," he said placidly, "and I have
no doubt I should have been if I hadn't happened to be born in that
nice house next door. I can't see any harm in it, anyhow."

"How can you say such things?" she remonstrated.

"Well," said the young man, "if you're born on the wrong side of
the wall, I can't see that it's wrong to climb over it."

"I never know what you will say or do next," she said.

"I don't often know myself," replied Mr. Crook; "but then I am
on the right side of the wall now."

"And which is the right side of the wall?" asked the young lady,
smiling.

"Whichever side you are on," said the young man named Crook.

As they went together through the laurels towards the front garden a motor horn sounded thrice, coming nearer and nearer, and a car of splendid speed, great elegance, and a pale green colour swept up to the front doors like a bird and stood throbbing.

"Hullo, hullo!" said the young man with the red tie, "here's somebody born on the right side, anyhow. I didn't know, Miss Adams, that your Santa Claus was so modern as this."

"Oh, that's my godfather, Sir Leopold Fischer. He always comes on Boxing Day."

Then, after an innocent pause, which unconsciously betrayed some lack of enthusiasm, Ruby Adams added:

"He is very kind."

John Crook, journalist, had heard of that eminent City magnate; and it was not his fault if the City magnate had not heard of him; for in certain articles in *The Clarion or The New Age* Sir Leopold had been dealt with austerely. But he said nothing and grimly watched the unloading of the motor-car, which was rather a long process. A large, neat chauffeur in green got out from the front, and a small, neat manservant in grey got out from the back, and between them they deposited Sir Leopold on the doorstep and began to unpack him, like some very carefully protected parcel. Rugs enough to stock a bazaar, furs of all the beasts of the forest, and scarves of all the colours of the rainbow were unwrapped one by one, till they revealed something resembling the human form; the form of a friendly, but foreign-looking old gentleman, with a grey goat-like beard and a beaming smile, who rubbed his big fur gloves together.

Long before this revelation was complete the two big doors of the porch had opened in the middle, and Colonel Adams (father of the furry young lady) had come out himself to invite his eminent guest inside. He was a tall, sunburnt and very silent man, who wore a red smoking-cap like a fez, making him look like one of the English Sirdars or Pashas in Egypt.[3] With him was his brother-in-law, lately come

---

[3] *Sirdar*, a word from the Urdu language of India, means "a leader", and was used at the time for the British Commander of Egyptian Armies; *pasha* (or *pacha*) is Turkish for a "high-ranking official".

from Canada, a big and rather boisterous young gentleman-farmer, with a yellow beard, by name James Blount. With him also was the more insignificant figure of the priest from the neighbouring Roman church; for the colonel's late wife had been a Catholic, and the children, as is common in such cases, had been trained to follow her. Everything seemed undistinguished about the priest, even down to his name, which was Brown; yet the colonel had always found something companionable about him, and frequently asked him to such family gatherings.

In the large entrance hall of the house there was ample room even for Sir Leopold and the removal of his wraps. Porch and vestibule, indeed, were unduly large in proportion to the house, and formed, as it were, a big room with the front door at one end, and the bottom of the staircase at the other. In front of the large hall fire, over which hung the colonel's sword, the process was completed and the company, including the saturnine Crook, presented to Sir Leopold Fischer. That venerable financier, however, still seemed struggling with portions of his well-lined attire, and at length produced from a very interior tail-coat pocket, a black oval case which he radiantly explained to be his Christmas present for his god-daughter. With an unaffected vain-glory that had something disarming about it he held out the case before them all; it flew open at a touch and half-blinded them. It was just as if a crystal fountain had spurted in their eyes. In a nest of orange velvet lay like three eggs, three white and vivid diamonds that seemed to set the very air on fire all round them. Fischer stood beaming benevolently and drinking deep of the astonishment and ecstasy of the girl, the grim admiration and gruff thanks of the colonel, the wonder of the whole group.

"I'll put 'em back now, my dear," said Fischer, returning the case to the tails of his coat. "I had to be careful of 'em coming down. They're the three great African diamonds called 'The Flying Stars,' because they've been stolen so often. All the big criminals are on the track; but even the rough men about in the streets and hotels could hardly have kept their hands off them. I might have lost them on the road here. It was quite possible."

"Quite natural, I should say," growled the man in the red tie. "I shouldn't blame 'em if they had taken 'em. When they ask for bread, and you don't even give them a stone, I think they might take the stone for themselves."

"I won't have you talking like that," cried the girl, who was in a curious glow. "You've only talked like that since you became a horrid what's-his-name. You know what I mean. What do you call a man who wants to embrace the chimney-sweep?"

"A saint," said Father Brown.

"I think," said Sir Leopold, with a supercilious smile, "that Ruby means a Socialist."

"A radical does not mean a man who lives on radishes," remarked Crook, with some impatience; "and a Conservative does not mean a man who preserves jam. Neither, I assure you, does a Socialist mean a man who desires a social evening with the chimney-sweep. A Socialist means a man who wants all the chimneys swept and all the chimney-sweeps paid for it."

"But who won't allow you," put in the priest in a low voice, "to own your own soot."

Crook looked at him with an eye of interest and even respect. "Does one want to own soot?" he asked.

"One might," answered Brown, with speculation in his eye. "I've heard that gardeners use it. And I once made six children happy at Christmas when the conjuror didn't come, entirely with soot—applied externally."

"Oh, splendid," cried Ruby. "Oh, I wish you'd do it to this company."

The boisterous Canadian, Mr. Blount, was lifting his loud voice in applause, and the astonished financier his (in some considerable deprecation), when a knock sounded at the double front doors. The priest opened them, and they showed again the front garden of evergreens, monkey-tree and all, now gathering gloom against a gorgeous violet sunset. The scene thus framed was so coloured and quaint, like a back scene in a play, that they forgot for a moment the insignificant figure standing in the door. He was dusty-looking and in a frayed coat, evidently a common messenger. "Any of you gentlemen Mr. Blount?" he asked, and held forward a letter doubtfully. Mr. Blount started, and stopped in his shout of assent. Ripping up the envelope with evident astonishment he read it; his face clouded a little, and then cleared, and he turned to his brother-in-law and host.

"I'm sick at being such a nuisance, colonel," he said, with the cheery colonial convention; "but would it upset you if an old acquaintance called on me here tonight on business? In point of fact it's Florian, that famous French acrobat and comic actor; I knew him years ago out West (he was a French-Canadian by birth), and he seems to have business for me, though I hardly guess what."

"Of course, of course," replied the colonel carelessly. "My dear chap, any friend of yours. No doubt he will prove an acquisition."

"He'll black his face, if that's what you mean," cried Blount, laughing. "I don't doubt he'd black everyone else's eyes. I don't care; I'm not refined. I like the jolly old pantomime where a man sits on his top hat."

"Not on mine, please," said Sir Leopold Fischer, with dignity.

"Well, well," observed Crook airily, "don't let's quarrel. There are lower jokes than sitting on a top hat."

Dislike of the red-tied youth, born of his predatory opinions and evident intimacy with the pretty god-child, led Fischer to say, in his most sarcastic, magisterial manner: "No doubt you have found something much lower than sitting on a top hat. What is it, pray?"

"Letting a top hat sit on you, for instance," said the Socialist.

"Now, now, now," cried the Canadian farmer with his barbarian benevolence, "don't let's spoil a jolly evening. What I say is, let's do something for the company tonight. Not blacking faces or sitting on hats, if you don't like those—but something of the sort. Why couldn't we have a proper old English pantomime—clown, columbine, and so on. I saw one when I left England at twelve years old, and it's blazed in my brain like a bonfire ever since. I came back to the old country only last year, and I find the thing's extinct. Nothing but a lot of snivelling fairy plays. I want a hot poker and a policeman made into sausages, and they give me princesses moralizing by moonlight, Blue Birds, or something.[4] Blue Beard's more in my line, and him I liked best when he turned into the pantaloon."

[4] Blount's reference is to *The Blue Bird* (1908), a children's fable and play by the Belgian dramatist, Maurice Maeterlink.

"I'm all for making a policeman into sausages," said John Crook. "It's a better definition of Socialism than some recently given. But surely the get-up would be too big a business."

"Not a scrap," cried Blount, quite carried away. "A harlequinade's the quickest thing we can do, for two reasons. First, one can gag to any degree; and, second, all the objects are household things—tables and towel-horses and washing baskets, and things like that."

"That's true," admitted Crook, nodding eagerly and walking about. "But I'm afraid I can't have my policeman's uniform. Haven't killed a policeman lately."

Blount frowned thoughtfully a space, and then smote his thigh. "Yes, we can!" he cried. "I've got Florian's address here, and he knows every *costumier* in London. I'll 'phone him to bring a police dress when he comes." And he went bounding away to the telephone.

"Oh, it's glorious, godfather," cried Ruby, almost dancing. "I'll be columbine and you shall be pantaloon."

The millionaire held himself stiff with a sort of heathen solemnity. "I think, my dear," he said, "you must get someone else for pantaloon."

"I will be pantaloon, if you like," said Colonel Adams, taking his cigar out of his mouth, and speaking for the first and last time.

"You ought to have a statue," cried the Canadian, as he came back, radiant, from the telephone. "There, we are all fitted. Mr. Crook shall be clown; he's a journalist and knows all the oldest jokes. I can be harlequin, that only wants long legs and jumping about. My friend Florian 'phones he's bringing the police costume; he's changing on the way. We can act it in this very hall, the audience sitting on those broad stairs opposite, one row above another. These front doors can be the back scene, either open or shut. Shut, you see an English interior. Open, a moonlit garden. It all goes by magic." And snatching a chance piece of billiard chalk from his pocket, he ran it across the hall floor, half-way between the front door and the staircase, to mark the line of the footlights.

How even such a banquet of bosh was got ready in the time remained a riddle. But they went at it with that mixture of recklessness and industry that lives when youth is in a house; and youth was in that house that night, though not all may have isolated the two faces and hearts from which it flamed. As always happens, the invention grew wilder and wilder through the very tameness of the *bourgeois* conventions from which it had to create. The columbine looked charming in an outstanding skirt that strangely resembled the large lamp-shade in the drawing-room. The clown and pantaloon made themselves white with flour from the cook, and red with rouge from some other domestic, who remained (like all true Christian benefactors) anonymous. The harlequin, already clad in silver paper out of cigar boxes, was, with difficulty, prevented from smashing the old Victorian lustre chandeliers, that he might cover himself with resplendent crystals. In fact he would certainly have done so, had not Ruby unearthed some old pantomime paste jewels she had worn at a fancy dress party as the Queen of Diamonds. Indeed, her uncle, James Blount, was getting almost out of hand in his excitement; he was like a schoolboy. He put a paper donkey's head unexpectedly on Father Brown, who bore it patiently, and even found some private manner of moving his ears. He even essayed to put the paper donkey's tail to the coat-tails of Sir Leopold Fischer. This, however, was frowned down. "Uncle is too absurd," cried Ruby to Crook, round whose shoulders she had seriously placed a string of sausages. "Why is he so wild?"

"He is harlequin to your columbine," said Crook. "I am only the clown who makes the old jokes."

"I wish you were the harlequin," she said, and left the string of sausages swinging.

Father Brown, though he knew every detail done behind the scenes, and had even evoked applause by his transformation of a pillow into a pantomime baby, went round to the front and sat among the audience with all the solemn expectation of a child at his first matinée. The spectators were few, relations, one or two local friends, and the servants; Sir Leopold sat in the front seat, his full and still fur-collared figure largely obscuring the view of the little cleric behind him; but it has never been settled by artistic authorities whether the cleric lost much. The pantomime was utterly chaotic, yet not contemptible; there ran through it a rage of improvisation which came chiefly from Crook the clown. Commonly he was a clever man, and he was inspired tonight with a wild omniscience, a folly wiser than the world, that which comes to a young man who has seen for an instant a particular expression on a particular face. He was supposed to be the clown, but he was really almost everything else, the author (so far as there was an author), the prompter, the scene-painter, the scene-shifter, and, above all, the orchestra. At abrupt intervals in the outrageous performance he would hurl himself in full costume at the piano and bang out some popular music equally absurd and appropriate.

The climax of this, as of all else, was the moment when the two front doors at the back of the scene flew open, showing the lovely moonlit garden, but showing more prominently the famous professional guest; the great Florian, dressed up as a policeman. The clown at the piano played the constabulary chorus in the "Pirates of Penzance," but it was drowned in the deafening applause, for every gesture of the great comic actor was an admirable though restrained version of the carriage and manner of the police. The harlequin leapt upon him and hit him over the helmet; the pianist playing "Where did you get that hat?" he faced about in admirably simulated astonishment, and then the leaping harlequin hit him again (the pianist suggesting a few bars of "Then we had another one"). Then the harlequin rushed right into the arms of the policeman and fell on top of him, amid a roar of applause. Then it was that the strange actor gave that celebrated imitation of a dead man, of which the fame still lingers round Putney. It was almost impossible to believe that a living person could appear so limp.

The athletic harlequin swung him about like a sack or twisted or tossed him about like an Indian club; all the time to the most maddeningly ludicrous tunes from the piano. When the harlequin heaved the comic constable heavily off the floor the clown played "I arise from dreams of thee." When he shuffled him across his back, "With my bundle on my shoulder," and when the harlequin finally let fall the policeman with a most convincing thud, the lunatic at the instrument struck into a jingling measure with some words which are still believed to have been, "I sent a letter to my love and on the way I dropped it."

At about this limit of mental anarchy Father Brown's view was obscured altogether; for the City magnate in front of him rose to his full height and thrust his hands savagely into all his pockets. Then he sat down nervously, still fumbling, and then stood up again. For an instant it seemed seriously likely that he would stride across the footlights; then he turned a glare at the clown playing the piano; and then he burst in silence out of the room.

The priest had only watched for a few more minutes the absurd but not inelegant dance of the amateur harlequin over his splendidly unconscious foe. With real though rude art, the harlequin danced slowly backwards out of the door into the garden, which was full of moonlight and stillness. The vamped dress of silver paper and paste, which had been too glaring in the footlights, looked more and more magical and silvery as it danced away under a brilliant moon. The audience was closing in with a cataract of applause, when Brown felt his arm abruptly touched, and he was asked in a whisper to come into the colonel's study.

He followed his summoner with increasing doubt, which was not dispelled by a solemn comicality in the scene of the study. There sat Colonel Adams, still unaffectedly dressed as a pantaloon, with the knobbed whalebone nodding above his brow, but with his poor old eyes sad enough to have sobered a Saturnalia. Sir Leopold Fischer was leaning against the mantelpiece and heaving with all the importance of panic.

"This is a very painful matter, Father Brown," said Adams. "The truth is, those diamonds we all saw this afternoon seem to have vanished from my friend's tail-coat pocket. And as you—"

"As I," supplemented Father Brown, with a broad grin, "was sitting just behind him—"

"Nothing of the sort shall be suggested," said Colonel Adams, with a firm look at Fischer, which rather implied that some such thing *had* been suggested. "I only ask you to give me the assistance that any gentleman might give."

"Which is turning out his pockets," said Father Brown, and proceeded to do so, displaying seven and sixpence, a return ticket, a small silver crucifix, a small breviary, and a stick of chocolate.

The colonel looked at him long, and then said, "Do you know, I should like to see the inside of your head more than the inside of your pockets. My daughter is one of your people, I know; well, she has lately—" and he stopped.

"She has lately," cried out old Fischer, "opened her father's house to a cut-throat Socialist, who says openly he would steal anything from a richer man. This is the end of it. Here is the richer man—and none the richer."

"If you want the inside of my head you can have it," said Brown rather wearily. "What it's worth you can say afterwards. But the first thing I find in that disused pocket is this; that men who mean to steal diamonds don't talk Socialism. They are more likely," he added demurely, "to denounce it."

Both the others shifted sharply, and the priest went on:

"You see, we know these people, more or less. That Socialist would no more steal a diamond than a Pyramid. We ought to look at once to the one man we don't know. The fellow acting the policeman— Florian. Where is he exactly at this minute, I wonder?"

The pantaloon sprang erect and strode out of the room. An interlude ensued, during which the millionaire stared at the priest, and the priest at his breviary; then the pantaloon returned and said, with *staccato* gravity, "The policeman is still lying on the stage. The curtain has gone up and down six times; he is still lying there."

Father Brown dropped his book and stood staring with a look of blank mental ruin. Very slowly a light began to creep back in his grey eyes, and then he made the scarcely obvious answer.

"Please forgive me, colonel, but when did your wife die?"

"My wife!" replied the staring soldier, "she died this year two months. Her brother James arrived just a week too late to see her."

The little priest bounded like a rabbit shot. "Come on!" he cried in quite unusual excitement. "Come on! We've got to go and look at that policeman!"

They rushed on to the now curtained stage, breaking rudely past the columbine and clown (who seemed whispering quite contentedly), and Father Brown bent over the prostrate comic policeman.

"Chloroform," he said as he rose; "I only guessed it just now."

There was a startled stillness, and then the colonel said slowly, "Please say seriously what all this means."

Father Brown suddenly shouted with laughter, then stopped, and only struggled with it for instants during the rest of his speech. "Gentlemen," he gasped, "there's not much time to talk. I must run after the criminal. But this great French actor who played the policeman—this clever corpse the harlequin waltzed with and dandled and threw about—he was—" His voice again failed him, and he turned his back to run.

"He was?" called Fischer inquiringly.

"A real policeman," said Father Brown, and ran away, into the dark.

There were hollows and bowers at the extreme end of that leafy garden, in which the laurels and other immortal shrubs showed against sapphire sky and silver moon, even in that midwinter, warm colours as of the south. The green gaiety of the waving laurels, the rich purple indigo of the night, the moon like a monstrous crystal, make an almost irresponsibly romantic picture; and among the top branches of the garden trees a strange figure is climbing, who looks not so much romantic as impossible. He sparkles from head to heel, as if clad in ten million moons; the real moon catches him at every movement and sets a new inch of him on fire. But he swings, flashing and successful, from the short tree in this garden to the tall, rambling tree in the other, and only stops there because a shade has slid under the smaller tree and has unmistakably called up to him.

"Well, Flambeau," says the voice, "you really look like a Flying Star; but that always means a Falling Star at last."

The silver, sparkling figure above seems to lean forward in the laurels and, confident of escape, listens to the little figure below.

"You never did anything better, Flambeau. It was clever to come from Canada (with a Paris ticket, I suppose) just a week after Mrs. Adams died, when one was in a mood to ask questions. It was cleverer to have marked down the Flying Stars and the very day of Fischer's coming. But there's no cleverness, but mere genius, in what followed. Stealing the stones, I suppose, was nothing to you. You could have done it by sleight of hand in a hundred other ways besides that pretence of putting a paper donkey's tail to Fischer's coat. But in the rest you eclipsed yourself."

The silvery figure among the green leaves seems to linger as if hypnotized, though his escape is easy behind him; he is staring at the man below.

"Oh, yes," says the man below, "I know all about it. I know you not only forced the pantomime, but put it to a double use. You were going to steal the stones quietly; news came by an accomplice that you were already suspected, and a capable police officer was coming to rout you up that very night. A common thief would have been thankful for the warning and fled; but you are a poet. You already had the clever notion of hiding the jewels in a blaze of false stage jewellery. Now, you saw that if the dress were a harlequin's the appearance of a policeman would be quite in keeping. The worthy officer started from Putney police-station to find you, and walked into the queerest trap ever set in this world. When the front door opened he walked straight on to the stage of a Christmas pantomime, where he could be kicked, clubbed, stunned and drugged by the dancing harlequin, amid roars of laughter from all the most respectable people in Putney. Oh, you will never do anything better. And now, by the way, you might give me back those diamonds."

The green branch on which the glittering figure swung, rustled as if in astonishment; but the voice went on:

"I want you to give them back, Flambeau, and I want you to give up this life. There is still youth and honour and humour in you; don't fancy they will last in that trade. Men may keep a sort of level of good, but no man has ever been able to keep on one level of evil. That road goes down and down. The kind man drinks and turns cruel; the frank man kills and lies about it. Many a man I've known started like you to be an honest outlaw, a merry robber of the rich, and ended stamped into slime. Maurice Blum started out as an anarchist of principle, a father of the poor; he ended a greasy spy and talebearer that both sides used and despised. Harry Burke started his free money movement sincerely enough; now he's sponging on a half-starved sister for endless brandies and sodas. Lord Amber went into wild society in a sort of chivalry; now he's paying blackmail to the lowest vultures in London. Captain Barillon was the great gentleman-apache before your time; he died in a madhouse, screaming with fear of the 'narks' and receivers that had betrayed him and hunted him down. I know the woods look very free behind you, Flambeau; I know that in a flash you could melt into them like a monkey. But some day you will be an old grey monkey, Flambeau. You will sit up in your tree forest cold at heart and close to death, and the tree-tops will be very bare."

Everything continued still, as if the small man below held the other in the tree in some long invisible leash; and he went on:

"Your downward steps have begun. You used to boast of doing nothing mean, but you are doing something mean tonight. You are leaving suspicion on an honest boy with a good deal against him already; you are separating him from the woman he loves and who loves him. But you will do meaner things than that before you die."

Three flashing diamonds fell from the tree to the turf. The small man stooped to pick them up, and when he looked up again the green cage of the tree was emptied of its silver bird.

The restoration of the gems (accidentally picked up by Father Brown, of all people) ended the evening in uproarious triumph; and Sir Leopold, in his height of good humour, even told the priest that though he himself had broader views, he could respect those whose creed required them to be cloistered and ignorant of this world.

THE INVISIBLE MAN

In the cool blue twilight of two steep streets in Camden Town, the shop at the corner, a confectioner's, glowed like the butt of a cigar. One should rather say, perhaps, like the butt of a firework, for the light was of many colours and some complexity, broken up by many mirrors and dancing on many gilt and gaily-coloured cakes and sweetmeats. Against this one fiery glass were glued the noses of many guttersnipes, for the chocolates were all wrapped in those red and gold and green metallic colours which are almost better than chocolate itself; and the huge white wedding-cake in the window was somehow at once remote and satisfying, just as if the whole North Pole were good to eat. Such rainbow provocations could naturally collect the youth of the neighbourhood up to the ages of ten or twelve. But this corner was also attractive to youth at a later stage; and a young man, not less than twenty-four, was staring into the same shop window. To him, also, the shop was of fiery charm, but this attraction was not wholly to be explained by chocolates; which, however, he was far from despising.

He was a tall, burly, red-haired young man, with a resolute face but a listless manner. He carried under his arm a flat, grey portfolio of black-and-white sketches, which he had sold with more or less success to publishers ever since his uncle (who was an admiral) had disinherited him for Socialism, because of a lecture which he had delivered against that economic theory. His name was John Turnbull Angus.

Entering at last, he walked through the confectioner's shop into the back room, which was a sort of pastry-cook restaurant, merely raising his hat to the young lady who was serving there. She was a dark, elegant, alert girl in black, with a high colour and very quick, dark eyes; and after the ordinary interval she followed him into the inner room to take his order.

His order was evidently a usual one. "I want, please," he said with precision, "one halfpenny bun and a small cup of black coffee." An instant before the girl could turn away he added, "Also, I want you to marry me."

The young lady of the shop stiffened suddenly, and said, "Those are jokes I don't allow."

The red-haired young man lifted grey eyes of an unexpected gravity.

"Really and truly," he said, "it's as serious—as serious as the half-penny bun. It is expensive, like the bun; one pays for it. It is indigestible, like the bun. It hurts."

The dark young lady had never taken her dark eyes off him, but seemed to be studying him with almost tragic exactitude. At the end of her scrutiny she had something like the shadow of a smile, and she sat down in a chair.

"Don't you think," observed Angus, absently, "that it's rather cruel to eat these halfpenny buns? They might grow up into penny buns. I shall give up these brutal sports when we are married."

The dark young lady rose from her chair and walked to the window, evidently in a state of strong but not unsympathetic cogitation. When at last she swung round again with an air of resolution she was bewildered to observe that the young man was carefully laying out on the table various objects from the shop-window. They included a pyramid of highly coloured sweets, several plates of sandwiches, and the two decanters containing that mysterious port and sherry which are peculiar to pastry-cooks. In the middle of this neat arrangement he had carefully let down the enormous load of white sugared cake which had been the huge ornament of the window.

"What on earth are you doing?" she asked.

"Duty, my dear Laura," he began.

"Oh, for the Lord's sake, stop a minute," she cried, "and don't talk to me in that way. I mean what is all that?"

"A ceremonial meal, Miss Hope."

"And what is *that*?" she asked impatiently, pointing to the mountain of sugar.

"The wedding-cake, Mrs. Angus," he said.

The girl marched to that article, removed it with some clatter, and put it back in the shop window; she then returned, and, putting her elegant elbows on the table, regarded the young man not unfavourably but with considerable exasperation.

"You don't give me any time to think," she said.

"I'm not such a fool," he answered; "that's my Christian humility."

She was still looking at him; but she had grown considerably graver behind the smile.

"Mr. Angus," she said steadily, "before there is a minute more of this nonsense I must tell you something about myself as shortly as I can."

"Delighted," replied Angus gravely. "You might tell me something about myself, too, while you are about it."

"Oh, do hold your tongue and listen," she said. "It's nothing that I'm ashamed of, and it isn't even anything that I'm specially sorry about. But what would you say if there were something that is no business of mine and yet is my nightmare?"

"In that case," said the man seriously, "I should suggest that you bring back the cake."

"Well, you must listen to the story first," said Laura, persistently. "To begin with, I must tell you that my father owned the inn called the 'Red Fish' at Ludbury, and I used to serve people in the bar."

"I have often wondered," he said, "why there was a kind of a Christian air about this one confectioner's shop."

"Ludbury is a sleepy, grassy little hole in the Eastern Counties, and the only kind of people who ever came to the 'Red Fish' were occasional commercial travellers, and for the rest, the most awful people you can see, only you've never seen them. I mean little, loungy men, who had just enough to live on, and had nothing to do but lean about in bar-rooms and bet on horses in bad clothes that were just too good for them. Even these wretched young rotters were not very common at our house; but there were two of them that were a lot too common—common in every sort of way. They both lived on money of their own, and were wearisomely idle and over-dressed. But yet I was a bit sorry for them, because I half believe they slunk into our little empty bar because each of them had a slight deformity; the sort of thing that some yokels laugh at. It wasn't exactly a deformity either; it was more an oddity. One of them was a surprisingly small man, something like a dwarf, or at least like a jockey. He was not at all jockeyish to look at, though; he had a round black head and a well-trimmed black beard, bright eyes like a bird's; he jingled money in his pockets; he jangled a great gold watch chain; and he never turned up except dressed just too much like a gentleman to be one. He was no fool, though, though a futile idler; he was curiously clever at all kinds of things that couldn't be the slightest use; a sort of impromptu conjuring; making fifteen matches set fire to each other like a regular firework; or cutting a banana or some such thing into a dancing doll. His name was Isidore Smythe; and I can see him still, with his little dark face, just coming up to the counter, making a jumping kangaroo out of five cigars.

"The other fellow was more silent and more ordinary; but somehow he alarmed me much more than poor little Smythe. He was very tall and slight, and light-haired; his nose had a high bridge, and he might almost have been handsome in a spectral sort of way; but he had one of the most appalling squints I have ever seen or heard of. When he looked straight at you, you didn't know where you were yourself, let alone what he was looking at. I fancy this sort of disfigurement embittered the poor chap a little; for while Smythe was ready to show off his monkey tricks anywhere, James Welkin (that was the squinting man's name) never did anything except soak in our bar parlour, and go for great walks by himself in the flat, grey country all round. All the same, I think Smythe, too, was a little sensitive about being so small, though he carried it off more smartly. And so it was that I was really puzzled, as well as startled, and very sorry, when they both offered to marry me in the same week.

"Well, I did what I've since thought was perhaps a silly thing. But, after all, these freaks were my friends in a way; and I had a horror of their thinking I refused them for the real reason, which was that they were so impossibly ugly. So I made up some gas of another sort, about never meaning to marry anyone who hadn't carved his way in the world. I said it was a point of principle with me not to live on money that was just inherited like theirs. Two days after I had talked in this well-meaning sort of way, the whole trouble began. The first thing I heard was that both of them had gone off to seek their fortunes, as if they were in some silly fairy tale.

"Well, I've never seen either of them from that day to this. But I've had two letters from the little man called Smythe, and really they were rather exciting."

"Ever heard of the other man?" asked Angus.

"No, he never wrote," said the girl, after an instant's hesitation. "Smythe's first letter was simply to say that he had started out walking with Welkin to London; but Welkin was such a good walker that the little man dropped out of it, and took a rest by the roadside. He happened to be picked up by some travelling show, and, partly because he was nearly a dwarf, and partly because he was really a clever little wretch, he got on quite well in the show business, and was soon sent up to the Aquarium, to do some tricks that I forget. That was his first letter. His second was much more of a startler, and I only got it last week."

The man called Angus emptied his coffee-cup and regarded her with mild and patient eyes. Her own mouth took a slight twist of laughter as she resumed, "I suppose you've seen on the hoardings all about this 'Smythe's Silent Service'? Or you must be the only person that hasn't. Oh, I don't know much about it, it's some clockwork invention for doing all the housework by machinery. You know the sort of thing, 'Press a button—A Butler who Never Drinks.' 'Turn a handle—Ten Housemaids who Never Flirt.' You must have seen the advertisements. Well, whatever these machines are, they are making pots of money; and they are making it all for that little imp whom I knew down in Ludbury. I can't help feeling pleased the poor little chap has fallen on his feet; but the plain fact is, I'm in terror of his turning up any minute and telling me he's carved his way in the world—as he certainly has."

"And the other man?" repeated Angus with a sort of obstinate quietude.

Laura Hope got to her feet suddenly. "My friend," she said, "I think you are a witch. Yes, you are quite right. I have not seen a line of the other man's writing; and I have no more notion than the dead of what or where he is. But it is of him that I am frightened. It is he who is all about my path. It is he who has half driven me mad. Indeed, I think he has driven me mad; for I have felt him where he could not have been, and I have heard his voice when he could not have spoken."

"Well, my dear," said the young man, cheerfully, "if he were Satan himself, he is done for now you have told somebody. One goes mad all alone, old girl. But when was it you fancied you felt and heard our squinting friend?"

"I heard James Welkin laugh as plainly as I hear you speak," said the girl, steadily. "There was nobody there, for I stood just outside the shop at the corner, and could see down both streets at once. I had forgotten how he laughed, though his laugh was as odd as his squint. I had not thought of him for nearly a year. But it's a solemn truth that a few seconds later the first letter came from his rival."

"Did you ever make the spectre speak or squeak, or anything?" asked Angus, with some interest.

Laura suddenly shuddered, and then said with an unshaken voice, "Yes. Just when I had finished reading the second letter from Isidore Smythe announcing his success, just then, I heard Welkin say, 'He shan't have you, though.' It was quite plain, as if he were in the room. It is awful; I think I must be mad."

"If you really were mad," said the young man, "you would think you must be sane. But certainly there seems to me to be something a little rum about this unseen gentleman. Two heads are better than one—I spare you allusions to any other organs—and really, if you would allow me, as a sturdy, practical man, to bring back the wedding-cake out of the window—"

Even as he spoke, there was a sort of steely shriek in the street outside, and a small motor, driven at devilish speed, shot up to the door of the shop and stuck there. In the same flash of time a small man in a shiny top hat stood stamping in the outer room.

Angus, who had hitherto maintained hilarious ease from motives of mental hygiene, revealed the strain of his soul by striding abruptly out of the inner room and confronting the new-comer. A glance at him was quite sufficient to confirm the savage guesswork of a man in love. This very dapper but dwarfish figure, with the spike of black beard carried insolently forward, the clever unrestful eyes, the neat but very nervous fingers, could be none other than the man just described to him, Isidore Smythe, who made dolls out of banana skins and match-boxes; Isidore Smythe, who made millions out of undrinking butlers and unflirting housemaids of metal. For a moment the two men, instinctively understanding each other's air of possession, looked at each other with that curious cold generosity which is the soul of rivalry.

Mr. Smythe, however, made no allusion to the ultimate ground of their antagonism, but said simply and explosively, "Has Miss Hope seen that thing on the window?"

"On the window?" repeated the staring Angus.

"There's no time to explain other things," said the small millionaire shortly. "There's some tomfoolery going on here that has to be investigated."

He pointed his polished walking-stick at the window, recently depleted by the bridal preparations of Mr. Angus; and that gentleman was astonished to see along the front of the glass a long strip of paper pasted, which had certainly not been on the window when he had looked through it some time before. Following the energetic Smythe outside into the street, he found that some yard and a half of stamp paper had been carefully gummed along the glass outside, and on this was written in straggly characters, "If you marry Smythe, he will die."

"Laura," said Angus, putting his big red head into the shop, "you're not mad."

"It's the writing of that fellow Welkin," said Smythe gruffly. "I haven't seen him for years, but he's always bothering me. Five times in the last fortnight he's had threatening letters left at my flat, and I can't even find out who leaves them, let alone if it is Welkin himself. The porter of the flats swears that no suspicious characters have been seen, and here he has pasted up a sort of dado on a public shop window, while the people in the shop—"

"Quite so," said Angus modestly, "while the the people in the shop were having tea. Well, sir, I can assure you I appreciate your common sense in dealing so directly with the matter. We can talk about other things afterwards. The fellow cannot be very far off yet, for I swear there was no paper there when I went last to the window, ten or fifteen minutes ago. On the other hand, he's too far off to be chased, as we don't even know the direction. If you'll take my advice, Mr. Smythe, you'll put this at once in the hands of some energetic inquiry man, private rather than public. I know an extremely clever fellow, who has set up in business five minutes from here in your car. His name's Flambeau, and though his youth was a bit stormy, he's a strictly honest man now, and his brains are worth money. He lives in Lucknow Mansions, Hampstead."

"That is odd," said the little man, arching his black eyebrows. "I live, myself, in Himalaya Mansions round the corner. Perhaps you might care to come with me; I can go to my rooms and sort out these queer Welkin documents, while you run round and get your friend the detective."

"You are very good," said Angus politely. "Well, the sooner we act the better."

Both men, with a queer kind of impromptu fairness, took the same sort of formal farewell of the lady, and both jumped into the brisk little car. As Smythe took the handles and they turned the great corner of the street, Angus was amused to see a gigantesque poster of "Smythe's Silent Service," with a picture of a huge headless iron doll, carrying a saucepan with the legend, "A Cook Who is Never Cross."

"I use them in my own flat," said the little black-bearded man, laughing, "partly for advertisements, and partly for real convenience. Honestly, and all above board, those big clockwork dolls of mine do bring you coals or claret or a timetable quicker than any live servants I've ever known, if you know which knob to press. But I'll never deny, between ourselves, that such servants have their disadvantages, too."

"Indeed?" said Angus; "is there something they can't do?"

"Yes," replied Smythe coolly; "they can't tell me who left those threatening letters at my flat."

The man's motor was small and swift like himself; in fact, like his domestic service, it was of his own invention. If he was an advertising quack, he was one who believed in his own wares. The sense of something tiny and flying was accentuated as they swept up long white curves of road in the dead but open daylight of evening. Soon the white curves came sharper and dizzier; they were upon ascending spirals, as they say in the modern religions. For, indeed, they were cresting a corner of London which is almost as precipitous as Edinburgh, if not quite so picturesque. Terrace rose above terrace, and the special tower of flats they sought, rose above them all to almost Egyptian height, gilt by the level sunset. The change, as they turned the corner and entered the crescent known as Himalaya Mansions, was as abrupt as the opening of a window; for they found that pile of flats sitting above London as above a green sea of slate. Opposite to the mansions, on the other side of the gravel crescent, was a bushy enclosure more like a steep hedge or dyke than a garden, and some way below that ran a strip of artificial water, a sort of canal, like the moat of that embowered fortress. As the car swept round the crescent it passed, at one corner, the stray stall of a man selling chestnuts; and right away at the other end of the curve, Angus could see a dim blue policeman walking slowly. These were the only human shapes in that high suburban solitude; but he had an irrational sense that they expressed the speechless poetry of London. He felt as if they were figures in a story.

The little car shot up to the right house like a bullet, and shot out its owner like a bomb shell. He was immediately inquiring of a tall commissionaire in shining braid, and a short porter in shirt sleeves, whether anybody or anything had been seeking his apartments. He was assured that nobody and nothing had passed these officials since his last inquiries; whereupon he and the slightly bewildered Angus were shot up in the lift like a rocket, till they reached the top floor.

"Just come in for a minute," said the breathless Smythe. "I want to show you those Welkin letters. Then you might run round the corner and fetch your friend." He pressed a button concealed in the wall, and the door opened of itself.

It opened on a long, commodious ante-room, of which the only arresting features, ordinarily speaking, were the rows of tall half-human mechanical figures that stood up on both sides like tailors' dummies. Like tailors' dummies they were headless; and like tailors' dummies they had a handsome unnecessary humpiness in the shoulders, and a pigeon-breasted protuberance of chest; but barring this, they were not much more like a human figure than any automatic machine at a station that is about the human height. They had two great hooks like arms, for carrying trays; and they were painted pea-green, or vermillion, or black for convenience of distinction; in every other way they were only automatic machines and nobody would have looked twice at them. On this occasion, at least, nobody did. For between the two rows of these domestic dummies lay something more interesting than most of the mechanics of the world. It was a white, tattered scrap of paper scrawled with red ink; and the agile inventor had snatched it up almost as soon as the door flew open. He handed it to Angus without a word. The red ink on it actually was not dry, and the message ran, "If you have been to see her today, I shall kill you."

There was a short silence, and then Isidore Smythe said quietly, "Would you like a little whisky? I rather feel as if I should."

"Thank you; I should like a little Flambeau," said Angus, gloomily. "This business seems to me to be getting rather grave. I'm going round at once to fetch him."

"Right you are," said the other, with admirable cheerfulness. "Bring him round here as quick as you can."

But as Angus closed the front door behind him he saw Smythe push back a button, and one of the clockwork images glided from its place and slid along a groove in the floor carrying a tray with syphon and decanter. There did seem something a trifle weird about leaving the little man alone among those dead servants, who were coming to life as the door closed.

Six steps down from Smythe's landing the man in shirt sleeves was doing something with a pail. Angus stopped to extract a promise, fortified with a prospective bribe, that he would remain in that place until the return with the detective, and would keep count of any kind of stranger coming up those stairs. Dashing down to the front hall he then laid similar charges of vigilance on the commssionaire at the front door, from whom he learned the simplifying circumstance that there was no back door. Not content with that, he captured the floating policeman and induced him to stand opposite the entrance and watch it; and finally paused an instant for a pennyworth of chestnuts, and an inquiry as to the probable length of the merchant's stay in the neighbourhood.

The chestnut seller, turning up the collar of his coat, told him he should probably be moving shortly, as he thought it was going to snow. Indeed, the evening was growing grey and bitter, but Angus, with all his eloquence, proceeded to nail the chestnut man to his post.

"Keep yourself warm on your own chestnuts," he said earnestly. "Eat up your whole stock; I'll make it worth your while. I'll give you a sovereign if you'll wait here till I come back, and then tell me whether any man, woman, or child has gone into that house where the commissionaire is standing."

He then walked away smartly, with a last look at the besieged tower.

"I've made a ring round that room, anyhow," he said. "They can't all four of them be Mr. Welkin's accomplices."

Lucknow Mansions were, so to speak, on a lower platform of that hill of houses, of which Himalaya Mansions might be called the peak. Mr. Flambeau's semi-official flat was on the ground floor, and presented in every way a marked contrast to the American machinery and cold hotel-like luxury of the flat of the Silent Service. Flambeau, who was a friend of Angus, received him in a rococo artistic den behind his office, of which the ornaments were sabres, harquebuses, Eastern curiosities, flasks of Italian wine, savage cooking-pots, a plumy Persian cat, and a small dusty-looking Roman Catholic priest, who looked particularly out of place.

"This is my friend, Father Brown," said Flambeau. "I've often wanted you to meet him. Splendid weather, this; a little cold for Southerners like me."

"Yes, I think it will keep clear," said Angus, sitting down on a violet-striped Eastern ottoman.

"No," said the priest quietly; "it has begun to snow."

And, indeed, as he spoke, the first few flakes, foreseen by the man of chestnuts, began to drift across the darkening window-pane.

"Well," said Angus heavily. "I'm afraid I've come on business, and rather jumpy business at that. The fact is, Flambeau, within a stone's throw of your house is a fellow who badly wants your help; he's perpetually being haunted and threatened by an invisible enemy—a scoundrel whom nobody has even seen." As Angus proceeded to tell the whole tale of Smythe and Welkin, beginning with Laura's story, and going on with his own, the supernatural laugh at the corner of two empty streets, the strange distinct words spoken in an empty room,

Flambeau grew more and more vividly concerned, and the little priest seemed to be left out of it, like a piece of furniture. When it came to the scribbled stamp-paper pasted on the window, Flambeau rose, seeming to fill the room with his huge shoulders.

"If you don't mind," he said, "I think you had better tell me the rest on the nearest road to this man's house. It strikes me, somehow, that there is no time to be lost."

"Delighted," said Angus, rising also, "though he's safe enough for the present, for I've set four men to watch the only hole to his burrow."

They turned out into the street, the small priest trundling after them with the docility of a small dog. He merely said, in a cheerful way, like one making conversation, "How quick the snow gets thick on the ground."

As they threaded the steep side streets already powdered with silver, Angus finished his story; and by the time they reached the crescent with the towering flats, he had leisure to turn his attention to the four sentinels. The chestnut seller, both before and after receiving a sovereign, swore stubbornly that he had watched the door and seen no visitor enter. The policeman was even more emphatic. He said he had had experience of crooks of all kinds, in top hats and in rags; he wasn't so green as to expect suspicious characters to look suspicious; he looked out for anybody, and, so help him, there had been nobody. And when all three men gathered round the gilded commissionaire, who still stood smiling astride of the porch, the verdict was more final still.

"I've got a right to ask any man, duke or dustman, what he wants in these flats," said the genial and gold-laced giant, "and I'll swear there's been nobody to ask since this gentleman went away."

The unimportant Father Brown, who stood back, looking modestly at the pavement, here ventured to say meekly, "Has nobody been up and down stairs, then, since the snow began to fall? It began while we were all round at Flambeau's."

"Nobody's been in here, sir, you can take it from me," said the official, with beaming authority.

"Then I wonder what that is?" said the priest, and stared at the ground blankly like a fish.

The others all looked down also; and Flambeau used a fierce exclamation and a French gesture. For it was unquestionably true that down the middle of the entrance guarded by the man in gold lace, actually between the arrogant, stretched legs of that colossus, ran a stringy pattern of grey footprints stamped upon the white snow.

"God!" cried Angus involuntarily; "the Invisible Man!" [1]

Without another word he turned and dashed up the stairs, with Flambeau following; but Father Brown still stood looking about him in the snow-clad street as if he had lost interest in his query.

Flambeau was plainly in a mood to break down the door with his big shoulders; but the Scotsman, with more reason, if less intuition, fumbled about on the frame of the door till he found the invisible button; and the door swung slowly open.

It showed substantially the same serried interior; the hall had grown darker, though it was still struck here and there with the last crimson shafts of sunset, and one or two of the headless machines had been moved from their places for this or that purpose, and stood here and there about the twilit place. The green and red of their coats were all darkened in the dusk; and their likeness to human shapes slightly increased by their very shapelessness. But in the middle of them all, exactly where the paper with the red ink had lain, there lay something that looked very like red ink spilled out of its bottle. But it was not red ink.

With a French combination of reason and violence Flambeau simply said "Murder!" and, plunging into the flat, had explored every corner and cupboard of it in five minutes. But if he expected to find a corpse he found none. Isidore Smythe simply was not in the place, either dead or alive. After the most tearing search the two men met each other in the outer hall, with streaming faces and staring eyes. "My friend," said Flambeau, talking French in his excitement, "not only is your murderer invisible, but he makes invisible also the murdered man."

Angus looked round at the dim room full of dummies, and in some Celtic corner of his Scotch soul a shudder started. One of the life-size

[1] Angus is thinking of the popular novel *The Invisible Man* (1897) by H. G. Wells about a scientist who had concocted a chemical potion to render himself invisible.

dolls stood immediately overshadowing the blood stain, summoned, perhaps, by the slain man an instant before he fell. One of the high-shouldered hooks that served the thing for arms, was a little lifted, and Angus had suddenly the horrid fancy that poor Smythe's own iron child had struck him down. Matter had rebelled, and these machines had killed their master. But even so, what had they done with him?

"Eaten him?" said the nightmare at his ear; and he sickened for an instant at the idea of rent, human remains absorbed and crushed into all that acephalous clockwork.

He recovered his mental health by an emphatic effort, and said to Flambeau, "Well, there it is. The poor fellow has evaporated like a cloud and left a red streak on the floor. The tale does not belong to this world."

"There is only one thing to be done," said Flambeau, "whether it belongs to this world or the other. I must go down and talk to my friend."

They descended, passing the man with the pail, who again asseverated that he had let no intruder pass, down to the commissionaire and the hovering chestnut man, who rigidly reasserted their own watchfulness. But when Angus looked round for his fourth confirmation he could not see it, and called out with some nervousness, "Where is the policeman?"

"I beg your pardon," said Father Brown; "that is my fault. I just sent him down the road to investigate something—that I just thought worth investigating."

"Well, we want him back pretty soon," said Angus abruptly, "for the wretched man upstairs has not only been murdered, but wiped out."

"How?" asked the priest.

"Father," said Flambeau, after a pause, "upon my soul I believe it is more in your department than mine. No friend or foe has entered the house, but Smythe is gone, as if stolen by the fairies. If that is not supernatural, I—"

As he spoke they were all checked by an unusual sight; the big blue policeman came round the corner of the crescent, running. He came straight up to Brown.

"You're right, sir," he panted, "they've just found poor Mr. Smythe's body in the canal down below."

Angus put his hand wildly to his head. "Did he run down and drown himself?" he asked.

"He never came down, I'll swear," said the constable, "and he wasn't drowned either, for he died of a great stab over the heart."

"And yet you saw no one enter?" said Flambeau in a grave voice.

"Let us walk down the road a little," said the priest.

As they reached the other end of the crescent he observed abruptly, "Stupid of me! I forgot to ask the policeman something. I wonder if they found a light brown sack."

"Why a light brown sack?" asked Angus, astonished.

"Because if it was any other coloured sack, the case must begin over again," said Father Brown; "but if it was a light brown sack, why, the case is finished."

"I am pleased to hear it," said Angus with hearty irony. "It hasn't begun, so far as I am concerned."

"You must tell us all about it," said Flambeau with a strange heavy simplicity, like a child.

Unconsciously they were walking with quickening steps down the long sweep of road on the other side of the high crescent, Father Brown leading briskly, though in silence. At last he said with an almost touching vagueness, "Well, I'm afraid you'll think it so prosy. We always begin at the abstract end of things, and you can't begin this story anywhere else.

"Have you ever noticed this—that people never answer what you say? They answer what you mean—or what they think you mean. Suppose one lady says to another in a country house, 'Is anybody staying with you?' the lady doesn't answer 'Yes; the butler, the three footmen, the parlourmaid, and so on,' though the parlourmaid may be in the room, or the butler behind her chair. She says, 'There is *nobody* staying with us,' meaning nobody of the sort you mean. But suppose a doctor inquiring into an epidemic asks, 'Who is staying in the house?' then the lady will remember the butler, the parlourmaid, and the rest. All language is used like that; you never get a question answered literally, even when you get it answered truly. When those four quite honest men said that no man had gone into the Mansions, they did not really mean that *no man* had gone into them. They meant no man whom they could suspect of being your man. A man did go into the house, and did come out of it, but they never noticed him."

"An invisible man?" inquired Angus, raising his red eyebrows.

"A mentally invisible man," said Father Brown.

A minute or two after he resumed in the same unassuming voice, like a man thinking his way. "Of course, you can't think of such a man, until you do think of him. That's where his cleverness comes in. But I came to think of him through two or three little things in the tale Mr. Angus told us. First, there was the fact that this Welkin went for long walks. And then there was the vast lot of stamp paper on the window. And then, most of all, there were the two things the young lady said—things that couldn't be true. Don't get annoyed," he added hastily, noting a sudden movement of the Scotsman's head; "she thought they were true all right, but they couldn't be true. A person *can't* be quite alone in a street a second before she receives a letter. She can't be quite alone in a street when she starts reading a letter just received. There must be somebody pretty near her; he must be mentally invisible."

"Why must there be somebody near her?" asked Angus.

"Because," said Father Brown, "barring carrier-pigeons, somebody must have brought her the letter."

"Do you really mean to say," asked Flambeau, with energy, "that Welkin carried his rival's letters to his lady?"

"Yes," said the priest. "Welkin carried his rival's letters to his lady. You see, he had to."

"Oh, I can't stand much more of this," exploded Flambeau. "Who is this fellow? What does he look like. What is the usual get-up of a mentally invisible man?"

"He is dressed rather handsomely in red, blue and gold," replied the priest promptly with precision, "and in this striking, and even showy costume he entered Himalaya Mansions under eight human eyes; he killed Smythe in cold blood, and came down into the street again carrying the dead body in his arms—"

"Reverend sir," cried Angus, standing still, "are you raving mad, or am I?"

"You are not mad," said Brown, "only a little unobservant. You have not noticed such a man as this, for example."

He took three quick strides forward, and put his hand on the shoulder of an ordinary passing postman who had bustled by them unnoticed under the shade of the trees.

"Nobody ever notices postmen, somehow," he said thoughtfully; "yet they have passions like other men, and even carry large bags where a small corpse can be stowed quite easily."

The postman, instead of turning naturally, had ducked and tumbled against the garden fence. He was a lean fair-bearded man of very ordinary appearance, but as he turned an alarmed face over his shoulder, all three men were fixed with an almost fiendish squint.

Flambeau went back to his sabres, purple rugs and Persian cat, having many things to attend to. John Turnbull Angus went back to the lady at the shop, with whom that imprudent young man contrives to be extremely comfortable. But Father Brown walked those snow-covered hills under the stars for many hours with a murderer, and what they said to each other will never be known.

THE HONOUR OF ISRAEL GOW

A stormy evening of olive and silver was closing in, as Father Brown, wrapped in a grey Scotch plaid, came to the end of a grey Scotch valley and beheld the strange castle of Glengyle. It stopped one end of the glen or hollow like a blind alley; and it looked like the end of the world. Rising in steep roofs and spires of seagreen slate in the manner of the old French-Scotch châteaux, it reminded an Englishman of the sinister steeple-hats of witches in fairy tales; and the pine woods that rocked round the green turrets looked, by comparison, as black as numberless flocks of ravens. This note of a dreamy, almost a sleepy devilry, was no mere fancy from the landscape. For there did rest on the place one of those clouds of pride and madness and mysterious sorrow which lie more heavily on the noble houses of Scotland than on any other of the children of men. For Scotland has a double dose of the poison called heredity; the sense of blood in the aristocrat, and the sense of doom in the Calvinist.

The priest had snatched a day from his business at Glasgow to meet his friend Flambeau, the amateur detective, who was at Glengyle Castle with another more formal officer investigating the life and death of the late Earl of Glengyle. That mysterious person was the last representative of a race whose valour, insanity, and violent cunning had made them terrible even among the sinister nobility of their nation in the sixteenth century. None were deeper in that labyrinthine ambition, in chamber within chamber of that palace of lies that was built up around Mary Queen of Scots.

The rhyme in the country-side attested the motive and the result of their machinations candidly:

> "As green sap to the simmer trees
> Is red gold to the Ogilvies."

For many centuries there had never been a decent lord in Glengyle Castle; and with the Victorian era one would have thought that all eccentricities were exhausted. The last Glengyle, however, satisfied his tribal tradition by doing the only thing that was left for him to do;

he disappeared. I do not mean that he went abroad; by all accounts he was still in the castle, if he was anywhere. But though his name was in the church register and the big red Peerage, nobody ever saw him under the sun.

If anyone saw him it was a solitary man-servant, something between a groom and a gardener. He was so deaf that the more business-like assumed him to be dumb; while the more penetrating declared him to be half-witted. A gaunt, red-haired labourer, with a dogged jaw and chin, but quite black blue eyes, he went by the name of Israel Gow, and was the one silent servant on that deserted estate. But the energy with which he dug potatoes, and the regularity with which he disappeared into the kitchen gave people an impression that he was providing for the meals of a superior, and that the strange earl was still concealed in the castle. If society needed any further proof that he was there, the servant persistently asserted that he was not at home. One morning the provost and the minister (for the Glengyles were Presbyterian) were summoned to the castle. There they found that the gardener, groom and cook had added to his many professions that of an undertaker, and had nailed up his noble master in a coffin. With how much or how little further inquiry this odd fact was passed, did not as yet very plainly appear; for the thing had never been legally investigated till Flambeau had gone north two or three days before. By then the body of Lord Glengyle (if it was the body) had lain for some time in the little churchyard on the hill.

As Father Brown passed through the dim garden and came under the shadow of the château, the clouds were thick and the whole air damp and thundery. Against the last stripe of the green-gold sunset he saw a black human silhouette; a man in a chimney-pot hat, with a big spade over his shoulder. The combination was queerly suggestive of a sexton; but when Brown remembered the deaf servant who dug potatoes, he thought it natural enough. He knew something of the Scotch peasant; he knew the respectability which might well feel it necessary to wear "blacks" for an official inquiry; he knew also the economy that would not lose an hour's digging for that. Even the man's start and suspicious stare as the priest went by were consonant enough with the vigilance and jealousy of such a type.

The great door was opened by Flambeau himself, who had with him a lean man with iron-grey hair and papers in his hand: Inspector Craven from Scotland Yard. The entrance hall was mostly stripped and empty; but the pale, sneering faces of one or two of the wicked Ogilvies looked down out of the black periwigs and blackening canvas.

Following them into an inner room, Father Brown found that the allies had been seated at a long oak table, of which their end was covered with scribbled papers, flanked with whisky and cigars. Through the whole of its remaining length it was occupied by detached objects arranged at intervals; objects about as inexplicable as any objects could be. One looked like a small heap of glittering broken glass. Another looked like a high heap of brown dust. A third appeared to be a plain stick of wood.

"You seem to have a sort of geological museum here," he said, as he sat down, jerking his head briefly in the direction of the brown dust and the crystalline fragments.

"Not a geological museum," replied Flambeau; "say a psychological museum."

"Oh, for the Lord's sake," cried the police detective laughing, "don't let's begin with such long words."

"Don't you know what psychology means?" asked Flambeau with friendly surprise. "Psychology means being off your chump."

"Still I hardly follow," replied the official.

"Well," said Flambeau, with decision, "I mean that we've only found out one thing about Lord Glengyle. He was a maniac."

The black silhouette of Gow with his top hat and spade passed the window, dimly outlined against the darkening sky. Father Brown stared passively at it and answered:

"I can understand there must have been something odd about the man, or he wouldn't have buried himself alive—nor been in such a hurry to bury himself dead. But what makes you think it was lunacy?"

"Well," said Flambeau; "you just listen to the list of things Mr. Craven has found in the house."

"We must get a candle," said Craven, suddenly. "A storm is getting up, and it's too dark to read."

"Have you found any candles," asked Brown smiling, "among your oddities?"

Flambeau raised a grave face, and fixed his dark eyes on his friend. "That is curious, too," he said. "Twenty-five candles, and not a trace of a candlestick."

In the rapidly darkening room and rapidly rising wind, Brown went along the table to where a bundle of wax candles lay among the other scrappy exhibits. As he did so he bent accidentally over the heap of red-brown dust; and a sharp sneeze cracked the silence.

"Hullo!" he said; "snuff!"

He took one of the candles, lit it carefully, came back and stuck it in the neck of the whisky bottle. The unrestful night air, blowing through the crazy window, waved the long flame like a banner. And on every side of the castle they could hear the miles and miles of black pine wood seething like a black sea around a rock.

"I will read the inventory," began Craven gravely, picking up one of the papers, "the inventory of what we found loose and unexplained in the castle. You are to understand that the place generally was dismantled and neglected; but one or two rooms had plainly been inhabited in a simple but not squalid style by somebody; somebody who was not the servant Gow. The list is as follows:

"First item. A very considerable hoard of precious stones, nearly all diamonds, and all of them loose, without any setting whatever. Of course, it is natural that the Ogilvies should have family jewels; but those are exactly the jewels that are almost always set in particular articles of ornament. The Ogilvies would seem to have kept theirs loose in their pockets, like coppers.

"Second item. Heaps and heaps of loose snuff, not kept in a horn, or even a pouch, but lying in heaps on the mantelpieces, on the sideboard, on the piano, anywhere. It looks as if the old gentleman would not take the trouble to look in a pocket or lift a lid.

"Third item. Here and there about the house curious little heaps of minute pieces of metal, some like steel springs and some in the form of microscopic wheels. As if they had gutted some mechanical toy.

"Fourth item. The wax candles, which have to be stuck in bottle necks because there is nothing else to stick them in. Now I wish you

to note how very much queerer all this is than anything we antici-
pated. For the central riddle we are prepared; we have all seen at a
glance that there was something wrong about the last earl. We have
come here to find out whether he really lived here, whether he really
died here, whether that red-haired scarecrow who did his burying
had anything to do with his dying. But suppose the worst in all this,
the most lurid or melodramatic solution you like. Suppose the servant
really killed the master, or suppose the master isn't really dead, or
suppose the master is dressed up as the servant, or suppose the servant
is buried for the master; invent what Wilkie Collins tragedy you like,
and you still have not explained a candle without a candlestick, or
why an elderly gentleman of good family should habitually spill snuff
on the piano. The core of the tale we could imagine; it is the fringes
that are mysterious. By no stretch of fancy can the human mind connect together snuff and diamonds and wax and loose clockwork."

"I think I see the connexion," said the priest. "This Glengyle was
mad against the French Revolution. He was an enthusiast for the
ancien régime, and was trying to re-enact literally the family life of
the last Bourbons. He had snuff because it was the eighteenth century luxury; wax candles, because they were the eighteenth century
lighting; the mechanical bits of iron represent the locksmith hobby
of Louis XVI; the diamonds are for the Diamond Necklace of Marie
Antoinette."

Both the other men were staring at him with round eyes. "What a
perfectly extraordinary notion!" cried Flambeau. "Do you really think
that is the truth?"

"I am perfectly sure it isn't," answered Father Brown, "only you
said that nobody could connect snuff and diamonds and clockwork
and candles. I give you that connexion off-hand. The real truth, I am
very sure, lies deeper."

He paused a moment and listened to the wailing of the wind in the
turrets. Then he said, "The late Earl of Glengyle was a thief. He lived
a second and darker life as a desperate housebreaker. He did not have
any candlesticks because he only used these candles cut short in the
little lantern he carried. The snuff he employed as the fiercest French
criminals have used pepper: to fling it suddenly in dense masses in the

face of a captor or pursuer. But the final proof is in the curious coincidence of the diamonds and the small steel wheels. Surely that makes everything plain to you? Diamonds and small steel wheels are the only two instruments with which you can cut out a pane of glass."

The bough of a broken pine tree lashed heavily in the blast against the windowpane behind them, as if in parody of a burglar, but they did not turn round. Their eyes were fastened on Father Brown.

"Diamonds and small wheels," repeated Craven ruminating. "Is that all that makes you think it the true explanation?"

"I don't think it the true explanation," replied the priest placidly; "but you said that nobody could connect the four things. The true tale, of course, is something much more humdrum. Glengyle had found, or thought he had found, precious stones on his estate. Somebody had bamboozled him with those loose brilliants, saying they were found in the castle caverns. The little wheels are some diamond-cutting affair. He had to do the thing very roughly and in a small way, with the help of a few shepherds or rude fellows on these hills. Snuff is the one great luxury of such Scotch shepherds; it's the one thing with which you can bribe them. They didn't have candlesticks because they didn't want them; they held the candles in their hands when they explored the caves."

"Is that all?" asked Flambeau after a long pause. "Have we got to the dull truth at last?"

"Oh, no," said Father Brown.

As the wind died in the most distant pine woods with a long hoot as of mockery Father Brown, with an utterly impassive face, went on:

"I only suggested that because you said one could not plausibly connect snuff with clockwork or candles with bright stones. Ten false philosophies will fit the universe; ten false theories will fit Glengyle Castle. But we want the real explanation of the castle and the universe. But are there no other exhibits?"

Craven laughed, and Flambeau rose smiling to his feet and strolled down the long table.

"Items five, six, seven, etc.," he said, "are certainly more varied than instructive. A curious collection, not of lead pencils, but of the lead out of lead pencils. A senseless stick of bamboo, with the top rather splintered. It might be the instrument of the crime. Only, there isn't any crime. The only other things are a few old missals and little Catholic pictures, which the Ogilvies kept, I suppose, from the Middle Ages—their family pride being stronger than their Puritanism. We only put them in the museum because they seem curiously cut about and defaced."

The heady tempest without drove a dreadful wrack of clouds across Glengyle and threw the long room into darkness as Father Brown picked up the little illuminated pages to examine them. He spoke before the drift of darkness had passed; but it was the voice of an utterly new man.

"Mr. Craven," said he, talking like a man ten years younger, "you have got a legal warrant, haven't you, to go up and examine that grave? The sooner we do it the better, and get to the bottom of this horrible affair. If I were you I should start now."

"Now," repeated the astonished detective, "and why now?"

"Because this is serious," answered Brown; "this is not spilt snuff or loose pebbles, that might be there for a hundred reasons. There is only one reason I know of for *this* being done; and the reason goes down to the roots of the world. These religious pictures are not just dirtied or torn or scrawled over, which might be done in idleness or bigotry, by children or by Protestants. These have been treated very carefully— and very queerly. In every place where the great ornamented name of God comes in the old illuminations it has been elaborately taken out. The only other thing that has been removed is the halo round the head of the Child Jesus. Therefore, I say, let us get our warrant and our spade and our hatchet, and go up and break open that coffin."

"What *do* you mean?" demanded the London officer.

"I mean," answered the little priest, and his voice seemed to rise slightly in the roar of the gale. "I mean that the great devil of the universe may be sitting on the top tower of this castle at this moment, as big as a hundred elephants, and roaring like the Apocalypse. There is black magic somewhere at the bottom of this."

"Black magic," repeated Flambeau in a low voice, for he was too enlightened a man not to know of such things; "but what can these other things mean?"

"Oh, something damnable, I suppose," replied Brown impatiently. "How should I know? How can I guess all their mazes down below? Perhaps you can make a torture out of snuff and bamboo. Perhaps lunatics lust after wax and steel filings. Perhaps there is a maddening drug made of lead pencils! Our shortest cut to the mystery is up the hill to the grave."

His comrades hardly knew that they had obeyed and followed him till a blast of the night wind nearly flung them on their faces in the garden. Nevertheless they had obeyed him like automata; for Craven found a hatchet in his hand, and the warrant in his pocket; Flambeau was carrying the heavy spade of the strange gardener; Father Brown was carrying the little gilt book from which had been torn the name of God.

The path up the hill to the churchyard was crooked but short; only under the stress of wind it seemed laborious and long. Far as the eye could see, farther and farther as they mounted the slope, were seas beyond seas of pines, now all aslope one way under the wind. And that universal gesture seemed as vain as it was vast, as vain as if that wind were whistling about some unpeopled and purposeless planet. Through all that infinite growth of grey-blue forests sang, shrill and high, that ancient sorrow that is in the heart of all heathen things. One could fancy that the voices from the under world of unfathomable foliage were cries of the lost and wandering pagan gods: gods who had gone roaming in that irrational forest, and who will never find their way back to heaven.

"You see," said Father Brown in low but easy tone, "Scotch people before Scotland existed were a curious lot. In fact, they're a curious lot still. But in the prehistoric times I fancy they really worshipped demons. That," he added genially, "is why they jumped at the Puritan theology."

"My friend," said Flambeau, turning in a kind of fury, "what does all that snuff mean?"

"My friend," replied Brown, with equal seriousness, "there is one mark of all genuine religions: materialism. Now, devil-worship is a perfectly genuine religion."

They had come up on the grassy scalp of the hill, one of the few bald spots that stood clear of the crashing and roaring pine forest. A mean enclosure, partly timber and partly wire, rattled in the tempest to tell them the border of the graveyard. But by the time Inspector Craven had come to the corner of the grave, and Flambeau had planted his spade point downwards and leaned on it, they were both almost as shaken as the shaky wood and wire. At the foot of the grave grew great tall thistles, grey and silver in their decay. Once or twice, when a ball of thistledown broke under the breeze and flew past him, Craven jumped slightly as if it had been an arrow.

Flambeau drove the blade of his spade through the whistling grass into the wet clay below. Then he seemed to stop and lean on it as on a staff.

"Go on," said the priest very gently. "We are only trying to find the truth. What are you afraid of?"

"I am afraid of finding it," said Flambeau.

The London detective spoke suddenly in a high crowing voice that was meant to be conversational and cheery. "I wonder why he really did hide himself like that. Something nasty, I suppose; was he a leper?"

"Something worse than that," said Flambeau.

"And what do you imagine," asked the other, "would be worse than a leper?"

"I don't imagine it," said Flambeau.

He dug for some dreadful minutes in silence, and then said in a choked voice, "I'm afraid of his not being the right shape."

"Nor was that piece of paper, you know," said Father Brown quietly, "and we survived even that piece of paper." [1]

Flambeau dug on with a blind energy. But the tempest had shouldered away the choking grey clouds that clung to the hills like smoke and revealed grey fields of faint starlight before he cleared the shape of a rude timber coffin, and somehow tipped it up upon the turf. Craven stepped forward with his axe; a thistle-top touched him, and he flinched. Then he took a firmer stride, and hacked and wrenched

---

[1] Father Brown has recalled his experience with the oddly cut sheet of paper that figures so prominently in "The Wrong Shape", a story that preceded "The Honour of Israel Gow" when they first appeared in *The Saturday Evening Post*. Evidently Chesterton and his editors forgot about this reference when they collected the stories and changed their order for *The Innocence of Father Brown*.

with an energy like Flambeau's till the lid was torn off, and all that was there lay glimmering in the grey starlight.

"Bones," said Craven; and then he added, "but it is a man," as if that were something unexpected.

"Is he," asked Flambeau in a voice that went oddly up and down, "is he all right?"

"Seems so," said the officer huskily, bending over the obscure and decaying skeleton in the box. "Wait a minute."

A vast heave went over Flambeau's huge figure. "And now I come to think of it," he cried, "why in the name of madness shouldn't he be all right? What is it gets hold of a man on these cursed cold mountains? I think it's the black, brainless repetition; all these forests, and over all an ancient horror of unconsciousness. It's like the dream of an atheist. Pine-trees and more pine-trees and millions more pine trees—"

"God!" cried the man by the coffin; "but he hasn't got a head."

While the others stood rigid the priest, for the first time, showed a leap of startled concern.

"No head!" he repeated. "*No head?*" as if he had almost expected some other deficiency.

Half-witted visions of a headless baby born to Glengyle, of a headless youth hiding himself in the castle, of a headless man pacing those ancient halls or that gorgeous garden, passed in panorama through their minds. But even in that stiffened instant the tale took no root in them and seemed to have no reason in it. They stood listening to the loud woods and the shrieking sky quite foolishly, like exhausted animals. Thought seemed to be something enormous that had suddenly slipped out of their grasp.

"There are three headless men," said Father Brown, "standing round this open grave."

The pale detective from London opened his mouth to speak, and left it open like a yokel, while a long scream of wind tore the sky; then he looked at the axe in his hands as if it did not belong to him, and dropped it.

"Father," said Flambeau in that infantile and heavy voice he used very seldom, "what are we to do?"

His friend's reply came with the pent promptitude of a gun going off.

"Sleep!" cried Father Brown. "Sleep. We have come to the end of the ways. Do you know what sleep is? Do you know that every man who sleeps believes in God? It is a sacrament; for it is an act of faith and it is a food. And we need a sacrament, if only a natural one. Something has fallen on us that falls very seldom on men; perhaps the worst thing that can fall on them."

Craven's parted lips came together to say, "What do you mean?"

The priest had turned his face to the castle as he answered:

"We have found the truth; and the truth makes no sense."

He went down the path in front of them with a plunging and reckless step very rare with him, and when they reached the castle again he threw himself upon sleep with the simplicity of a dog.

Despite his mystic praise of slumber, Father Brown was up earlier than anyone else except the silent gardener; and was found smoking a big pipe and watching that expert at his speechless labours in the kitchen garden. Towards daybreak the rocking storm had ended in roaring rains, and the day came with a curious freshness. The gardener seemed even to have been conversing, but at sight of the detectives he planted his spade sullenly in a bed and, saying something about his breakfast, shifted along the lines of cabbages and shut himself in the kitchen. "He's a valuable man, that," said Father Brown. "He does the potatoes amazingly. Still," he added, with a dispassionate charity, "he has his faults; which of us hasn't? He doesn't dig this bank quite regularly. There, for instance," and he stamped suddenly on one spot. "I'm really very doubtful about that potato."

"And why?" asked Craven, amused with the little man's new hobby.

"I'm doubtful about it," said the other, "because old Gow was doubtful about it himself. He put his spade in methodically in every place but just this. There must be a mighty fine potato just here."

Flambeau pulled up the spade and impetuously drove it into the place. He turned up, under a load of soil, something that did not look like a potato, but rather like a monstrous, over-domed mushroom. But it struck the spade with a cold click; it rolled over like a ball, and grinned up at them.

"The Earl of Glengyle," said Brown sadly, and looked down heavily at the skull.

Then, after a momentary meditation, he plucked the spade from Flambeau, and, saying, "We must hide it again," clamped the skull down in the earth. Then he leaned his little body and huge head on the great handle of the spade, that stood up stiffly in the earth, and his eyes were empty and his forehead full of wrinkles. "If one could only conceive," he muttered, "the meaning of this last monstrosity." And leaning on the large spade handle, he buried his brows in his hands, as men do in church.

All the corners of the sky were brightening into blue and silver; the birds were chattering in the tiny garden trees; so loud it seemed as if the trees themselves were talking. But the three men were silent enough.

"Well, I give it all up," said Flambeau at last boisterously. "My brain and this world don't fit each other; and there's an end of it. Snuff, spoilt Prayer Books, and the insides of musical boxes—what—"

Brown threw up his bothered brow and rapped on the spade handle with an intolerance quite unusual with him. "Oh, tut, tut, tut, tut, tut!" he cried. "All that is as plain as a pikestaff. I understood the snuff and clockwork, and so on, when I first opened my eyes this morning. And since then I've had it out with old Gow, the gardener, who is neither so deaf nor so stupid as he pretends. There's nothing amiss about the loose items. I was wrong about the torn mass-book, too; there's no harm in that. But it's this last business. Desecrating graves and stealing dead men's heads—surely there's harm in that? Surely there's black magic still in that? That doesn't fit in to the quite simple story of the snuff and the candles." And, striding about again, he smoked moodily.

"My friend," said Flambeau, with a grim humour, "you must be careful with me and remember I was once a criminal. The great advantage of that estate was that I always made up the story myself, and acted it as quick as I chose. This detective business of waiting about is too much for my French impatience. All my life, for good or evil, I have done things at the instant; I always fought duels the next morning; I always paid bills on the nail; I never even put off a visit to the dentist—"

Father Brown's pipe fell out of his mouth and broke into three pieces on the gravel path. He stood rolling his eyes, the exact picture of an idiot. "Lord, what a turnip I am!" he kept saying. "Lord, what a turnip!" Then, in a somewhat groggy kind of way, he began to laugh.

"The dentist!" he repeated. "Six hours in the spiritual abyss, and all because I never thought of the dentist! Such a simple, such a beautiful and peaceful thought! Friends, we have passed a night in hell; but now the sun is risen, the birds are singing, and the radiant form of the dentist consoles the world."

"I will get some sense out of this," cried Flambeau, striding forward, "if I use the tortures of the Inquisition."

Father Brown repressed what appeared to be a momentary disposition to dance on the now sunlit lawn and cried quite piteously, like a child, "Oh, let me be silly a little. You don't know how unhappy I have been. And now I know that there has been no deep sin in this business at all. Only a little lunacy, perhaps—and who minds that?"

He spun round once more, then faced them with gravity.

"This is not a story of crime," he said; "rather it is the story of a strange and crooked honesty. We are dealing with the one man on earth, perhaps, who has taken no more than his due. It is a study in the savage living logic that has been the religion of this race.

"That old local rhyme about the house of Glengyle—

> "'As green sap to the simmer trees
> Is red gold to the Ogilvies'—

was literal as well as metaphorical. It did not merely mean that the Glengyles sought for wealth; it was also true that they literally gathered gold; they had a huge collection of ornaments and utensils in that metal. They were, in fact, misers whose mania took that turn. In the light of that fact, run through all the things we found in the castle. Diamonds without their gold rings; candles without their gold candlesticks; snuff without the gold snuff-boxes; pencil-leads without the gold pencil-cases; a walking stick without its gold top; clockwork without the gold clocks—or rather watches. And, mad as it sounds, because the halos and the name of God in the old missals were of real gold; these also were taken away."

The garden seemed to brighten, the grass to grow gayer in the strengthening sun, as the crazy truth was told. Flambeau lit a cigarette as his friend went on.

"Were taken away," continued Father Brown; "were taken away— but not stolen. Thieves would never have left this mystery. Thieves would have taken the gold snuff-boxes, snuff and all; the gold pencil-cases, lead and all. We have to deal with a man with a peculiar conscience, but certainly a conscience. I found that mad moralist this morning in the kitchen garden yonder, and I heard the whole story.

"The late Archibald Ogilvie was the nearest approach to a good man ever born at Glengyle. But his bitter virtue took the turn of the misanthrope; he moped over the dishonesty of his ancestors, from which, somehow, he generalised a dishonesty of all men. More especially he distrusted philanthropy or free-giving; and he swore if he could find one man who took his exact rights he should have all the gold of Glengyle. Having delivered this defiance to humanity he shut himself up, without the smallest expectation of its being answered. One day, however, a deaf and seemingly senseless lad from a distant village brought him a belated telegram; and Glengyle, in his acrid pleasantry, gave him a new farthing. At least he thought he had done so, but when he turned over his change he found the new farthing still there and a sovereign gone. The accident offered him vistas of sneering speculation. Either way, the boy would show the greasy greed of the species. Either he would vanish, a thief steal-ing a coin; or he would sneak back with it virtuously, a snob seek-ing a reward. In the middle of that night Lord Glengyle was knocked up out of his bed—for he lived alone—and forced to open the door to the deaf idiot. The idiot brought with him, not the sovereign, but exactly nineteen shillings and eleven-pence three-farthings in change.

"Then the wild exactitude of this action took hold on the mad lord's brain like fire. He swore he was Diogenes, that had long sought an honest man, and at last had found one. He made a new will, which I have seen. He took the literal youth into his huge, neglected house, and trained him up as his solitary servant and—after an odd manner—his heir. And whatever that queer creature understands, he understood absolutely his lord's two fixed ideas: first, that the letter of right is everything; and second, that he himself was to have the gold of Glengyle. So far, that is all; and that is simple. He has stripped the house of gold, and taken not a grain that was not gold; not so much as a grain of snuff. He lifted the gold leaf off an old illumination, fully satisfied that he left the rest unspoilt. All that I understood; but I could not understand this skull business. I was really uneasy about that human head buried among the potatoes. It distressed me—till Flambeau said the word.

"It will be all right. He will put the skull back in the grave, when he has taken the gold out of the tooth."

And, indeed, when Flambeau crossed the hill that morning, he saw that strange being, the just miser, digging at the desecrated grave, the plaid round his throat thrashing out in the mountain wind; the sober top hat on his head.

THE WRONG SHAPE

Certain of the great roads going north out of London continue far into the country a sort of attenuated and interrupted spectre of a street, with great gaps in the building, but preserving the line. Here will be a group of shops, followed by a fenced field or paddock, and then a famous public-house, and then perhaps a market garden or a nursery garden, and then one large private house, and then another field and another inn, and so on. If anyone walks along one of these roads he will pass a house which will probably catch his eye, though he may not be able to explain its attraction. It is a long, low house, running parallel with the road, painted mostly white and pale green, with a veranda and sun-blinds, and porches capped with those quaint sort of cupolas like wooden umbrellas that one sees in some old-fashioned houses. In fact, it is an old-fashioned house, very English and very suburban in the good old wealthy Clapham sense. And yet the house has a look of having been built chiefly for the hot weather. Looking at its white paint and sun-blinds one thinks vaguely of pugarees and even of palm trees. I cannot trace the feeling to its root; perhaps the place was built by an Anglo-Indian.

Anyone passing this house, I say, would be namelessly fascinated by it; would feel that it was a place about which some story was to be told. And he would have been right, as you shall shortly hear. For this is the story—the story of the strange things that did really happen in it in the Whitsuntide of the year 18—.

Anyone passing the house on the Thursday before Whit-Sunday at about half-past four p.m. would have seen the front door open, and Father Brown, of the small church of St. Mungo, come out smoking a large pipe in company with a very tall French friend of his called Flambeau, who was smoking a very small cigarette. These persons may or may not be of interest to the reader, but the truth is that they were not the only interesting things that were displayed when the front door of the white-and-green house was opened. There are further peculiarities about this house, which must be described to start with, not only that the reader may understand this tragic tale, but also that he may realise what it was that the opening of the door revealed.

The whole house was built upon the plan of a T, but a T with a very long cross piece and a very short tail piece. The long cross piece was the frontage that ran along in face of the street, with the front door in the middle; it was two stories high, and contained nearly all the important rooms. The short tail piece, which ran out at the back immediately opposite the front door, was one story high, and consisted only of two long rooms, the one leading into the other. The first of these two rooms was the study in which the celebrated Mr. Quinton wrote his wild Oriental poems and romances. The farther room was a glass conservatory full of tropical blossoms of quite unique and almost monstrous beauty, and on such afternoons as these was glowing with gorgeous sunlight. Thus when the hall door was open, many a passer-by literally stopped to stare and gasp; for he looked down a perspective of rich apartments to something really like a transformation scene in a fairy play: purple clouds and golden suns and crimson stars that were at once scorchingly vivid and yet transparent and far away.

Leonard Quinton, the poet, had himself most carefully arranged this effect; and it is doubtful whether he so perfectly expressed his personality in any of his poems. For he was a man who drank and bathed in colours, who indulged his lust for colour somewhat to the neglect of form—even of good form. This it was that had turned his genius so wholly to eastern art and imagery; to those bewildering carpets or blinding embroideries in which all the colours seem fallen into a fortunate chaos, having nothing to typify or to teach. He had attempted, not perhaps with complete artistic success, but with acknowledged imagination and invention, to compose epics and love stories reflecting the riot of violent and even cruel colour; tales of tropical heavens of burning gold or blood-red copper; of eastern heroes who rode with twelve-turbaned mitres upon elephants painted purple or peacock green; of gigantic jewels that a hundred negroes could not carry, but which burned with ancient and strange-hued fires.

In short (to put the matter from the more common point of view), he dealt much in eastern heavens, rather worse than most western hells;

in eastern monarchs, whom we might possibly call maniacs; and in eastern jewels which a Bond Street jeweler (if the hundred staggering negroes brought them into his shop) might possibly not regard as genuine. Quinton was a genius, if a morbid one; and even his morbidity appeared more in his life than in his work. In temperament he was weak and waspish, and his health had suffered heavily from oriental experiments with opium. His wife—a handsome, hard-working, and, indeed, over-worked woman—objected to the opium, but objected much more to a live Indian hermit in white and yellow robes, whom her husband had insisted on entertaining for months together, a Virgil to guide his spirit through the heavens and the hells of the east.

It was out of this artistic household that Father Brown and his friend stepped on to the door-step; and to judge from their faces, they stepped out of it with much relief. Flambeau had known Quinton in wild student days in Paris, and they had renewed the acquaintance for a week-end; but apart from Flambeau's more responsible developments of late, he did not get on well with the poet now. Choking oneself with opium and writing little erotic verses on vellum was not his notion of how a gentleman should go to the devil. As the two paused on the doorstep, before taking a turn in the garden, the front garden gate was thrown open with violence, and a young man with a billy-cock hat on the back of his head tumbled up the steps in his eagerness. He was a dissipated-looking youth with a gorgeous red necktie all awry, as if he had slept in it, and he kept fidgeting and lashing about with one of those little jointed canes.

"I say," he said breathlessly, "I want to see old Quinton. I must see him. Has he gone?"

"Mr. Quinton is in, I believe," said Father Brown, cleaning his pipe, "but I do not know if you can see him. The doctor is with him at present."

The young man, who seemed not to be perfectly sober, stumbled into the hall; and at the same moment the doctor came out of Quinton's study, shutting the door and beginning to put on his gloves.

"See Mr. Quinton?" said the doctor coolly. "No, I'm afraid you can't. In fact, you mustn't on any account. Nobody must see him; I've just given him his sleeping draught."

"No, but look here, old chap," said the youth in the red tie, trying affectionately to capture the doctor by the lapels of his coat. "Look here. I'm simply sewn up, I tell you. I—"

"It's no good, Mr. Atkinson," said the doctor, forcing him to fall back; "when you can alter the effects of a drug I'll alter my decision," and, settling on his hat, he stepped out into the sunlight with the other two. He was a bull-necked, good-tempered little man with a small moustache, inexpressibly ordinary, yet giving an impression of capability.

The young man in the billycock, who did not seem to be gifted with any tact in dealing with people beyond the general idea of clutching hold of their coats, stood outside the door, as dazed as if he had been thrown out bodily, and silently watched the other three walk away together through the garden.

"That was a sound, spanking lie I told just now," remarked the medical man, laughing. "In point of fact, poor Quinton doesn't have his sleeping draught for nearly half an hour. But I'm not going to have him bothered with that little beast, who only wants to borrow money that he wouldn't pay back if he could. He's a dirty little scamp, though he is Mrs. Quinton's brother, and she's as fine a woman as ever walked."

"Yes," said Father Brown. "She's a good woman."

"So I propose to hang about the garden till the creature has cleared off," went on the doctor, "and then I'll go in to Quinton with the medicine. Atkinson can't get in, because I locked the door."

"In that case, Dr. Harris," said Flambeau, "we might as well walk round at the back by the end of the conservatory. There's no entrance to it that way but it's worth seeing, even from the outside."

"Yes, and I might get a squint at my patient," laughed the doctor, "for he prefers to lie on an ottoman right at the end of the conservatory amid all those blood-red poinsettias; it would give me the creeps. But what are you doing?"

Father Brown had stopped for a moment, and picked up out of the long grass, where it had almost been wholly hidden, a queer, crooked Oriental knife, inlaid exquisitely in coloured stones and metals.

"What is this?" asked Father Brown, regarding it with some disfavour.

"Oh, Quinton's, I suppose," said Dr. Harris carelessly; "he has all sorts of Chinese knickknacks about the place. Or perhaps it belongs to the mild Hindoo of his whom he keeps on a string."

"What Hindoo?" asked Father Brown, still staring at the dagger in his hand.

"Oh, some Indian conjurer," said the doctor lightly; "a fraud, of course."

"You don't believe in magic?" asked Father Brown without looking up.

"Oh crikey! magic!" said the doctor.

"It's very beautiful," said the priest in a low, dreaming voice; "the colours are very beautiful. But it's the wrong shape."

"What for?" asked Flambeau, staring.

"For anything. It's the wrong shape in the abstract. Don't you ever feel that about Eastern art? The colours are intoxicatingly lovely; but the shapes are mean and bad—deliberately mean and bad. I have seen wicked things in a Turkey carpet."

"*Mon Dieu!*" cried Flambeau, laughing.

"They are letters and symbols in a language I don't know; but I know they stand for evil words," went on the priest, his voice growing lower and lower. "The lines go wrong on purpose—like serpents doubling to escape."

"What the devil are you talking about?" said the doctor with a loud laugh.

Flambeau spoke quietly to him in answer. "The Father sometimes gets this mystic's cloud on him," he said; "but I give you fair warning that I have never known him have it except when there was some evil quite near."

"Oh, rats!" said the scientist.

"Why, look at it," cried Father Brown, holding out the crooked knife at arm's length, as if it were some glittering snake. "Don't you see it is the wrong shape? Don't you see that it has no hearty and plain purpose? It does not point like a spear. It does not sweep like a scythe. It does not *look* like a weapon. It looks like an instrument of torture."

"Well, as you don't seem to like it," said the jolly Harris, "it had better be taken back to its owner. Haven't we come to the end of this confounded conservatory yet? This house is the wrong shape, if you like."

"You don't understand," said Father Brown, shaking his head. "The shape of this house is quaint—it is even laughable. But there is nothing *wrong* about it."

As they spoke they came round the curve of glass that ended the conservatory, an uninterrupted curve, for there was neither door nor window by which to enter at that end. The glass, however, was clear, and the sun still bright, though beginning to set; and they could see not only the flamboyant blossoms inside, but the frail figure of the poet in a brown velvet coat lying languidly on the sofa, having, apparently, fallen half asleep over a book. He was a pale, slight man, with loose, chestnut hair and a fringe of beard that was the paradox of his face, for the beard made him look less manly. These traits were well known to all three of them; but even had it not been so, it may be doubted whether they would have looked at Quinton just then. Their eyes were riveted on another object.

Exactly in their path, immediately outside the round end of the glass building, was standing a tall man, whose drapery fell to his feet in faultless white, and whose bare, brown skull, face, and neck gleamed in the setting sun like splendid bronze. He was looking through the glass at the sleeper, and he was more motionless than a mountain.

"Who is that?" cried Father Brown, stepping back with a hissing intake of his breath.

"Oh, it is only that Hindoo humbug," growled Harris; "but I don't know what the deuce he's doing here."

"It looks like hypnotism," said Flambeau, biting his black moustache.

"Why are you unmedical fellows always talking bosh about hypnotism?" cried the doctor. "It looks a deal more like burglary."

"Well, we will speak to it, at any rate," said Flambeau, who was always for action. One long stride took him to the place where the Indian stood. Bowing from his great height, which overtopped even the Oriental's, he said with placid impudence:

"Good evening, sir. Do you want anything?"

Quite slowly, like a great ship turning into a harbour, the great yellow face turned, and looked at last over its white shoulder. They were startled to see that its yellow eyelids were quite sealed, as in

sleep. "Thank you," said the face in excellent English. "I want nothing." Then, half opening the lids, so as to show a slit of opalescent
eyeball, he repeated, "I want nothing." Then he opened his eyes wide
with a startling stare, said, "I want nothing," and went rustling away
into the rapidly darkening garden.

"The Christian is more modest," muttered Father Brown; "he wants
something."

"What on earth was he doing?" asked Flambeau, knitting his black
brows and lowering his voice.

"I should like to talk to you later," said Father Brown.

The sunlight was still a reality, but it was the red light of evening,
and the bulk of the garden trees and bushes grew blacker and blacker
against it. They turned round the end of the conservatory, and walked
in silence down the other side to get round to the front door. As they
went they seemed to wake something, as one startles a bird, in the
deeper corner between the study and the main building; and again
they saw the white-robed fakir slide out of the shadow, and slip round
towards the front door. To their surprise, however, he had not been
alone. They found themselves abruptly pulled up and forced to banish their bewilderment by the appearance of Mrs. Quinton, with her
heavy golden hair and square pale face, advancing on them out of the
twilight. She looked a little stern, but was entirely courteous.

"Good evening, Dr. Harris," was all she said.

"Good evening, Mrs. Quinton," said the little doctor heartily. "I
am just going to give your husband his sleeping draught."

"Yes," she said in a clear voice. "I think it is quite time." And she
smiled at them, and went sweeping into the house.

"That woman's over-driven," said Father Brown; "that's the kind
of woman that does her duty for twenty years, and then does something dreadful."

The little doctor looked at him for the first time with an eye of
interest. "Did you ever study medicine?" he asked.

"You have to know something of the mind as well as the body,"
answered the priest; "we have to know something of the body as well
as the mind."

"Well," said the doctor, "I think I'll go and give Quinton his
stuff."

They had turned the corner of the front façade, and were approaching the front doorway. As they turned into it they saw the man in the white robe for the third time. He came so straight towards the front door that it seemed quite incredible that he had not just come out of the study opposite to it. Yet they knew that the study door was locked.

Father Brown and Flambeau, however, kept this weird contradiction to themselves, and Dr. Harris was not a man to waste his thoughts on the impossible. He permitted the omnipresent Asiatic to make his exit, and then stepped briskly into the hall. There he found a figure which he had already forgotten. The inane Atkinson was still hanging about, humming and poking things with his knobby cane. The doctor's face had a spasm of disgust and decision, and he whispered rapidly to his companion, "I must lock the door again, or this rat will get in. But I shall be out again in two minutes."

He rapidly unlocked the door and locked it again behind him, just balking a blundering charge from the young man in the billycock. The young man threw himself impatiently on a hall chair. Flambeau looked at a Persian illumination on the wall; Father Brown, who seemed in a sort of daze, dully eyed the door. In about four minutes the door was opened again. Atkinson was quicker this time. He sprang forward, held the door open for an instant, and called out, "Oh, I say, Quinton, I want—"

From the other end of the study came the clear voice of Quinton, in something between a yawn and a yell of weary laughter.

"Oh, I know what you want. Take it, and leave me in peace. I'm writing a song about peacocks."

Before the door closed half a sovereign came flying through the aperture; and Atkinson, stumbling forward, caught it with singular dexterity.

"So that's settled," said the doctor, and, locking the door savagely, he led the way out into the garden.

"Poor Leonard can get a little peace now," he added to Father Brown; "he's locked in all by himself for an hour or two."

"Yes," answered the priest; "and his voice sounded jolly enough when we left him." Then he looked gravely round the garden, and saw the loose figure of Atkinson standing and jingling the half-sovereign in his pocket, and beyond, in the purple twilight, the figure of the Indian sitting bolt upright upon a bank of grass with his face turned towards the setting sun. Then he said abruptly, "Where is Mrs. Quinton?"

"She has gone up to her room," said the doctor. "That is her shadow on the blind."

Father Brown looked up, and frowningly scrutinised a dark outline at the gas-lit window.

"Yes," he said, "that is her shadow," and he walked a yard or two and threw himself upon a garden seat.

Flambeau sat down beside him; but the doctor was one of those energetic people who live naturally on their legs. He walked away, smoking, into the twilight, and the two friends were left together.

"My father," said Flambeau in French, "what is the matter with you?"

Father Brown was silent and motionless for half a minute then he said: "Superstition is irreligious, but there is something in the air of this place. I think it's that Indian—at least, partly."

He sank into silence, and watched the distant outline of the Indian, who still sat rigid as if in prayer. At first sight he seemed motionless, but as Father Brown watched him he saw that the man swayed ever so slightly with a rhythmic movement, just as the dark tree-tops swayed ever so slightly in the little wind that was creeping up the dim garden paths and shuffling the fallen leaves a little.

The landscape was growing rapidly dark, as if for a storm, but they could still see all the figures in their various places. Atkinson was leaning against a tree, with a listless face; Quinton's wife was still at her window; the doctor had gone strolling round the end of the conservatory; they could see his cigar like a will-o'-the-wisp; and the fakir still sat rigid and yet rocking, while the trees above him began to rock and almost to roar. Storm was certainly coming.

"When that Indian spoke to us," went on Brown in a conversational undertone, "I had a sort of vision, a vision of him and all his universe. Yet he only said the same thing three times. When first he said, 'I want nothing,' it meant only that he was impenetrable, that Asia does not give itself away. Then he said again, 'I want nothing,' and I knew that he meant that he was sufficient to himself, like a cosmos, that he needed no God, neither admitted any sins. And when he said the third time, 'I want nothing,' he said it with blazing eyes. And I knew that he meant literally what he said; that nothing was his desire and his home; that he was weary for nothing as for wine; that annihilation, the mere destruction of everything or anything—"

Two drops of rain fell; and for some reason Flambeau started and looked up, as if they had stung him. And the same instant the doctor down by the end of the conservatory began running towards them, calling out something as he ran.

As he came among them like a bombshell the restless Atkinson happened to be taking a turn nearer to the house front; and the doctor clutched him by the collar in a convulsive grip. "Foul play!" he cried; "what have you been doing to him, you dog?"

The priest had sprung erect, and had the voice of steel of a soldier in command.

"No fighting," he cried coolly; "we are enough to hold anyone we want to. What is the matter, doctor?"

"Things are not right with Quinton," said the doctor, quite white. "I could just see him through the glass, and I don't like the way he's lying. It's not as I left him, anyhow."

"Let us go in to him," said Father Brown shortly. "You can leave Mr. Atkinson alone. I have had him in sight since we heard Quinton's voice."

"I will stop here and watch him," said Flambeau hurriedly. "You go in and see."

The doctor and the priest flew to the study door, unlocked it, and fell into the room. In doing so they nearly fell over the large mahogany table in the centre at which the poet usually wrote; for the place was lit only by a small fire kept for the invalid. In the middle of this table lay a single sheet of paper, evidently left there on purpose. The doctor snatched it up, glanced at it, handed it to Father Brown, and crying, "Good God, look at that!" plunged towards the glass room beyond, where the terrible tropic flowers still seemed to keep a crimson memory of the sunset.

Father Brown read the words three times before he put down the paper. The words were, "I die by my own hand; yet I die murdered!" They were in the quite inimitable, not to say illegible, handwriting of Leonard Quinton.

Then Father Brown, still keeping the paper in his hand, strode towards the conservatory, only to meet his medical friend coming back with a face of assurance and collapse. "He's done it," said Harris.

They went together through the gorgeous unnatural beauty of cactus and azalea and found Leonard Quinton, poet and romancer, with his head hanging downward off his ottoman and his red curls sweeping the ground. Into his left side was thrust the queer dagger that they had picked up in the garden, and his limp hand still rested on the hilt.

Outside, the storm had come at one stride, like the night in Coleridge,[1] and garden and glass roof were darkening with driving rain. Father Brown seemed to be studying the paper more than the corpse; he held it close to his eyes; and seemed trying to read it in the twilight. Then he held it up against the faint light, and, as he did so, lightning stared at them for an instant so white that the paper looked black against it.

Darkness full of thunder followed, and after the thunder Father Brown's voice said out of the dark, "Doctor, this paper is the wrong shape."

"What do you mean?" asked Doctor Harris, with a frowning stare.

"It isn't square," answered Brown. "It has a sort of edge snipped off at the corner. What does it mean?"

"How the deuce should I know?" growled the doctor. "Shall we move the poor chap, do you think? He's quite dead."

"No," answered the priest; "we must leave him as he lies and send for the police." But he was still scrutinising the paper.

As they went back through the study he stopped by the table and picked up a small pair of nail scissors. "Ah," he said with a sort of relief, "this is what he did it with. But yet—" And he knitted his brows.

"Oh, stop fooling with that scrap of paper," said the doctor emphatically. "It was a fad of his. He had hundreds of them. He cut all his paper like that," as he pointed to a stack of sermon paper still unused on another and smaller table. Father Brown went up to it and held up a sheet. It was the same irregular shape.

"Quite so," he said. "And here I see the corners that were snipped off." And to the indignation of his colleague he began to count them.

"That's all right," he said, with an apologetic smile. "Twenty-three sheets cut and twenty-two corners cut off them. And as I see you are impatient we will rejoin the others."

[1] The allusion is to Coleridge's "The Rime of the Ancient Mariner" (1798): "The Sun's rim dips; the stars rush out: / At one stride comes the dark;" (lines 199–200).

"Who is to tell his wife?" asked Dr. Harris. "Will you go and tell her now, while I send a servant for the police?"

"As you will," said Father Brown indifferently. And he went out to the hall door.

Here also he found a drama, though of a more grotesque sort. It showed nothing less than his big friend Flambeau in an attitude to which he had long been unaccustomed, while upon the pathway at the bottom of the steps was sprawling with his boots in the air the amiable Atkinson, his billycock hat and walking-cane sent flying in opposite directions along the path. Atkinson had at length wearied of Flambeau's almost paternal custody, and had endeavoured to knock him down, which was by no means a smooth game to play with the Roi des Apaches,[2] even after that monarch's abdication.

Flambeau was about to leap upon his enemy and secure him once more, when the priest patted him easily on the shoulder.

"Make it up with Mr. Atkinson, my friend," he said. "Beg a mutual pardon and say 'Good night.' We need not detain him any longer." Then, as Atkinson rose somewhat doubtfully and gathered his hat and stick and went towards the garden gate, Father Brown said in a more serious voice, "Where is that Indian?"

They all three (for the doctor had joined them) turned involuntarily towards the dim grassy bank amid the tossing trees, purple with twilight, where they had last seen the brown man swaying in his strange prayers. The Indian was gone.

"Confound him," said the doctor, stamping furiously. "Now I know that it was that nigger[3] that did it."

"I thought you didn't believe in magic," said Father Brown quietly.

---

[2] *Roi des Apaches* is a reference to Flambeau's previous life in the Parisian underworld, whose fierce brawlers and ruffians Émile Darsy and other turn-of-the-century French journalists had dubbed "Apaches".

[3] Today the slang epithet "nigger" is universally acknowledged to be unforgivably offensive and insulting. In the England of Chesterton's day, although the word was disparaging, its use was considered acceptable. This edition of the Father Brown stories is intended to offer Chesterton's texts as they originally appeared, and his use of this word does not imply that he held (or that the editor or publisher hold) opinions or feelings that such usage implies today.

"No more I did," said the doctor, rolling his eyes. "I only know that I loathed that yellow devil when I thought he was a sham wizard. And I shall loathe him more if I come to think he was a real one."

"Well, his having escaped is nothing," said Flambeau. "For we could have proved nothing and done nothing against him. One hardly goes to the parish constable with a story of suicide imposed by witchcraft or auto-suggestion."

Meanwhile Father Brown had made his way into the house, and now went to break the news to the wife of the dead man.

When he came out again he looked a little pale and tragic; but what passed between them in that interview was never known, even when all was known.

Flambeau, who was talking quietly with the doctor, was surprised to see his friend reappear so soon at his elbow; but Brown took no notice, and merely drew the doctor apart. "You have sent for the police, haven't you?" he asked.

"Yes," answered Harris. "They ought to be here in ten minutes."

"Will you do me a favour?" said the priest quietly. "The truth is, I make a collection of these curious stories, which often contain, as in the case of our Hindoo friend, elements which can hardly be put into a police report. Now, I want you to write out a report of this case for my private use. Yours is a clever trade," he said, looking at the doctor gravely and steadily in the face. "I sometimes think that you know some details of this matter which you have not thought fit to mention. Mine is a confidential trade like yours, and I will treat anything you write for me in strict confidence. But write the whole."

The doctor, who had been listening thoughtfully with his head a little on one side, looked the priest in the face for an instant, and said, "All right," and went into the study, closing the door behind him.

"Flambeau," said Father Brown, "there is a long seat there under the veranda, where we can smoke, out of the rain. You are my only friend in the world, and I want to talk to you. Or, perhaps, be silent with you."

They established themselves comfortably in the veranda seat; Father Brown, against his common habit, accepted a good cigar and smoked it steadily in silence, while the rain shrieked and rattled on the roof of the veranda.

"My friend," he said at length, "this is a very queer case. A very queer case."

"I should think it was," said Flambeau, with something like a shudder.

"You call it queer, and I call it queer," said the other, "and yet we mean quite opposite things. The modern mind always mixes up two different ideas: mystery in the sense of what is marvellous, and mystery in the sense of what is complicated. That is half its difficulty about miracles. A miracle is startling; but it is simple. It is simple because it *is* a miracle. It is power coming directly from God (or the devil) instead of indirectly through nature or human wills. Now you mean that this business is marvellous because it is miraculous, because it is witchcraft worked by a wicked Indian. Understand, I do not say that it was not spiritual or diabolic. Heaven and hell only know by what surrounding influences strange sins come into the lives of men. But for the present my point is this: If it was pure magic, as you think, then it is marvellous; but it is not mysterious—that is, it is not complicated. The quality of a miracle is mysterious, but its manner is simple. Now, the manner of this business has been the reverse of simple."

The storm that had slackened for a little seemed to be swelling again, and there came heavy movements as of faint thunder. Father Brown let fall the ash of his cigar and went on:

"There has been in this incident," he said, "a twisted, ugly, complex quality that does not belong to the straight bolts either of heaven or hell. As one knows the crooked track of a snail, I know the crooked track of a man."

The white lightning opened its enormous eye in one wink, the sky shut up again, and the priest went on:

"Of all these crooked things, the crookedest was the shape of that piece of paper. It was crookeder than the dagger that killed him."

"You mean the paper on which Quinton confessed his suicide," said Flambeau.

"I mean the paper on which Quinton wrote, 'I die by my own hand,' " answered Father Brown. "The shape of that paper, my friend, was the wrong shape; the wrong shape, if ever I have seen it in this wicked world."

"It only had a corner snipped off," said Flambeau, "and I understand that all Quinton's paper was cut that way."

"It was a very odd way," said the other, "and a very bad way, to my taste and fancy. Look here, Flambeau, this Quinton—God receive his soul!—was perhaps a bit of a cur in some ways, but he really was an artist, with the pencil as well as the pen. His handwriting, though hard to read, was bold and beautiful. I can't prove what I say; I can't prove anything. But I tell you with the full force of conviction that he could never have cut that mean little piece off a sheet of paper. If he had wanted to cut down paper for some purpose of fitting in, or binding up, or what not, he would have made quite a different slash with the scissors. Do you remember the shape? It was a mean shape. It was a wrong shape. Like this. Don't you remember?"

And he waved his burning cigar before him in the darkness, making irregular squares so rapidly that Flambeau really seemed to see them as fiery hieroglyphics upon the darkness—hieroglyphics such as his friend had spoken of, which are undecipherable, yet can have no good meaning.

"But," said Flambeau, as the priest put his cigar in his mouth again and leaned back, staring at the roof. "Suppose somebody else did use the scissors. Why should somebody else, cutting pieces off his sermon paper, make Quinton commit suicide?"

Father Brown was still leaning back and staring at the roof, but he took his cigar out of his mouth and said, "Quinton never did commit suicide."

Flambeau stared at him. "Why, confound it all," he cried; "then why did he confess to suicide?"

The priest leaned forward again, settled his elbows on his knees, looked at the ground, and said in a low distinct voice, "He never did confess to suicide."

Flambeau laid his cigar down. "You mean," he said, "that the writing was forged?"

"No," said Father Brown; "Quinton wrote it all right."

"Well, there you are," said the aggravated Flambeau; "Quinton wrote, 'I die by my own hand,' with his own hand on a plain piece of paper."

"Of the wrong shape," said the priest calmly.

"Oh, the shape be damned!" cried Flambeau. "What has the shape to do with it?"

"There were twenty-three snipped papers," resumed Brown unmoved, "and only twenty-two pieces snipped off. Therefore one of the pieces had been destroyed, probably that from the written paper. Does that suggest anything to you?"

A light dawned on Flambeau's face, and he said, "There was something else written by Quinton, some other words. 'They will tell you I die by my own hand,' or 'Do not believe that—'"

"Hotter, as the children say," said his friend. "But the piece was hardly half an inch across; there was no room for one word, let alone five. Can you think of anything hardly bigger than a comma which the man with hell in his heart had to tear away as a testimony against him?"

"I can think of nothing," said Flambeau at last.

"What about quotation marks?" said the priest, and flung his cigar far into the darkness like a shooting star.

All words had left the other man's mouth, and Father Brown said, like one going back to fundamentals:

"Leonard Quinton was a romancer, and was writing an Oriental romance about wizardry and hypnotism. He—"

At this moment the door opened briskly behind them and the doctor came out with his hat on. He put a long envelope into the priest's hands.

"That's the document you wanted," he said, "and I must be getting home. Good night."

"Good night," said Father Brown, as the doctor walked briskly to the gate. He had left the front door open, so that a shaft of gaslight fell upon them. In the light of this Brown opened the envelope and read the following words:

"DEAR FATHER BROWN,—*Vicisti Galilæe!*[4] Otherwise, damn your eyes, which are very penetrating ones. Can it be possible that there is something in all that stuff of yours after all?

[4] *Vicisti, Galilæe* were said to be the last words of the Roman Emperor Julian, "the Apostate" (ca. 331–363), meaning, "You have conquered me, Galilean."

"I am a man who has ever since boyhood believed in Nature and in all natural functions and instincts, whether men called them moral or immoral. Long before I became a doctor, when I was a schoolboy keeping mice and spiders, I believed that to be a good animal is the best thing in the world. But just now I am shaken; I have believed in Nature; but it seems as if Nature could betray a man. Can there be anything in your bosh? I am really getting morbid.

"I loved Quinton's wife. What was there wrong in that? Nature told me to, and it's love that makes the world go round. I also thought, quite sincerely, that she would be happier with a clean animal like me than with that tormenting little lunatic. What was there wrong in that? I was only facing facts, like a man of science. She would have been happier.

"According to my own creed I was quite free to kill Quinton, which was the best thing for everybody, even himself. But as a healthy animal I had no notion of killing myself. I resolved, therefore, that I would never do it until I saw a chance that would leave me scot free. I saw that chance this morning.

"I have been three times, all told, into Quinton's study today. The first time I went in he would talk about nothing but the weird tale, called 'The Curse of a Saint,' which he was writing, which was all about how some Indian hermit made an English colonel kill himself by thinking about him. He showed me the last sheets, and even read me the last paragraph, which was something like this, 'The conqueror of the Punjab, a mere yellow skeleton, but still gigantic, managed to lift himself on his elbow and gasp in his nephew's ear, "I die by my own hand, yet I die murdered!"' It so happened, by one chance out of a hundred, that those last words were written at the top of a new sheet of paper. I left the room, and went out into the garden intoxicated with a frightful opportunity.

"We walked round the house, and two more things happened in my favour. You suspected an Indian, and you found a dagger which the Indian might most probably use. Taking the opportunity to stuff it in my pocket I went back to Quinton's study, locked the door, and gave him his sleeping draught. He was against answering Atkinson at all, but I urged him to call out and quiet the fellow, because I wanted a clear proof that Quinton was alive when I left the room for the second time. Quinton lay down in the conservatory, and I came through the study. I am a quick man with my hands, and in a minute and a half I had done what I wanted to do. I had emptied all the first part of Quinton's romance into the fireplace, where it burnt to ashes. Then I saw that the quotation marks wouldn't do, so I snipped them off, and to make it seem likelier, snipped the whole quire to match. Then I came out with the knowledge that Quinton's confession of suicide lay on the front table, while Quinton lay alive, but asleep, in the conservatory beyond.

"The last act was a desperate one; you can guess it: I pretended to have seen Quinton dead and rushed to his room. I delayed you with the paper; and, being a quick man with my hands, killed Quinton while you were looking at his confession of suicide. He was half-asleep, being drugged, and I put his own hand on the knife and drove it into his body. The knife was of so queer a shape that no one but an operator could have calculated the angle that would reach his heart. I wonder if you noticed this.

"When I had done it the extraordinary thing happened. Nature deserted me. I felt ill. I felt just as if I had done something wrong. I think my brain is breaking up; I feel some sort of desperate pleasure in thinking I have told the thing to somebody; that I shall not have to be alone with it if I marry and have children. What is the matter with me? ... Madness ... or can one have remorse, just as if one were in Byron's poems! I cannot write any more.—JAMES ERSKINE HARRIS."

Father Brown carefully folded up the letter and put it in his breast pocket just as there came a loud peal at the gate bell, and the wet waterproofs of several policeman gleamed in the road outside.

THE SINS OF PRINCE SARADINE

When Flambeau took his month's holiday from his office in Westminster he took it in a small sailing-boat, so small that it passed much of its time as a rowing-boat. He took it, moreover, in little rivers in the Eastern counties, rivers so small that the boat looked like a magic boat, sailing on land through meadows and cornfields. The vessel was just comfortable for two people; there was room only for necessities, and Flambeau had stocked it with such things as his special philosophy considered necessary. They reduced themselves, apparently, to four essentials: tins of salmon, if he should want to eat; loaded revolvers, if he should want to fight; a bottle of brandy, presumably in case he should faint; and a priest, presumably in case he should die. With this light luggage he crawled down the little Norfolk rivers, intending to reach the Broads at last, but meanwhile delighting in the overhanging gardens and meadows, the mirrored mansions or villages, lingering to fish in the pools and corners, and in some sense hugging the shore.

Like a true philosopher, Flambeau had no aim in his holiday; but, like a true philosopher, he had an excuse. He had a sort of half purpose, which he took just so seriously that its success would crown the holiday, but just so lightly that its failure would not spoil it. Years ago, when he had been a king of thieves and the most famous figure in Paris, he had often received wild communications of approval, denunciation, or even love; but one had, somehow, stuck in his memory. It consisted simply of a visiting-card, in an envelope with an English postmark. On the back of the card was written in French and in green ink, "If you ever retire and become respectable, come and see me. I want to meet you, for I have met all the other great men of my time. That trick of yours of getting one detective to arrest the other was the most splendid scene in French history." On the front of the card was engraved in the formal fashion, "Prince Saradine, Reed House, Reed Island, Norfolk."

He had not troubled much about the prince then, beyond ascertaining that he had been a brilliant and fashionable figure in southern

Italy. In his youth, it was said, he had eloped with a married woman of high rank; the escapade was scarcely startling in his social world, but it had clung to men's minds because of an additional tragedy: the alleged suicide of the insulted husband, who appeared to have flung himself over a precipice in Sicily. The prince then lived in Vienna for a time, but his more recent years seemed to have been passed in perpetual and restless travel. But when Flambeau, like the prince himself, had left European celebrity and settled in England, it occurred to him that he might pay a surprise visit to this eminent exile in the Norfolk Broads. Whether he should find the place he had no idea; and, indeed, it was sufficiently small and forgotten. But, as things fell out, he found it much sooner than he expected.

They had moored their boat one night under a bank veiled in high grasses and short pollarded trees. Sleep, after heavy sculling, had come to them early, and by a corresponding accident they awoke before it was light. To speak more strictly, they awoke before it was daylight; for a large lemon moon was only just setting in the forest of high grass above their heads, and the sky was of a vivid violet-blue, nocturnal but bright. Both men had simultaneously a reminiscence of childhood, of the elfin and adventurous time when tall weeds close over us like woods. Standing up thus against the large low moon, the daisies really seemed to be giant daisies, the dandelions to be giant dandelions. Somehow it reminded them of the dado of a nursery wallpaper. The drop of the river-bed sufficed to sink them under the roots of all shrubs and flowers and make them gaze upwards at the grass.

"By Jove!" said Flambeau; "it's like being in fairyland."

Father Brown sat bolt upright in the boat and crossed himself. His movement was so abrupt that his friend asked him, with a mild stare, what was the matter.

"The people who wrote the mediæval ballads," answered the priest, "knew more about fairies than you do. It isn't only nice things that happen in fairyland."

"Oh, bosh!" said Flambeau. "Only nice things could happen under such an innocent moon. I am for pushing on now and seeing what does really come. We may die and rot before we ever see again such a moon or such a mood."

"All right," said Father Brown. "I never said it was always wrong to enter fairyland. I only said it was always dangerous."

They pushed slowly up the brightening river; the glowing violet of the sky and the pale gold of the moon grew fainter and fainter, and faded into that vast colourless cosmos that precedes the colours of the dawn. When the first faint stripes of red and gold and grey split the horizon from end to end they were broken by the black bulk of a town or village which sat on the river just ahead of them. It was already an easy twilight, in which all things were visible, when they came under the hanging roofs and bridges of this riverside hamlet. The houses, with their long, low, stooping roofs, seemed to come down to drink at the river, like huge grey and red cattle. The broadening and whitening dawn had already turned to working daylight before they saw any living creature on the wharves and bridges of that silent town. Eventually they saw a very placid and prosperous man in his shirt sleeves, with a face as round as the recently sunken moon, and rays of red whisker around the low arc of it, who was leaning on a post above the sluggish tide. By an impulse not to be analysed, Flambeau rose to his full height in the swaying boat and shouted at the man to ask if he knew Reed Island or Reed House. The prosperous man's smile grew slightly more expansive, and he simply pointed up the river towards the next bend of it. Flambeau went ahead without further speech.

The boat took many such grassy corners and followed many such reedy and silent reaches of river; but before the search had become monotonous they had swung round a specially sharp angle and come into the silence of a sort of pool or lake, the sight of which instinctively arrested them. For in the middle of this wider piece of water, fringed on every side with rushes, lay a long, low islet along which ran a long, low house or bungalow built of bamboo or some kind of tough tropic cane. The upstanding rods of bamboo which made the walls were pale yellow, the sloping rods that made the roof were of darker red or brown, otherwise the long house was a thing of repetition and monotony. The early morning breeze rustled the reeds round the island and sang in the strange ribbed house as in a giant pan-pipe.

"By George!" cried Flambeau; "here is the place, after all! Here is Reed Island, if ever there was one. Here is Reed House, if it is anywhere. I believe that fat man with whiskers was a fairy."

"Perhaps," remarked Father Brown impartially. "If he was, he was a bad fairy."

But even as he spoke the impetuous Flambeau had run his boat ashore in the rattling reeds, and they stood on the long, quaint islet beside the old and silent house.

The house stood with its back, as it were, to the river and the only landing-stage; the main entrance was on the other side, and looked down the long island garden. The visitors approached it, therefore, by a small path running round nearly three sides of the house, close under the low eaves. Through three different windows on three different sides they looked in on the same long, well-lit room, panelled in light wood, with a large number of looking-glasses, and laid out as for an elegant lunch. The front door, when they came round to it at last, was flanked by two turquoise-blue flower pots. It was opened by a butler of the drearier type—long, lean, grey and listless—who murmured that Prince Saradine was from home at present, but was expected hourly; the house being kept ready for him and his guests. The exhibition of the card with the scrawl of green ink awoke a flicker of life in the parchment face of this depressed retainer, and it was with a certain shaky courtesy that he suggested that the strangers should remain. "His Highness may be here any minute," he said, "and would be distressed to have just missed any gentleman he had invited. We have orders always to keep a little cold lunch for him and his friends, and I am sure he would wish it to be offered."

Moved with curiosity to this minor adventure, Flambeau assented gracefully, and followed the old man, who ushered him ceremoniously into the long, lightly panelled room. There was nothing very notable about it, except the rather unusual alternation of many long, low windows with many long, low oblongs of looking-glass, which gave a singular air of lightness and unsubstantialness to the place. It was somehow like lunching out of doors. One or two pictures of a quiet kind hung in the corners, one a large grey photograph of a very young man in uniform, another a red chalk sketch of two long-haired boys. Asked by Flambeau whether the soldierly person was the prince, the butler answered shortly in the negative; it was the prince's younger brother, Captain Stephen Saradine, he said. And with that the old man seemed to dry up suddenly and lose all taste for conversation.

After lunch had tailed off with exquisite coffee and liqueurs, the guests were introduced to the garden, the library, and the housekeeper—a dark, handsome lady, of no little majesty, and rather like a plutonic Madonna. It appeared that she and the butler were the only survivors of the prince's original foreign *ménage*, all the other servants now in the house being new and collected in Norfolk by the housekeeper. This latter lady went by the name of Mrs. Anthony, but she spoke with a slight Italian accent, and Flambeau did not doubt that Anthony was a Norfolk version of some more Latin name. Mr. Paul, the butler, also had a faintly foreign air, but he was in tongue and training English, as are many of the most polished men-servants of the cosmopolitan nobility.

Pretty and unique as it was, the place had about it a curious luminous sadness. Hours passed in it like days. The long, well-windowed rooms were full of daylight, but it seemed a dead daylight. And through all other incidental noises, the sound of talk, the clink of glasses, or the passing feet of servants, they could hear on all sides of the house the melancholy noise of the river.

"We have taken a wrong turning and come to a wrong place," said Father Brown, looking out of the window at the grey-green sedges and the silver flood. "Never mind; one can sometimes do good by being the right person in the wrong place."

Father Brown, though commonly a silent, was an oddly sympathetic little man, and in those few but endless hours he unconsciously sank deeper into the secrets of Reed House than his professional friend. He had that knack of friendly silence which is so essential to gossip; and saying scarcely a word, he probably obtained from his new acquaintances all that in any case they would have told. The butler indeed was naturally uncommunicative. He betrayed a sullen and almost animal affection for his master, who, he said, had been very badly treated. The chief offender seemed to be his highness's brother, whose name alone would lengthen the old man's lantern jaws and pucker his parrot nose into a sneer. Captain Stephen was a ne'er-do-well, apparently, and had drained his benevolent brother of hundreds and thousands; forced him to fly from fashionable life and live quietly in this retreat. That was all Paul, the butler, would say, and Paul was obviously a partisan.

The Italian housekeeper was somewhat more communicative, being, as Brown fancied, somewhat less content. Her tone about her master was faintly acid; though not without a certain awe. Flambeau and his friend were standing in the room of the looking-glasses examining the red sketch of the two boys, when the housekeeper swept in swiftly on some domestic errand. It was a peculiarity of this glittering, glass-panelled place that anyone entering was reflected in four or five mirrors at once; and Father Brown, without turning round, stopped in the middle of a sentence of family criticism. But Flambeau, who had his face close up to the picture, was already saying in a loud voice, "The brothers Saradine, I suppose. They both look innocent enough. It would be hard to say which is the good brother and which the bad." Then, realising the lady's presence, he turned the conversation with some triviality, and strolled out into the garden. But Father Brown still gazed steadily at the red crayon sketch; and Mrs. Anthony still gazed steadily at Father Brown.

She had large and tragic brown eyes, and her olive face glowed darkly with a curious and painful wonder—as of one doubtful of a stranger's identity or purpose. Whether the little priest's coat and creed touched some southern memories of confession, or whether she fancied he knew more than he did, she said to him in a low voice as to a fellow plotter, "He is right enough in one way, your friend. He says it would be hard to pick out the good and bad brothers. Oh, it would be hard, it would be mighty hard, to pick out the good one."

"I don't understand you," said Father Brown, and began to move away.

The woman took a step nearer to him, with thunderous brows and a sort of savage stoop, like a bull lowering his horns.

"There isn't a good one," she hissed. "There was badness enough in the captain taking all that money, but I don't think there was much goodness in the prince giving it. The captain's not the only man with something against him."

A light dawned on the cleric's averted face, and his mouth formed silently the word "blackmail." Even as he did so the woman turned an abrupt white face over her shoulder and almost fell. The door had opened soundlessly and the pale Paul stood like a ghost in the doorway. By the weird trick of the reflecting walls, it seemed as if five Pauls had entered by five doors simultaneously.

"His Highness," he said, "has just arrived."

In the same flash the figure of a man had passed outside the first window, crossing the sunlit pane like a lighted stage. An instant later he passed at the second window and the many mirrors repainted in successive frames the same eagle profile and marching figure. He was erect and alert, but his hair was white and his complexion of an odd ivory yellow. He had that short, curved Roman nose which generally goes with long, lean cheeks and chin, but these were partly masked by moustache and imperial. The moustache was much darker than the beard, giving an effect slightly theatrical, and he was dressed up to the same dashing part, having a white top hat, an orchid in his coat, a yellow waistcoat and yellow gloves which he flapped and swung as he walked. When he came round to the front door they heard the stiff Paul open it, and heard the new arrival say cheerfully, "Well, you see I have come." The stiff Mr. Paul bowed and answered in his inaudible manner; for a few minutes their conversation could not be heard. Then the butler said, "Everything is at your disposal"; and the glove-flapping Prince Saradine came gaily into the room to greet them. They beheld once more that spectral scene—five princes entering a room with five doors.

The prince put the white hat and yellow gloves on the table and offered his hand quite cordially.

"Delighted to see you here, Mr. Flambeau," he said. "Know you very well by reputation, if that's not an indiscreet remark."

"Not at all," answered Flambeau, laughing. "I am not sensitive. Very few reputations are gained by unsullied virtue."

The prince flashed a sharp look at him to see if the retort had any personal point; then he laughed also and offered chairs to everyone, including himself.

"Pleasant little place, this, I think," he said with a detached air. "Not much to do, I fear; but the fishing is really good."

The priest, who was staring at him with the grave stare of a baby, was haunted by some fancy that escaped definition. He looked at the grey, carefully curled hair, yellow white visage, and slim, somewhat foppish figure. These were not unnatural, though perhaps a shade *prononcé*, like the outfit of a figure behind the footlights. The nameless interest lay in something else, in the very framework of the face; Brown was tormented with a half memory of having seen it somewhere before. The man looked like some old friend of his dressed up. Then he suddenly remembered the mirrors, and put his fancy down to some psychological effect of that multiplication of human masks.

Prince Saradine distributed his social attentions between his guests with great gaiety and tact. Finding the detective of a sporting turn and eager to employ his holiday, he guided Flambeau and Flambeau's boat down to the best fishing spot in the stream, and was back in his own canoe in twenty minutes to join Father Brown in the library and plunge equally politely into the priest's more philosophic pleasures. He seemed to know a great deal both about the fishing and the books, though of these not the most edifying; he spoke five or six languages, though chiefly the slang of each. He had evidently lived in varied cities and very motley societies, for some of his cheerfullest stories were about gambling hells and opium dens, Australian bushrangers or Italian brigands. Father Brown knew that the once celebrated Saradine had spent his last few years in almost ceaseless travel, but he had not guessed that the travels were so disreputable or so amusing.

Indeed, with all his dignity of a man of the world, Prince Saradine radiated to such sensitive observers as the priest, a certain atmosphere of the restless and even the unreliable. His face was fastidious, but his eye was wild; he had little nervous ticks, like a man shaken by drink or drugs; and he neither had, nor professed to have, his hand on the helm of household affairs. All these were left to the two old servants, especially to the butler, who was plainly the central pillar of the house. Mr. Paul, indeed, was not so much a butler as a sort of steward, or even, chamberlain; he dined privately, but with almost as much pomp as his master; he was feared by all the servants; and he consulted with the prince decorously, but somewhat unbendingly—rather as if he were the prince's solicitor. The sombre housekeeper was a mere shadow in comparison; indeed, she seemed to efface herself and wait only on the butler, and Brown heard no more of those volcanic whispers which had half told him of the younger brother who blackmailed the elder. Whether the prince was really being thus bled by the absent captain, he could not be certain, but there was something insecure and secretive about Saradine that made the tale by no means incredible.

When they went once more into the long hall with the windows and the mirrors, yellow evening was dropping over the waters and the willowy banks; and a bittern sounded in the distance like an elf upon his dwarfish drum. The same singular sentiment of some sad and evil fairyland crossed the priest's mind again like a little grey cloud. "I wish Flambeau were back," he muttered.

"Do you believe in doom?" asked the restless Prince Saradine suddenly.

"No," answered his guest. "I believe in Doomsday."

The prince turned from the window and stared at him in a singular manner, his face in shadow against the sunset. "What do you mean?" he asked.

"I mean that we here are on the wrong side of the tapestry," answered Father Brown. "The things that happen here do not seem to mean anything; they mean something somewhere else. Somewhere else retribution will come on the real offender. Here it often seems to fall on the wrong person."

The prince made an inexplicable noise like an animal; in his shadowed face the eyes were shining queerly. A new and shrewd thought exploded silently in the other's mind. Was there another meaning in Saradine's blend of brilliancy and abruptness? Was the prince—Was he perfectly sane? He was repeating, "The wrong person—the wrong person," many more times than was natural in a social exclamation.

Then Father Brown awoke tardily to a second truth. In the mirrors before him he could see the silent door standing open, and the silent Mr. Paul standing in it, with his usual pallid impassiveness.

"I thought it better to announce at once," he said, with the same stiff respectfulness as of an old family lawyer, "a boat rowed by six men has come to the landing-stage, and there's a gentleman sitting in the stern."

"A boat!" repeated the prince; "a gentleman?" and he rose to his feet.

There was a startled silence punctuated only by the odd noise of the bird in the sedge; and then, before anyone could speak again, a new face and figure passed in profile round the three sunlit windows, as the prince had passed an hour or two before. But except for the accident that both outlines were aquiline, they had little in common. Instead of the new white topper of Saradine, was a black one of antiquated or foreign shape; under it was a young and very solemn face, clean shaven, blue about its resolute chin, and carrying a faint suggestion of the young Napoleon. The association was assisted by something old and odd about the whole get-up, as of a man who had never troubled to change the fashions of his fathers. He had a shabby blue frock coat, a red, soldierly looking waistcoat, and a kind of coarse white trousers common among the early Victorians, but strangely incongruous today. From all this old clothes-shop his olive face stood out strangely young and monstrously sincere.

"The deuce!" said Prince Saradine, and clapping on his white hat he went to the front door himself, flinging it open on the sunset garden.

By that time the new-comer and his followers were drawn up on the lawn like a small stage army. The six boatmen had pulled the boat well up on shore, and were guarding it almost menacingly, holding their oars erect like spears. They were swarthy men, and some of them wore earrings. But one of them stood forward beside the olive-faced young man in the red waistcoat, and carried a large black case of unfamiliar form.

"Your name," said the young man, "is Saradine?"

Saradine assented rather negligently.

The newcomer had dull, dog-like brown eyes, as different as possible from the restless and glittering grey eyes of the prince. But once again Father Brown was tortured with a sense of having seen somewhere a replica of the face; and once again he remembered the repetitions of the glass-panelled room, and put down the coincidence to that. "Confound this crystal palace!" he muttered. "One sees everything too many times. It's like a dream."

"If you are Prince Saradine," said the young man, "I may tell you that my name is Antonelli."

"Antonelli," repeated the prince languidly. "Somehow I remember the name."

"Permit me to present myself," said the young Italian.

With his left hand he politely took off his old-fashioned top hat; with his right he caught Prince Saradine so ringing a crack across the face that the white top hat rolled down the steps and one of the blue flower-pots rocked upon its pedestal.

The prince, whatever he was, was evidently not a coward; he sprang at his enemy's throat and almost bore him backwards to the grass. But his enemy extricated himself with a singularly inappropriate air of hurried politeness.

"That is all right," he said, panting and in halting English. "I have insulted. I will give satisfaction. Marco, open the case."

The man beside him with the earrings and the big black case proceeded to unlock it. He took out of it two long Italian rapiers, with splendid steel hilts and blades, which he planted point downwards in the lawn. The strange young man standing facing the entrance with his yellow and vindictive face, the two swords standing up in the turf like two crosses in a cemetery, and the line of the ranked rowers behind, gave it all an odd appearance of being some barbaric court of justice. But everything else was unchanged, so sudden had been the interruption. The sunset gold still glowed on the lawn, and the bittern still boomed as announcing some small but dreadful destiny.

"Prince Saradine," said the man called Antonelli, "when I was an infant in the cradle you killed my father and stole my mother; my father was the more fortunate. You did not kill him fairly, as I am going to kill you. You and my wicked mother took him driving to a lonely pass in Sicily, flung him down a cliff, and went on your way. I could imitate you if I chose, but imitating you is too vile. I have followed you all over the world, and you have always fled from me. But this is the end of the world—and of you. I have you now, and I give you the chance you never gave my father. Choose one of those swords."

Prince Saradine, with contracted brows, seemed to hesitate a moment, but his ears were still singing with the blow, and he sprang forward and snatched at one of the hilts. Father Brown had also sprung forward, striving to compose the dispute; but he soon found his personal presence made matters worse.

Saradine was a French freemason and a fierce atheist, and a priest moved him by the law of contraries. And for the other man neither priest nor layman moved him at all. This young man with the Bonaparte face and the brown eyes was something far sterner than a puritan—a pagan. He was a simple slayer from the morning of the earth; a man of the stone age—a man of stone.

One hope remained, the summoning of the household; and Father Brown ran back into the house. He found, however, that all the under-servants had been given a holiday ashore by the autocrat Paul, and that only the sombre Mrs. Anthony moved uneasily about the long rooms. But the moment she turned a ghastly face upon him, he resolved one of the riddles of the house of mirrors. The heavy brown eyes of Antonelli were the heavy brown eyes of Mrs. Anthony; and in a flash he saw half the story.

"Your son is outside," he said, without wasting words; "either he or the prince will be killed. Where is Mr. Paul?"

"He is at the landing-stage," said the woman faintly. "He is—he is—signalling for help."

"Mrs. Anthony," said Father Brown seriously, "there is no time for nonsense. My friend has his boat down the river fishing. Your son's boat is guarded by your son's men. There is only this one canoe; what is Mr. Paul doing with it?"

"Santa Maria! I do not know," she said; and swooned all her length on the matted floor.

Father Brown lifted her to a sofa, flung a pot of water over her, shouted for help, and then rushed down to the landing-stage of the little island. But the canoe was already in mid-stream, and old Paul was pulling and pushing it up the river with an energy incredible at his years.

"I will save my master," he cried, his eyes blazing maniacally. "I will save him yet!"

Father Brown could do nothing but gaze after the boat as it struggled up-stream and pray that the old man might waken the little town in time.

"A duel is bad enough," he muttered, rubbing up his rough dust-coloured hair, "but there's something wrong about this duel, even as a duel. I feel it in my bones. But what can it be?"

As he stood staring at the water, a wavering mirror of sunset, he heard from the other end of the island garden a small but unmistakable sound—the cold concussion of steel. He turned his head.

Away on the farthest cape or headland of the long islet, on a strip of turf beyond the last rank of roses, the duellists had already crossed swords. Evening above them was a dome of virgin gold, and, distant as they were, every detail was picked out. They had cast off their coats, but the yellow waistcoat and white hair of Saradine, the red waistcoat and white trousers of Antonelli, glittered in the level light like the colours of the dancing clockwork dolls. The two swords sparkled from point to pommel like two diamond pins. There was something frightful in the two figures appearing so little and so gay. They looked like two butterflies trying to pin each other to a cork.

Father Brown ran as hard as he could, his little legs going like a wheel. But when he came to the field of combat he found he was both too late and too early—too late to stop the strife, under the shadow of the grim Sicilians leaning on their oars, and too early to anticipate any disastrous issue of it. For the two men were singularly well matched, the prince using his skill with a sort of cynical confidence, the Sicilian using his with a murderous care. Few finer fencing matches can ever have been seen in crowded amphitheatres than that which tinkled and sparkled on that forgotten island in the reedy river. The dizzy fight was balanced so long that hope began to revive in the protesting priest; by all common probability Paul must soon come back with the police. It would be some comfort even if Flambeau came back from his fishing, for Flambeau, physically speaking, was worth four other men. But there was no sign of Flambeau, and, what was much queerer, no sign of Paul or the police. No other raft or stick was left to float on; in that lost island in that vast nameless pool, they were cut off as on a rock in the Pacific.

Almost as he had the thought the ringing of the rapiers quickened to a rattle, the prince's arms flew up, and the point shot out behind between his shoulder-blades. He went over with a great whirling movement, almost like one throwing the half of a boy's cart-wheel. The sword flew from his hand like a shooting star, and dived into the distant river. And he himself sank with so earth-shaking a subsidence that he broke a big rose-tree with his body and shook up into the sky a cloud of red earth—like the smoke of some heathen sacrifice. The Sicilian had made blood-offering to the ghost of his father.

The priest was instantly on his knees by the corpse; but only to make too sure that it was a corpse. As he was still trying some last hopeless tests he heard for the first time voices from farther up the river, and saw a police boat shoot up to the landing-stage, with constables and other important people, including the excited Paul. The little priest rose with a distinctly dubious grimace.

"Now, why on earth," he muttered, "why on earth couldn't he have come before?"

Some seven minutes later the island was occupied by an invasion of townsfolk and police, and the latter had put their hands on the victorious duellist, ritually reminding him that anything he said might be used against him.

"I shall not say anything," said the monomaniac, with a wonderful and peaceful face. "I shall never say anything more. I am very happy, and I only want to be hanged."

Then he shut his mouth as they led him away, and it is the strange but certain truth that he never opened it again in this world, except to say "Guilty" at his trial.

Father Brown had stared at the suddenly crowded garden, the arrest of the man of blood, the carrying away of the corpse after its examination by the doctor, rather as one watches the break-up of some ugly dream; he was motionless, like a man in a nightmare. He gave his name and address as a witness, but declined their offer of a boat to the shore, and remained alone in the island garden, gazing at the broken rose bush and the whole green theatre of that swift and inexplicable tragedy. The light died along the river; mist rose in the marshy banks; a few belated birds flitted fitfully across.

Stuck stubbornly in his sub-consciousness (which was an unusually lively one) was an unspeakable certainty that there was something still unexplained. This sense that had clung to him all day could not be fully explained by his fancy about "looking-glass land." Somehow he had not seen the real story, but some game or masque. And yet people do not get hanged or run through the body for the sake of a charade.

As he sat on the steps of the landing-stage ruminating he grew conscious of the tall, dark streak of a sail coming silently down the shining river, and sprang to his feet with such a backrush of feeling that he almost wept.

"Flambeau!" he cried, and shook his friend by both hands again and again, much to the astonishment of that sportsman, as he came on shore with his fishing tackle. "Flambeau," he said, "so you're not killed?"

"Killed!" repeated the angler in great astonishment. "And why should I be killed?"

"Oh, because nearly everybody else is," said his companion rather wildly. "Saradine got murdered, and Antonelli wants to be hanged, and his mother's fainted, and I, for one, don't know whether I'm in this world or the next. But, thank God, you're in the same one." And he took the bewildered Flambeau's arm.

As they turned from the landing-stage they came under the eaves of the low bamboo house, and looked in through one of the windows, as they had done on their first arrival. They beheld a lamp-lit interior well calculated to arrest their eyes. The table in the long dining-room had been laid for dinner when Saradine's destroyer had fallen like a storm-bolt on the island. And the dinner was now in placid progress, for Mrs. Anthony sat somewhat sullenly at the foot of the table, while at the head of it was Mr. Paul, the *major domo*, eating and drinking of the best, his bleared, bluish eyes standing queerly out of his face, his gaunt countenance inscrutable, but by no means devoid of satisfaction.

With a gesture of powerful impatience, Flambeau rattled at the window, wrenched it open, and put an indignant head into the lamp-lit room.

"Well!" he cried; "I can understand you may need some refreshment, but really to steal your master's dinner while he lies murdered in the garden—"

"I have stolen a great many things in a long and pleasant life," replied the strange old gentleman placidly; "this dinner is one of the few things I have not stolen. This dinner and this house and garden happen to belong to me."

A thought flashed across Flambeau's face. "You mean to say," he began, "that the will of Prince Saradine—"

"I am Prince Saradine," said the old man, munching a salted almond.

Father Brown, who was looking at the birds outside, jumped as if he were shot, and put in at the window a pale face like a turnip.

"You are *what?*" he repeated in a shrill voice.

"Paul Prince Saradine, *à vos ordres,*" said the venerable person politely, lifting a glass of sherry. "I live here very quietly, being a domestic kind of fellow; and for the sake of modesty I am called Mr. Paul, to distinguish me from my unfortunate brother Mr. Stephen. He died, I hear, recently—in the garden. Of course, it is not my fault if enemies pursue him to this place. It is owing to the regrettable irregularity of his life. He was not a domestic character."

He relapsed into silence, and continued to gaze at the opposite wall just above the bowed and sombre head of the woman. They saw plainly the family likeness that had haunted them in the dead man. Then his old shoulders began to heave and shake a little, as if he were choking, but his face did not alter.

"My God!" cried Flambeau after a pause; "he's laughing!"

"Come away," said Father Brown, who was quite white. "Come away from this house of hell. Let us get into an honest boat again."

Night had sunk on rushes and river by the time they had pushed off from the island, and they went down-stream in the dark, warming themselves with two big cigars that glowed like crimson ships' lanterns. Father Brown took his cigar out of his mouth and said:

"I suppose you can guess the whole story now? After all, it's a primitive story. A man had two enemies. He was a wise man. And so he discovered that two enemies are better than one."

"I do not follow that," answered Flambeau.

"Oh, it's really simple," rejoined his friend. "Simple, though anything but innocent. Both the Saradines were scamps, but the prince, the elder, was the sort of scamp that gets to the top, and the younger, the captain, was the sort that sinks to the bottom. This squalid officer fell from beggar to blackmailer, and one ugly day he got his hold upon his brother the prince. Obviously it was for no light matter, for Prince Paul Saradine was frankly 'fast,' and had no reputation to lose as to the mere sins of society. In plain fact, it was a hanging matter, and Stephen literally had a rope round his brother's neck. He had somehow discovered the truth about the Sicilian affair, and could prove that Paul murdered old Antonelli in the mountains. The captain raked in the hush money heavily for ten years, until even the prince's splendid fortune began to look a little foolish.

"But Prince Saradine bore another burden besides his blood-sucking brother. He knew that the son of Antonelli, a mere child at the time of the murder, had been trained in savage Sicilian loyalty, and lived only to avenge his father, not with the gibbet (for he lacked Stephen's legal proof), but with the old weapons of vendetta. The boy had practised arms with a deadly perfection, and about the time that he was old enough to use them Prince Saradine began, as the society papers said, to travel. The fact is that he began to flee for his life, passing from place to place like a hunted criminal; but with one relentless man upon his trail. That was Prince Paul's position, and by no means a pretty one. The more money he spent on eluding Antonelli the less he had to silence Stephen. The more he gave to silence Stephen the less chance there was of finally escaping Antonelli. Then it was that he showed himself a great man—a genius like Napoleon.

"Instead of resisting his two antagonists, he surrendered suddenly to both of them. He gave way like a Japanese wrestler, and his foes fell prostrate before him. He gave up the race round the world, and he gave up his address to young Antonelli; then he gave up everything to his brother. He sent Stephen money enough for smart clothes and easy travel, with a letter saying roughly, 'This is all I have left. You have cleaned me out. I still have a little house in Norfolk, with servants and a cellar, and if you want more from me you must take that. Come and take possession if you like, and I will live there quietly as your friend or agent or anything.' He knew that the Sicilian had never seen the Saradine brothers save, perhaps, in pictures; he knew they were somewhat alike, both having grey, pointed beards. Then he shaved his own face and waited. The trap worked. The unhappy captain, in his new clothes, entered the house in triumph as a prince, and walked upon the Sicilian's sword.

"There was one hitch, and it is to the honour of human nature. Evil spirits like Saradine often blunder by never expecting the virtues of mankind. He took it for granted that the Italian's blow, when it came, would be dark, violent and nameless, like the blow it avenged; that the victim would be knifed at night, or shot from behind a hedge, and so die without speech. It was a bad minute for Prince Paul when Antonelli's chivalry proposed a formal duel, with all its possible explanations. It was then that I found him putting off in his boat with wild eyes. He was fleeing, bareheaded, in an open boat before Antonelli should learn who he was.

"But, however agitated, he was not hopeless. He knew the adventurer and he knew the fanatic. It is quite probable that Stephen, the adventurer, would hold his tongue, through his mere histrionic pleasure in playing a part, his lust for clinging to his new cosy quarters, his rascal's trust in luck, and his fine fencing. It was certain that Antonelli, the fanatic, would hold his tongue, and be hanged without telling tales of his family. Paul hung about on the river till he knew the fight was over. Then he roused the town, brought the police, saw his two vanquished enemies taken away forever, and sat down smiling to his dinner."

"Laughing, God help us!" said Flambeau with a strong shudder. "Do they get such ideas from Satan?"

"He got that idea from you," answered the priest.

"God forbid!" ejaculated Flambeau. "From me? What do you mean?"

The priest pulled a visiting-card from his pocket and held it up in the faint glow of his cigar; it was scrawled with green ink.

"Don't you remember his original invitation to you?" he asked, "and the compliment to your criminal exploit? 'That trick of yours,' he says, 'of getting one detective to arrest the other?' He has just copied your trick. With an enemy on each side of him he slipped swiftly out of the way and let them collide and kill each other."

Flambeau tore Prince Saradine's card from the priest's hands and rent it savagely in small pieces.

"There's the last of that old skull and crossbones," he said as he scattered the pieces upon the dark and disappearing waves of the stream; "but I should think it would poison the fishes."

The last gleam of white card and green ink was drowned and darkened; a faint and vibrant colour as of morning changed the sky, and the moon behind the grasses grew paler. They drifted in silence.

"Father," said Flambeau suddenly, "do you think it was all a dream?"

The priest shook his head, whether in dissent or agnosticism, but remained mute. A smell of hawthorn and of orchards came to them through the darkness, telling them that a wind was awake; the next moment it swayed their little boat and swelled their sail, and carried them onward down the winding river to happier places and the homes of harmless men.

THE HAMMER OF GOD

The little village of Bohun Beacon was perched on a hill so steep that the tall spire of its church seemed only like the peak of a small mountain. At the foot of the church stood a smithy, generally red with fires and always littered with hammers and scraps of iron; opposite to this, over a rude cross of cobbled paths, was "The Blue Boar," the only inn of the place. It was upon this crossway in the lifting of a leaden and silver daybreak, that two brothers met in the street and spoke; though one was beginning the day and the other finishing it. The Rev. and Hon. Wilfred Bohun was very devout, and was making his way to some austere exercises of prayer or contemplation at dawn. Colonel the Hon. Norman Bohun, his elder brother, was by no means devout, and was sitting in evening-dress on the bench outside "The Blue Boar," drinking what the philosophic observer was free to regard either as his last glass on Tuesday or his first on Wednesday. The colonel was not particular.

The Bohuns were one of the very few aristocratic families really dating from the Middle Ages, and their pennon had actually seen Palestine. But it is a great mistake to suppose that such houses stand high in chivalric tradition. Few except the poor preserve traditions. Aristocrats live not in traditions but in fashions. The Bohuns had been Mohocks under Queen Anne and Mashers under Queen Victoria.[1]

But, like more than one of the really ancient houses, they had rotted in the last two centuries into mere drunkards and dandy degenerates, till there had even come a whisper of insanity. Certainly there was something hardly human about the colonel's wolfish pursuit of pleasure, and his chronic resolution not to go home till morning had a touch of the hideous clarity of insomnia. He was a tall, fine animal, elderly, but with hair startlingly yellow. He would have looked merely blond and leonine, but his blue eyes were sunk so deep in his face that

---

[1] "Mohock" was an eighteenth-century word for the murderous, thrill-seeking aristocrats of London, and "masher" was a disparaging term in the 1880s for a self-styled womanizer who exhibited exaggerated manners and wore dandyish clothes.

they looked black. They were a little too close together. He had very long yellow moustaches: on each side of them a fold or furrow from nostril to jaw, so that a sneer seemed to cut into his face. Over his evening clothes he wore a curiously pale yellow coat that looked more like a very light dressing gown than an overcoat, and on the back of his head was stuck an extraordinary broad-brimmed hat of a bright green colour, evidently some oriental curiosity caught up at random. He was proud of appearing in such incongruous attires—proud of the fact that he always made them look congruous.

His brother the curate had also the yellow hair and the elegance, but he was buttoned up to the chin in black, and his face was clean-shaven, cultivated and a little nervous. He seemed to live for nothing but his religion; but there were some who said (notably the blacksmith, who was a Presbyterian) that it was a love of Gothic architecture rather than of God, and that his haunting of the church like a ghost was only another and purer turn of the almost morbid thirst for beauty which sent his brother raging after women and wine. This charge was doubtful, while the man's practical piety was indubitable. Indeed, the charge was mostly an ignorant misunder-standing of the love of solitude and secret prayer, and was founded on his being often found kneeling, not before the altar, but in pecu-liar places, in the crypts or gallery, or even in the belfry. He was at the moment about to enter the church through the yard of the smithy, but stopped and frowned a little as he saw his brother's cav-ernous eyes staring in the same direction. On the hypothesis that the colonel was interested in the church he did not waste any spec-ulations. There only remained the blacksmith's shop, and though the blacksmith was a Puritan and none of his people, Wilfred Bohun had heard some scandals about a beautiful and rather celebrated wife. He flung a suspicious look across the shed, and the colonel stood up laughing to speak to him.

"Good morning, Wilfred," he said. "Like a good landlord I am watching sleeplessly over my people. I am going to call on the blacksmith."

Wilfred looked at the ground and said, "The blacksmith is out. He is over at Greenford."

"I know," answered the other with silent laughter; "that is why I am calling on him."

"Norman," said the cleric, with his eye on a pebble in the road, "are you ever afraid of thunderbolts?"

"What do you mean?" asked the colonel. "Is your hobby meteorology?"

"I mean," said Wilfred, without looking up, "do you ever think that God might strike you in the street?"

"I beg your pardon," said the colonel; "I see your hobby is folklore."

"I know your hobby is blasphemy," retorted the religious man, stung in the one live place of his nature. "But if you do not fear God, you have good reason to fear man."

The elder raised his eyebrows politely. "Fear man?" he said.

"Barnes the blacksmith is the biggest and strongest man for forty miles round," said the clergyman sternly. "I know you are no coward or weakling, but he could throw you over the wall."

This struck home, being true, and the lowering line by mouth and nostril darkened and deepened. For a moment he stood with the heavy sneer on his face. But in an instant Colonel Bohun had recovered his own cruel good humour and laughed, showing two dog-like front teeth under his yellow moustache. "In that case, my dear Wilfred," he said quite carelessly, "it was wise for the last of the Bohuns to come out partially in armour."

And he took off the queer round hat covered with green, showing that it was lined within with steel. Wilfred recognised it indeed as a light Japanese or Chinese helmet torn down from a trophy that hung in the old family hall.

"It was the first to hand," explained his brother airily; "always the nearest hat—and the nearest woman."

"The blacksmith is away at Greenford," said Wilfred quietly; "the time of his return is unsettled."

And with that he turned and went into the church with bowed head, crossing himself like one who wishes to be quit of an unclean spirit. He was anxious to forget such grossness in the cool twilight of his tall Gothic cloisters; but on that morning it was fated that his still round of religious exercises should be everywhere arrested by small shocks. As he entered the church, hitherto always empty at that hour, a kneeling figure rose hastily to its feet and came towards the full daylight of the doorway. When the curate saw it he stood still with surprise. For the early worshipper was none other than the village idiot, a nephew of the blacksmith, one who neither would nor could care for the church or for anything else. He was always called "Mad Joe," and seemed to have no other name; he was a dark, strong, slouching lad, with a heavy white face, dark straight hair, and a mouth always open. As he passed the priest, his moon-calf countenance gave no hint of what he had been doing or thinking of. He had never been known to pray before. What sort of prayers was he saying now? Extraordinary prayers surely.

Wilfred Bohun stood rooted to the spot long enough to see the idiot go out into the sunshine, and even to see his dissolute brother hail him with a sort of avuncular jocularity. The last thing he saw was the colonel throwing pennies at the open mouth of Joe, with the serious appearance of trying to hit it.

This ugly sunlight picture of the stupidity and cruelty of the earth sent the ascetic finally to his prayers for purification and new thoughts. He went up to a pew in the gallery, which brought him under a coloured window which he loved and which always quieted his spirit; a blue window with an angel carrying lilies. There he began to think less about the half-wit, with his livid face and mouth like a fish. He began to think less of his evil brother, pacing like a lean lion in his horrible hunger. He sank deeper and deeper into those cold and sweet colours of silver blossoms and sapphire sky.

In this place half an hour afterwards he was found by Gibbs, the village cobbler, who had been sent for him in some haste. He got to his feet with promptitude, for he knew that no small matter would have brought Gibbs into such a place at all. The cobbler was, as in many villages, an atheist, and his appearance in church was a shade more extraordinary than Mad Joe's. It was a morning of theological enigmas.

"What is it?" asked Wilfred Bohun rather stiffly, but putting out a trembling hand for his hat.

The atheist spoke in a tone that, coming from him, was quite startlingly respectful, and even, as it were, huskily sympathetic.

"You must excuse me, sir," he said in a hoarse whisper, "but we didn't think it right not to let you know at once. I'm afraid a rather dreadful thing has happened, sir. I'm afraid your brother—"

Wilfred clenched his frail hands. "What devilry has he done now?" he cried in involuntary passion.

"Why sir," said the cobbler, coughing, "I'm afraid he's done nothing, and won't do anything. I'm afraid he's done for. You had really better come down, sir."

The curate followed the cobbler down a short winding stair which brought them out at an entrance rather higher than the street. Bohun saw the tragedy in one glance, flat underneath him like a plan. In the yard of the smithy were standing five or six men, mostly in black, one in an inspector's uniform. They included the doctor, the Presbyterian minister, and the priest from the Roman Catholic chapel to which the blacksmith's wife belonged. The latter was speaking to her, indeed, very rapidly, in an undertone, as she, a magnificent woman with red-gold hair, was sobbing blindly on a bench. Between these two groups, and just clear of the main heap of hammers, lay a man in evening dress, spread-eagled and flat on his face. From the height above Wilfred could have sworn to every item of his costume and appearance, down to the Bohun rings upon his fingers; but the skull was only a hideous splash, like a star of blackness and blood.

Wilfred Bohun gave but one glance, and ran down the steps into the yard. The doctor, who was the family physician, saluted him, but he scarcely took any notice. He could only stammer out, "My brother is dead. What does it mean? What is this horrible mystery?" There was an unhappy silence; and then the cobbler, the most outspoken man present, answered, "Plenty of horror, sir," he said, "but not much mystery."

"What do you mean?" asked Wilfred, with a white face.

"It's plain enough," answered Gibbs. "There is only one man for forty miles round that could have struck such a blow as that, and he's the man that had most reason to."

"We must not prejudge anything," put in the doctor, a tall, black-bearded man, rather nervously; "but it is competent for me to corroborate what Mr. Gibbs says about the nature of the blow, sir; it is an incredible blow. Mr. Gibbs says that only one man in this district could have done it. I should have said myself that nobody could have done it."

A shudder of superstition went through the slight figure of the curate. "I can hardly understand," he said.

"Mr. Bohun," said the doctor in a low voice, "metaphors literally fail me. It is inadequate to say that the skull was smashed to bits like an egg-shell. Fragments of bone were driven into the body and the ground like bullets into a mud wall. It was the hand of a giant."

He was silent a moment, looking grimly through his glasses; then he added, "The thing has one advantage—that it clears most people of suspicion at one stroke. If you or I or any normally made man in the country were accused of this crime, we should be acquitted as an infant would be acquitted of stealing the Nelson Column."

"That's what I say," repeated the cobbler obstinately, "there's only one man that could have done it, and he's the man that would have done it. Where's Simeon Barnes, the blacksmith?"

"He's over at Greenford," faltered the curate.

"More likely over in France," muttered the cobbler.

"No; he is in neither of those places," said a small and colourless voice, which came from the little Roman priest who had joined the group. "As a matter of fact, he is coming up the road at this moment."

The little priest was not an interesting man to look at, having stubbly brown hair and a round and stolid face. But if he had been as splendid as Apollo no one would have looked at him at that moment. Everyone turned round and peered at the pathway which wound across the plain below, along which was indeed walking, at his own huge stride and with a hammer on his shoulder, Simeon the smith. He was a bony and gigantic man, with deep, dark, sinister eyes and a dark chin beard. He was walking and talking quietly with two other men; and though he was never specially cheerful, he seemed quite at his ease.

"My God!" cried the atheistic cobbler; "and there's the hammer he did it with."

"No," said the inspector, a sensible-looking man with a sandy moustache, speaking for the first time. "There's the hammer he did it with, over there by the church wall. We have left it and the body exactly as they are."

All glanced round, and the short priest went across and looked down in silence at the tool where it lay. It was one of the smallest and the lightest of the hammers, and would not have caught the eye among the rest; but on the iron edge of it were blood and yellow hair.

After a silence the short priest spoke without looking up, and there was a new note in his dull voice. "Mr. Gibbs was hardly right," he said, "in saying that there is no mystery. There is at least the mystery of why so big a man should attempt so big a blow with so little a hammer."

"Oh, never mind that," cried Gibbs, in a fever. "What are we to do with Simeon Barnes?"

"Leave him alone," said the priest quietly. "He is coming here of himself. I know these two men with him. They are very good fellows from Greenford, and they have come over about the Presbyterian chapel."

Even as he spoke the tall smith swung round the corner of the church and strode into his own yard. Then he stood there quite still, and the hammer fell from his hand. The inspector, who had preserved impenetrable propriety, immediately went up to him.

"I won't ask you, Mr. Barnes," he said, "whether you know anything about what has happened here. You are not bound to say. I hope you don't know, and that you will be able to prove it. But I must go through the form of arresting you in the King's name for the murder of Colonel Norman Bohun."

"You are not bound to say anything," said the cobbler in officious excitement. "They've got to prove everything. They haven't proved yet that it is Colonel Bohun, with the head all smashed up like that."

"That won't wash," said the doctor aside to the priest. "That's out of detective stories. I was the colonel's medical man, and I knew his body better than he did. He had very fine hands, but quite peculiar ones. The second and third fingers were the same in length. Oh, that's the colonel right enough."

As he glanced at the brained corpse upon the ground the iron eyes of the motionless blacksmith followed them and rested there also.

"Is Colonel Bohun dead?" said the smith quite calmly. "Then he's damned."

"Don't say anything! Oh, don't say anything," cried the atheist cobbler, dancing about in an ecstasy of admiration of the English legal system. For no man is such a legalist as the good Secularist.

The blacksmith turned on him over his shoulder the august face of a fanatic.

"It is well for you infidels to dodge like foxes because the world's law favours you," he said; "but God guards His own in His pocket, as you shall see this day."

Then he pointed to the colonel and said, "When did this dog die in his sins?"

"Moderate your language," said the doctor.

"Moderate the Bible's language, and I'll moderate mine. When did he die?"

"I saw him alive at six o'clock this morning," stammered Wilfred Bohun.

"God is good," said the smith. "Mr. Inspector, I have not the slightest objection to being arrested. It is you who may object to arresting me. I don't mind leaving the court without a stain on my character. You do mind, perhaps, leaving the court with a bad set-back in your career."

The solid inspector for the first time looked at the blacksmith with a lively eye—as did everybody else, except the short, strange priest, who was still looking down at the little hammer that had dealt the dreadful blow.

"There are two men standing outside this shop," went on the blacksmith with ponderous lucidity, "good tradesmen in Greenford whom you all know, who will swear that they saw me from before midnight till daybreak and long after in the committee-room of our Revival Mission, which sits all night, we save souls so fast. In Greenford itself twenty people could swear to me for all that time. If I were a heathen, Mr. Inspector, I would let you walk on to your downfall; but, as a Christian man, I feel bound to give you your chance and ask you whether you will hear my alibi now or in court."

The inspector seemed for the first time disturbed and said, "Of course I should be glad to clear you altogether now."

The smith walked out of his yard with the same long and easy stride, and returned to his two friends from Greenford, who were indeed friends of nearly everyone present. Each of them said a few words which no one ever thought of disbelieving. When they had spoken the innocence of Simeon stood up as solid as the great church above them.

One of those silences struck the group which are more strange and insufferable than any speech. Madly, in order to make conversation, the curate said to the Catholic priest:

"You seem very much interested in that hammer, Father Brown."

"Yes, I am," said Father Brown; "why is it such a small hammer?"

The doctor swung round on him.

"By George, that's true," he cried; "who would use a little hammer with ten larger hammers lying about?"

Then he lowered his voice in the curate's ear and said, "Only the kind of person that can't lift a large hammer. It is not a question of force or courage between the sexes. It's a question of lifting power in the shoulders. A bold woman could commit ten murders with a light hammer and never turn a hair. She could not kill a beetle with a heavy one."

Wilfred Bohun was staring at him with a sort of hypnotised horror, while Father Brown listened with his head a little on one side, really interested and attentive. The doctor went on with more hissing emphasis:

"Why do those idiots always assume that the only person who hates the wife's lover is the wife's husband? Nine times out of ten the person who most hates the wife's lover is the wife. Who knows what insolence or treachery he had shown her—look there?"

He made a momentary gesture towards the red-haired woman on the bench. She had lifted her head at last and the tears were drying on her splendid face. But the eyes were fixed on the corpse with an electric glare that had in it something of idiocy.

The Rev. Wilfred Bohun made a limp gesture as if waving away all desire to know; but Father Brown, dusting off his sleeve some ashes blown from the furnace, spoke in his indifferent way.

"You are like so many doctors," he said; "your mental science is really suggestive. It is your physical science that is utterly impossible. I agree that the woman wants to kill the co-respondent much more than the petitioner does. And I agree that a woman will always pick up a small hammer instead of a big one. But the difficulty is one of physical impossibility. No woman ever born could have smashed a man's skull out flat like that." Then he added reflectively, after a pause, "These people haven't grasped the whole of it. The man was actually wearing an iron helmet, and the blow scattered it like broken glass. Look at that woman. Look at her arms."

Silence held them all up again, and then the doctor said rather sulkily, "Well, I may be wrong; there are objections to everything. But I stick to the main point. No man but an idiot would pick up that little hammer if he could use a big hammer."

With that the lean and quivering hands of Wilfred Bohun went up to his head and seemed to clutch his scanty yellow hair. After an instant they dropped, and he cried, "That was the word I wanted; you have said the word."

Then he continued, mastering his discomposure, "The words you said were, 'No man but an idiot would pick up the small hammer.'"

"Yes," said the doctor. "Well?"

"Well," said the curate, "no man but an idiot did." The rest stared at him with eyes arrested and riveted, and he went on in a febrile and feminine agitation.

"I am a priest," he cried unsteadily, "and a priest should be no shedder of blood. I—I mean that he should bring no one to the gallows. And I thank God that I see the criminal clearly now—because he is a criminal who cannot be brought to the gallows."

"You will not denounce him?" inquired the doctor.

"He would not be hanged if I did denounce him," answered Wilfred with a wild but curiously happy smile. "When I went into the church this morning I found a madman praying there—that poor Joe, who has been wrong all his life. God knows what he prayed; but with such strange folk it is not incredible to suppose that their prayers are all upside down. Very likely a lunatic would pray before killing a man. When I last saw poor Joe he was with my brother. My brother was mocking him."

"By Jove!" cried the doctor, "this is talking at last. But how do you explain—"

The Rev. Wilfred was almost trembling with the excitement of his own glimpse of the truth. "Don't you see; don't you see," he cried feverishly, "that is the only theory that covers both the queer things, that answers both the riddles. The two riddles are the little hammer and the big blow. The smith might have struck the big blow, but he would not have chosen the little hammer. His wife would have chosen the little hammer, but she could not have struck the big blow. But the madman might have done both. As for the little hammer—why, he was mad and might have picked up anything. And for the big blow, have you never heard, doctor, that a maniac in his paroxysm may have the strength of ten men?"

The doctor drew a deep breath and then said, "By golly, I believe you've got it."

Father Brown had fixed his eyes on the speaker so long and steadily as to prove that his large grey, ox-like eyes were not quite so insignificant as the rest of his face. When silence had fallen he said with marked respect, "Mr. Bohun, yours is the only theory yet propounded which holds water every way and is essentially unassailable. I think, therefore, that you deserve to be told, on my positive knowledge, that it is not the true one." And with that the odd little man walked away and stared again at the hammer.

"That fellow seems to know more than he ought to," whispered the doctor peevishly to Wilfred. "Those popish priests are deucedly sly."

"No, no," said Bohun, with a sort of wild fatigue. "It was the lunatic. It was the lunatic."

The group of the two clerics and the doctor had fallen away from the more official group containing the inspector and the man he had arrested. Now, however, that their own party had broken up, they heard voices from the others. The priest looked up quietly and then looked down again as he heard the blacksmith say in a loud voice:

"I hope I've convinced you, Mr. Inspector. I'm a strong man, as you say, but I couldn't have flung my hammer bang here from Greenford. My hammer hasn't any wings that it should come flying half a mile over hedges and fields."

The inspector laughed amicably and said, "No; I think you can be considered out of it, though it's one of the rummiest coincidences I ever saw. I can only ask you to give us all the assistance you can in finding a man as big and strong as yourself. By George! you might be useful, if only to hold him! I suppose you yourself have no guess at the man?"

"I may have a guess," said the pale smith, "but it is not at a man." Then, seeing the scared eyes turn towards his wife on the bench, he put his huge hand on her shoulder and said, "Nor a woman either."

"What do you mean?" asked the inspector jocularly. "You don't think cows use hammers, do you?"

"I think no thing of flesh held that hammer," said the blacksmith in a stifled voice; "mortally speaking, I think the man died alone."

Wilfred made a sudden forward movement and peered at him with burning eyes.

"Do you mean to say, Barnes," came the sharp voice of the cobbler, "that the hammer jumped up of itself and knocked the man down?"

"Oh, you gentlemen may stare and snigger," cried Simeon; "you clergymen who tell us on Sunday in what a stillness the Lord smote Sennacherib. I believe that One who walks invisible in every house defended the honour of mine, and laid the defiler dead before the door of it. I believe the force in that blow was just the force there is in earthquakes, and no force less."

Wilfred said, with a voice utterly undescribable, "I told Norman myself to beware of the thunderbolt."

"That agent is outside my jurisdiction," said the inspector with a slight smile.

"You are not outside His," answered the smith; "see you to it." And, turning his broad back, he went into the house.

The shaken Wilfred was led away by Father Brown, who had an easy and friendly way with him. "Let us get out of this horrid place, Mr. Bohun," he said. "May I look inside your church? I hear it's one of the oldest in England. We take some interest, you know," he added with a comical grimace, "in old English churches." [2]

---

[2] Father Brown's grimace shows that he is thinking of Henry VIII's Suppression of 1536–1539 in which hundreds of Roman Catholic abbeys and churches were dissolved, their ownership transferred to the crown. The properties were subsequently sold to the English gentry to expand the royal treasury.

Wilfred Bohun did not smile, for humour was never his strong point. But he nodded rather eagerly, being only too ready to explain the Gothic splendours to someone more likely to be sympathetic than the Presbyterian blacksmith or the atheist cobbler.

"By all means," he said; "let us go in at this side." And he led the way into the high side entrance at the top of the flight of steps. Father Brown was mounting the first step to follow him when he felt a hand on his shoulder, and turned to behold the dark, thin figure of the doctor, his face darker yet with suspicion.

"Sir," said the physician harshly, "you appear to know some secrets in this black business. May I ask if you are going to keep them to yourself?"

"Why, doctor," answered the priest, smiling quite pleasantly, "there is one very good reason why a man of my trade would keep things to himself when he is not sure of them, and that is that it is so constantly his duty to keep them to himself when he is sure of them. But if you think I have been discourteously reticent with you or anyone, I will go to the extreme limit of my custom. I will give you two very large hints."

"Well, sir?" said the doctor gloomily.

"First," said Father Brown quietly, "the thing is quite in your own province. It is a matter of physical science. The blacksmith is mistaken, not perhaps in saying that the blow was divine, but certainly in saying that it came by a miracle. It was no miracle, doctor, except in so far as man is himself a miracle, with his strange and wicked and yet half-heroic heart. The force that smashed that skull was a force well known to scientists—one of the most frequently debated of the laws of nature."

The doctor, who was looking at him with frowning intentness, only said, "And the other hint?"

"The other hint is this," said the priest, "Do you remember the blacksmith, though he believes in miracles, talking scornfully of the impossible fairy tale that his hammer had wings and flew half a mile across country?"

"Yes," said the doctor, "I remember that."

"Well," added Father Brown, with a broad smile, "that fairy tale was the nearest thing to the real truth that has been said today." And with that he turned his back and stumped up the steps after the curate.

The Reverend Wilfred, who had been waiting for him, pale and impatient, as if this little delay were the last straw for his nerves, led him immediately to his favourite corner of the church, that part of the gallery closest to the carved roof and lit by the wonderful window with the angel. The little Latin priest explored and admired everything exhaustively, talking cheerfully but in a low voice all the time. When in the course of his investigation he found the side exit and the winding stair down which Wilfred had rushed to find his brother dead, Father Brown ran not down but up, with the agility of a monkey, and his clear voice came from an outer platform above.

"Come up here, Mr. Bohun," he called. "The air will do you good." Bohun followed him, and came out on a kind of stone gallery or balcony outside the building, from which one could see the illimitable plain in which their small hill stood, wooded away to the purple horizon and dotted with villages and farms. Clear and square, but quite small beneath them, was the blacksmith's yard, where the inspector still stood taking notes and the corpse still lay like a smashed fly.

"Might be the map of the world, mightn't it?" said Father Brown.

"Yes," said Bohun very gravely, and nodded his head.

Immediately beneath and about them the lines of the Gothic building plunged outwards into the void with a sickening swiftness akin to suicide. There is that element of Titan energy in the architecture of the Middle Ages that, from whatever aspect it be seen, it always seems to be rushing away, like the strong back of some maddened horse. This church was hewn out of ancient and silent stone, bearded with old fungoids and stained with the nests of birds. And yet, when they saw it from below, it sprang like a fountain at the stars; and when they saw it, as now, from above, it poured like a cataract into a voiceless pit. For these two men on the tower were left alone with the most terrible aspect of the Gothic: the monstrous foreshortening and disproportion, the dizzy perspectives, the glimpses of great things small and small things great; a topsy-turvydom of stone in the mid-air. Details of stone, enormous by their proximity, were relieved against a pattern of fields and farms, pygmy in their distance. A carved bird or beast at a corner seemed like some vast walking or flying dragon wasting the pastures and villages below. The whole atmosphere was dizzy and dangerous, as if men were upheld in air amid the gyrating wings of colossal genii; and the whole of that old church, as tall and rich as a cathedral, seemed to sit upon the sunlit country like a cloudburst.

"I think there is something rather dangerous about standing on these high places even to pray," said Father Brown. "Heights were made to be looked at, not to be looked from."

"Do you mean that one may fall over?" asked Wilfred.

"I mean that one's soul may fall if one's body doesn't," said the other priest.

"I scarcely understand you," remarked Bohun indistinctly.

"Look at that blacksmith, for instance," went on Father Brown calmly; "a good man, but not a Christian—hard, imperious, unforgiving. Well, his Scotch religion was made up by men who prayed on hills and high crags, and learnt to look down on the world more than to look up at heaven. Humility is the mother of giants. One sees great things from the valley; only small things from the peak."

"But he—he didn't do it," said Bohun tremulously.

"No," said the other in an odd voice; "we know he didn't do it."

After a moment he resumed, looking tranquilly out over the plain with his pale grey eyes. "I knew a man," he said, "who began by worshipping with others before the altar, but who grew fond of high and lonely places to pray from, corners or niches in the belfry or the spire. And once in one of those dizzy places, where the whole world seemed to turn under him like a wheel, his brain turned also, and he fancied he was God. So that though he was a good man, he committed a great crime."

Wilfred's face was turned away, but his bony hands turned blue and white as they tightened on the parapet of stone.

"He thought it was given to *him* to judge the world and strike down the sinner. He would never have had such a thought if he had been kneeling, with other men upon a floor. But he saw all men walking about like insects. He saw one especially strutting just below him, insolent and evident by a bright green hat—a poisonous insect."

Rooks cawed round the corners of the belfry; but there was no other sound till Father Brown went on.

"This also tempted him, that he had in his hand one of the most awful engines of nature; I mean gravitation, that mad and quickening rush by which all earth's creatures fly back to her heart when released. See, the inspector is strutting just below us in the smithy. If I were to toss a pebble over this parapet it would be something like a bullet by the time it struck him. If I were to drop a hammer—even a small hammer—"

Wilfred Bohun threw one leg over the parapet, and Father Brown had him in a minute by the collar.

"Not by that door," he said quite gently; "that door leads to hell."

Bohun staggered back against the wall, and stared at him with frightful eyes.

"How do you know all this?" he cried. "Are you a devil?"

"I am a man," answered Father Brown gravely; "and therefore have all devils in my heart. Listen to me," he said after a short pause. "I know what you did—at least, I can guess the great part of it. When you left your brother you were racked with no unrighteous rage to the extent even that you snatched up the small hammer, half inclined to kill him with his foulness on his mouth. Recoiling, you thrust it under your buttoned coat instead, and rushed into the church. You pray wildly in many places, under the angel window, upon the platform above, and on a higher platform still, from which you could see the colonel's Eastern hat like the back of a green beetle crawling about. Then something snapped in your soul, and you let God's thunderbolt fall."

Wilfred put a weak hand to his head, and asked in a low voice, "How did you know that his hat looked like a green beetle?"

"Oh, that," said the other with the shadow of a smile, "that was common sense. But hear me further. I say I know all this; but no one else shall know it. The next step is for you; I shall take no more steps; I will seal this with the seal of confession. If you ask me why, there are many reasons, and only one that concerns you. I leave things to you because you have not yet gone very far wrong, as assassins go. You did not help to fix the crime on the smith when it was easy; or on his wife, when that was easy. You tried to fix it on the imbecile, because you knew that he could not suffer. That was one of the gleams that it is my business to find in assassins. And now come down into the village, and go your own way as free as the wind; for I have said my last word."

They went down the winding stairs in utter silence, and came out into the sunlight by the smithy. Wilfred Bohun carefully unlatched the wooden gate of the yard, and going up to the inspector, said, "I wish to give myself up; I have killed my brother."

THE EYE OF APOLLO

That singular smoky sparkle, at once a confusion and a transparency, which is the strange secret of the Thames, was changing more and more from its grey to its glittering extreme as the sun climbed to the zenith over Westminster, and the two men crossed Westminster Bridge. One man was very tall and the other very short; they might even have been fantastically compared to the arrogant clock-tower of Parliament and the humbler humped shoulders of the Abbey, for the short man was in clerical dress. The official description of the tall man was M. Hercule Flambeau, private detective, and he was going to his new offices in a new pile of flats facing the Abbey entrance. The official description of the short man was the Reverend J. Brown,[1] attached to St. Francis Xavier's Church, Camberwell, and he was coming from a Camberwell deathbed to see the new offices of his friend.

The building was American in its sky-scraping altitude, and American also in the oiled elaboration of its machinery of telephones and lifts. But it was barely finished and still understaffed; only three tenants had moved in; the office just above Flambeau was occupied, as also was the office just below him; the two floors above that and the three floors below were entirely bare. But the first glance at the new tower of flats caught something much more arresting. Save for a few relics of scaffolding, the one glaring object was erected outside the office just above Flambeau's. It was an enormous gilt effigy of the human eye, surrounded with rays of gold, and taking up as much room as two or three office windows.

"What on earth is that?" asked Father Brown, and stood still.

"Oh, a new religion," said Flambeau, laughing; "one of those new religions that forgive your sins by saying you never had any. Rather like Christian Science, I should think. The fact is that a fellow calling himself Kalon (I don't know what his name is, except that it can't be that) has taken the flat just above me. I have two lady typewriters

---

[1] The initial "J" of this "official" description appears in the British first edition of *The Innocence of Father Brown* (1911). It was removed in subsequent editions.

underneath me, and this enthusiastic old humbug on top. He calls himself the New Priest of Apollo, and he worships the sun."

"Let him look out," said Father Brown. "The sun was the cruellest of all the gods. But what does that monstrous eye mean?"

"As I understand it, it is a theory of theirs," answered Flambeau, "that a man can endure anything if his mind is quite steady. Their two great symbols are the sun and the open eye; for they say that if a man were really healthy he could stare at the sun."

"If a man were really healthy," said Father Brown, "he would not bother to stare at it."

"Well, that's all I can tell you about the new religion," went on Flambeau carelessly. "It claims, of course, that it can cure all physical diseases."

"Can it cure the one spiritual disease?" asked Father Brown, with a serious curiosity.

"And what is the one spiritual disease?" asked Flambeau, smiling.

"Oh, thinking one is quite well," said his friend.

Flambeau was more interested in the quiet little office below him than in the flamboyant temple above. He was a lucid Southerner, incapable of conceiving himself as anything but a Catholic or an atheist; and new religions of a bright and pallid sort were not much in his line. But humanity was always in his line, especially when it was good-looking; moreover, the ladies downstairs were characters in their way. The office was kept by two sisters, both slight and dark, one of them tall and striking. She had a dark, eager and aquiline profile, and was one of those women whom one always thinks of in profile, as of the clean-cut edge of some weapon. She seemed to cleave her way through life. She had eyes of startling brilliancy, but it was the brilliancy of steel rather than of diamonds; and her straight, slim figure was a shade too stiff for its grace. Her younger sister was like her shortened shadow, a little greyer, paler, and more insignificant. They both wore a business-like black, with little masculine cuffs and collars. There are thousands of such curt, strenuous ladies in the offices of London, but the interest of these lay rather in their real than their apparent position.

For Pauline Stacey, the elder, was actually the heiress of a crest and half a county, as well as great wealth; she had been brought up in castles and gardens, before a frigid fierceness (peculiar to the modern woman) had driven her to what she considered a harsher and a higher existence. She had not, indeed, surrendered her money; in that there would have been a romantic or monkish abandon quite alien to her masterful utilitarianism. She held her wealth, she would say, for use upon practical social objects. Part of it she had put into her business, the nucleus of a model typewriting emporium; part of it was distributed in various leagues and causes for the advancement of such work among women. How far Joan, her sister and partner, shared this slightly prosaic idealism no one could be very sure. But she followed her leader with a dog-like affection which was somehow more attractive, with its touch of tragedy, than the hard, high spirits of the elder. For Pauline Stacey had nothing to say to tragedy; she was understood to deny its existence.

Her rigid rapidity and cold impatience had amused Flambeau very much on the first occasion of his entering the flats. He had lingered outside the lift in the entrance hall waiting for the lift-boy, who generally conducts strangers to the various floors. But this bright-eyed falcon of a girl had openly refused to endure such official delay. She said sharply that she knew all about the lift, and was not dependent on boys—or on men either. Though her flat was only three floors above, she managed in the few seconds of ascent to give Flambeau a great many of her fundamental views in an off-hand manner; they were to the general effect that she was a modern working woman and loved modern working machinery. Her bright black eyes blazed with abstract anger against those who rebuke mechanic science and ask for the return of romance. Everyone, she said, ought to be able to manage machines, just as she could manage the lift. She seemed almost to resent the fact of Flambeau opening the lift-door for her; and that gentleman went up to his own apartments smiling with somewhat mingled feelings at the memory of such spit-fire self-dependence.

She certainly had a temper, of a snappy, practical sort; the gestures of her thin, elegant hands were abrupt or even destructive. Once Flambeau entered her office on some typewriting business, and found she had just flung a pair of spectacles belonging to her sister into the middle of the floor and stamped on them. She was already in the rapids of an ethical tirade about the "sickly medical notions" and the morbid admission of weakness implied in such an apparatus. She dared her sister to bring such artificial, unhealthy rubbish into the place again. She asked if she was expected to wear wooden legs or false hair or glass eyes; and as she spoke her eyes sparkled like the terrible crystal.

Flambeau, quite bewildered with this fanaticism, could not refrain from asking Miss Pauline (with direct French logic) why a pair of spectacles was a more morbid sign of weakness than a lift, and why, if science might help us in the one effort, it might not help us in the other.

"That is *so* different," said Pauline Stacey, loftily. "Batteries and motors and all those things are marks of the force of man—yes, Mr. Flambeau, and the force of women, too! We shall take our turn at these great engines that devour distance and defy time. That is high and splendid—that is really science. But these nasty props and plasters the doctors sell—why, they are just badges of poltroonery. Doctors stick on legs and arms as if we were born cripples and sick slaves. But I was freeborn, Mr. Flambeau! People only think they need these things because they have been trained in fear instead of being trained in power and courage, just as the silly nurses tell children not to stare at the sun, and so they can't do it without blinking. But why among the stars should there be one star I may not see? The sun is not my master, and I will open my eyes and stare at him whenever I choose."

"Your eyes," said Flambeau, with a foreign bow, "will dazzle the sun." He took pleasure in complimenting this strange stiff beauty, partly because it threw her a little off her balance. But as he went upstairs to his floor he drew a deep breath and whistled, saying to himself, "So she has got into the hands of that conjurer upstairs with his golden eye." For, little as he knew or cared about the new religion of Kalon, he had heard of his special notion about sun-gazing.

He soon discovered that the spiritual bond between the floors above and below him was close and increasing. The man who called himself Kalon was a magnificent creature, worthy, in a physical sense, to be the pontiff of Apollo. He was nearly as tall even as Flambeau, and very much better looking, with a golden beard, strong blue eyes, and a mane flung back like a lion's. In structure he was the blond beast of

Nietzsche,[2] but all this animal beauty was heightened, brightened and softened by genuine intellect and spirituality. If he looked like one of the great Saxon kings, he looked like one of the kings that were also saints. And this despite the cockney incongruity of his surroundings; the fact that he had an office half-way up a building in Victoria Street; that the clerk (a commonplace youth in cuffs and collars) sat in the outer room, between him and the corridor; that his name was on a brass plate, and the gilt emblem of his creed hung above the street, like the advertisement of an oculist. All this vulgarity could not take away from the man called Kalon the vivid oppression and inspiration that came from his soul and body. When all was said, a man in the presence of this quack did feel in the presence of a great man. Even in the loose jacket-suit of linen that he wore as a workshop dress in his office he was a fascinating and formidable figure; and when robed in the white vestments and crowned with the golden circlet, in which he daily saluted the sun, he really looked so splendid that the laughter of the street people sometimes died suddenly on their lips. For three times in the day the new sun-worshipper went out on his little balcony, in the face of all Westminster, to say some litany to his shining lord: once at daybreak, once at sunset, and once at the shock of noon. And it was while the shock of noon still shook faintly from the towers of Parliament and parish church that Father Brown, the friend of Flambeau, first looked up and saw the white priest of Apollo.

Flambeau had seen quite enough of these daily salutations of Phœbus, and plunged into the porch of the tall building without even looking for his clerical friend to follow. But Father Brown, whether from a professional interest in ritual or a strong individual interest in tomfoolery, stopped and stared up at the balcony of the sun-worshipper, just as he might have stopped and stared up at a Punch and Judy. Kalon the Prophet was already erect, with argent garments and uplifted hands, and the sound of his strangely penetrating voice could be heard all the way down the busy street uttering his solar litany. He was already

---

[2] The "blond beast" referred to is the vital animal of Friedrich Nietzsche's *Geneology of Morals* (1887); the phrase later became identified with the notion of Germanic racial supremacy.

in the middle of it; his eyes were fixed upon the flaming disk. It is doubtful if he saw anything or anyone on this earth; it is substantially certain that he did not see a stunted, round-faced priest who, in the crowd below, looked up at him with blinking eyes. That was perhaps the most startling difference between even these two far divided men. Father Brown could not look at anything without blinking; but the priest of Apollo could look on the blaze at noon without a quiver of the eyelid.

"O sun," cried the prophet, "O star that art too great to be allowed among the stars! O fountain that flowest quietly in that secret spot that is called space. White Father of all white unwearied things, white flames and white flowers and white peaks. Father, who art more innocent than all thy most innocent and quiet children; primal purity, into the peace of which——"

A rush and crash like the reversed rush of a rocket was cloven with a strident and incessant yelling. Five people rushed into the gate of the mansions as three people rushed out, and for an instant they all deafened each other. The sense of some utterly abrupt horror seemed for a moment to fill half the street with bad news—bad news that was all the worse because no one knew what it was. Two figures remained still after the crash of commotion: the fair priest of Apollo on the balcony above, and the ugly priest of Christ below him.

At last the tall figure and titanic energy of Flambeau appeared in the doorway of the mansions and dominated the little mob. Talking at the top of his voice like a fog-horn, he told somebody or anybody to go for a surgeon; and as he turned back into the dark and thronged entrance his friend Father Brown slipped in insignificantly after him. Even as he ducked and dived through the crowd he could still hear the magnificent melody and monotony of the solar priest still calling on the happy god who is the friend of fountains and flowers.

Father Brown found Flambeau and some six other people standing round the enclosed space into which the lift commonly descended. But the lift had not descended. Something else had descended; something that ought to have come by a lift.

For the last four minutes Flambeau had looked down on it; had seen the brained and bleeding figure of that beautiful woman who

denied the existence of tragedy. He had never had the slightest doubt
that it was Pauline Stacey; and, though he had sent for a doctor, he
had not the slightest doubt that she was dead.

He could not remember for certain whether he had liked her or
disliked her; there was so much both to like and dislike. But she had
been a person to him, and the unbearable pathos of details and habit
stabbed him with all the small daggers of bereavement. He remembered her pretty face and priggish speeches with a sudden secret vividness which is all the bitterness of death. In an instant like a bolt
from the blue, like a thunderbolt from nowhere, that beautiful and
defiant body had been dashed down the open well of the lift to death
at the bottom. Was it suicide? With so insolent an optimist it seemed
impossible. Was it murder? But who was there in those hardly inhabited flats to murder anybody? In a rush of raucous words, which he
meant to be strong and suddenly found weak, he asked where was
that fellow Kalon. A voice, habitually heavy, quiet and full, assured
him that Kalon for the last fifteen minutes had been away up on his
balcony worshipping his god. When Flambeau heard the voice, and
felt the hand of Father Brown, he turned his swarthy face and said
abruptly:

"Then, if he has been up there all the time, who can have done it?"

"Perhaps," said the other, "we might go upstairs and find out. We
have half an hour before the police will move."

Leaving the body of the slain heiress in charge of the surgeons,
Flambeau dashed up the stairs to the typewriting office, found it utterly
empty, and then dashed up to his own. Having entered that, he abruptly
returned with a new and white face to his friend.

"Her sister," he said, with an unpleasant seriousness, "her sister
seems to have gone out for a walk."

Father Brown nodded. "Or, she may have gone up to the office of
that sun man," he said. "If I were you I should just verify that, and
then let us talk it over in your office. No," he added suddenly, as if
remembering something, "shall I ever get over that stupidity of mine?
Of course, in their office downstairs."

Flambeau stared; but he followed the little father downstairs to the
empty flat of the Staceys, where that impenetrable pastor took a large

red-leather chair in the very entrance, from which he could see the stairs and landings, and waited. He did not wait very long. In about four minutes three figures descended the stairs, alike only in their solemnity. The first was Joan Stacey, the sister of the dead woman— evidently she *had* been upstairs in the temporary temple of Apollo; the second was the priest of Apollo himself, his litany finished, sweeping down the empty stairs in utter magnificence—something in his white robes, beard and parted hair had the look of Doré's Christ leaving the Pretorium;[3] the third was Flambeau, black browed and somewhat bewildered.

Miss Joan Stacey, dark, with a drawn face and hair prematurely touched with grey, walked straight to her own desk and set out her papers with a practical flap. The mere action rallied everyone else to sanity. If Miss Joan Stacey was a criminal, she was a cool one. Father Brown regarded her for some time with an odd little smile, and then, without taking his eyes off her, addressed himself to somebody else.

"Prophet," he said, presumably addressing Kalon, "I wish you would tell me a lot about your religion."

"I shall be proud to do it," said Kalon, inclining his still crowned head, "but I am not sure that I understand."

"Why, it's like this," said Father Brown, in his frankly doubtful way, "We are taught that if a man has really bad first principles, that must be partly his fault. But, for all that, we can make some difference between a man who insults his quite clear conscience and a man with a conscience more or less clouded with sophistries. Now, do you really think that murder is wrong at all?"

"Is this an accusation?" asked Kalon very quietly.

"No," answered Brown, equally gently, "it is the speech for the defence."

In the long and startled stillness of the room the prophet of Apollo slowly rose; and really it was like the rising of the sun. He filled that room with his light and life in such a manner that a man felt he could

[3] The Praetorium was the palace in which King Herod questioned Jesus, who is pictured leaving there in one of French illustrator Gustave Doré's engravings for *La Sainte Bible* (1866) where the commanding presence of Christ includes the robe, divided beard, and the long, parted hair referred to here.

as easily have filled Salisbury Plain. His robed form seemed to hang
the whole room with classic draperies; his epic gesture seemed to
extend it into grander perspectives, till the little black figure of the
modern cleric seemed to be a fault and an intrusion, a round, black
blot upon some splendour of Hellas.

"We meet at last, Caiaphas," said the prophet. "Your church and
mine are the only realities on this earth. I adore the sun, and you the
darkening of the sun; you are the priest of the dying and I of the
living God. Your present work of suspicion and slander is worthy of
your coat and creed. All your church is but a black police; you are
only spies and detectives seeking to tear from men confessions of guilt,
whether by treachery or torture. You would convict men of crime, I
would convict them of innocence. You would convince them of sin,
I would convince them of virtue.

"Reader of the books of evil, one more word before I blow away
your baseless nightmares for ever. Not even faintly could you understand how little I care whether you can convict me or no. The things
you call disgrace and horrible hanging are to me no more than an ogre
in a child's toy-book to a man once grown up. You said you were
offering the speech for the defence. I care so little for the cloudland of
this life that I will offer you the speech for the prosecution. There is
but one thing that can be said against me in this matter, and I will say
it myself. The woman that is dead was my love and my bride; not
after such manner as your tin chapels call lawful, but by a law purer
and sterner than you will ever understand. She and I walked another
world from yours, and trod places of crystal while you were plodding
through tunnels and corridors of brick. Well, I know that policemen,
theological and otherwise, always fancy that where there has been
love there must soon be hatred; so there you have the first point made
for the prosecution. But the second point is stronger; I do not grudge
it you. Not only is it true that Pauline loved me, but it is also true that
this very morning, before she died, she wrote at that table a will leaving me and my new church half a million. Come, where are the handcuffs? Do you suppose I care what foolish things you do with me?
Penal servitude will only be like waiting for her at a wayside station.
The gallows will only be going to her in a headlong car."

He spoke with the brain-shaking authority of an orator, and Flambeau and Joan Stacey stared at him in an amazed admiration. Father Brown's face seemed to express nothing but extreme distress; he looked at the ground with one wrinkle of pain across his forehead. The prophet of the sun leaned easily against the mantelpiece and resumed:

"In a few words I have put before you the whole case against me—the only possible case against me. In fewer words still I will blow it to pieces, so that not a trace of it remains. As to whether I have committed this crime, the truth is in one sentence: I could not have committed this crime. Pauline Stacey fell from this floor to the ground at five minutes past twelve. A hundred people will go into the witness-box and say that I was standing out upon the balcony of my own rooms above from just before the stroke of noon to a quarter-past—the usual period of my public prayers. My clerk (a respectable youth from Clapham, with no sort of connexion with me) will swear that he sat in my outer office all the morning, and that no communication passed through. He will swear that I arrived a full ten minutes before the hour, fifteen minutes before any whisper of the accident, and that I did not leave the office or the balcony all that time. No one ever had so complete an alibi; I could subpœna half Westminster. I think you had better put the handcuffs away again. The case is at an end.

"But last of all, that no breath of this idiotic suspicion remain in the air, I will tell you all you want to know. I believe I do know how my unhappy friend came by her death. You can, if you choose, blame me for it, or my faith and philosophy at least; but you certainly cannot lock me up. It is well known to all students of the higher truths that certain adepts and *illuminati* have in history attained the power of levitation—that is, of being self-sustained upon the empty air. It is but a part of that general conquest of matter which is the main element in our occult wisdom. Poor Pauline was of an impulsive and ambitious temper. I think, to tell the truth, she thought herself somewhat deeper in the mysteries than she was; and she has often said to me, as we went down in the lift together, that if one's will were strong enough, one could float down as harmlessly as a feather. I solemnly believe that in some ecstasy of noble thoughts she attempted the miracle. Her will, or faith, must have failed her at the crucial instant, and the lower law of matter had its horrible revenge. There is the whole story, gentlemen, very sad and, as you think, very presumptuous and wicked, but certainly not criminal or in any way connected with me. In the short-hand of the police-courts, you had better call it suicide. I shall always call it heroic failure for the advance of science and the slow scaling of heaven."

It was the first time Flambeau had ever seen Father Brown vanquished. He still sat looking at the ground, with a painful and corrugated brow, as if in shame. It is impossible to avoid the feeling which the prophet's winged words had fanned, that here was a sullen, professional suspector of men overwhelmed by a prouder and purer spirit of natural liberty and health. At last he said, blinking as if in bodily distress, "Well, if that is so, sir, you need do no more than take the testamentary paper you spoke of and go. I wonder where the poor lady left it."

"It will be over there on her desk by the door, I think," said Kalon, with that massive innocence of manner that seemed to acquit him wholly. "She told me specially she would write it this morning, and I actually saw her writing as I went up in the lift to my own room."

"Was her door open then?" asked the priest, with his eye on a corner of the matting.

"Yes," said Kalon calmly.

"Ah! it has been open ever since," said the other, and resumed his silent study of the mat.

"There is a paper over here," said the grim Miss Joan, in a somewhat singular voice. She had passed over to her sister's desk by the doorway, and was holding a sheet of blue foolscap in her hand. There was a sour smile on her face that seemed unfit for such a scene or occasion, and Flambeau looked at her with a darkening brow.

Kalon the prophet stood away from the paper with that royal unconsciousness that had carried him through. But Flambeau took it out of the lady's hand, and read it with the utmost amazement. It did, indeed, begin in the formal manner of a will, but after the words "I give and bequeath all of which I die possessed" the writing abruptly stopped with a set of scratches, and there was no trace of the name of any legatee. Flambeau, in wonder, handed this truncated testament to his clerical friend, who glanced at it and silently gave it to the priest of the sun.

An instant afterwards that pontiff, in his splendid sweeping draperies, had crossed the room in two great strides, and was towering over Joan Stacey, his blue eyes standing from his head.

"What monkey tricks have you been playing here?" he cried. "That's not all Pauline wrote."

They were startled to hear him speak in quite a new voice, with a Yankee shrillness in it; all his grandeur and good English had fallen from him like a cloak.

"That is the only thing on her desk," said Joan, and confronted him steadily with the same smile of evil favour.

Of a sudden the man broke out into blasphemies and cataracts of incredulous words. There was something shocking about the dropping of his mask; it was like a man's real face falling off.

"See here!" he cried in broad American, when he was breathless with cursing, "I may be an adventurer, but I guess you're a murderess. Yes, gentlemen, here's your death explained, and without any levitation. The poor girl is writing a will in my favour; her cursed sister comes in, struggles for the pen, drags her to the well, and throws her down before she can finish it. Sakes! I reckon we want the handcuffs after all."

"As you have truly remarked," replied Joan, with ugly calm, "your clerk is a very respectable young man, who knows the nature of an oath; and he will swear in any court that I was up in your office arranging some typewriting work for five minutes before and five minutes after my sister fell. Mr. Flambeau will tell you he found me there."

There was a silence.

"Why, then," cried Flambeau, "Pauline was alone when she fell, and it was suicide!"

"She was alone when she fell," said Father Brown, "but it was not suicide."

"Then how did she die?" asked Flambeau impatiently.

"She was murdered."

"But she was all alone," objected the detective.

"She was murdered when she was all alone," answered the priest.

All the rest stared at him, but he remained sitting in the same old dejected attitude, with a wrinkle in his round forehead and an appearance of impersonal shame and sorrow; his voice was colourless and sad.

"What I want to know," cried Kalon, with an oath, "is when the police are coming for this bloody and wicked sister. She's killed her flesh and blood; she's robbed me of half a million that was just as sacredly mine as—"

"Come, come, prophet," interrupted Flambeau, with a kind of sneer; "remember that all this world is a cloudland."

The hierophant of the sun-god made an effort to climb back on to his pedestal. "It is not the mere money," he cried, "though that would equip the cause throughout the world. It is also my beloved one's wishes. To Pauline all this was holy. In Pauline's eyes—"

Father Brown suddenly sprang erect, so that his chair fell over flat behind him. He was deathly pale, yet he seemed fired with a hope; his eyes shone.

"That's it!" he cried in a clear voice. "That's the way to begin. In Pauline's eyes—"

The tall prophet retreated before the tiny priest in an almost mad disorder. "What do you mean? How dare you?" he cried repeatedly.

"In Pauline's eyes," repeated the priest, his own shining more and more. "Go on—in God's name, go on. The foulest crime the fiends ever prompted feels lighter after confession; and I implore you to confess. Go on, go on—in Pauline's eyes—"

"Let me go, you devil!" thundered Kalon, struggling like a giant in bonds. "Who are you, you cursed spy, to weave your spiders' webs round me, and peep and peer? Let me go."

"Shall I stop him?" asked Flambeau, bounding towards the exit, for Kalon had already thrown the door wide open.

"No; let him pass," said Father Brown, with a strange deep sigh that seemed to come from the depths of the universe. "Let Cain pass by, for he belongs to God."

There was a long-drawn silence in the room when he had left it, which was to Flambeau's fierce wits one long agony of interrogation. Miss Joan Stacey very coolly tidied the papers on her desk.

"Father," said Flambeau at last, "it is my duty, not my curiosity only—it is my duty to find out, if I can, who committed the crime."

"Which crime?" asked Father Brown.

"The one we are dealing with, of course," replied his impatient friend.

"We are dealing with two crimes," said Brown, "crimes of very different weight—and by very different criminals."

Miss Joan Stacey, having collected and put away her papers, proceeded to lock up her drawer. Father Brown went on, noticing her as little as she noticed him.

"The two crimes," he observed, "were committed against the same weakness of the same person, in a struggle for her money. The author of the larger crime found himself thwarted by the smaller crime; the author of the smaller crime got the money."

"Oh, don't go on like a lecturer," groaned Flambeau; "put it in a few words."

"I can put it in one word," answered his friend.

Miss Joan Stacey skewered her business-like black hat on to her head with a business-like black frown before a little mirror, and, as the conversation proceeded, took her handbag and umbrella in an unhurried style, and left the room.

"The truth is in one word, and a short one," said Father Brown. "Pauline Stacey was blind."

"Blind!" repeated Flambeau, and rose slowly to his whole huge stature.

"She was subject to it by blood," Brown proceeded. "Her sister would have started eye glasses if Pauline would have let her; but it was her special philosophy or fad that one must not encourage such diseases by yielding to them. She would not admit the cloud; or she tried to dispel it by will. So her eyes got worse and worse with straining; but the worst strain was to come. It came with this precious prophet, or whatever he calls himself, who taught her to stare at the hot sun with the naked eye. It was called accepting Apollo. Oh, if these new pagans would only be old pagans, they would be a little wiser! The old pagans knew that mere naked Nature-worship must have a cruel side. They knew that the eye of Apollo can blast and blind."

There was a pause, and the priest went on in a gentle and even broken voice, "Whether or no that devil deliberately made her blind, there is no doubt that he deliberately killed her through her blindness. The very simplicity of the crime is sickening. You know he and she went up and down in those lifts without official help; you know also how smoothly and silently the lifts slide. Kalon brought the lift to the girl's landing, and saw her, through the open door, writing in her slow, sightless way the will she had promised him. He called out to her cheerily that he had the lift ready for her, and she was to come out when she was ready. Then he pressed a button and shot soundlessly up to his own floor, walked through his own office, out on to his own balcony, and was safely praying before the crowded street when the poor girl, having finished her work, ran gaily out to where her lover and lift were to receive her, and stepped —"

"Don't!" cried Flambeau.

"He ought to have got half a million by pressing that button," continued the little father, in the colourless voice in which he talked of such horrors. "But that went smash. It went smash because there happened to be another person who also wanted the money, and who also knew the secret about poor Pauline's sight. There was one thing about that will that I think nobody noticed: although it was unfinished and without a signature, the other Miss Stacey and some servant of hers had already signed it as witnesses. Joan had signed first, saying Pauline could finish it later, with a typical feminine contempt for legal forms. Therefore, Joan wanted her sister to sign the will without real witnesses. Why? I thought of the blindness, and felt sure she had wanted Pauline to sign in solitude because she had wanted her not to sign at all.

"People like the Staceys always use fountain pens; but this was specially natural to Pauline. By habit and her strong will and her memory she could still write almost as well as if she saw; but she could not tell when her pen needed dipping. Therefore, her fountain pens were carefully filled by her sister—all except this fountain pen. This was carefully *not* filled by her sister; the remains of the ink held out for a few lines and then failed altogether. And the prophet lost five hundred thousand pounds and committed one of the most brutal and brilliant murders in human history for nothing."

Flambeau went to the open door and heard the official police ascending the stairs. He turned and said, "You must have followed everything devilish close to have traced the crime to Kalon in ten minutes."

Father Brown gave a sort of start.

"Oh! to him," he said. "No; I had to follow rather close to find out about Miss Joan and the fountain pen. But I knew Kalon was the criminal before I came into the front door."

"You must be joking!" cried Flambeau.

"I'm quite serious," answered the priest. "I tell you I knew he had done it, even before I knew what he had done."

"But why?"

"These pagan stoics," said Brown reflectively, "always fail by their strength. There came a crash and a scream down the street, and the priest of Apollo did not start or look round. I did not know what it was. But I knew that he was expecting it."

THE SIGN OF THE BROKEN SWORD

The thousand arms of the forest were grey, and its million fingers silver. In a sky of dark green-blue-like slate the stars were bleak and brilliant like splintered ice. All that thickly wooded and sparsely tenanted countryside was stiff with a bitter and brittle frost. The black hollows between the trunks of the trees looked like bottomless, black caverns of that heartless Scandinavian hell, a hell of incalculable cold.[1] Even the square stone tower of the church looked northern to the point of heathenry, as if it were some barbaric tower among the sea rocks of Iceland. It was a queer night for anyone to explore a churchyard. But, on the other hand, perhaps it was worth exploring.

It rose abruptly out of the ashen wastes of forest in a sort of hump or shoulder of green turf that looked grey in the starlight. Most of the graves were on a slant, and the path leading up to the church was as steep as a staircase. On the top of the hill, in the one flat and prominent place, was the monument for which the place was famous. It contrasted strangely with the featureless graves all round, for it was the work of one of the greatest sculptors of modern Europe; and yet his fame was at once forgotten in the fame of the man whose image he had made. It showed, by touches of the small silver pencil of starlight, the massive metal figure of a soldier recumbent, the strong hands sealed in an everlasting worship, the great head pillowed upon a gun. The venerable face was bearded, or rather whiskered, in the old, heavy Colonel Newcome fashion. The uniform, though suggested with the few strokes of simplicity, was that of modern war. By his right side lay a sword, of which the tip was broken off; on the left side lay a Bible. On glowing summer afternoons wagonettes came full of Americans and cultured suburbans to see the sepulchre; but even then they felt the vast forest land with its one dumpy dome of churchyard and church as a place oddly dumb and neglected. In this freezing darkness of mid-winter one would think he might be left alone with the stars.

[1] The Scandinavian hell is Niflheim ("mist-home"), the icy netherworld of Norse mythology, a region of endless night and unlimited cold.

Nevertheless, in the stillness of those stiff woods a wooden gate creaked, and two dim figures dressed in black climbed up the little path to the tomb.

So faint was that frigid starlight that nothing could have been traced about them except that while they both wore black, one man was enormously big, and the other (perhaps by contrast) almost startlingly small. They went up to the great graven tomb of the historic warrior, and stood for a few minutes staring at it. There was no human, perhaps no living, thing for a wide circle; and a morbid fancy might well have wondered if they were human themselves. In any case, the beginning of their conversation might have seemed strange. After the first silence the small man said to the other:

"Where does a wise man hide a pebble?"

And the tall man answered in a low voice, "On the beach."

The small man nodded, and after a short silence said: "Where does a wise man hide a leaf?"

And the other answered, "In the forest."

There was another stillness, and then the tall man resumed: "Do you mean that when a wise man has to hide a real diamond he has been known to hide it among sham ones?" [2]

"No, no," said the little man with a laugh, "we will let bygones be bygones."

He stamped his cold feet for a second or two, and then said, "I'm not thinking of that at all, but of something else; something rather peculiar. Just strike a match, will you?"

The big man fumbled in his pocket, and soon a scratch and a flare painted gold the whole flat side of the monument. On it was cut in black letters the well-known words which so many Americans had reverently read, "Sacred to the Memory of General Sir Arthur St. Clare, Hero and Martyr, who Always Vanquished his Enemies and Always Spared Them, and Was Treacherously Slain by Them at Last. May God in Whom he Trusted both Reward and Revenge him."

[2] Flambeau refers to the subterfuge he himself used successfully in the story "The Flying Stars".

The match burnt the big man's fingers, blackened, and dropped. He was about to strike another, but his small companion stopped him. "That's all right, Flambeau, old man; I saw what I wanted. Or, rather, I didn't see what I didn't want. And now we must walk a mile and a half along the road to the next inn, and I will try to tell you all about it. For Heaven knows a man should have fire and ale when he dares tell such a story."

They descended the precipitous path, they relatched the rusty gate, and set off at a stamping, ringing walk down the frozen forest road. They had gone a full quarter of a mile before the smaller man spoke again. He said, "Yes; the wise man hides a pebble on the beach. But what does he do if there is no beach? Do you know anything of the great St. Clare trouble?"

"I know nothing about English generals, Father Brown," answered the large man, laughing, "though a little about English policemen. I only know that you have dragged me a precious long dance to all the shrines of this fellow, whoever he is. One would think he got buried in six different places. I've seen a memorial to General St. Clare in Westminster Abbey. I've seen a ramping equestrian statue of General St. Clare on the Embankment. I've seen a medallion of St. Clare in the street he was born in, and another in the street he lived in; and now you drag me after dark to his coffin in the village churchyard. I am beginning to be a bit tired of his magnificent personality, especially as I don't in the least know who he was. What are you hunting for in all these crypts and effigies?"

"I am only looking for one word," said Father Brown. "A word that isn't there."

"Well," asked Flambeau, "are you going to tell me anything about it?"

"I must divide it into two parts," remarked the priest. "First there is what everybody knows; and then there is what I know. Now, what everybody knows is short and plain enough. It is also entirely wrong."

"Right you are," said the big man called Flambeau cheerfully. "Let's begin at the wrong end. Let's begin with what everybody knows, which isn't true."

"If not wholly untrue, it is at least very inadequate," continued Brown; "for in point of fact, all that the public knows amounts precisely to this: The public knows that Arthur St. Clare was a great and successful English general. It knows that after splendid yet careful campaigns both in India and Africa he was in command against Brazil when the great Brazilian patriot Olivier issued his ultimatum. It knows that on that occasion St. Clare with a very small force attacked Olivier with a very large one, and was captured after heroic resistance. And it knows that after his capture, and to the abhorrence of the civilised world, St. Clare was hanged on the nearest tree. He was found swinging there after the Brazilians had retired, with his broken sword hung round his neck."

"And that popular story is untrue?" suggested Flambeau.

"No," said his friend quietly, "that story is quite true, so far as it goes."

"Well, I think it goes far enough!" said Flambeau, "but if the popular story is true, what is the mystery?"

They had passed many hundreds of grey and ghostly trees before the little priest answered. Then he bit his finger reflectively and said, "Why, the mystery is a mystery of psychology. Or, rather, it is a mystery of two psychologies. In that Brazilian business two of the most famous men of modern history acted flat against their characters. Mind you, Olivier and St. Clare were both heroes—the old thing, and no mistake; it was like the fight between Hector and Achilles. Now, what would you say to an affair in which Achilles was timid and Hector was treacherous?"

"Go on," said the large man impatiently as the other bit his finger again.

"Sir Arthur St. Clare was a soldier of the old religious type—the type that saved us during the Mutiny," continued Brown.[3] "He was always more for duty than for dash; and with all his personal courage was decidedly a prudent commander, particularly indignant at any

[3] Father Brown is referring to such aggressive leaders as Brigadier General John Nicholson who subdued a number of rebellious native regiments during the Indian mutiny of 1857.

needless waste of soldiers. Yet in this last battle he attempted something that a baby could see was absurd. One need not be a strategist to see it was as wild as wind; just as one need not be a strategist to keep out of the way of a motor-bus. Well, that is the first mystery; what had become of the English general's head? The second riddle is, what had become of the Brazilian general's heart? President Olivier might be called a visionary or a nuisance; but even his enemies admitted that he was magnanimous to the point of knight errantry. Almost every other prisoner he had ever captured had been set free or even loaded with benefits. Men who had really wronged him came away touched by his simplicity and sweetness. Why the deuce should he diabolically revenge himself only once in his life; and then for the one particular blow that could not have hurt him? Well, there you have it. One of the wisest men in the world acted like an idiot for no reason. One of the best men in the world acted like a fiend for no reason. That's the long and the short of it; and I leave it to you, my boy."

"No, you don't," said the other with a snort. "I leave it to you; and you jolly well tell me all about it."

"Well," resumed Father Brown, "it's not fair to say that the public impression is just what I've said, without adding that two things have happened since. I can't say they threw a new light; for nobody can make sense of them. But they threw a new kind of darkness; they threw the darkness in new directions. The first was this. The family physician of the St. Clares quarrelled with that family, and began publishing a violent series of articles, in which he said that the late general was a religious maniac; but as far as the tale went, this seemed to mean little more than a religious man. Anyhow, the story fizzled out. Everyone knew, of course, that St. Clare had some of the eccentricities of puritan piety. The second incident was much more arresting. In the luckless and unsupported regiment which made that rash attempt at the Black River there was a certain Captain Keith, who was at that time engaged to St. Clare's daughter, and who afterwards married her. He was one of those who were captured by Olivier, and, like all the rest except the general, appears to have been bounteously treated and promptly set free. Some twenty years afterwards this man, then Lieutenant-Colonel Keith, published a sort of autobiography called 'A British Officer in Burmah and Brazil.'

In the place where the reader looks eagerly for some account of the mystery of St. Clare's disaster may be found the following words: 'Everywhere else in this book I have narrated things exactly as they occurred, holding as I do the old-fashioned opinion that the glory of England is old enough to take care of itself. The exception I shall make is in this matter of the defeat by the Black River; and my reasons, though private, are honourable and compelling. I will, however, add this in justice to the memories of two distinguished men. General St. Clare has been accused of incapacity on this occasion; I can at least testify that this action, properly understood, was one of the most brilliant and sagacious of his life. President Olivier by similar report is charged with savage injustice. I think it due to the honour of an enemy to say that he acted on this occasion with even more than his characteristic good feeling. To put the matter popularly, I can assure my countrymen that St. Clare was by no means such a fool nor Olivier such a brute as he looked. This is all I have to say; nor shall any earthly consideration induce me to add a word to it.' "

A large frozen moon like a lustrous snowball began to show through the tangle of twigs in front of them, and by its light the narrator had been able to refresh his memory of Captain Keith's text from a scrap of printed paper. As he folded it up and put it back in his pocket Flambeau threw up his hand with a French gesture.

"Wait a bit, wait a bit," he cried excitedly. "I believe I can guess it at the first go."

He strode on, breathing hard, his black head and bull neck forward, like a man winning a walking race. The little priest, amused and interested, had some trouble in trotting beside him. Just before them the trees fell back a little to left and right, and the road swept downwards across a clear, moonlit valley, till it dived again like a rabbit into the wall of another wood. The entrance to the farther forest looked small and round, like the black hole of a remote railway tunnel. But it was within some hundred yards, and gaped like a cavern before Flambeau spoke again.

"I've got it," he cried at last, slapping his thigh with his great hand. "Four minutes' thinking, and I can tell your whole story myself."

"All right," assented his friend. "You tell it."

Flambeau lifted his head, but lowered his voice. "General Sir Arthur St. Clare," he said, "came of a family in which madness was hereditary; and his whole aim was to keep this from his daughter, and even, if possible, from his future son-in-law. Rightly or wrongly, he thought the final collapse was close, and resolved on suicide. Yet ordinary suicide would blazon the very idea he dreaded. As the campaign approached the clouds came thicker on his brain; and at last in a mad moment he sacrificed his public duty to his private. He rushed rashly into battle, hoping to fall by the first shot. When he found that he had only attained capture and discredit, the sealed bomb in his brain burst, and he broke his own sword and hanged himself."

He stared firmly at the grey façade of forest in front of him, with the one black gap in it, like the mouth of the grave, into which their path plunged. Perhaps something menacing in the road thus suddenly swallowed reinforced his vivid vision of the tragedy, for he shuddered.

"A horrid story," he said.

"A horrid story," repeated the priest with bent head. "But not the real story."

Then he threw back his head with a sort of despair and cried, "Oh, I wish it had been."

The tall Flambeau faced round and stared at him.

"Yours is a clean story," cried Father Brown, deeply moved. "A sweet, pure, honest story, as open and white as that moon. Madness and despair are innocent enough. There are worse things, Flambeau."

Flambeau looked up wildly at the moon thus invoked; and from where he stood one black tree-bough curved across it exactly like a devil's horn.

"Father—Father," cried Flambeau with the French gesture and stepping yet more rapidly forward, "do you mean it was worse than that?"

"Worse than that," said the other like a grave echo.[4] And they plunged into the black cloister of the woodland, which ran by them in a dim tapestry of trunks, like one of the dark corridors in a dream.

---

[4] In the original magazine presentation, oddly enough, the wording is, "said Paul." For American editions of *The Innocence of Father Brown*, the phrase was changed to "said the priest." In the British editions, as here, the phrase is "said the other."

They were soon in the most secret entrails of the wood, and felt close about them the foliage that they could not see, when the priest said again:

"Where does a wise man hide a leaf? In the forest. But what does he do if there is no forest?"

"Well, well," cried Flambeau irritably, "what does he do?"

"He grows a forest to hide it in," said the priest in an obscure voice. "A fearful sin."

"Look here," cried his friend impatiently, for the dark wood and the dark sayings got a little on his nerves; "will you tell me this story or not? What other evidence is there to go on?"

"There are three more bits of evidence," said the other, "that I have dug up in holes and corners; and I will give them in logical rather than chronological order. First of all, of course, our authority for the issue and event of the battle is in Olivier's own dispatches, which are lucid enough. He was entrenched with two or three regiments on the heights that swept down to the Black River, on the other side of which was lower and more marshy ground. Beyond this again was gently rising country, on which was the first English outpost, supported by others which lay, however, considerably in its rear. The British forces as a whole were greatly superior in numbers; but this particular regiment was just far enough from its base to make Olivier consider the project of crossing the river to cut it off. By sunset, however, he had decided to retain his own position, which was a specially strong one. At daybreak next morning he was thunderstruck to see that this stray handful of English, entirely unsupported from their rear, had flung themselves across the river, half by the bridge to the right, and the other half by a ford higher up, and were massed upon the marshy bank below him.

"That they should attempt an attack with such numbers against such a position was incredible enough; but Olivier noticed something yet more extraordinary. For instead of attempting to seize more solid ground, this mad regiment, having put the river in its rear by one wild charge, did nothing more, but stuck there in the mire like flies in treacle. Needless to say, the Brazilians blew great gaps in them with artillery, which they could only return with spirited but lessening

rifle fire. Yet they never broke; and Olivier's curt account ends with
a strong tribute of admiration for the mystic valour of these imbeciles.
'Our line then advanced finally,' writes Olivier, 'and drove them into
the river; we captured General St. Clare himself and several other
officers. The colonel and the major had both fallen in the battle. I
cannot resist saying that few finer sights can have been seen in history
than the last stand of this extraordinary regiment; wounded officers
picking up the rifles of dead soldiers, and the general himself facing
us on horseback bareheaded and with a broken sword.' On what happened to the general afterwards Olivier is as silent as Captain Keith."

"Well," grunted Flambeau, "get on to the next bit of evidence."

"The next evidence," said Father Brown, "took some time to find,
but it will not take long to tell. I found at last in an almshouse down
in the Lincolnshire Fens an old soldier who not only was wounded at
the Black River, but had actually knelt beside the colonel of the regiment when he died. This latter was a certain Colonel Clancy, a big
bull of an Irishman; and it would seem that he died almost as much of
rage as of bullets. He, at any rate, was not responsible for that ridiculous raid; it must have been imposed on him by the general. His last
edifying words, according to my informant, were these: 'And there
goes the damned old donkey with the end of his sword knocked off.
I wish it was his head.' You will remark that everyone seems to have
noticed this detail about the broken sword blade, though most people
regard it somewhat more reverently than did the late Colonel Clancy.
And now for the third fragment."

Their path through the woodland began to go upward, and the
speaker paused a little for breath before he went on. Then he continued in the same business-like tone:

"Only a month or two ago a certain Brazilian official died in
England, having quarrelled with Olivier and left his country. He was
a well-known figure both here and on the Continent, a Spaniard named
Espado; I knew him myself, a yellow-faced old dandy, with a hooked
nose. For various private reasons I had permission to see the documents he had left; he was a Catholic, of course, and I had been with
him towards the end. There was nothing of his that lit up any corner
of the black St. Clare business, except five or six common exercise

books filled with the diary of some English soldier. I can only suppose that it was found by the Brazilians on one of those that fell.
Anyhow, it stopped abruptly the night before the battle.

"But the account of that last day in the poor fellow's life was certainly worth reading. I have it on me; but it's too dark to read it here,
and I will give you a résumé. The first part of that entry is full of
jokes, evidently flung about among the men, about somebody called
the Vulture. It does not seem as if this person, whoever he was, was
one of themselves, nor even an Englishman; neither is he exactly spoken of as one of the enemy. It sounds rather as if he were some local
go-between and non-combatant; perhaps a guide or a journalist. He
has been closeted with old Colonel Clancy; but is more often seen
talking to the major. Indeed, the major is somewhat prominent in this
soldier's narrative; a lean, dark-haired man, apparently, of the name of
Murray—a north of Ireland man and a Puritan. There are continual
jests about the contrast between this Ulsterman's austerity and the
conviviality of Colonel Clancy. There is also some joke about the
Vulture wearing bright-coloured clothes.

"But all these levities are scattered by what may well be called the note
of a bugle. Behind the English camp and almost parallel to the river,
ran one of the few great roads of that district. Westward the road curved
round towards the river, which it crossed by the bridge before mentioned. To the east the road swept backwards into the wilds, and some
two miles along it was the next English outpost. From this direction there
came along the road that evening a glitter and clatter of light cavalry,
in which even the simple diarist could recognise with astonishment the
general with his staff. He rode the great white horse which you have
seen so often in illustrated papers and Academy pictures; and you may
be sure that the salute they gave him was not merely ceremonial. He,
at least, wasted no time on ceremony, but, springing from the saddle
immediately, mixed with the group of officers, and fell into emphatic
though confidential speech. What struck our friend the diarist most
was his special disposition to discuss matters with Major Murray; but,
indeed, such a selection, so long as it was not marked, was in no way
unnatural. The two men were made for sympathy; they were men who
'read their Bibles'; they were both the old Evangelical type of officer.

However this may be, it is certain that when the general mounted again he was still talking earnestly to Murray; and that as he walked his horse slowly down the road towards the river, the tall Ulsterman still walked by his bridle rein in earnest debate. The soldiers watched the two until they vanished behind a clump of trees where the road turned towards the river. The colonel had gone back to his tent, and the men to their pickets; the man with the diary lingered for another four minutes, and saw a marvellous sight.

"The great white horse which had marched slowly down the road, as it had marched in so many processions, flew back, galloping up the road towards them as if it were mad to win a race. At first they thought it had run away with the man on its back; but they soon saw that the general, a fine rider, was himself urging it to full speed. Horse and man swept up to them like a whirlwind; and then, reining up the reeling charger, the general turned on them a face like flame, and called for the colonel like the trumpet that wakes the dead.

"I conceive that all the earthquake events of that catastrophe tumbled on top of each other rather like lumber in the minds of men such as our friend with the diary. With the dazed excitement of a dream, they found themselves falling—literally falling—into their ranks, and learned that an attack was to be led at once across the river. The general and the major, it was said, had found out something at the bridge, and there was only just time to strike for life. The major had gone back at once to call up the reserve along the road behind; it was doubtful if even with that prompt appeal help could reach them in time. But they must pass the stream that night, and seize the heights by morning. It is with the very stir and throb of that romantic nocturnal march that the diary suddenly ends."

Father Brown had mounted ahead; for the woodland path grew smaller, steeper, and more twisted, till they felt as if they were ascending a winding staircase. The priest's voice came from above out of the darkness.

"There was one other little and enormous thing. When the general urged them to their chivalric charge he drew half his sword from the scabbard; and then, as if ashamed of such melodrama, thrust it back again. The sword again, you see."

A half-light broke through the network of boughs above them, flinging the ghost of a net about their feet; for they were mounting again to the faint luminosity of the naked night. Flambeau felt truth all round him as an atmosphere, but not as an idea. He answered with bewildered brain, "Well, what's the matter with the sword? Officers generally have swords, don't they?"

"They are not often mentioned in modern war," said the other dispassionately; "but in this affair one falls over the blessed sword everywhere."

"Well, what is there in that?" growled Flambeau; "it was a twopence coloured sort of incident; the old man's blade breaking in his last battle. Anyone might bet the papers would get hold of it—as they have. On all these tombs and things it's shown broken at the point. I hope you haven't dragged me through this blasted Polar expedition merely because two men with an eye for a picture saw St. Clare's broken sword."

"No," cried Father Brown, with a sharp voice like a pistol shot; "but who saw his unbroken sword?"

"What do you mean?" cried the other, and stood still under the stars. They had come abruptly out of the grey gates of the wood.

"I say, who saw his unbroken sword?" repeated Father Brown obstinately. "Not the writer of the diary, anyhow; the general sheathed it in time."

Flambeau looked about him in the moonlight, as a man struck blind might look in the sun; and his friend went on, for the first time with eagerness:

"Flambeau," he cried, "I cannot prove it, even after hunting through the tombs. But I am sure of it. Let me add just one more tiny fact that tips the whole thing over. The colonel, by a strange chance, was one of the first struck by a bullet. He was struck long before the troops came to close quarters. But he saw St. Clare's sword broken. Why was it broken? How was it broken? My friend, it was broken before the battle."

"Oh!" said his friend, with a sort of forlorn jocularity; "and pray where is the other piece?"

"I can tell you," said the priest promptly. "In the north-east corner of the cemetery of the Protestant Cathedral at Belfast."

"Indeed?" inquired the other. "Have you looked for it?"

"I couldn't," replied Brown, with frank regret. "There's a great marble monument on top of it; a monument to the heroic Major Murray, who fell fighting gloriously at the famous Battle of the Black River."

Flambeau seemed suddenly galvanised into existence. "You mean," he cried hoarsely, "that General St. Clare hated Murray, and murdered him on the field of battle because—"

"You are still full of good and pure thoughts," said the other. "It was worse than that."

"Well," said the large man, "my stock of evil imagination is used up."

The priest seemed really doubtful where to begin, and at last he said again:

"Where would a wise man hide a leaf? In the forest."

The other did not answer.

"If there were no forest, he would make a forest. And if he wished to hide a dead leaf, he would make a dead forest."

There was still no reply, and the priest added still more mildly and quietly:

"And if a man had to hide a dead body, he would make a field of dead bodies to hide it in."

Flambeau began to stamp forward with an intolerance of delay in time or space; but Father Brown went on as if he were continuing the last sentence:

"Sir Arthur St. Clare, as I have already said, was a man who read his Bible. That was what was the matter with *him*. When will people understand that it is useless for a man to read his Bible unless we also reads everybody else's Bible? A printer reads a Bible for misprints. A Mormon reads his Bible and finds polygamy; a Christian Scientist reads his, and finds we have no arms and legs. St. Clare was an old Anglo-Indian Protestant soldier. Now, just think what that might mean; and, for Heaven's sake, don't cant about it. It might mean a man physically formidable living under a tropic sun in an Oriental society, and soaking himself without sense or guidance in an Oriental Book. Of course, he read the Old Testament rather than the New. Of course, he found in the Old Testament anything that he wanted—lust, tyranny, treason. Oh, I dare say he was honest, as you call it. But what is the good of a man being honest in his worship of dishonesty?

"In each of the hot and secret countries to which that man went he kept a harem, he tortured witnesses, he amassed shameful gold; but certainly he would have said with steady eyes that he did it to the glory of the Lord. My own theology is sufficiently expressed by asking which Lord? Anyhow, there is this about such evil, that it opens door after door in hell, and always into smaller and smaller chambers. This is the real case against crime, that a man does not become wilder and wilder, but only meaner and meaner. St. Clare was soon suffocated by difficulties of bribery and blackmail; and needed more and more cash. And by the time of the battle of the Black River he had fallen from world to world to that place which Dante makes the lowest floor of the universe."

"What do you mean?" asked his friend again.

"I mean *that*," retorted the cleric, and suddenly pointed at a puddle sealed with ice that shone in the moon. "Do you remember whom Dante put in the last circle of ice?"

"The traitors," said Flambeau, and shuddered. As he looked round at the inhuman landscape of trees, with taunting and almost obscene outlines, he could almost fancy he was Dante, and the priest with the rivulet of a voice was, indeed, a Virgil leading him through a land of eternal sins.

The voice went on, "Olivier, as you know, was quixotic, and would not permit a secret service and spies. The thing, however, was done, like many other things, behind his back. It was managed by my old friend Espado; he was the bright-clad fop, whose hook nose got him called the Vulture. Posing as a sort of philanthropist at the front, he felt his way through the English Army, and at last got his fingers on its one corrupt man—please God!—and that man at the top. St. Clare was in foul need of money, and mountains of it. The discredited family doctor was threatening those extraordinary exposures that afterwards began and were broken off; tales of monstrous and prehistoric things in Park Lane; things done by an English Evangelical that smelt like human sacrifice and hordes of slaves. Money was wanted, too, for his daughter's dowry; for to him the fame of wealth was as sweet as wealth itself. He snapped the last thread, whispered the word to Brazil, and wealth poured in from the enemies of England. But another man had talked to Espado the Vulture as well as he. Somehow the dark, grim young major from Ulster had guessed the hideous truth; and when they walked slowly together down that road towards the bridge Murray was telling the general that he must resign instantly, or be court-martialled and shot. The general temporised with him till they came to the fringe of tropic trees by the bridge; and there by the singing river and the sunlit palms (for I can see the picture) the general drew his sabre and plunged it through the body of the major."

The wintry road curved over a ridge in cutting frost, with cruel black shapes of bush and thicket; but Flambeau fancied that he saw beyond it faintly the edge of an aureole that was not starlight and moonlight, but some fire such as is made by men. He watched it as the tale drew to its close.

"St. Clare was a hell-hound, but he was a hound of breed. Never, I'll swear, was he so lucid and so strong as when poor Murray lay a cold lump at his feet. Never in all his triumphs, as Captain Keith said truly, was the great man so great as he was in this last world-despised defeat. He looked coolly at his weapon to wipe off the blood; he saw the point he had planted between his victim's shoulders had broken off in the body. He saw quite calmly as, through a club windowpane, all that must follow. He saw that men must find the unaccountable corpse; must extract the unaccountable sword-point; must notice the unaccountable broken sword—or absence of sword. He had killed, but not silenced. But his imperious intellect rose against the facer—there was one way yet. He could make the corpse less unaccountable. He could create a hill of corpses to cover this one. In twenty minutes eight hundred English soldiers were marching down to their death."

The warmer glow behind the black winter wood grew richer and brighter, and Flambeau strode on to reach it. Father Brown also quickened his stride; but he seemed merely absorbed in his tale.

"Such was the valour of that English thousand, and such the genius of their commander, that if they had at once attacked the hill, even their mad march might have met some luck. But the evil mind that played with them like pawns had other aims and reasons. They must remain in the marshes by the bridge at least till British corpses should be a common sight there. Then for the last grand scene, the silver-haired soldier-saint would give up his shattered sword to save further slaughter. Oh, it was well organised for an impromptu. But I think (I cannot prove), I think that it was while they stuck there in the bloody mire that someone doubted—and someone guessed."

He was mute a moment, and then said, "There is a voice from nowhere that tells me the man who guessed was the lover ... the man to wed the old man's child."

"But what about Olivier and the hanging?" asked Flambeau.

"Olivier, partly from chivalry, partly from policy, seldom encumbered his march with captives," explained the narrator. "He released everybody in most cases. He released everybody in this case."

"Everybody but the general," said the tall man.

"Everybody," said the priest.

Flambeau knitted his black brows. "I don't grasp it all yet," he said.

"There is another picture, Flambeau," said Brown in his more mystical undertone. "I can't prove it; but I can do more—I can see it. There is a camp breaking up on the bare, torrid hills at morning, and Brazilian uniforms massed in blocks and columns to march. There is the red shirt and long black beard of Olivier, which blows as he stands, his broad-brimmed hat in his hand. He is saying farewell to the great enemy he is setting free—the simple, snow-headed English veteran, who thanks him in the name of his men. The English remnant stand behind at attention; beside them are stores and vehicles for the retreat. The drums roll; the Brazilians are moving; the English are still like statues. So they abide till the last hum and flash of the enemy have faded from the tropic horizon. Then they alter their postures all at once, like dead men coming to life; they turn their fifty faces upon the general—faces not to be forgotten."

Flambeau gave a great jump. "Ah," he cried. "You don't mean—"

"Yes," said Father Brown in a deep, moving voice. "It was an English hand that put the rope round St. Clare's neck; I believe the hand that put the ring on his daughter's finger. They were English hands that dragged him up to the tree of shame; the hands of men that had adored him and followed him to victory. And they were English souls (God pardon and endure us all!) who stared at him swinging in that foreign sun on the green gallows of palm, and prayed in their hatred that he might drop off it into hell."

As the two topped the ridge there burst on them the strong scarlet light of a red-curtained English inn. It stood sideways in the road, as if standing aside in the amplitude of hospitality. Its three doors stood open with invitation; and even where they stood they could hear the hum and laughter of humanity happy for a night.

"I need not tell you more," said Father Brown. "They tried him in the wilderness and destroyed him; and then, for the honour of England and of his daughter, they took an oath to seal up for ever the story of the traitor's purse and the assassin's sword blade. Perhaps—Heaven help them—they tried to forget it. Let us try to forget it, anyhow; here is our inn."

"With all my heart," said Flambeau, and was just striding into the bright, noisy bar when he stepped back and almost fell on the road.

"Look there, in the devil's name!" he cried, and pointed rigidly at the square wooden sign that overhung the road. It showed dimly the crude shape of a sabre hilt and a shortened blade; and was inscribed in false archaic lettering, "The Sign of the Broken Sword."

"Were you not prepared?" asked Father Brown gently. "He is the god of this country; half the inns and parks and streets are named after him and his story."

"I thought we had done with the leper," cried Flambeau, and spat on the road.

"You will never have done with him in England," said the priest, looking down, "while brass is strong and stone abides. His marble statues will erect the souls of proud, innocent boys for centuries, his village tomb will smell of loyalty as of lilies. Millions who never knew him shall love him like a father—this man whom the last few that knew him dealt with like dung. He shall be a saint; and the truth shall never be told of him, because I have made up my mind at last. There is so much good and evil in breaking secrets, that I put my conduct to a test. All these newspapers will perish; the anti-Brazil boom is already over; Olivier is already honoured everywhere. But I told myself that if anywhere, by name, in metal or marble that will endure like the pyramids, Colonel Clancy, or Captain Keith, or President Olivier, or any innocent man was wrongly blamed, then I would speak. If it were only that St. Clare was wrongly praised, I would be silent. And I will."

They plunged into the red-curtained tavern, which was not only cosy, but even luxurious inside. On a table stood a silver model of the tomb of St. Clare, the silver head bowed, the silver sword broken. On the walls were coloured photographs of the same scene, and of the system of wagonettes that took tourists to see it. They sat down on the comfortable padded benches.

"Come, it's cold," cried Father Brown; "let's have some wine or beer."

"Or brandy," said Flambeau.

THE THREE TOOLS OF DEATH

Both calling and conviction Father Brown knew better than most of us that every man is dignified when he is dead. But even he felt a pang of incongruity when he was knocked up at daybreak and told that Sir Aaron Armstrong had been murdered. There was something absurd and unseemly about secret violence in connexion with so entirely entertaining and popular a figure. For Sir Aaron Armstrong was entertaining to the point of being comic; and popular in such a manner as to be almost legendary. It was like hearing that Sunny Jim had hanged himself;[1] or that Mr. Pickwick had died in Hanwell. For though Sir Aaron was a philanthropist, and thus dealt with the darker side of our society, he prided himself on dealing with it in the brightest possible style. His political and social speeches were cataracts of anecdotes and "loud laughter"; his bodily health was of a bursting sort; his ethics were all optimism; and he dealt with the Drink problem (his favourite topic) with that immortal or even monotonous gaiety which is so often a mark of the prosperous total abstainer.

The established story of his conversion was familiar on the more puritanic platforms and pulpits, how he had been, when only a boy, drawn away from Scotch theology to Scotch whisky, and how he had risen out of both and become (as he modestly put it) what he was. Yet his wide white beard, cherubic face, and sparkling spectacles, at the numberless dinners and congresses where they appeared, made it hard to believe, somehow, that he had ever been anything so morbid as either a dram-drinker or a Calvinist. He was, one felt, the most seriously merry of all the sons of men.

He had lived on the rural skirt of Hampstead in a handsome house, high but not broad, a modern and prosaic tower. The narrowest of its narrow sides overhung the steep green bank of a railway, and was shaken by passing trains. Sir Aaron Armstrong, as he boisterously explained, had no nerves. But if the train had often given a shock to

---

[1] Sunny Jim was an exceedingly cheerful character in breakfast-cereal advertisements of the day.

the house, that morning the tables were turned, and it was the house that gave a shock to the train.

The engine slowed down and stopped just beyond that point where an angle of the house impinged upon the sharp slope of turf. The arrest of most mechanical things must be slow; but the living cause of this had been very rapid. A man clad completely in black, even (it was remembered) to the dreadful detail of black gloves, appeared on the ridge above the engine, and waved his black hands like some sable windmill. This in itself would hardly have stopped even a lingering train. But there came out of him a cry which was talked of afterwards as something utterly unnatural and new. It was one of those shouts that are horribly distinct even when we cannot hear what is shouted. The word in this case was "Murder!"

But the engine-driver swears he would have pulled up just the same if he had heard only the dreadful and definite accent and not the word.

The train once arrested, the most superficial stare could take in many features of the tragedy. The man in black on the green bank was Sir Aaron Armstrong's man-servant Magnus. The baronet in his optimism had often laughed at the black gloves of this dismal attendant; but no one was likely to laugh at him just now.

So soon as an inquirer or two had stepped off the line and across the smoky hedge, they saw, rolled down almost to the bottom of the bank, the body of an old man in a yellow dressing-gown with a very vivid scarlet lining. A scrap of rope seemed caught about his leg, entangled presumably in a struggle. There was a smear or so of blood, though very little; but the body was bent or broken into a posture impossible to any living thing. It was Sir Aaron Armstrong. A few more bewildered moments brought out a big fair-bearded man, whom some travellers could salute as the dead man's secretary, Patrick Royce, once well known in Bohemian society and even famous in the Bohemian arts. In a manner more vague, but even more convincing, he echoed the agony of the servant. By the time the third figure of that household, Alice Armstrong, daughter of the dead man, had come already tottering and wavering into the garden, the engine-driver had put a stop to his stoppage. The whistle had blown and the train had panted on to get help from the next station.

Father Brown had been thus rapidly summoned at the request of Patrick Royce, the big ex-Bohemian secretary. Royce was an Irishman by birth; and that casual kind of Catholic that never remembers his religion until he is really in a hole. But Royce's request might have been less promptly complied with if one of the official detectives had not been a friend and admirer of the unofficial Flambeau; and it was impossible to be a friend of Flambeau without hearing numberless stories about Father Brown. Hence, while the young detective (whose name was Merton) led the little priest across the fields to the railway, their talk was more confidential than could be expected between two total strangers.

"As far as I can see," said Mr. Merton candidly, "there is no sense to be made of it at all. There is nobody one can suspect. Magnus is a solemn old fool; far too much of a fool to be an assassin. Royce has been the baronet's best friend for years; and his daughter undoubtedly adored him. Besides, it's all too absurd. Who would kill such a cheery old chap as Armstrong? Who could dip his hands in the gore of an after-dinner speaker? It would be like killing Father Christmas."

"Yes, it was a cheery house," assented Father Brown. "It was a cheery house while he was alive. Do you think it will be cheery now he is dead?"

Merton started a little and regarded his companion with an enlivened eye. "Now he is dead?" he repeated.

"Yes," continued the priest stolidly; "*he* was cheerful. But did he communicate his cheerfulness? Frankly, was anyone else in the house cheerful but he?"

A window in Merton's mind let in that strange light of surprise in which we see for the first time things we have known all along. He had often been to the Armstrong's, on little police jobs of the philanthropist; and, now he came to think of it, it was in itself a depressing house. The rooms were very high and very cold; the decoration mean and provincial; the draughty corridors were lit by electricity that was bleaker than moonlight. And though the old man's scarlet face and silver beard had blazed like a bonfire in each room or passage in turn, it did not leave any warmth behind it. Doubtless this spectral discomfort in the place was partly due to the very vitality and exuberance of its owner; he needed no stoves or lamps, he would say, but carried his own warmth with him. But when Merton recalled the other inmates, he was compelled to confess that they also were as shadows of their lord. The moody man-servant, with his monstrous black gloves, was almost a nightmare; Royce, the secretary, was solid enough, a big bull of a man, in tweeds, with a short beard; but the straw-coloured beard was startlingly salted with grey like the tweeds, and the broad forehead was barred with premature wrinkles. He was good-natured enough also, but it was a sad sort of good-nature, almost a heart-broken sort—he had the general air of being some sort of failure in life. As for Armstrong's daughter, it was almost incredible that she was his daughter; she was so pallid in colour and sensitive in outline. She was graceful, but there was a quiver in the very shape of her that was like the lines of an aspen. Merton had sometimes wondered if she had learnt to quail at the crash of the passing trains.

"You see," said Father Brown, blinking modestly, "I'm not sure that the Armstrong cheerfulness is so very cheerful—for other people. You say that nobody could kill such a happy old man, but I'm not sure; *ne nos inducas in tentationem.* If ever I murdered somebody," he added quite simply, "I dare say it might be an Optimist."

"Why?" cried Merton, amused. "Do you think people dislike cheerfulness?"

"People like frequent laughter," answered Father Brown, "but I don't think they like a permanent smile. Cheerfulness without humour is a very trying thing."

They walked some way in silence along the windy grassy bank by the rail, and just as they came under the far-flung shadow of the tall Armstrong house, Father Brown said suddenly, like a man throwing away a troublesome thought rather than offering it seriously: "Of course, drink is neither good nor bad in itself. But I can't help sometimes feeling that men like Armstrong want an occasional glass of wine to sadden them."

Merton's official superior, a grizzled and capable detective named Gilder, was standing on the green bank waiting for the coroner, talking to Patrick Royce, whose big shoulders and bristly beard and hair towered above him. This was the more noticeable because Royce walked always with a sort of powerful stoop, and seemed to be going about his small clerical and domestic duties in a heavy and humbled style, like a buffalo drawing a go-cart.

He raised his head with unusual pleasure at the sight of the priest, and took him a few paces apart. Meanwhile Merton was addressing the older detective respectfully indeed, but not without a certain boyish impatience.

"Well, Mr. Gilder, have you got much farther with the mystery?"

"There is no mystery," replied Gilder, as he looked under dreamy eyelids at the rooks.

"Well, there is for me, at any rate," said Merton, smiling.

"It is simple enough, my boy," observed the senior investigator, stroking his grey, pointed beard. "Three minutes after you'd gone for Mr. Royce's parson the whole thing came out. You know that pasty-faced servant in the black gloves who stopped the train?"

"I should know him anywhere. Somehow he rather gave me the creeps."

"Well," drawled Gilder, "when the train had gone on again, that man had gone, too. Rather a cool criminal, don't you think, to escape by the very train that went off for the police?"

"You're pretty sure, I suppose," remarked the young man, "that he really did kill his master?"

"Yes, my son, I'm pretty sure," replied Gilder drily, "for the trifling reason that he has gone off with twenty thousand pounds in papers that were in his master's desk. No, the only thing worth calling a difficulty is how he killed him. The skull seems broken as with some big weapon, but there's no weapon at all lying about, and the murderer would have found it awkward to carry it away, unless the weapon was too small to be noticed."

"Perhaps the weapon was too big to be noticed," said the priest, with an odd little giggle.

Gilder looked round at his wild remark, and rather sternly asked Brown what he meant.

"Silly way of putting it, I know," said Father Brown apologetically. "Sounds like a fairy tale. But poor Armstrong was killed with a giant's club, a great green club, too big to be seen, and which we call the earth. He was broken against this green bank we are standing on."

"How do you mean?" asked the detective quickly.

Father Brown turned his moon face up to the narrow façade of the house and blinked hopelessly up. Following his eyes, they saw that right at the top of this otherwise blind back quarter of the building, an attic window stood open.

"Don't you see," he explained, pointing a little awkwardly like a child, "he was thrown down from there?"

Gilder frowningly scrutinised the window, and then said, "Well, it is certainly possible. But I don't see why you are so sure about it."

Brown opened his grey eyes wide. "Why," he said, "there's a bit of rope round the dead man's leg. Don't you see that other bit of rope up there caught at the corner of the window?"

At that height the thing looked like the faintest particle of dust or hair, but the shrewd old investigator was satisfied. "You're quite right, sir," he said to Father Brown; "that is certainly one to you."

Almost as he spoke a special train with one carriage took the curve of the line on their left, and, stopping, disgorged another group of policemen, in whose midst was the hangdog visage of Magnus, the absconded servant.

"By Jove! they've got him," cried Gilder, and stepped forward with quite a new alertness.

"Have you got the money?" he cried to the first policeman.

The man looked him in the face with a rather curious expression and said, "No." Then he added, "At least, not here."

"Which is the inspector, please?" asked the man called Magnus.

When he spoke everybody instantly understood how this voice had stopped a train. He was a dull-looking man with flat black hair, a colourless face, and a faint suggestion of the East in the level slits in his eyes and mouth. His blood and name, indeed, had remained dubious, ever since Sir Aaron had "rescued" him from a waitership in a London restaurant, and (as some said) from more infamous things. But his voice was as vivid as his face was dead. Whether through exactitude in a foreign language, or in deference to his master (who had been somewhat deaf), Magnus's tones had a peculiarly ringing and piercing quality, and the whole group quite jumped when he spoke.

"I always knew this would happen," he said aloud with brazen blandness. "My poor old master made game of me for wearing black; but I always said I should be ready for his funeral."

And he made a momentary movement with his two dark-gloved hands.

"Sergeant," said Inspector Gilder, eyeing the black hands with wrath, "aren't you putting the bracelets on this fellow; he looks pretty dangerous."

"Well, sir," said the sergeant, with the same odd look of wonder, "I don't know that we can."

"What do you mean?" asked the other sharply. "Haven't you arrested him?"

A faint scorn widened the slit-like mouth, and the whistle of an approaching train seemed oddly to echo the mockery.

"We arrested him," replied the sergeant gravely, "just as he was coming out of the police-station at Highgate, where he had deposited all his master's money in the care of Inspector Robinson."

Gilder looked at the man-servant in utter amazement. "Why on earth did you do that?" he asked of Magnus.

"To keep it safe from the criminal, of course," replied that person placidly.

"Surely," said Gilder, "Sir Aaron's money might have been safely left with Sir Aaron's family."

The tail of his sentence was drowned in the roar of the train as it went rocking and clanking; but through all the hell of noises to which that unhappy house was periodically subject, they could hear the syllables of Magnus's answer, in all their bell-like distinctness, "I have no reason to feel confidence in Sir Aaron's family."

All the motionless men had the ghostly sensation of the presence of some new person; and Merton was scarcely surprised when he looked up and saw the pale face of Armstrong's daughter over Father Brown's shoulder. She was still young and beautiful in a silvery style, but her hair was of so dusty and hueless a brown that in some shadows it seemed to have turned totally grey.

"Be careful what you say," said Royce gruffly, "you'll frighten Miss Armstrong."

"I hope so," said the man with the clear voice.

As the woman winced and everyone else wondered, he went on, "I am somewhat used to Miss Armstrong's tremors. I have seen her trembling off and on for years. And some said she was shaking with cold and some she was shaking with fear, but I know she was shaking with hate and wicked anger—fiends that have had their feast this morning. She would have been away by now with her lover and all the money but for me. Ever since my poor old master prevented her from marrying that tipsy blackguard —"

"Stop," said Gilder very sternly. "We have nothing to do with your family fancies or suspicions. Unless you have some practical evidence, your mere opinions —"

"Oh, I'll give you practical evidence," cut in Magnus, in his hacking accent. "You'll have to subpœna me, Mr. Inspector, and I shall have to tell the truth. And the truth is this: An instant after the old man was pitched bleeding out of the window, I ran into the attic, and found his daughter swooning on the floor with a red dagger still in her hand. Allow me to hand that also to the proper authorities." He took from his tail-pocket a long horn-hilted knife with a red smear on it, and handed it politely to the sergeant. Then he stood back again, and his slits of eyes almost faded from his face in one fat Chinese sneer.

Merton felt an almost bodily sickness at the sight of him; and he muttered to Gilder, "Surely you would take Miss Armstrong's word against his?"

Father Brown suddenly lifted a face so absurdly fresh that it looked somehow as if he had just washed it. "Yes," he said, radiating innocence, "but is Miss Armstrong's word against his?"

The girl uttered a startled, singular little cry; everyone looked at her. Her figure was rigid as if paralysed; only her face within its frame of faint brown hair was alive with an appalling surprise. She stood like one of a sudden lassooed and throttled.

"This man," said Mr. Gilder gravely, "actually says that you were found grasping a knife, insensible, after the murder."

"He says the truth," answered Alice.

The next fact of which they were conscious was that Patrick Royce strode with his great stooping head into their ring and uttered the singular words, "Well, if I've got to go, I'll have a bit of pleasure first." His huge shoulder heaved and he sent an iron fist smash into Magnus's bland Mongolian visage, laying him on the lawn as flat as a starfish. Two or three of the police instantly put their hands on Royce; but to the rest it seemed as if all reason had broken up and the universe were turning into a brainless harlequinade.

"None of that, Mr. Royce," Gilder had called out authoritatively. "I shall arrest you for assault."

"No you won't," answered the secretary in a voice like an iron gong, "you will arrest me for murder."

Gilder threw an alarmed glance at the man knocked down; but since that outraged person was already sitting up and wiping a little blood off a substantially uninjured face, he only said shortly, "What do you mean?"

"It is quite true, as this fellow says," explained Royce, "that Miss Armstrong fainted with a knife in her hand. But she had not snatched the knife to attack her father, but to defend him."

"To defend him," repeated Gilder gravely. "Against whom?"

"Against me," answered the secretary.

Alice looked at him with a complex and baffling face; then she said in a low voice, "After it all, I am still glad you are brave."

"Come upstairs," said Patrick Royce heavily, "and I will show you the whole cursed thing."

The attic, which was the secretary's private place (and rather a small cell for so large a hermit), had indeed all the vestiges of a violent drama. Near the centre of the floor lay a large revolver as if flung away; nearer to the left was rolled a whisky bottle, open but not quite empty. The cloth of the little table lay dragged and trampled, and a length of cord, like that found on the corpse, was cast wildly across the window-sill. Two vases were smashed on the mantelpiece and one on the carpet.

"I was drunk," said Royce. And this simplicity in the prematurely battered man somehow had the pathos of the first sin of a baby.

"You all know about me," he continued huskily; "everybody knows how my story began, and it may as well end like that, too. I was called a clever man once, and might have been a happy one; Armstrong saved the remains of a brain and body from the taverns, and was always kind to me in his own way, poor fellow! Only he wouldn't let me marry Alice here; and it will always be said that he was right enough. Well, you can form your own conclusions, and you won't want me to go into details. That is my whisky bottle half emptied in the corner; that is my revolver quite emptied on the carpet. It was the rope from my box that was found on the corpse, and it was from my window the corpse was thrown. You need not set detectives to grub up my tragedy; it is a common enough weed in this world. I give myself to the gallows; and, by God, that is enough!"

At a sufficiently delicate sign the police gathered round the large man to lead him away; but their unobtrusiveness was somewhat staggered by the remarkable appearance of Father Brown, who was on his hands and knees on the carpet in the doorway, as if engaged in some kind of undignified prayers. Being a person utterly insensible to the social figure he cut, he remained in this posture, but turned a bright round face up at the company, presenting the appearance of a quadruped with a very comic human head.

"I say," he said good-naturedly, "this really won't do at all, you know. At the beginning you said we'd found no weapon. But now we're finding too many; there's the knife to stab, and the rope to strangle, and the pistol to shoot; and after all he broke his neck by falling out of a window! It won't do. It's not economical." And he shook his head at the ground as a horse does grazing.

Inspector Gilder had opened his mouth with serious intentions, but before he could speak the grotesque figure on the floor had gone on quite volubly.

"And now three quite impossible things. First, these holes in the carpet, where the six bullets have gone in. Why on earth should anybody fire at the carpet? A drunken man lets fly at his enemy's head, the thing that's grinning at him. He doesn't pick a quarrel with his feet, or lay siege to his slippers. And then there's the rope"—and having done with the carpet the speaker lifted his hands and put them in his pockets, but continued unaffectedly on his knees—"in what conceivable intoxication would anybody try to put a rope round a man's neck and finally put it round his leg? Royce, anyhow, was not so drunk as that, or he would be sleeping like a log by now. And, plainest of all, the whisky bottle. You suggest a dipsomaniac fought for the whisky bottle, and then having won, rolled it away in a corner, spilling one half and leaving the other. That is the very last thing a dipsomaniac would do."

He scrambled awkwardly to his feet, and said to the self-accused murderer in tones of limpid penitence, "I'm awfully sorry, my dear sir, but your tale is really rubbish."

"Sir," said Alice Armstrong in a low tone to the priest, "can I speak to you alone for a moment?"

This request forced the communicative cleric out of the gangway, and before he could speak in the next room, the girl was talking with strange incisiveness.

"You are a clever man," she said, "and you are trying to save Patrick, I know. But it's no use. The core of all this is black, and the more things you find out the more there will be against the miserable man I love."

"Why?" asked Brown, looking at her steadily.

"Because," she answered equally steadily, "I saw him commit the crime myself."

"Ah!" said the unmoved Brown, "and what did he do?"

"I was in this room next to them," she explained; "both doors were closed, but I suddenly heard a voice, such as I had never heard on earth, roaring 'Hell, hell, hell,' again and again, and then the two doors shook with the first explosion of the revolver. Thrice again the thing banged before I got the two doors open and found the room full of smoke; but the pistol was smoking in my poor, mad Patrick's hand; and I saw him fire the last murderous volley with my own eyes. Then he leapt on my father, who was clinging in terror to the window-sill, and, grappling, tried to strangle him with the rope, which he threw over his head, but which slipped over his struggling shoulders to his feet. Then it tightened round one leg and Patrick dragged him along like a maniac. I snatched a knife from the mat, and, rushing between them, managed to cut the rope before I fainted."

"I see," said Father Brown, with the same wooden civility. "Thank you."

As the girl collapsed under her memories, the priest passed stiffly into the next room, where he found Gilder and Merton alone with Patrick Royce, who sat in a chair, handcuffed. There he said to the Inspector submissively:

"Might I say a word to the prisoner in your presence; and might he take off those funny cuffs for a minute?"

"He is a very powerful man," said Merton in an undertone. "Why do you want them taken off?"

"Why, I thought," replied the priest humbly, "that perhaps I might have the very great honour of shaking hands with him."

Both detectives stared, and Father Brown added, "Won't you tell them about it, sir?"

The man on the chair shook his tousled head, and the priest turned impatiently.

"Then I will," he said. "Private lives are more important than public reputations. I am going to save the living, and let the dead bury their dead."

He went to the fatal window and blinked out of it as he went on talking.

"I told you that in this case there were too many weapons and only one death. I tell you now that they were not weapons, and were not used to cause death. All those grisly tools, the noose, the bloody knife, the exploding pistol, were instruments of a curious mercy. They were not used to kill Sir Aaron, but to save him."

"To save him!" repeated Gilder. "And from what?"

"From himself," said Father Brown. "He was a suicidal maniac."

"*What?*" cried Merton in an incredulous tone. "And the Religion of Cheerfulness —"

"It is a cruel religion," said the priest, looking out of the window. "Why couldn't they let him weep a little, like his fathers before him? His plans stiffened, his views grew cold; behind that merry mask was the empty mind of the atheist. At last, to keep up his hilarious public level, he fell back on that dram-drinking he had abandoned long ago. But there is this horror about alcoholism in a sincere teetotaler: that he pictures and expects that psychological inferno from which he has warned others. It leapt upon poor Armstrong prematurely, and by this morning he was in such a case that he sat here and cried he was in hell, in so crazy a voice that his daughter did not know it. He was mad for death, and with the monkey tricks of the mad he had scattered round him death in many shapes—a running noose and his friend's revolver and a knife. Royce entered accidentally and acted in a flash. He flung the knife on the mat behind him, snatched up the revolver, and having no time to unload it, emptied it shot after shot all over the floor. The suicide saw a fourth shape of death, and made a dash for the window. The rescuer did the only thing he could—ran after him with the rope and tried to tie him hand and foot. Then it was that the unlucky girl ran in, and misunderstanding the struggle, strove to slash her father free. At first she only slashed poor Royce's knuckles, from which has come all the blood in this little affair. But, of course, you noticed that he left blood, but no wound, on that servant's face? Only before the poor woman swooned, she did hack her father loose, so that he went crashing through that window into eternity."

There was a long stillness slowly broken by the metallic noises of Gilder unlocking the handcuffs of Patrick Royce, to whom he said, "I think you should have told the truth, sir. You and the young lady are worth more than Armstrong's obituary notices."

"Confound Armstrong's notices," cried Royce roughly. "Don't you see it was because she mustn't know?"

"Mustn't know what?" asked Merton.

"Why, that she killed her father, you fool!" roared the other. "He'd have been alive now but for her. It might craze her to know that."

"No, I don't think it would," remarked Father Brown as he picked up his hat. "I rather think I should tell her. Even the most murderous blunders don't poison life like sins; anyhow, I think you may both be the happier now. I've got to go back to the Deaf School."

As he went out on to the gusty grass an acquaintance from Highgate stopped him and said:

"The Coroner has arrived. The inquiry is just going to begin."

"I've got to get back to the Deaf School," said Father Brown. "I'm sorry I can't stop for the inquiry."

THE WISDOM OF
FATHER BROWN

1914

To
LUCIAN OLDERSHAW

THE ABSENCE OF MR. GLASS

The consulting-rooms of Dr. Orion Hood, the eminent criminologist and specialist in certain moral disorders, lay along the sea-front at Scarborough, in a series of very large and well-lighted French windows, which showed the North Sea like one endless outer wall of blue-green marble. In such a place the sea had something of the monotony of a blue-green dado: for the chambers themselves were ruled throughout by a terrible tidiness not unlike the terrible tidiness of the sea. It must not be supposed that Dr. Hood's apartments excluded luxury, or even poetry. These things were there, in their place; but one felt that they were never allowed out of their place. Luxury was there: there stood upon a special table eight or ten boxes of the best cigars; but they were built upon a plan so that the strongest were always nearest the wall and the mildest nearest the window. A tantalus containing three kinds of spirit, all of a liqueur excellence, stood always on this table of luxury; but the fanciful have asserted that the whisky, brandy, and rum seemed always to stand at the same level. Poetry was there: the left-hand corner of the room was lined with as complete a set of English classics as the right hand could show of English and foreign physiologists. But if one took a volume of Chaucer or Shelley from that rank, its absence irritated the mind like a gap in a man's front teeth. One could not say the books were never read; probably they were, but there was a sense of their being chained to their places, like the Bibles in the old churches. Dr. Hood treated his private bookshelf as if it were a public library. And if this strict scientific intangibility steeped even the shelves laden with lyrics and ballads and the tables laden with drink and tobacco, it goes without saying that yet more of such heathen holiness protected the other shelves that held the specialist's library, and the other tables that sustained the frail and even fairylike instruments of chemistry or mechanics. Dr. Orion Hood paced the length of his string of apartments, bounded—as the boys' geographies say—on the east by the North Sea and on the west by the serried ranks of his sociological and criminologist library. He was clad in an artist's velvet, but with none of an artist's negligence; his hair

241

was heavily shot with grey, but growing thick and healthy; his face was lean, but sanguine and expectant. Everything about him and his room indicated something at once rigid and restless, like that great Northern Sea by which (on pure principles of hygiene) he had built his home.

Fate, being in a funny mood, pushed the door open and introduced into those long, strict, sea-flanked apartments one who was perhaps the most startling opposite of them and their master. In answer to a curt but civil summons, the door opened inwards and there shambled into the room a shapeless little figure, which seemed to find its own hat and umbrella as unmanageable as a mass of luggage. The umbrella was a black and prosaic bundle long past repair, the hat was a broad-curved black hat, clerical but not common in England, the man was the very embodiment of all that is homely and helpless.

The doctor regarded the new-comer with a restrained astonishment, not unlike that he would have shown if some huge but obviously harmless sea-beast had crawled into his room. The new-comer regarded the doctor with that beaming but breathless geniality which characterises a corpulent charwoman who has just managed to stuff herself into an omnibus. It is a rich confusion of social self-congratulation and bodily disarray. His hat tumbled to the carpet, his heavy umbrella slipped between his knees with a thud; he reached after the one and ducked after the other, but with an unimpaired smile on his round face spoke simultaneously as follows:

"My name is Brown. Pray excuse me. I've come about that business of the MacNabs. I have heard you often help people out of such troubles. Pray excuse me if I am wrong."

By this time he had sprawlingly recovered the hat, and made an odd little bobbing bow over it, as if setting everything quite right.

"I hardly understand you," replied the scientist, with a cold intensity of manner. "I fear you have mistaken the chambers. I am Dr. Hood, and my work is almost entirely literary and educational. It is true that I have sometimes been consulted by the police in cases of peculiar difficulty and importance, but —"

"Oh, this is of the greatest importance," broke in the little man called Brown. "Why, her mother won't let them get engaged." And he leaned back in his chair in radiant rationality.

The brows of Dr. Hood were drawn down darkly, but the eyes under them were bright with something that might be anger or might be amusement. "And still," he said, "I do not quite understand."

"You see, they want to get married," said the man with the clerical hat. "Maggie MacNab and young Todhunter want to get married. Now, what can be more important than that?"

The great Orion Hood's scientific triumphs had deprived him of many things—some said of his health, others of his God; but they had not wholly despoiled him of his sense of the absurd. At the last plea of the ingenuous priest a chuckle broke out of him from inside, and he threw himself into an arm-chair in an ironical attitude of the consulting physician.

"Mr. Brown," he said gravely, "it is quite fourteen and a half years since I was personally asked to test a personal problem: then it was the case of an attempt to poison the French President at a Lord Mayor's Banquet. It is now, I understand, a question of whether some friend of yours called Maggie is a suitable fiancée for some friend of hers called Todhunter. Well, Mr. Brown, I am a sportsman. I will take it on. I will give the MacNab family my best advice, as good as I gave the French Republic and the King of England—no, better: fourteen years better. I have nothing else to do this afternoon. Tell me your story."

The little clergyman called Brown thanked him with unquestionable warmth, but still with a queer kind of simplicity. It was rather as if he were thanking a stranger in a smoking-room for some trouble in passing the matches, than as if he were (as he was) practically thanking the Curator of Kew Gardens for coming with him into a field, to find a four-leaved clover. With scarcely a semi-colon after his hearty thanks, the little man began his recital:

"I told you my name was Brown; well, that's the fact, and I'm the priest of the little Catholic Church I dare say you've seen beyond those straggly streets, where the town ends towards the north. In the last and straggliest of those streets which runs along the sea like a sea-wall there is a very honest but rather sharp-tempered member of my flock, a widow called MacNab. She has one daughter, and she lets lodgings, and between her and the daughter, and between her and the lodgers; well, I dare say there is a great deal to be said on both sides. At present she has only one lodger, the young man called Todhunter; but he has given more trouble than all the rest, for he wants to marry the young woman of the house."

"And the young woman of the house," asked Dr. Hood, with huge and silent amusement, "what does she want?"

"Why, she wants to marry him," cried Father Brown, sitting up eagerly. "That is just the awful complication."

"It is indeed a hideous enigma," said Dr. Hood.

"This young James Todhunter," continued the cleric, "is a very decent man so far as I know; but then nobody knows very much. He is a bright, brownish little fellow, agile like a monkey, clean-shaven like an actor, and obliging like a born courtier. He seems to have quite a pocketful of money, but nobody knows what his trade is. Mrs. MacNab, therefore (being of a pessimistic turn), is quite sure it is something dreadful, and probably connected with dynamite. The dynamite must be of a shy and noiseless sort, for the poor fellow only shuts himself up for several hours of the day and studies something behind a locked door. He declares his privacy is temporary and justified, and promises to explain before the wedding. That is all that anyone knows for certain, but Mrs. MacNab will tell you a great deal more than even she is certain of. You know how the tales grow like grass on such a patch of ignorance as that. There are tales of two voices heard talking in the room; though, when the door is opened, Todhunter is always found alone. There are tales of a mysterious tall man in a silk hat, who once came out of the sea-mists and apparently out of the sea, stepping softly across the sandy fields and through the small back garden at twilight, till he was heard talking to the lodger at his open back window. The colloquy seemed to end in a quarrel: Todhunter dashed down his window with violence, and the man in the high hat melted into the sea-fog again. This story is told by the family with the fiercest mystification, but I really think Mrs. MacNab prefers her own original tale: that the Other Man (or whatever it is) crawls out every night from the big box in the corner, which is kept locked all day. You see, therefore, how this sealed door of Todhunter's is treated as the gate of all the fancies and monstrosities of the *Thousand and One Nights*. And yet there is the little fellow in his respectable black jacket, as punctual and innocent as a parlour clock. He pays his rent to the tick; he is practically a teetotaller; he is tirelessly kind with the younger children, and can keep them amused for a day on end; and, last and most urgent of all, he has made himself equally popular with the eldest daughter, who is ready to go to church with him to-morrow."

A man warmly concerned with any large theories has always a relish for applying them to any triviality. The great specialist, having condescended to the priest's simplicity, condescended expansively. He settled himself with comfort in his arm-chair and began to talk in the tone of a somewhat absent-minded lecturer:

"Even in a minute instance, it is best to look first to the main tendencies of Nature. A particular flower may not be dead in early winter, but the flowers are dying; a particular pebble may never be wetted with the tide, but the tide is coming in. To the scientific eye all human history is a series of collective movements, destructions or migrations, like the massacre of flies in winter or the return of birds in spring. Now the root fact in all history is Race. Race produces religion; Race produces legal and ethical wars. There is no stronger case than that of the wild, unworldly and perishing stock which we commonly call the Celts, of whom your friends the MacNabs are specimens. Small, swarthy, and of this dreamy and drifting blood, they accept easily the superstitious explanation of any incidents, just as they still accept (you will excuse me for saying) that superstitious explanation of all incidents which you and your Church represent. It is not remarkable that such people, with the sea moaning behind them and the Church (excuse me again) droning in front of them, should put fantastic features into what are probably plain events. You, with your small parochial responsibilities, see only this particular Mrs. MacNab, terrified with this particular tale of two voices and a tall man out of the sea. But the man with the scientific imagination sees, as it were, the whole clans of MacNabs scattered over the whole world, in its ultimate average as uniform as a tribe of birds. He sees thousands of

Mrs. MacNabs, in thousands of houses, dropping their little drop of morbidity in the tea-cups of their friends; he sees —"[1]

Before the scientist could conclude his sentence, another and more impatient summons sounded from without; someone with swishing skirts was marshalled hurriedly down the corridor, and the door opened on a young girl, decently dressed but disordered and red-hot with haste. She had sea-blown blonde hair, and would have been entirely beautiful if her cheekbones had not been, in the Scotch manner, a little high in relief as well as in colour. Her apology was almost as abrupt as a command.

"I'm sorry to interrupt you, sir," she said; "but I had to follow Father Brown at once; it's nothing less than life or death."

Father Brown began to get to his feet in some disorder. "Why, what has happened, Maggie?" he said.

"James has been murdered, for all I can make out," answered the girl, still breathing hard from her rush. "That man Glass has been with him again; I heard them talking, through the door quite plain. Two separate voices; for James speaks low, with a burr, and the other voice was high and quavery."

"That man Glass?" repeated the priest in some perplexity.

"I know his name is Glass," answered the girl, in great impatience. "I heard it through the door. They were quarrelling—about money, I think—for I heard James say again and again, 'That's right, Mr. Glass,' and 'No, Mr. Glass,' and then, 'Two or three, Mr. Glass.' But we're talking too much; you must come at once, and there may be time yet."

"But time for what?" asked Dr. Hood, who had been studying the young lady with marked interest. "What is there about Mr. Glass and his money troubles that should impel such urgency?"

"I tried to break down the door and couldn't," answered the girl shortly. "Then I ran round to the back-yard, and managed to climb

---

[1] Dr. Hood's crude racial ideology was much in vogue when this story was written in 1912. It traces back to the theories of the Swedish biologist Charles Linnaeus (1797–1778), who was the first to attribute character traits to race; and to Francis Galton (1822–1911), the British scientist who founded Eugenics, the "science" of improving the human species by eliminating "inferior" races through selective breeding.

on to the window-sill that looks into the room. It was all dim, and seemed to be empty, but I swear I saw James lying huddled up in a corner, as if he were drugged or strangled."

"This is very serious," said Father Brown, gathering his errant hat and umbrella and standing up; "in point of fact, I was just putting your case before this gentleman, and his view —"

"Has been largely altered," said the scientist gravely. "I do not think this young lady is so Celtic as I had supposed. As I have nothing else to do, I will put on my hat and stroll down the town with you."

In a few minutes all three were approaching the dreary tail of the MacNabs' street; the girl with the stern and breathless stride of the mountaineer, the criminologist with a lounging grace (which was not without a certain leopard-like swiftness), and the priest at an energetic trot entirely devoid of distinction. The aspect of this edge of the town was not entirely without justification for the doctor's hints about desolate moods and environments. The scattered houses stood farther and farther apart in a broken string along the seashore, the afternoon was closing with a premature and partly lurid twilight; the sea was of an inky purple and murmuring ominously. In the scrappy back garden of the MacNabs which ran down towards the sand, two black, barren-looking trees stood up like demon hands held up in astonishment, and as Mrs. MacNab ran down the street to meet them with lean hands similarly spread, and her fierce face in shadow, she was a little like a demon herself. The doctor and the priest made scant reply to her shrill reiterations of her daughter's story, with more disturbing details of her own, to the divided vows of vengeance against Mr. Glass for murdering, and against Mr. Todhunter for being murdered, or against the latter for having dared to want to marry her daughter, and for not having lived to do it. They passed through the narrow passages in the front of the house until they came to the lodger's door at the back, and there Dr. Hood, with the trick of an old detective, put his shoulder sharply to the panel and burst in the door.

It opened on a scene of silent catastrophe. No one seeing it, even for a flash, could doubt that the room had been the theatre of some thrilling collision between two, or perhaps more, persons. Playing-cards lay littered across the table or fluttered about the floor as if a game had been interrupted. Two wine glasses stood ready for wine on a side-table, but a third lay smashed in a star of crystal upon the carpet. A few feet from it lay what looked like a long knife or short sword, straight, but with an ornamental and pictured handle; its dull blade just caught a grey glint from the dreary window behind, which showed the black trees against the leaden level of the sea. Towards the opposite corner of the room was rolled a gentleman's silk top hat, as if it had just been knocked off his head; so much so, indeed, that one almost looked to see it still rolling. And in the corner behind it, thrown like a sack of potatoes, but corded like a railway trunk, lay Mr. James Todhunter, with a scarf across his mouth, and six or seven ropes knotted round his elbows and ankles. His brown eyes were alive and shifted alertly.

Dr. Orion Hood paused for one instant on the door mat and drank in the whole scene of voiceless violence. Then he stepped swiftly across the carpet, picked up the tall silk hat, and gravely put it upon the head of the yet pinioned Todhunter. It was so much too large for him that it almost slipped down on to his shoulders.

"Mr. Glass's hat," said the doctor, returning with it and peering into the inside with a pocket lens. "How to explain the absence of Mr. Glass and the presence of Mr. Glass's hat? For Mr. Glass is not a careless man with his clothes. This hat is of a stylish shape and systematically brushed and burnished, though not very new. An old dandy, I should think."

"But, good heavens!" called out Miss MacNab, "aren't you going to untie the man first?"

"I say 'old' with intention, though not with certainty," continued the expositor; "my reason for it might seem a little far-fetched. The hair of human beings falls out in very varying degrees, but almost always falls out slightly, and with the lens I should see the tiny hairs in a hat recently worn. It has none, which leads me to guess that Mr. Glass is bald. Now when this is taken with the high-pitched and querulous voice which Miss MacNab described so vividly (patience my dear lady, patience), when we take the hairless head together with the tone common in senile anger, I should think we may deduce some advance in years. Nevertheless, he was probably vigorous, and he was almost certainly tall. I might rely in some degree on the story of his previous appearance at the window, as a tall man in a silk hat, but I think I have more exact indication. This wine-glass has been smashed all over the place, but one of its splinters lies on the high bracket beside the mantelpiece. No such fragment could have fallen there if the vessel had been smashed in the hand of a comparatively short man like Mr. Todhunter."

"By the way," said Father Brown, "might it not be as well to untie Mr. Todhunter?"

"Our lesson from the drinking vessels does not end here," proceeded the specialist. "I may say at once that it is possible that the man Glass was bald or nervous through dissipation rather than age. Mr. Todhunter, as has been remarked, is a quiet, thrifty gentleman, essentially an abstainer. These cards and wine cups are no part of his normal habit; they have been produced for a particular companion. But, as it happens, we may go farther. Mr. Todhunter may or may not possess this wine-service, but there is no appearance of his possessing any wine. What, then, were these vessels to contain? I would at once suggest some brandy or whisky, perhaps of a luxurious sort, from a flask in the pocket of Mr. Glass. We have thus something like a picture of the man, or at least of the type: tall, elderly, fashionable, but somewhat frayed, certainly fond of play and strong waters, and perhaps rather too fond of them. Mr. Glass is a gentleman not unknown on the fringes of society."

"Look here," cried the young woman, "if you don't let me pass to untie him I'll run outside and scream for the police."

"I should not advise you, Miss MacNab," said Dr. Hood gravely, "to be in any hurry to fetch the police. Father Brown, I seriously ask you to compose your flock, for their sakes not for mine. Well, we have seen something of the figure and quality of Mr. Glass; what are the chief facts known of Mr. Todhunter? They are substantially three: that he is economical, that he is more or less wealthy, and that he has a secret. Now, surely it is obvious that these are the three chief marks of the kind of man who is blackmailed. And surely it is equally obvious that the faded finery, the profligate habits and the shrill irritation of Mr. Glass are the unmistakable marks of the kind of man who blackmails him. We have the two typical figures of a tragedy of hush money: on the one hand, the respectable man with a mystery; on the other, the west-end vulture with a scent for a mystery. These two men have met here today and have quarrelled, using blows and a bare weapon."

"Are you going to take those ropes off?" asked the girl stubbornly.

Dr. Hood replaced the silk hat carefully on the side table, and went across to the captive. He studied him intently, even moving him a little and half-turning him round by the shoulders, but he only answered:

"No, I think these ropes will do very well till your friends the police bring the handcuffs."

Father Brown, who had been looking dully at the carpet, lifted his round face and said, "What do you mean?"

The man of science had picked up the peculiar dagger-sword from the carpet and was examining it intently as he answered.

"Because you find Mr. Todhunter tied up," he said, "you all jump to the conclusion that Mr. Glass had tied him up; and then, I suppose, escaped. There are four objections to this. First, why should a gentleman so dressy as our friend Glass leave his hat behind him, if he left of his own free will? Second," he continued, moving towards the window, "this is the only exit, and it is locked on the inside. Third, this blade here has a tiny touch of blood at the point, but there is no wound on Mr. Todhunter. Mr. Glass took that wound away with him, dead or alive. Add to all this primary probability. It is much more likely that the blackmailed person would try to kill his incubus, rather than that the blackmailer would try to kill the goose that lays his golden eggs. There, I think, we have a pretty complete story."

"But the ropes?" inquired the priest, whose eyes had remained open with a rather vacant admiration.

"Ah, the ropes," said the expert with a singular intonation. "Miss MacNab very much wanted to know why I did not set Mr. Todhunter free from his ropes. Well, I will tell her. I did not do it because Mr. Todhunter can set himself free from them at any minute he chooses."

"*What?*" cried the audience in quite different notes of astonishment.

"I have looked at all the knots on Mr. Todhunter," reiterated Hood quietly. "I happen to know something about knots; they are quite a branch of criminal science. Every one of those knots he has made himself and could loosen himself; not one of them would have been made by an enemy really trying to pinion him. The whole of this affair of the ropes is a clever fake, to make us think him the victim of the struggle instead of the wretched Glass, whose corpse may be hidden in the garden or stuffed up the chimney."

There was a rather depressed silence; the room was darkening, the sea-blighted boughs of the garden trees looked leaner and blacker than ever, yet they seemed to have come nearer to the window. One could almost fancy they were sea-monsters like crakens or cuttlefish, writhing polypi who had crawled up from the sea to see the end of this tragedy, even as he, the villain and victim of it, the terrible man in the tall hat, had once crawled up from the sea. For the whole air was dense with the morbidity of blackmail, which is the most morbid of human things, because it is a crime concealing a crime; a black plaster on a blacker wound.

The face of the little Catholic priest, which was commonly complacent and even comic, had suddenly become knotted with a curious frown. It was not the blank curiosity of his first innocence. It was rather that creative curiosity which comes when a man has the beginnings of an idea. "Say it again, please," he said in a simple, bothered manner; "do you mean that Todhunter can tie himself up all alone and untie himself all alone?"

"That is what I mean," said the doctor.

"Jerusalem!" ejaculated Brown suddenly, "I wonder if it could possibly be that!"

He scuttled across the room rather like a rabbit, and peered with quite a new impulsiveness into the partially covered face of the captive. Then he turned his own rather fatuous face to the company. "Yes, that's it!" he cried in a certain excitement. "Can't you see it in the man's face? Why, look at his eyes!"

Both the Professor and the girl followed the direction of his glance. And though the broad black scarf completely masked the lower half

of Todhunter's visage, they did grow conscious of something struggling and intense about the upper part of it.

"His eyes do look queer," cried the young woman, strongly moved.
"You brutes; I believe it's hurting him!"

"Not that, I think," said Dr. Hood; "the eyes have certainly a singular expression. But I should interpret those transverse wrinkles as
expressing rather such slight psychological abnormality —"

"Oh, bosh!" cried Father Brown, "can't you see he's laughing?"

"Laughing!" repeated the doctor, with a start, "but what on earth
can he be laughing at?"

"Well," replied the Reverend Brown apologetically, "not to put
too fine a point on it, I think he is laughing at you. And indeed, I'm
a little inclined to laugh at myself, now I know about it."

"Now you know about what?" asked Hood, in some exasperation.

"Now I know," replied the priest, "the profession of Mr. Todhunter."

He shuffled about the room looking at one object after another
with what seemed to be a vacant stare, and then invariably bursting
into an equally vacant laugh, a highly irritating process for those who
had to watch it. He laughed very much over the hat, still more uproar-
iously over the broken glass, but the blood on the sword point sent
him into mortal convulsions of amusement. Then he turned to the
fuming specialist.

"Dr. Hood," he cried enthusiastically, "you are a great poet! You
have called an uncreated being out of the void. How much more
godlike that is than if you had only ferreted out the mere facts!
Indeed, the mere facts are rather commonplace and comic by
comparison."

"I have no notion what you are talking about," said Dr. Hood
rather haughtily; "my facts are all inevitable, though necessarily incom-
plete. A place may be permitted to intuition, perhaps (or poetry if
you prefer the term), but only because the corresponding details cannot as yet be ascertained. In the absence of Mr. Glass —"

"That's it, that's it," said the little priest, nodding quite eagerly,
"that's the first idea to get fixed; the absence of Mr. Glass. He is so
extremely absent. I suppose," he added reflectively, "that there was
never anybody so absent as Mr. Glass."

"Do you mean he is absent from the town?" demanded the doctor.

"I mean he is absent from everywhere," answered Father Brown; "he is absent from the Nature of Things, so to speak."

"Do you seriously mean," said the specialist with a smile, "that there is no such person?"

The priest made a sign of assent. "It does seem a pity," he said.

Orion Hood broke into a contemptuous laugh. "Well," he said, "before we go on to the hundred and one other evidences, let us take the first proof we found; the first fact we fell over when we fell into this room. If there is no Mr. Glass, whose hat is this?"

"It is Mr. Todhunter's," replied Brown.

"But it doesn't fit him," cried Hood impatiently. "He couldn't possibly wear it!"

Father Brown shook his head with ineffable mildness. "I never said he could wear it," he answered, "I said it was his hat. Or, if you insist on a shade of difference, a hat that is his."

"And what is the shade of difference?" asked the criminologist with a slight sneer.

"My good sir," cried the mild little man, with his first movement akin to impatience, "if you will walk down the street to the nearest hatter's shop, you will see that there is, in common speech, a difference between a man's hat and the hats that are his."

"But a hatter," protested Hood, "can get money out of his stock of new hats. What could Todhunter get out of this one old hat?"

"Rabbits," replied Father Brown promptly.

"What?" cried Dr. Hood.

"Rabbits, ribbons, sweetmeats, goldfish, rolls of coloured paper," said the reverend gentleman with rapidity. "Didn't you see it all when you found out the faked ropes? It's just the same with the sword. Mr. Todhunter hasn't got a scratch on him, as you say; but he's got a scratch in him, if you follow me."

"Do you mean inside Mr. Todhunter's clothes?" inquired Mrs. MacNab sternly.

"I do not mean inside Mr. Todhunter's clothes," said Father Brown. "I mean inside Mr. Todhunter."

"Well, what in the name of Bedlam do you mean?"

"Mr. Todhunter," explained Father Brown placidly, "is learning to be a professional conjurer, as well as juggler, ventriloquist, and expert in the rope trick. The conjuring explains the hat. It is without traces of hair, not because it is worn by the prematurely bald Mr. Glass, but because it has never been worn by anybody. The juggling explains the three glasses, which Todhunter was teaching himself to throw up and catch in rotation. But, being only at the stage of practice, he smashed one glass against the ceiling. And the juggling also explains the sword, which it was Mr. Todhunter's professional pride and duty to swallow. But, again, being at the stage of practice, he very slightly grazed the inside of his throat with the weapon. Hence he has a wound inside him, which I am sure (from the expression of his face) is not a serious one. He was also practising the trick of a release from ropes, like the Davenport Brothers, and he was just about to free himself when we all burst into the room.[2] The cards, of course, are for card tricks, and they are scattered on the floor because he had just been practising one of those dodges of sending them flying through the air. He merely kept his trade secret, because he had to keep his tricks secret, like any other conjurer. But the mere fact of an idler in a top hat having once looked in at his back window, and been driven away by him with great indignation, was enough to set us all on a wrong track of romance, and make us imagine his whole life overshadowed by the silk-hatted spectre of Mr. Glass."

"But what about the two voices?" asked Maggie, staring.

"Have you never heard a ventriloquist?" asked Father Brown. "Don't you know they speak first in their natural voice, and then answer themselves in just that shrill, squeaky, unnatural voice that you heard?"

There was a long silence, and Dr. Hood regarded the little man who had spoken with a dark and attentive smile. "You are certainly a very ingenious person," he said; "it could not have been done better in a book. But there is just one part of Mr. Glass you have not succeeded in explaining away, and that is his name. Miss MacNab distinctly heard him so addressed by Mr. Todhunter."

[2] Father Brown refers to the rope trick of the notorious Davenport Brothers, Ira and William, American confidence men and escape artists of the 1860s.

The Rev. Mr. Brown broke into a rather childish giggle. "Well, that," he said, "that's the silliest part of the whole silly story. When our juggling friend here threw up the three glasses in turn, he counted them aloud as he caught them, and also commented aloud when he failed to catch them. What he really said was, 'One, two and three—missed a glass; one, two—missed a glass.' And so on."

There was a second of stillness in the room, and then everyone with one accord burst out laughing. As they did so the figure in the corner complacently uncoiled all the ropes and let them fall with a flourish. Then, advancing into the middle of the room with a bow, he produced from his pocket a big bill printed in blue and red, which announced that ZALADIN, the World's Greatest Conjurer, Contortionist, Ventriloquist and Human Kangaroo, would be ready with an entirely new series of Tricks at the Empire Pavilion, Scarborough, on Monday next at eight o'clock precisely.

THE PARADISE OF THIEVES

The great Muscari, most original of the young Tuscan poets, walked swiftly into his favourite restaurant, which overlooked the Mediterranean, was covered by an awning and fenced by little lemon and orange trees. Waiters in white aprons were already laying out on white tables the insignia of an early and elegant lunch; and this seemed to increase a satisfaction that already touched the top of swagger. Muscari had an eagle nose like Dante, his hair and neckerchief were dark and flowing; he carried a black cloak, and might almost have carried a black mask, so much did he bear with him a sort of Venetian melodrama. He acted as if a troubadour had still a definite social office, like a bishop. He went as near as his century permitted to walking the world literally like Don Juan, with rapier and guitar.

For he never travelled without a case of swords, with which he had fought many brilliant duels, or without a corresponding case of his mandolin, with which he had actually serenaded Miss Ethel Harrogate, the highly-conventional daughter of a Yorkshire banker, on a holiday. Yet he was neither a charlatan nor a child; but a hot, logical Latin who liked a certain thing and was it. His poetry was as straightforward as anyone else's prose. He desired fame or wine or the beauty of women with a torrid directness inconceivable among the cloudy ideals or cloudy compromises of the north; to vaguer races his intensity smelt of danger or even crime. Like fire or the sea, he was too simple to be trusted.

The banker and his beautiful English daughter were staying at the hotel attached to Muscari's restaurant; that was why it was his favourite restaurant. A glance flashed round the room told him at once, however, that the English party had not descended. The restaurant was glittering, but still comparatively empty. Two priests were talking at a table in a corner, but Muscari (an ardent Catholic) took no more notice of them than of a couple of crows. But from a yet farther seat, partly concealed behind a dwarf tree golden with oranges, there rose and advanced towards the poet a person whose costume was the most aggressive opposite to his own.

This figure was clad in tweeds of a piebald check, with a pink tie, a sharp collar and protuberant yellow boots. He contrived, in the true tradition of 'Arry at Margate, to look at once startling and commonplace.[1] But as the Cockney apparition drew nearer, Muscari was astounded to observe that the head was distinctly different from the body. It was an Italian head, fuzzy, swarthy and very vivacious, that rose abruptly out of the standing collar like cardboard and the comic pink tie. In fact it was a head he knew. He recognised it, above all the dire erection of English holiday array, as the face of an old but forgotten friend named Ezza. This youth had been a prodigy at college, and European fame was promised him when he was barely fifteen; but when he appeared in the world he failed, first publicly as a dramatist and a demagogue, and then privately for years on end as an actor, a traveller, a commission agent or a journalist. Muscari had known him last behind the footlights; he was but too well attuned to the excitements of that profession, and it was believed that some moral calamity had swallowed him up.

"Ezza!" cried the poet, rising and shaking hands in a pleasant astonishment. "Well, I've seen you in many costumes in the green room; but I never expected to see you dressed up as an Englishman."

"This," answered Ezza gravely, "is not the costume of an Englishman, but of the Italian of the future."

"In that case," remarked Muscari, "I confess I prefer the Italian of the past."

"That is your old mistake, Muscari," said the man in tweeds, shaking his head. "And the mistake of Italy. In the sixteenth century we Tuscans made the morning: we had the newest steel, the newest carving, the newest chemistry. Why should we not now have the newest factories, the newest motors, the newest finance—and the newest clothes?"

"Because they are not worth having," answered Muscari. "You cannot make Italians really progressive; they are too intelligent. Men who see the short cut to good living will never go by the new elaborate roads."

[1] The reference is to the brassy vulgarity of a character in comic poems by E.J. Milliken, a staff writer for *Punch* magazine in the 1880s.

"Well, to me Marconi, not D'Annunzio, is the star of Italy," said the other.[2] "That is why I have become a Futurist—and a courier."

"A courier!" cried Muscari, laughing. "Is that the last of your list of trades? And whom are you conducting?"

"Oh, a man of the name of Harrogate, and his family, I believe."

"Not the banker in this hotel?" inquired the poet, with some eagerness.

"That's the man," answered the courier.

"Does it pay well?" asked the troubadour innocently.

"It will pay me," said Ezza, with a very enigmatic smile. "But I am a rather curious sort of courier." Then, as if changing the subject, he said abruptly, "He has a daughter—and a son."

"The daughter is divine," affirmed Muscari, "the father and son are, I suppose, human. But granted his harmless qualities, doesn't that banker strike you as a splendid instance of my argument? Harrogate has millions in his safes, and I have—the hole in my pocket. But you daren't say—you can't say—that he's cleverer than I, or bolder than I, or even more energetic. He's not clever; he's got eyes like blue buttons; he's not energetic, he moves from chair to chair like a paralytic. He's a conscientious, kindly old blockhead; but he's got money simply because he collects money, as a boy collects stamps. You're too strong-minded for business, Ezza. You won't get on. To be clever enough to get all that money, one must be stupid enough to want it."

"I'm stupid enough for that," said Ezza gloomily. "But I should suggest a suspension of your critique of the banker, for here he comes."

Mr. Harrogate, the great financier, did indeed enter the room, but nobody looked at him. He was a massive elderly man with a boiled blue eye and faded grey-sandy moustaches; but for his heavy stoop he might have been a colonel. He carried several unopened letters in his hand. His son Frank was a really fine lad, curly haired, sun burnt and strenuous; but nobody looked at him either. All eyes, as usual, were riveted, for the moment at least, upon Ethel Harrogate, whose golden

[2] Guglielmo Marconi (1874–1937) was the inventor of the wireless telegraph, and Gabriele D'Annunzio (1863–1938) was an innovative novelist, playwright, and poet.

Greek head and colour of the dawn seemed set purposely above that sapphire sea, like a goddess's. The poet Muscari drew a deep breath as if he were drinking something; as indeed he was. He was drinking the Classic; which his fathers made. Ezza studied her with a gaze equally intense and far more baffling.

Miss Harrogate was specially radiant and ready for conversation on this occasion; and her family had fallen into the easier Continental habit, allowing the stranger Muscari and even the courier Ezza to share their table and their talk. In Ethel Harrogate conventionality crowned itself with a perfection and splendour of its own. Proud of her father's prosperity, fond of her fashionable pleasures, a fond daughter but an arrant flirt, she was all these things with a sort of golden good-nature that made her very pride pleasing and her worldly respectability a fresh and hearty thing.

They were in an eddy of excitement about some alleged peril in the mountain path they were to attempt that week. The danger was not from rock and avalanche, but from something yet more romantic. Ethel had been earnestly assured that brigands, the true cutthroats of the modern legend, still haunted that ridge and held that pass of the Apennines.

"They say," she cried, with the awful relish of a schoolgirl, "that all that country isn't ruled by the King of Italy, but by the King of Thieves. Who is the King of Thieves?"

"A great man," replied Muscari, "worthy to rank with your own Robin Hood, signorina. Montano, the King of Thieves, was first heard of in the mountains some ten years ago, when people said brigands were extinct. But his wild authority spread with the swiftness of a silent revolution. Men found his fierce proclamations nailed in every mountain village; his sentinels, gun in hand, in every mountain ravine. Six times the Italian Government tried to dislodge him; and was defeated in six pitched battles as if by Napoleon."

"Now that sort of thing," observed the banker weightily, "would never be allowed in England; perhaps after all we had better choose another route. But the courier thought it perfectly safe."

"It is perfectly safe," said the courier contemptuously; "I have been over it twenty times. There may have been some old jail-bird called a

King in the time of our grandmothers; but he belongs to history, if not to fable. Brigandage is utterly stamped out."

"It can never be utterly stamped out," Muscari answered, "because armed revolt is a reaction natural to southerners. Our peasants are like the mountains, rich in grace and green gaiety, but with the fires beneath. There is a point of human despair where the northern poor take to drink—and our own poor take to daggers."

"A poet is privileged," replied Ezza, with a sneer. "If Signor Muscari were English he would still be looking for highwaymen in Wandsworth. Believe me, there is no more danger of being captured in Italy than of being scalped in Boston."

"Then you propose to attempt it?" asked Mr. Harrogate, frowning.

"Oh, it sounds rather dreadful," cried the girl, turning her glorious eyes on Muscari. "Do you really think the pass is dangerous?"

Muscari threw back his black mane. "I know it is dangerous," he said. "I am crossing it tomorrow."

The young Harrogate was left behind for a moment, emptying a glass of white wine and lighting a cigarette, as the beauty retired with the banker, the courier and the poet, distributing peals of silvery satire. At about the same instant the two priests in the corner rose; the taller, a white-haired Italian, taking his leave. The shorter priest turned and walked towards the banker's son; and the latter was astonished to realise that though a Roman priest the man was an Englishman. He vaguely remembered meeting him at the social crushes of some of his Catholic friends. But the man spoke before his memories could collect themselves.

"Mr. Frank Harrogate, I think," he said. "I have had an introduction, but I do not mean to presume on it. The odd thing I have to say will come far better from a stranger. Mr. Harrogate, I say one word and go: take care of your sister in her great sorrow."

Even for Frank's truly fraternal indifference the radiance and derision of his sister still seemed to sparkle and ring; he could hear her laughter still from the garden of the hotel; and he stared at his sombre adviser in puzzledom.

"Do you mean the brigands?" he asked, and then, remembering a vague fear of his own, "or can you be thinking of Muscari?"

"One is never thinking of the real sorrow," said the strange priest. "One can only be kind when it comes."

And he passed promptly from the room, leaving the other almost with his mouth open.

A day or two afterwards a coach containing the company was really crawling and staggering up the spurs of the menacing mountain range. Between Ezza's cheery denial of the danger and Muscari's boisterous defiance of it, the financial family were firm in their original purpose; and Muscari made his mountain journey coincide with theirs. A more surprising feature was the appearance at the coast-town station of the little priest of the restaurant; he alleged merely that business led him also to cross the mountains of the midland. But young Harrogate could not but connect his presence with the mystical fears and warnings of yesterday.

The coach was a kind of commodious wagonette, invented by the modernist talent of the courier, who dominated the expedition with his scientific activity and breezy wit. The theory of danger from thieves was banished from thought and speech; though so far conceded in formal act that some slight protection was employed. The courier and the young banker carried loaded revolvers, and Muscari (with much boyish gratification) buckled on a kind of cutlass under his black cloak.

He had planted his person at a flying leap next to the lovely Englishwoman; on the other side of her sat the priest, whose name was Brown and who was fortunately a silent individual; the courier and the father and son were on the *banc* behind. Muscari was in towering spirits, seriously believing in the peril, and his talk to Ethel might well have made her think him a maniac. But there was something in the crazy and gorgeous ascent, amid crags like peaks loaded with woods like orchards, that dragged her spirit up along with his into purple preposterous heavens with wheeling suns. The white road climbed like a white cat; it spanned sunless chasms like a tight-rope; it was flung round far-off headlands like a lasso.

And yet however high they went, the desert still blossomed like the rose. The fields were burnished in sun and wind with the colour of kingfisher and parrot and humming-bird; the hues of a hundred flowering flowers. There are no lovelier meadows and woodlands than the English; no nobler crests or chasms than those of Snowdon and Glencoe. But Ethel Harrogate had never before seen the southern parks tilted on the splintered northern peaks; the gorge of Glencoe laden with the fruits of Kent. There was nothing here of that chill and desolation that in Britain one associates with high and wild scenery. It was rather like a mosaic palace, rent with earthquakes; or like a Dutch tulip garden blown to the stars with dynamite.

"It's like Kew Garden's on Beachy Head," said Ethel.

"It is our secret," answered he, "the secret of the volcano; that is also the secret of the revolution—that a thing can be violent and yet fruitful."

"You are rather violent yourself," and she smiled at him.

"And yet rather fruitless," he admitted; "if I die tonight I die unmarried and a fool."

"It is not my fault if you have come," she said after a difficult silence.

"It is never your fault," answered Muscari; "it was not your fault that Troy fell."

As he spoke they came under overwhelming cliffs that spread almost like wings above a corner of peculiar peril. Shocked by the big shadow on the narrow ledge, the horses stirred doubtfully. The driver leapt to the earth to hold their heads, and they became ungovernable. One horse reared up to his full height—the titanic and terrifying height of a horse when he becomes a biped. It was just enough to alter the equilibrium; the whole coach heeled over like a ship and crashed through the fringe of bushes over the cliff. Muscari threw an arm round Ethel, who clung to him, and shouted aloud. It was for such moments that he lived.

At the moment when the gorgeous mountain walls went round the poet's head like a purple windmill, a thing happened which was superficially even more startling. The elderly and lethargic banker sprang erect in the coach and leapt over the precipice before the tilted vehicle could take him there. In the first flash it looked as wild as suicide; but in the second it was as sensible as a safe investment. The Yorkshireman had evidently more promptitude as well as more sagacity than Muscari had given him credit for. For he landed in a lap of land which might have been specially padded with turf and clover to receive him. As it happened, indeed, the whole company were equally lucky, if less dignified in their form of ejection. Immediately under this abrupt turn of the road was a grassy and flowery hollow like a sunken meadow; a sort of green velvet pocket in the long, green, trailing garments of the hills. Into this they were all tipped or tumbled with little damage, save that their smallest baggage and even the contents of their pockets were scattered in the grass around them. The wrecked coach still hung above, entangled in the tough hedge, and the horses plunged painfully down the slope. The first to sit up was the little priest, who scratched his head with a face of foolish wonder; Frank Harrogate heard him say to himself, "Now why on earth have we fallen just here?"

He blinked at the litter around him, and recovered his own very clumsy umbrella. Beyond it lay the broad sombrero fallen from the head of Muscari, and beside it a sealed business letter which, after a glance at the address, he returned to the elder Harrogate. On the other side of him the grass partly hid Miss Ethel's sunshade, and just beyond it lay a curious little glass bottle hardly two inches long. The priest picked it up; in a quick, unobtrusive manner he uncorked and sniffed it, and his heavy face turned the colour of clay.

"Heaven deliver us!" he muttered, "it can't be hers! Has her sorrow come on her already?" He slipped it into his own waistcoat pocket. "I think I'm justified," he said, "till I know a little more."

He gazed painfully at the girl, at that moment being raised out of the flowers by Muscari, who was saying, "We have fallen into heaven; it is a sign. Mortals climb up and they fall down; but it is only gods and goddesses who can fall upwards."

And indeed she rose out of the sea of colours so beautiful and happy a vision that the priest felt his suspicion shaken and shifted. "After all," he thought, "perhaps the poison isn't hers; perhaps it's one of Muscari's melodramatic tricks."

Muscari set the lady lightly on her feet, made her an absurdly theatrical bow, and then, drawing his cutlass, hacked hard at the taut reins of the horses, so that they scrambled to their feet and stood in the grass trembling. When he had done so a most remarkable thing occurred. A very quiet man, very poorly dressed and extremely sunburnt, came out of the bushes and took hold of the horses' heads. He had a queer-shaped knife, very broad and crooked, buckled on his belt; there was nothing else remarkable about him, except his sudden and silent appearance. The poet asked him who he was, and he did not answer.

Looking around him at the confused and startled group in the hollow, Muscari then perceived that another tanned and tattered man, with a short gun under his arm, was looking at them from the ledge just below, leaning his elbows on the edge of the turf. Then he looked up at the road from which they had fallen and saw, looking down on them, the muzzles of four other carbines and four other brown faces with bright but quite motionless eyes.

"The brigands!" cried Muscari, with a kind of monstrous gaiety. "This was a trap. Ezza, if you will oblige me by shooting the coachman first, we can cut our way out yet. There are only six of them."

"The coachman," said Ezza, who was standing grimly with his hands in his pockets, "happens to be a servant of Mr. Harrogate's."

"Then shoot him all the more," cried the poet impatiently; "he was bribed to upset his master. Then put the lady in the middle, and we will break the line up there—with a rush."

And, wading in wild grass and flowers, he advanced fearlessly on the four carbines; but finding that no one followed except young Harrogate, he turned, brandishing his cutlass to wave the others on. He beheld the courier still standing slightly astride in the centre of the grassy ring, his hands in his pockets; and his lean, ironical Italian face seemed to grow longer and longer in the evening light.

"You thought, Muscari, I was the failure among our schoolfellows," he said, "and you thought you were the success. But I have succeeded more than you and fill a bigger place in history. I have been acting epics while you have been writing them."

"Come on, I tell you!" thundered Muscari from above. "Will you stand there talking nonsense about yourself with a woman to save and three strong men to help you? What do you call yourself?"

"I call myself Montano," cried the strange courier in a voice equally loud and full. "I am the King of Thieves, and I welcome you all to my summer palace."

And even as he spoke five more silent men with weapons ready came out of the bushes, and looked towards him for their orders. One of them held a large paper in his hand.

"This pretty little nest where we are all picnicking," went on the courier-brigand, with the same easy yet sinister smile, "is, together with some caves underneath it, known by the name of the Paradise of Thieves. It is my principal stronghold on these hills; for (as you have doubtless noticed) the eyrie is invisible both from the road above and from the valley below. It is something better than impregnable; it is unnoticeable. Here I mostly live, and here I shall certainly die, if the gendarmes ever track me here. I am not the kind of criminal that 'reserves his defence,' but the better kind that reserves his last bullet."

All were staring at him thunderstruck and still, except Father Brown, who heaved a huge sigh as of relief and fingered the little phial in his pocket. "Thank God!" he muttered, "that's much more probable. The poison belongs to this robber-chief, of course. He carries it so that he may never be captured, like Cato." [3]

The King of Thieves was, however, continuing his address with the same kind of dangerous politeness. "It only remains for me," he said, "to explain to my guests the social conditions upon which I have the pleasure of entertaining them. I need not expound the quaint old ritual of ransom, which it is incumbent upon me to keep up; and even this only applies to a part of the company. The Reverend Father Brown and the celebrated Signor Muscari I shall release tomorrow at dawn and escort to my outposts. Poets and priests, if you will pardon my simplicity of speech, never have any money. And so (since it is impossible to get anything out of them), let us seize the opportunity to show our admiration for classic literature and our reverence for Holy Church."

[3] Father Brown has in mind Cato the Younger (95–46 B.C.), the Roman Stoic and supporter of Pompey who chose suicide rather than surrender to Julius Cæsar.

He paused with an unpleasing smile; and Father Brown blinked repeatedly at him, and seemed suddenly to be listening with great attention. The brigand captain took the large paper from the attendant brigand and, glancing it over, continued, "My other intentions are clearly set forth in this public document, which I will hand round in a moment; and which after that will be posted on a tree by every village in the valley, and every cross-road in the hills. I will not weary you with the verbalism, since you will be able to check it; the substance of my proclamation is this. I announce first that I have captured the English millionaire, the colossus of finance, Mr. Samuel Harrogate. I next announce that I have found on his person notes and bonds for two thousand pounds, which he has given up to me. Now since it would be really immoral to announce such a thing to a credulous public if it had not occurred, I suggest it should occur without further delay. I suggest that Mr. Harrogate senior should now give me the two thousand pounds in his pocket."

The banker looked at him under lowering brows, red-faced and sulky, but seemingly cowed. That leap from the falling carriage seemed to have used up his last virility. He had held back in a hang-dog style when his son and Muscari had made a bold movement to break out of the brigand trap. And now his red and trembling hand went reluctantly to his breast-pocket, and passed a bundle of papers and envelopes to the brigand.

"Excellent!" cried that outlaw gaily, "so far we are all cosy. I resume the points of my proclamation, so soon to be published to all Italy. The third item is that of ransom. I am asking from the friends of the Harrogate family a ransom of three thousand pounds; which I am sure is almost insulting to that family in its moderate estimate of their importance. Who would not pay triple this sum for another day's association with such a domestic circle? I will not conceal from you that the document ends with certain legal phrases about the unpleasant things that may happen if the money is not paid; but meanwhile, ladies and gentlemen, let me assure you that I am comfortably off here for accommodation, wine and cigars, and bid you for the present a sportsmanlike welcome to the luxuries of the Paradise of Thieves."

All the time that he had been speaking the dubious-looking men with carbines and dirty slouch hats had been gathering silently in such preponderating numbers that even Muscari was compelled to recognise his sally with the sword as hopeless. He glanced around him; but the girl had already gone over to soothe and comfort her father, for her natural affection for his person was as strong or stronger than her somewhat snobbish pride in his success. Muscari, with the illogicality of a lover, admired this filial devotion and yet was irritated by it. He slapped his sword back in the scabbard and went and flung himself somewhat sulkily on one of the green banks. The priest sat down within a yard or two, and Muscari turned his aquiline eye and nose on him in an instantaneous irritation.

"Well," said the poet tartly, "do people still think me too romantic? Are there, I wonder, any brigands left in the mountains?"

"There may be," said Father Brown agnostically.

"What do you mean?" asked the other sharply.

"I mean I am puzzled," replied the priest. "I am puzzled about Ezza or Montano or whatever his name is. He seems to me much more inexplicable as a brigand even than he was as a courier."

"But in what way?" persisted his companion. "Santa Maria! I should have thought the brigand was plain enough."

"I find three curious difficulties," said the priest in a quiet voice. "I should like to have your opinion on them. First of all I must tell you I was lunching in that restaurant at the seaside. As four of you left the room, you and Miss Harrogate went ahead, talking and laughing; the banker and the courier came behind, speaking sparely and rather low. But I could not help hearing Ezza say these words—'Well, let her have a little fun; you know the blow may smash her any minute.' Mr. Harrogate answered nothing; so the words must have had some meaning. On the impulse of the moment I warned her brother that she might be in peril; I said nothing of its nature, for I did not know. But if it meant this capture in the hills, the thing is nonsense. Why should the brigand-courier warn his patron, even by a hint, when it was his whole put purpose to lure him into the mountain-mousetrap? It could not have meant that. But if not, what is this other disaster, known both to courier and banker, which hangs over Miss Harrogate's head?"

"Disaster to Miss Harrogate!" ejaculated the poet, sitting up with some ferocity. "Explain yourself; go on."

"All my riddles, however, revolve round our bandit chief," resumed the priest reflectively. "And here is the second of them. Why did he put so prominently in his demand for ransom the fact that he had taken two thousand pounds from his victim on the spot? It had no faintest tendency to evoke the ransom. Quite the other way, in fact. Harrogate's friends would be far likelier to fear for his fate if they thought the thieves were poor and desperate. Yet the spoliation on the spot was emphasised and even put first in the demand. Why should Ezza Montano want so specially to tell all Europe that he had picked the pocket before he levied the blackmail?"

"I cannot imagine," said Muscari, rubbing up his black hair for once with an unaffected gesture. "You may think you enlighten me, but you are leading me deeper in the dark. What may be the third objection to the King of the Thieves?"

"The third objection," said Father Brown, still in meditation, "is this bank we are sitting on. Why does our brigand-courier call this his chief fortress and the Paradise of Thieves? It is certainly a soft spot to fall on and a sweet spot to look at. It is also quite true, as he says, that it is invisible from valley and peak, and is therefore a hiding-place. But it is not a fortress. It never could be a fortress. I think it would be the worst fortress in the world. For it is actually commanded from above by the common high-road across the mountains— the very place where the police would most probably pass. Why, five shabby short guns held us helpless here about half an hour ago. The quarter of a company of any kind of soldiers could have blown us over the precipice. Whatever is the meaning of this odd little nook of grass and flowers, it is not an entrenched position. It is something else; it has some other strange sort of importance; some value that I do not understand. It is more like an accidental theatre or a natural green-room; it is like the scene for some romantic comedy; it is like ... ."

As the little priest's words lengthened and lost themselves in a dull and dreamy sincerity, Muscari, whose animal senses were alert and impatient, heard a new noise in the mountains. Even for him the sound was as yet very small and faint; but he could have sworn the evening breeze bore with it something like the pulsation of horses' hoofs and a distant hallooing.

At the same moment, and long before the vibration had touched the less-experienced English ears, Montano the brigand ran up the bank above them and stood in the broken hedge, steadying himself against a tree and peering down the road. He was a strange figure as he stood there; for he had assumed a flapped fantastic hat and swinging baldric and cutlass in his capacity of bandit king, but the bright prosaic tweed of the courier showed through in patches all over him.

The next moment he turned his olive, sneering face and made a movement with his hand. The brigands scattered at the signal, not in confusion, but in what was evidently a kind of guerilla discipline. Instead of occupying the road along the ridge, they sprinkled themselves along the side of it behind the trees and the hedge, as if watching unseen for an enemy. The noise beyond grew stronger, beginning to shake the mountain road; and a voice could be clearly heard calling out orders. The brigands swayed and huddled, cursing and whispering, and the evening air was full of little metallic noises as they cocked their pistols or loosened their knives or trailed their scabbards over the stones. Then the noises from both quarters seemed to meet on the road above; branches broke, horses neighed, men cried out.

"A rescue!" cried Muscari, springing to his feet and waving his hat: "the gendarmes are on them! Now for freedom and a blow for it! Now to be rebels against robbers! Come, don't let us leave everything to the police; that is so dreadfully modern. Fall on the rear of these ruffians. The gendarmes are rescuing us; come, friends, let us rescue the gendarmes!"

And throwing his hat over the trees, he drew his cutlass once more and began to escalade the slope up to the road. Frank Harrogate jumped up and ran across to help him, revolver in hand, but was astounded to hear himself imperatively recalled by the raucous voice of his father, who seemed to be in great agitation.

"I won't have it," said the banker in a choking voice; "I command you not to interfere."

"But, father," said Frank very warmly, "an Italian gentleman has led the way. You wouldn't have it said that the English hung back."

"It is useless," said the older man, who was trembling violently, "it is useless. We must submit to our lot."

Father Brown looked at the banker; then he put his hand instinctively as if on his heart, but really on the little bottle of poison; and a great light came into his face like the light of the revelation of death.

Muscari meanwhile, without waiting for support, had crested the bank up to the road, and struck the brigand king heavily on the shoulder, causing him to stagger and swing round. Montano also had his cutlass unsheathed, and Muscari, without further speech, sent a slash at his head which he was compelled to catch and parry. But even as the two short blades crossed and clashed the King of Thieves deliberately dropped his point and laughed.

"What's the good, old man?" he said in spirited Italian slang; "this damned farce will soon be over."

"What do you mean, you shuffler?" panted the fire-eating poet. "Is your courage a sham as well as your honesty?"

"Everything about me is a sham," responded the ex-courier in complete good-humour. "I am an actor; and if I ever had a private character, I have forgotten it. I am no more a genuine brigand than I am a genuine courier. I am only a bundle of masks, and you can't fight a duel with that." And he laughed with boyish pleasure and fell into his old straddling attitude, with his back to the skirmish up the road.

Darkness was deepening under the mountain walls, and it was not easy to discern much of the progress of the struggle, save that tall men were pushing their horses' muzzles through a clinging crowd of brigands, who seemed more inclined to harass and hustle the invaders than to kill them. It was more like a town crowd preventing the passage of the police than anything the poet had ever pictured as the last stand of doomed and outlawed men of blood. Just as he was rolling his eyes in bewilderment he felt a touch on his elbow, and found the odd little priest standing there like a small Noah with a large hat, and requesting the favour of a word or two.

"Signor Muscari," said the cleric, "in this queer crisis personalities may be pardoned. I may tell you without offence of a way in which you will do more good than by helping the gendarmes, who are bound to break through in any case. You will permit me the impertinent intimacy; but do you care about that girl? Care enough to marry her and make her a good husband, I mean?"

"Yes," said the poet quite simply.

"Does she care about you?"

"I think so," was the equally grave reply.

"Then go over there and offer yourself," said the priest, "offer her everything you can; offer her heaven and earth if you've got them. The time is short."

"Why?" asked the astonished man of letters.

"Because," said Father Brown, "her Doom is coming up the road."

"Nothing is coming up the road," argued Muscari, "except the rescue."

"Well, you go over there," said his adviser, "and be ready to rescue her from the rescue."

Almost as he spoke the hedges were broken all along the ridge by a rush of the escaping brigands. They dived into bushes and thick grass like defeated men pursued; and the great cocked hats of the mounted gendarmerie were seen passing along above the broken hedge. Another order was given; there was a noise of dismounting, and a tall officer with a cocked hat, a grey imperial and a paper in his hand appeared in the gap that was the gate of the Paradise of Thieves. There was a momentary silence, broken in an extraordinary way by the banker, who cried out in a hoarse and strangled voice, "Robbed! I've been robbed!"

"Why, that was hours ago," cried his son in astonishment, "when you were robbed of two thousand pounds."

"Not of two thousand pounds," said the financier, with an abrupt and terrible composure, "only of a small bottle."

The policeman with the grey imperial was striding across the green hollow. Encountering the King of the Thieves in his path, he clapped him on the shoulder with something between a caress and a buffet and gave him a push that sent him staggering away. "You'll get into trouble, too," he said, "if you play these tricks."

Again to Muscari's artistic eye it seemed scarcely like the capture of a great outlaw at bay. Passing on, the policeman halted before the

Harrogate group and said, "Samuel Harrogate, I arrest you in the name of the law for embezzlement of the funds of the Hull and Huddersfield Bank."

The great banker nodded with an odd air of business assent, seemed to reflect a moment, and before they could interpose took a half turn and a step that brought him to the edge of the outer mountain wall. Then, flinging up his hands, he leapt, exactly as he leapt out of the coach. But this time he did not fall into a little meadow just beneath; he fell a thousand feet below, to become a wreck of bones in the valley.

The anger of the Italian policeman, which he expressed volubly to Father Brown, was largely mixed with admiration. "It was like him to escape us at last," he said. "*He* was a great brigand if you like. This last trick of his I believe to be absolutely unprecedented. He fled with the company's money to Italy, and actually got himself captured by sham brigands in his own pay, so as to explain both the disappearance of the money and the disappearance of himself. That demand for ransom was really taken seriously by most of the police. But for years he's been doing things as good as that, quite as good as that. He will be a serious loss to his family."

Muscari was leading away the unhappy daughter, who held hard to him, as she did for many a year after. But even in that tragic wreck he could not help having a smile and a hand of half-mocking friendship for the indefensible Ezza Montano. "And where are you going next?" he asked him over his shoulder.

"Birmingham," answered the actor, puffing a cigarette. "Didn't I tell you I was a Futurist? I really do believe in those things if I believe in anything. Change, bustle and new things every morning. I am going to Manchester, Liverpool, Leeds, Hull, Huddersfield, Glasgow, Chicago—in short, to enlightened, energetic, civilised society!"

"In short," said Muscari, "to the real Paradise of Thieves."

THE DUEL OF DR. HIRSCH

M. Maurice Brun and M. Armand Armagnac were crossing the sunlit Champs Elysées with a kind of vivacious respectability. They were both short, brisk and bold. They both had black beards that did not seem to belong to their faces, after the strange French fashion which makes real hair look like artificial. M. Brun had a dark wedge of beard apparently affixed under his lower lip. M. Armagnac, by way of a change, had two beards; one sticking out from each corner of his emphatic chin. They were both young. They were both atheists, with a depressing fixity of outlook but great mobility of exposition. They were both pupils of the great Dr. Hirsch, scientist, publicist and moralist.

M. Brun had become prominent by his proposal that the common expression "Adieu" should be obliterated from all the French classics and a slight fine imposed for its use in private life. "Then," he said, "the very name of your imagined God will have echoed for the last time in the ear of man." M. Armagnac specialised rather in a resistance to militarism, and wished the chorus of the Marseillaise altered from "Aux armes, citoyens" to "Aux grèves, citoyens." But his anti-militarism was of a peculiar and Gallic sort. An eminent and very wealthy English Quaker, who had come to see him to arrange for the disarmament of the whole planet, was rather distressed by Armagnac's proposal that (by way of beginning) the soldiers should shoot their officers.

And indeed it was in this regard that the two men differed most from their leader and father in philosophy. Dr. Hirsch, though born in France and covered with the most triumphant favours of French education, was temperamentally of another type; mild, dreamy, humane, and, despite his sceptical system, not devoid of transcendentalism. He was, in short, more like a German than a Frenchman; and much as they admired him, something in the subconsciousness of these Gauls was irritated at his pleading for peace in so peaceful a manner. To their party throughout Europe, however, Paul Hirsch was a saint of science. His large and daring cosmic theories advertised his austere life and innocent, if somewhat frigid, morality; he held something of the position of Darwin doubled with the position of Tolstoy. But he was neither an anarchist nor an antipatriot; his views on disarmament were moderate and evolutionary—the Republican Government put considerable confidence in him as to various chemical improvements. He had lately even discovered a noiseless explosive, the secret of which the Government was carefully guarding.

His house stood in a handsome street near the Elysée—a street which in that strong summer seemed almost as full of foliage as the park itself; a row of chestnuts shattered the sunshine, interrupted only in one place where a large café ran out into the street. Almost opposite to this were the white and green blinds of the great scientist's house, an iron balcony, also painted green, running along in front of the first-floor windows. Beneath this was the entrance into a kind of court, gay with shrubs and tiles, into which the two Frenchmen passed in animated talk.

The door was opened to them by the doctor's old servant Simon, who might very well have passed for a doctor himself, having a strict suit of black, spectacles, grey hair, and a confidential manner. In fact, he was a far more presentable man of science than his master Dr. Hirsch, who was a forked radish of a fellow, with just enough bulb of a head to make his body insignificant. With all the gravity of a great physician handling a prescription, he handed a letter to M. Armagnac. That gentleman ripped it up with a racial impatience, and rapidly read the following:

"I cannot come down to speak to you. There is a man in this house whom I refuse to meet. He is a Chauvinist officer, Dubosc. He is sitting on the stairs. He has been kicking the furniture about in all the other rooms; I have locked myself in my study, opposite that café. If you love me, go over to the café and wait at one of the tables outside. I will try to send him over to you. I want you to answer him and deal with him. I cannot meet him myself. I cannot: I will not.

"There is going to be another Dreyfus case.

"P. HIRSCH."

M. Armagnac looked at M. Brun. M. Brun borrowed the letter, read it, and looked at M. Armagnac. Then both betook themselves briskly to one of the little tables under the chestnuts opposite, where they procured two tall glasses of horrible green absinthe, which they could drink apparently in any weather and at any time. Otherwise the café seemed empty, except for one soldier drinking coffee at one table, and at another a large man drinking a small syrup and a priest drinking nothing.

Maurice Brun cleared his throat and said, "Of course we must help the master in every way, but —"

There was an abrupt silence, and Armagnac said, "He may have excellent reasons for not meeting the man himself, but —"

Before either could complete a sentence, it was evident that the invader had been expelled from the house opposite. The shrubs under the archway swayed and burst apart, as that unwelcome guest was shot out of them like a cannon-ball.

He was a sturdy figure in a small and tilted Tyrolean felt hat, a figure that had indeed something generally Tyrolean about it. The man's shoulders were big and broad, but his legs were neat and active in knee-breeches and knitted stockings. His face was brown like a nut; he had very bright and restless brown eyes; his dark hair was brushed back stiffly in front and cropped close behind, outlining a square and powerful skull; and he had a huge black moustache like the horns of a bison. Such a substantial head is generally based on a bull neck; but this was hidden by a big coloured scarf, swathed round up the man's ears and falling in front inside his jacket like a sort of fancy waistcoat. It was a scarf of strong dead colours, dark red and old gold and purple, probably of Oriental fabrication. Altogether the man had something a shade barbaric about him; more like a Hungarian squire than an ordinary French officer. His French, however, was obviously that of a native; and his French patriotism was so impulsive as to be slightly absurd. His first act when he burst out of the archway was to call in a clarion voice down the street, "Are there any Frenchmen here?" as if he were calling for Christians in Mecca.

Armagnac and Brun instantly stood up; but they were too late. Men were already running from the street corners; there was a small but ever-clustering crowd. With the prompt French instinct for the politics of the street, the man with the black moustache had already run across to a corner of the café, sprung on one of the tables, and seizing a branch of chestnut to steady himself, shouted as Camille Desmoulins once shouted when he scattered the oak-leaves among the populace.[1]

"Frenchmen!" he volleyed, "I cannot speak! God help me, that is why I am speaking! The fellows in their filthy parliaments who learn to speak also learn to be silent—silent as that spy cowering in the house opposite! Silent as he is when I beat on his bedroom door! Silent as he is now, though he hears my voice across this street and shakes where he sits! Oh, they can be silent eloquently—the politicians! But the time has come when we that cannot speak *must* speak. You are betrayed to the Prussians. Betrayed at this moment. Betrayed by that man. I am Jules Dubosc, Colonel of artillery, Belfort. We caught a German spy in the Vosges yesterday, and a paper was found on him—a paper I hold in my hand. Oh, they tried to hush it up; but I took it direct to the man who wrote it—the man in that house! It is in his hand. It is signed with his initials. It is a direction for finding the secret of this new Noiseless Powder. Hirsch invented it; Hirsch wrote this note about it. This note is in German, and was found in a German's pocket. 'Tell the man the formula for powder is in grey envelope in first drawer to the left of Secretary's desk, War Office, in red ink. He must be careful. P. H.'"

He rattled short sentences like a quick-firing gun, but he was plainly the sort of man who is either mad or right. The mass of the crowd was Nationalist, and already in threatening uproar; and a minority of equally angry Intellectuals, led by Armagnac and Brun, only made the majority more militant.

"If this is a military secret," shouted Brun, "why do you yell about it in the street?"

"I will tell you why I do!" roared Dubosc above the roaring crowd. "I went to this man in straight and civil style. If he had any explanation, it could have been given in complete confidence. He refuses to

---

[1] Camille Desmoulins (1760–1794), the most notable of Parisian tabletop orators on the eve of the French Revolution, wore an identifying knot of leaves in his hat, which was then imitated in the green cockade of the citizens' militia.

explain. He refers me to two strangers in a café as to two flunkeys. He has thrown me out of the house, but I am going back into it, with the people of Paris behind me!"

A shout seemed to shake the very façade of mansions and two stones flew, one breaking a window above the balcony. The indignant Colonel plunged once more under the archway and was heard crying and thundering inside. Every instant the human sea grew wider and wider; it surged up against the rails and steps of the traitor's house; it was already certain that the place would be burst into like the Bastille, when the broken French window opened and Dr. Hirsch came out on the balcony. For an instant the fury half turned to laughter; for he was an absurd figure in such a scene. His long bare neck and sloping shoulders were the shape of a champagne bottle, but that was the only festive thing about him. His coat hung on him as on a peg; he wore his carrot-coloured hair long and weedy; his cheeks and chin were fully fringed with one of those irritating beards that begin far from the mouth. He was very pale, and he wore blue spectacles.

Livid as he was, he spoke with a sort of prim decision; so that the mob fell silent in the middle of his third sentence.

"... only two things to say to you now. The first is to my foes, the second to my friends. To my foes I say: It is true I will not meet M. Dubosc, though he is storming outside this very room. It is true I have asked two other men to confront him for me. And I will tell you why! Because I will not and must not see him—because it would be against all rules of dignity and honour to see him. Before I am triumphantly cleared before a court, there is another arbitration this gentleman owes me as a gentleman; and in referring him to my seconds I am strictly —"

Armagnac and Brun were waving their hats wildly, and even the Doctor's enemies roared applause at this unexpected defiance. Once more a few sentences were inaudible, but they could hear him say, "To my friends—I myself should always prefer weapons purely intellectual, and to these an evolved humanity will certainly confine itself. But our own most precious truth is the fundamental force of matter and heredity. My books are successful; my theories are unrefuted; but I suffer in politics from a prejudice almost physical in the French. I cannot speak like Clemenceau and Déroulède, for their words are like echoes of their pistols.[2] The French ask for a duellist as the English ask for a sportsman. Well, I give my proofs: I will pay this barbaric bribe, and then go back to reason for the rest of my life."

Two men were instantly found in the crowd itself to offer their services to Colonel Dubosc, who came out presently, satisfied. One was the common soldier with the coffee, who said simply, "I will act for you, sir. I am the Duc de Valognes." The other was the big man, whom his friend the priest sought at first to dissuade; and then walked away alone.

In the early evening a light dinner was spread at the back of the Café Charlemagne. Though unroofed by any glass or gilt plaster, the guests were nearly all under a delicate and irregular roof of leaves; for the ornamental trees stood so thick around and among the tables as to give something of the dimness and the dazzle of a small orchard. At one of the central tables a very stumpy little priest sat in complete solitude and applied himself to a pile of whitebait with the gravest sort of enjoyment. His daily living being very plain, he had a peculiar taste for sudden and isolated luxuries; he was an abstemious epicure. He did not lift his eyes from his plate, round which red pepper, lemons, brown bread and butter, etc., were rigidly ranked, until a tall shadow fell across the table, and his friend Flambeau sat down opposite. Flambeau was gloomy.

"I'm afraid I must chuck this business," said he heavily; "I'm all on the side of the French soldiers like Dubosc, and I'm all against the French atheists like Hirsch. But it seems to me in this case we've made a mistake. The Duke and I thought it as well to investigate the charge, and I must say I'm glad we did."

"Is the paper a forgery, then?" asked the priest.

"That's just the odd thing," replied Flambeau. "It's exactly like Hirsch's writing, and nobody can point out any mistake in it. But it wasn't written by Hirsch. If he's a French patriot he didn't write

---

[2] Dr. Hirsch links the statesman Georges Clemenceau (1841–1929) with the soldier-journalist Paul Déroulède (1846–1914) because the two were both combative orators with a reputation for dueling, and, indeed, had once dueled one another.

it, because it gives information to Germany. And if he's a German spy he didn't write it, well—because it doesn't give information to Germany."

"You mean the information is wrong?" asked Father Brown.

"Wrong," replied the other, "and wrong exactly where Doctor Hirsch would have been right—about the hiding-place of his own secret formula in his own official department. By favour of Hirsch and the authorities, the Duke and I have actually been allowed to inspect the secret drawer at the War Office where the Hirsch formula is kept. We are the only people who have ever known it, except the inventor himself and the minister for War; but the Minister permitted it to save Hirsch from fighting. After that we really can't support Dubosc if his revelation is a mare's nest."

"And it is?" asked Father Brown.

"It is," said his friend gloomily. "It is a clumsy forgery by somebody who knew nothing of the real hiding-place. It says the paper is in the cupboard on the right of the Secretary's desk. As a fact, the cupboard with the secret drawer is some way to the left of the desk. It says the grey envelope contains a long document written in red ink. It isn't written in red ink, but in ordinary black ink. It's manifestly absurd to say that Hirsch can have made a mistake about a paper that nobody knew of but himself; or can have tried to help a foreign thief by telling him to fumble in the wrong drawer. I think we must chuck it up and apologise to old Carrots."

Father Brown seemed to cogitate; he lifted a little whitebait on his fork. "You are sure the grey envelope was in the left cupboard?" he asked.

"Positive," replied Flambeau. "The grey envelope—it was a white envelope really—was—"

Father Brown put down the small silver fish and the fork and stared across at his companion. "What?" he asked, in an altered voice.

"Well, what?" repeated Flambeau, eating heartily.

"It was *not* grey," said the priest. "Flambeau, you frighten me."

"What the deuce are you frightened of?"

"I'm frightened of a white envelope," said the other seriously. "If it had only just been grey! Hang it all, it might as well have been grey.

But if it *was* white, the whole business is black. The Doctor has been dabbling in some of the old brimstone after all."

"But I tell you he couldn't have written such a note!" cried Flambeau. "The note is utterly wrong about the facts. And, innocent or guilty, Dr. Hirsch knew all about the facts."

"The man who wrote that note knew all about the facts," said his clerical companion soberly. "He could never have got 'em so wrong without knowing about 'em. You have to know an awful lot to be wrong on every subject—like the devil."

"Do you mean —?"

"I mean a man telling lies on chance would have told some of the truth," said his friend firmly. "Suppose someone sent you to find a house with a green door and a blue blind, with a front garden but no back garden, with a dog but no cat, and where they drank coffee but not tea. You would say if you found no such house that it was all made up. But I say no. I say if you found a house where the door was blue and the blind green, where there was a back garden and no front garden, where cats were common and dogs instantly shot, where tea was drunk in quarts and coffee forbidden—then you would know you had found the house. The man must have known that particular house to be so accurately inaccurate."

"But what could it mean?" demanded the diner opposite.

"I can't conceive," said Brown; "I don't understand this Hirsch affair at all. As long as it was only the left drawer instead of the right, and red ink instead of black, I thought it must be the chance blunders of a forger, as you say. But three is a mystical number; it finishes things. It finishes this. That the direction about the drawer, the colour of ink, the colour of envelope, should *none* of them be right by accident, that *can't* be a coincidence. It wasn't."

"What was it, then? Treason?" asked Flambeau, resuming his dinner.

"I don't know that either," answered Brown, with a face of blank bewilderment. "The only thing I can think of.... Well, I never understood that Dreyfus case. I can always grasp moral evidence easier than the other sorts. I go by a man's eyes and voice, don't you know, and whether his family seems happy, and by what subjects he chooses—and avoids. Well, I was puzzled in the Dreyfus case. Not by the horrible things imputed both ways; I know (though it's not modern to say so) that human nature in the highest places is still capable of being Cenci or Borgia. No; what puzzled me was the *sincerity* of both parties. I don't mean the political parties; the rank and file are always roughly honest, and often duped. I mean the persons of the play. I mean the conspirators, if they were conspirators. I mean the traitor, if he was a traitor. I mean the men who *must* have known the truth. Now Dreyfus went on like a man who *knew* he was a wronged man. And yet the French statesmen and soldiers went on as if they *knew* he wasn't a wronged man, but simply a wrong 'un. I don't mean they behaved well, I mean they behaved as if they were sure. I can't describe these things; I know what I mean."

"I wish I did," said his friend. "And what has it to do with old Hirsch?"

"Suppose a person in a position of trust," went on the priest, "began to give the enemy information because it was false information. Suppose he even thought he was saving his country by misleading the foreigner. Suppose this brought him into spy circles, and little loans were made to him, and little ties tied on to him. Suppose he kept up his contradictory position in a confused way by never telling the foreign spies the truth, but letting it more and more be guessed. The better part of him (what was left of it) would still say, 'I have not helped the enemy; I said it was the left drawer.' The meaner part of him would already be saying, 'But they may have the sense to see that means the right.' I think it is psychologically possible—in an enlightened age, you know."

"It may be psychologically possible," answered Flambeau, "and it certainly would explain Dreyfus being certain he was wronged and his judges being sure he was guilty. But it won't wash historically, because Dreyfus's document (if it was his document) was literally correct."

"I wasn't thinking of Dreyfus," said Father Brown.

Silence had sunk around them with the emptying of the tables; it was already late, though the sunlight still clung to everything, as if accidentally entangled in the trees. In the stillness Flambeau shifted his seat sharply, making an isolated and echoing noise—and threw his elbow over the angle of it. "Well," he said, rather harshly, "if Hirsch is not better than a timid treason-monger. . . ."

"You mustn't be too hard on them," said Father Brown gently. "It's not entirely their fault; but they have no instincts. I mean those things that make a woman refuse to dance with a man or a man to touch an investment. They've been taught that it's all a matter of degree."

"Anyhow," cried Flambeau impatiently, "he's not a patch on my principal; and I shall go through with it. Old Dubosc may be a bit mad, but he's a sort of patriot after all."

Father Brown continued to consume whitebait.

Something in the stolid way he did so caused Flambeau's fierce black eyes to ramble over his companion afresh. "What's the matter with you?" Flambeau demanded. "Dubosc's all right in that way. You don't doubt him?"

"My friend," said the small priest, laying down his knife and fork in a kind of cold despair, "I doubt everything. Everything, I mean, that has happened today. I doubt the whole story, though it has been acted before my face. I doubt every sight that my eyes have seen since morning. There is something in this business quite different from the ordinary police mystery where one man is more or less lying and the other man more or less telling the truth. Here both men. . . . Well! I've told you the only theory I can think of that could satisfy anybody. It doesn't satisfy me."

"Nor me either," replied Flambeau frowning, while the other went on eating fish with an air of entire resignation. "If all you can suggest is that notion of a message conveyed by contraries, I call it uncommonly clever, but . . . well, what would you call it?"

"I should call it thin," said the priest promptly. "I should call it uncommonly thin. But that's the queer thing about the whole business. The lie is like a schoolboy's. There are only three versions, Dubosc's and Hirsch's and that fancy of mine. Either that note was written by a French officer to ruin a French official; or it was written by the French official to help German officers; or it was written by the French official to mislead German officers. Very well. You'd expect a secret paper passing between such people, officials

or officers, to look quite different from that. You'd expect, probably a cipher, certainly abbreviations; most certainly scientific and
strictly professional terms. But this thing's elaborately simple, like a
penny dreadful, 'In the purple grotto you will find the golden casket.' It looks as if ... as it if it were meant to be seen through at
once."

Almost before they could take it in a short figure in French uniform had walked up to their table like the wind, and sat down with a
sort of thump.

"I have extraordinary news," said the Duc de Valognes. "I have just
come from this Colonel of ours. He is packing up to leave the country, and he asks us to make his excuses *sur le terrain.*"

"What?" cried Flambeau, with an incredulity quite frightful—
"*apologise?*"

"Yes," said the Duke gruffly; "then and there—before everybody—
when the swords are drawn. And you and I have to do it while he is
leaving the country."

"But what *can* this mean?" cried Flambeau. "He can't be afraid of
that little Hirsch! Confound it!" he cried, in a kind of rational rage,
"nobody *could* be afraid of Hirsch!"

"I believe it's some plot!" snapped Valognes—"some plot of the
Jews and freemasons. It's meant to work up glory for Hirsch...."

The face of Father Brown was commonplace, but curiously con-
tented; it could shine with ignorance as well as with knowledge. But
there was always one flash when the foolish mask fell, and the wise
mask fitted itself in its place; and Flambeau, who knew his friend,
knew that his friend had suddenly understood. Brown said nothing,
but finished his plate of fish.

"Where did you last see our precious Colonel?" asked Flambeau,
irritably.

"He's round at the Hôtel Saint Louis by the Élysée, where we drove
with him. He's packing up, I tell you."

"Will he be there still, do you think?" asked Flambeau, frowning at
the table.

"I don't think he can get away yet," replied the Duke; "he's packing to go a long journey...."

"No," said Father Brown quite simply, but suddenly standing up, "for a very short journey. For one of the shortest, in fact. But we may still be in time to catch him if we go there in a motor-cab."

Nothing more could be got out of him until the cab swept round the corner by the Hôtel Saint Louis, where they got out, and he led the party up a side lane already in deep shadow with the growing dusk. Once when the Duke impatiently asked whether Hirsch was guilty of treason or not, he answered rather absently, "No; only of ambition—like Cæsar." Then he somewhat inconsequently added, "He lives a very lonely life; he has had to do everything for himself."

"Well, if he's ambitious, he ought to be satisfied now," said Flambeau rather bitterly. "All Paris will cheer him now our cursed Colonel has turned tail."

"Don't talk so loud," said Father Brown, lowering his voice; "your cursed Colonel is just in front."

The other two started and shrank farther back into the shadow of the wall, for the sturdy figure of their runaway principal could indeed be seen shuffling along in the twilight in front, a bag in each hand. He looked much the same as when they first saw him, except that he had changed his picturesque mountaineering knickers for a conventional pair of trousers. It was clear he was already escaping from the hotel.

The lane down which they followed him was one of those that seem to be at the back of things, and look like the wrong side of the stage scenery. A colourless continuous wall ran down one flank of it, interrupted at intervals by dull-hued and dirt-stained doors, all shut fast and featureless save for the chalk scribbles of some passing *gamin*. The tops of trees, mostly rather depressing evergreens, showed at intervals over the top of the wall, and beyond them in the grey and purple gloaming could be seen the back of some long terrace of tall Parisian houses, really comparatively close, but somehow looking as inaccessible as a range of marble mountains. On the other side of the lane ran the high gilt railings of a gloomy park.

Flambeau was looking round him in rather a weird way. "Do you know," he said, "there is something about this place that —"

"Hullo!" called out the Duke sharply, "that fellow's disappeared. Vanished, like a blasted fairy!"

"He has a key," explained their clerical friend. "He's only gone into one of these garden doors," and as he spoke they heard one of the dull wooden doors close again with a click in front of them.

Flambeau strode up to the door thus shut almost in his face, and stood in front of it for a moment, biting his black moustache in a fury of curiosity. Then he threw up his long arms and swung himself aloft like a monkey and stood on the top of the wall, his enormous figure dark against the purple sky, like the dark tree-tops.

The Duke looked at the priest. "Dubosc's escape is more elaborate than we thought," he said, "but I suppose he is escaping from France."

"He is escaping from everywhere," answered Father Brown.

Valognes's eyes brightened, but his voice sank. "Do you mean suicide?" he asked.

"You will not find his body," replied the other.

A kind of cry came from Flambeau on the wall above. "My God," he exclaimed in French, "I know what this place is now! Why, it's the back of the street where old Hirsch lives. I thought I could recognise the back of a house as well as the back of a man."

"And Dubosc's gone in there!" cried the Duke, smiting his hip. "Why, they'll meet after all!" And with sudden Gallic vivacity he hopped up on the wall beside Flambeau and sat there positively kicking his legs with excitement. The priest alone remained below, leaning against the wall, with his back to the whole theatre of events, and looking wistfully across to the park palings and the twinkling, twilight trees.

The Duke, however stimulated, had the instincts of an aristocrat, and desired rather to stare at the house than to spy on it; but Flambeau, who had the instincts of a burglar (and a detective), had already swung himself from the wall into the fork of a straggling tree from which he could crawl quite close to the only illuminated window in the back of the high dark house. A red blind had been pulled down over the light, but pulled crookedly, so that it gaped on one side, and by risking his neck along a branch that looked as treacherous as a twig, Flambeau could just see Colonel Dubosc walking about in a brilliantly lighted and luxurious bedroom. But close as Flambeau was to the house, he heard the words of his colleagues by the wall, and repeated them in a low voice.

"Yes, they will meet now after all!"

"They will never meet," said Father Brown. "Hirsch was right when he said that in such an affair the principals must not meet. Have you read a queer psychological story by Henry James, of two persons who so perpetually missed meeting each other by accident that they began to feel quite frightened of each other, and think it was fate? This is something of the kind, but more curious."

"There are people in Paris who will cure them of such morbid fancies," said Valognes vindictively. "They will jolly well have to meet if we capture them and force them to fight."

"They will not meet on the Day of Judgment," said the priest. "If God Almighty held the truncheon of the lists, if St. Michael blew the trumpet for the swords to cross—even then, if one of them stood ready, the other would not come."

"Oh, what does all this mysticism mean?" cried the Duc de Valognes, impatiently; "why on earth shouldn't they meet like other people?"

"They are the opposite of each other," said Father Brown, with a queer kind of smile. "They contradict each other. They cancel out, so to speak."

He continued to gaze at the darkening trees opposite, but Valognes turned his head sharply at a suppressed exclamation from Flambeau. That investigator, peering into the lighted room, had just seen the Colonel, after a pace or two, proceed to take his coat off. Flambeau's first thought was that this really looked like a fight; but he soon dropped the thought for another. The solidity and squareness of Dubosc's chest and shoulders was all a powerful piece of padding, and came off with his coat. In his shirt and trousers he was a comparatively slim gentleman, who walked across the bedroom to the bathroom with no more pugnacious purpose than that of washing himself. He bent over a basin, dried his dripping hands and face on a towel, and turned again so that the strong light fell on his face. His brown complexion had gone, his big black moustache had gone; he was clean-shaven and very pale. Nothing remained of the Colonel but his bright hawk-like, brown eyes. Under the wall Father Brown was going on in heavy meditation, as if to himself:

"It is all just like what I was saying to Flambeau. These opposites won't do. They don't work. They don't fight. If it's white instead of black, and solid instead of liquid, and so on all along the line—then there's something wrong, Monsieur, there's something wrong. One of these men is fair and the other dark, one stout and the other slim, one strong and the other weak. One has a moustache and no beard, so you can't see his mouth; the other has a beard and no moustache, so you can't see his chin. One has hair cropped to his skull, but a scarf to hide his neck; the other has low shirt collars, but long hair to hide his skull. It's all too neat and correct, Monsieur, and there's something wrong. Things made so opposite are things that cannot quarrel. Wherever the one sticks out the other sinks in. Like a face and a mask, like a lock and a key...."

Flambeau was peering into the house with a visage as white as a sheet. The occupant of the room was standing with his back to him, but in front of a looking-glass, and had already fitted round his face a sort of framework of rank red hair, hanging disordered from the head and clinging round the jaws and chin while leaving the mocking mouth uncovered. Seen thus in the glass, the white face looked like the face of Judas laughing horribly and surrounded by capering flames of hell. For a spasm Flambeau saw the fierce red-brown eyes dancing, then they were covered with a pair of blue spectacles. Slipping on a loose black coat, the figure vanished towards the front of the house. A few moments later a roar of popular applause from the street beyond announced that Dr. Hirsch had once more appeared upon the balcony.

THE MAN IN THE PASSAGE

Two men appeared simultaneously at the two ends of a sort of passage running along the side of the Apollo Theatre in the Adelphi. The evening daylight in the streets was large and luminous, opalescent and empty. The passage was comparatively long and dark, so each man could see the other as a mere black silhouette at the other end. Nevertheless, each man knew the other, even in that inky outline; for they were both men of striking appearance, and they hated each other.

The covered passage opened at one end on one of the steep streets of the Adelphi, and at the other on a terrace overlooking the sunset-coloured river. One side of the passage was a blank wall, for the building it supported was an old unsuccessful theatre restaurant, now shut up. The other side of the passage contained two doors, one at each end. Neither was what was commonly called the stage door; they were a sort of special and private stage doors, used by very special performers, and in this case by the star actor and actress in the Shakespearean performance of the day. Persons of that eminence often like to have such private exits and entrances, for meeting friends or avoiding them.

The two men in question were certainly two such friends, men who evidently knew the doors and counted on their opening, for each approached the door at the upper end with equal coolness and confidence. Not, however, with equal speed; but the man who walked fast was the man from the other end of the tunnel, so they both arrived before the secret stage door almost at the same instant. They saluted each other with civility, and waited a moment before one of them, the sharper walker, who seemed to have the shorter patience, knocked at the door.

In this and everything else each man was opposite and neither could be called inferior. As private persons, both were handsome, capable, and popular. As public persons, both were in the first public rank. But everything about them, from their glory to their good looks, was of a diverse and incomparable kind. Sir Wilson Seymour was the kind of man whose importance is known to everybody who knows. The more you mixed with the innermost ring in every polity or profession, the more often you met Sir Wilson Seymour. He was the one intelligent man on twenty unintelligent committees—on every sort of subject, from the reform of the Royal Academy to the project of bimetallism for Greater Britain. In the arts especially he was omnipotent. He was so unique that nobody could quite decide whether he was a great aristocrat who had taken up art, or a great artist whom the aristocrats had taken up. But you could not meet him for five minutes without realising that you had really been ruled by him all your life.

His appearance was "distinguished" in exactly the same sense; it was at once conventional and unique. Fashion could have found no fault with his high silk hat; yet it was unlike anyone else's hat—a little higher, perhaps, and adding something to his natural height. His tall, slender figure had a slight stoop, yet it looked the reverse of feeble. His hair was silver-grey, but he did not look old; it was worn longer than the common, yet he did not look effeminate; it was curly but it did not look curled. His carefully pointed beard made him look more manly and militant rather than otherwise, as it does in those old admirals of Velazquez with whose dark portraits his house was hung.[1] His grey gloves were a shade bluer, his silver-knobbed cane a shade longer than scores of such gloves and canes flapped and flourished about the theatres and the restaurants.

The other man was not so tall, yet would have struck nobody as short, but merely as strong and handsome. His hair also was curly, but fair and cropped close to a strong, massive head—the sort of head you break a door with, as Chaucer said of the Miller's. His military moustache and the carriage of his shoulders showed him as a soldier, but he had a pair of those peculiar, frank, and piercing blue eyes which are more common in sailors. His face was somewhat square, his jaw was square, his shoulders were square, even his jacket was square. Indeed, in the wild school of caricature then current, Mr. Max Beerbohm had represented him as a proposition in the fourth book of Euclid.

[1] A reference to Diego Velazquez (1599–1660), portrait painter for the Spanish royal court, and to his early style, which was somber and austere.

For he also was a public man, though with quite another sort of success. You did not have to be in the best society to have heard of Captain Cutler, of the siege of Hong-Kong, and the great march across China. You could not get away from hearing of him wherever you were; his portrait was on every other postcard; his maps and battles in every other illustrated paper; songs in his honour in every other music-hall turn or on every other barrel-organ. His fame, though probably more temporary, was ten times more wide, popular, and spontaneous than the other man's. In thousands of English homes he appeared enormous above England, like Nelson. Yet he had infinitely less power in England than Sir Wilson Seymour.

The door was opened to them by an aged servant or "dresser," whose broken-down face and figure and black shabby coat and trousers contrasted queerly with the glittering interior of the great actress's dressing-room. It was fitted and filled with looking-glasses at every angle of refraction, so that they looked like the hundred facets of one huge diamond—if one could get inside a diamond. The other features of luxury, a few flowers, a few coloured cushions, a few scraps of stage costume, were multiplied by all the mirrors into the madness of the Arabian Nights, and danced and changed places perpetually as the shuffling attendant shifted a mirror outwards or shot one back against the wall.

They both spoke to the dingy dresser by name, calling him Parkinson, and asking for the lady as Miss Aurora Rome. Parkinson said she was in the other room, but he would go and tell her. A shade crossed the brow of both visitors; for the other room was the private room of the great actor with whom Miss Aurora was performing, and she was of the kind that does not inflame admiration without inflaming jealousy. In about half a minute, however, the inner door opened, and she entered as she always did, even in private life, so that the very silence seemed to be a roar of applause, and one well deserved. She was clad in a somewhat strange garb of peacock green and peacock blue satins, that gleamed like blue and green metals, such as delight children and æsthetes, and her heavy, hot brown hair framed one of those magic faces which are dangerous to all men, but especially to boys and to men growing grey. In company with her male colleague, the great American actor, Isidore Bruno, she was producing a particularly poetical and fantastic interpretation of the *Midsummer Night's Dream*, in which the artistic prominence was given to Oberon and Titania, or in other words to Bruno and herself. Set in dreamy and exquisite scenery, and moving in mystical dances, the green costume, like burnished beetle-wings, expressed all the elusive individuality of an elfin queen. But when personally confronted in what was still broad daylight, a man looked only at the woman's face.

She greeted both men with the beaming and baffling smile which kept so many males at the same just dangerous distance from her. She accepted some flowers from Cutler, which were as tropical and expensive as his victories; and another sort of present from Sir Wilson Seymour, offered later on and more nonchalantly by that gentleman. For it was against his breeding to show eagerness, and against his conventional unconventionality to give anything so obvious as flowers. He had picked up a trifle, he said, which was rather a curiosity; it was an ancient Greek dagger of the Mycenean Epoch, and might well have been worn in the time of Theseus and Hippolyta. It was made of brass like all the Heroic weapons, but, oddly enough, sharp enough to prick anyone still. He had really been attracted to it by the leaf-like shape; it was as perfect as a Greek vase. If it was of any interest to Miss Rome or could come in anywhere in the play, he hoped she would —

The inner door burst open and a big figure appeared, who was more of a contrast to the explanatory Seymour than even Captain Cutler. Nearly six-foot-six, and of more than theatrical thews and muscles, Isidore Bruno, in the gorgeous leopard skin and golden-brown garments of Oberon, looked like a barbaric god. He leaned on a sort of hunting-spear, which across a theatre looked a slight, silvery wand, but which in the small and comparatively crowded room looked as plain as a pikestaff—and as menacing. His vivid, black eyes rolled volcanically, his bronzed face, handsome as it was, showed at that moment a combination of high cheekbones with set white teeth, which recalled certain American conjectures about his origin in the Southern plantations.

"Aurora," he began, in that deep voice like a drum of passion that had moved so many audiences, "will you —"

He stopped indecisively because a sixth figure had suddenly presented itself just inside the doorway—a figure so incongruous in the scene as to be almost comic. It was a very short man in the black uniform of the Roman secular clergy, and looking (especially in such a presence as Bruno's and Aurora's) rather like the wooden Noah out of an ark. He did not, however, seem conscious of any contrast, but said with dull civility, "I believe Miss Rome sent for me."

A shrewd observer might have remarked that the emotional temperature rather rose at so unemotional an interruption. The detachment of a professional celibate seemed to reveal to the others that they stood round the woman as a ring of amorous rivals; just as a stranger coming in with frost on his coat will reveal that a room is like a furnace. The presence of the one man who did not care about her increased Miss Rome's sense that everybody else was in love with her, and each in a somewhat dangerous way: the actor with all the appetite of a savage and a spoilt child; the soldier with all the simple selfishness of a man of will rather than mind; Sir Wilson with that daily hardening concentration with which old Hedonists take to a hobby; nay, even the abject Parkinson, who had known her before her triumphs, and who followed her about the room with eyes or feet, with the dumb fascination of a dog.

A shrewd person might also have noted a yet odder thing. The man like a black wooden Noah (who was not wholly without shrewdness) noted it with a considerable but contained amusement. It was evident that the great Aurora, though by no means indifferent to the admiration of the other sex, wanted at this moment to get rid of all the men who admired her and be left alone with the man who did not—did not admire her in that sense, at least; for the little priest did admire and even enjoy the firm feminine diplomacy with which she set about her task. There was, perhaps, only one thing that Aurora Rome was clever about, and that was one half of humanity—the other half. The little priest watched, like a Napoleonic campaign, the swift precision of her policy for expelling all while banishing none. Bruno, the big actor, was so babyish that it was easy to send him off in brute sulks, banging the door. Cutler, the British officer, was pachydermatous to ideas, but punctilious about behaviour. He would ignore all hints, but he would die rather than ignore a definite commission from a lady. As to old Seymour he had to be treated differently; he had to be left to the last. The only way to move him was to appeal to him in confidence as an old friend, to let him into the secret of the clearance. The priest did really admire Miss Rome as she achieved all these three objects in one selected action.

She went across to Captain Cutler and said in her sweetest manner, "I shall value all these flowers because they must be your favourite flowers. But they won't be complete, you know, without my favourite flower. *Do* go over to that shop round the corner and get me some lilies-of-the-valley, and then it will be *quite lovely*."

The first object of her diplomacy, the exit of the enraged Bruno, was at once achieved. He had already handed his spear in a lordly style like a sceptre to the piteous Parkinson, and was about to assume one of the cushioned seats like a throne. But at this open appeal to his rival there glowed in his opal eyeballs all the sensitive insolence of the slave; he knotted his enormous brown fists for an instant, and then, dashing open the door, disappeared into his own apartments beyond. But meanwhile Miss Rome's experiment in mobilising the British Army had not succeeded so simply, as seemed probable. Cutler had indeed risen stiffly and suddenly, and walked towards the door, hatless, as if at a word of command. But perhaps there was something ostentatiously elegant about the languid figure of Seymour leaning against one of the looking-glasses that brought him up short at the entrance, turning his head this way and that like a bewildered bulldog.

"I must show this stupid man where to go," said Aurora in a whisper to Seymour, and ran out to the threshold to speed the parting guest.

Seymour seemed to be listening, elegant and unconscious as was his posture, and he seemed relieved when he heard the lady call out some last instructions to the Captain, and then turn sharply and run laughing down the passage towards the other end, the end on the terrace above the Thames. Yet a second or two after, Seymour's brow darkened again. A man in his position has so many rivals, and he remembered that at the other end of the passage was the corresponding entrance to Bruno's private room. He did not lose his dignity;

he said some civil words to Father Brown about the revival of Byzantine architecture in the Westminster Cathedral, and then, quite naturally, strolled out himself into the upper end of the passage. Father Brown and Parkinson were left alone, and they were neither of them men with a taste for superfluous conversation. The dresser went round the room, pulling out looking-glasses and pushing them in again, his dingy dark coat and trousers looking all the more dismal since he was still holding the festive fairy spear of King Oberon. Every time he pulled out the frame of a new glass, a new black figure of Father Brown appeared; the absurd glass chamber was full of Father Browns, upside down in the air like angels, turning somersaults like acrobats, turning their backs to everybody like very rude persons.

Father Brown seemed quite unconscious of this cloud of witnesses, but followed Parkinson with an idly attentive eye till he took himself and his absurd spear into the farther room of Bruno. Then he abandoned himself to such abstract meditations as always amused him—calculating the angles of the mirrors, the angles of each refraction, the angle at which each must fit into the wall ... when he heard a strong but strangled cry.

He sprang to his feet and stood rigidly listening. At the same instant Sir Wilson Seymour burst back into the room, white as ivory. "Who's that man in the passage?" he cried. "Where's that dagger of mine?"

Before Father Brown could turn in his heavy boots, Seymour was plunging about the room looking for the weapon. And before he could possibly find that weapon or any other, a brisk running of feet broke upon the pavement outside, and the square face of Cutler was thrust into the same doorway. He was still grotesquely grasping a bunch of lilies-of-the-valley. "What's this?" he cried. "What's that creature down the passage? Is this some of your tricks?"

"My tricks!" hissed his pale rival, and made a stride towards him.

In the instant of time in which all this happened Father Brown stepped out into the top of the passage, looked down it, and at once walked briskly towards what he saw.

At this the other two men dropped their quarrel and darted after him, Cutler calling out, "What are you doing? Who are you?"

"My name is Brown," said the priest sadly, as he bent over something and straightened himself again. "Miss Rome sent for me, and I came as quickly as I could. I have come too late."

The three men looked down, and in one of them at least the life died in that late light of afternoon. It ran along the passage like a path of gold, and in the midst of it Aurora Rome lay lustrous in her robes of green and gold, with her dead face turned upwards. Her dress was torn away as in a struggle, leaving the right shoulder bare, but the wound from which the blood was welling was on the other side. The brass dagger lay flat and gleaming a yard or so away.

There was a blank stillness for a measurable time; so that they could hear far off a flower-girl's laugh outside Charing Cross, and someone whistling furiously for a taxicab in one of the streets off the Strand. Then the Captain, with a movement so sudden that it might have been passion or play-acting, took Sir Wilson Seymour by the throat.

Seymour looked at him steadily without either fight or fear. "You need not kill me," he said in a voice quite cold; "I shall do that on my own account."

The Captain's hand hesitated and dropped; and the other added with the same icy candour, "If I find I haven't the nerve to do it with that dagger, I can do it in a month with drink."

"Drink isn't good enough for me," replied Cutler, "but I'll have blood for this before I die. Not yours—but I think I know whose."

And before the others could appreciate his intention he snatched up the dagger, sprang at the other door at the lower end of the passage, burst it open, bolt and all, and confronted Bruno in his dressing-room. As he did so, old Parkinson tottered in his wavering way out of the door and caught sight of the corpse lying in the passage. He moved shakily towards it; looked at it weakly with a working face; then moved shakily back into the dressing-room again, and sat down suddenly on one of the richly cushioned chairs. Father Brown instantly ran across to him, taking no notice of Cutler and the colossal actor, though the room already rang with their blows and they began to struggle for the dagger. Seymour, who retained some practical sense, was whistling for the police at the end of the passage.

When the police arrived it was to tear the two men from an almost apelike grapple; and, after a few formal inquiries, to arrest Isidore Bruno upon a charge of murder, brought against him by his furious opponent. The idea that the great national hero of the hour had arrested a wrongdoer with his own hand doubtless had its weight with the police, who are not without elements of the journalist. They treated Cutler with a certain solemn attention, and pointed out that he had got a slight slash on the hand. Even as Cutler bore him back across tilted chair and table, Bruno had twisted the dagger out of his grasp and disabled him just below the wrist. The injury was really slight, but till he was removed from the room the half-savage prisoner stared at the running blood with a steady smile.

"Looks a cannibal sort of chap, don't he?" said the constable confidentially to Cutler.

Cutler made no answer, but said sharply a moment after, "We must attend to the ... the death ..." and his voice escaped from articulation.

"The two deaths," came in the voice of the priest from the farther side of the room. "This poor fellow was gone when I got across to him." And he stood looking down at old Parkinson, who sat in a black huddle on the gorgeous chair. He also had paid his tribute, not without eloquence, to the woman who had died.

The silence was first broken by Cutler, who seemed not untouched by a rough tenderness. "I wish I was him," he said huskily. "I remember he used to watch her wherever she walked more than—anybody. She was his air, and he's dried up. He's just dead."

"We are all dead," said Seymour in a strange voice, looking down the road.

They took leave of Father Brown at the corner of the road, with some random apologies for any rudeness they might have shown. Both their faces were tragic, but also cryptic.

The mind of the little priest was always a rabbit-warren of wild thoughts that jumped too quickly for him to catch them. Like the white tail of a rabbit he had the vanishing thought that he was certain of their grief, but not so certain of their innocence.

"We had better all be going," said Seymour heavily; "we have done all we can to help."

"Will you understand my motives," asked Father Brown quietly, "if I say you have done all you can to hurt?"

They both started as if guiltily, and Cutler said sharply, "To hurt whom?"

"To hurt yourselves," answered the priest. "I would not add to your troubles if it weren't common justice to warn you. You've done nearly everything you could do to hang yourselves, if this actor should be acquitted. They'll be sure to subpœna me; I shall be bound to say that after the cry was heard each of you rushed into the room in a wild state and began quarrelling about a dagger. As far as my words on oath can go, you might either of you have done it. You hurt yourselves with that; and then Captain Cutler must have hurt himself with the dagger."

"Hurt myself!" exclaimed the Captain, with contempt. "A silly little scratch."

"Which drew blood," replied the priest, nodding. "We know there's blood on the brass now. And so we shall never know whether there was blood on it before."

There was a silence; and then Seymour said, with an emphasis quite alien to his daily accent, "But I saw a man in the passage."

"I know you did," answered the cleric Brown, with a face of wood; "so did Captain Cutler. That's what seems so improbable."

Before either could make sufficient sense of it even to answer, Father Brown had politely excused himself and gone stumping up the road with his stumpy old umbrella.

As modern newspapers are conducted, the most honest and most important news is the police news. If it be true that in the twentieth century more space was given to murder than to politics, it is for the excellent reason that murder is a more serious subject. But even this would hardly explain the enormous omnipresence and widely distributed detail of "The Bruno Case," or "The Passage Mystery," in the Press of London and the provinces. So vast was the excitement that for some weeks the Press really told the truth; and the reports of examination and cross-examination, if interminable, even if intolerable, are at least reliable. The true reason, of course, was the coincidence of persons. The victim was a popular actress; the accused was a popular actor; and the accused had been caught red-handed, as it were, by the most popular soldier of the patriotic season. In those extraordinary circumstances the Press was paralysed into probity and accuracy; and the rest of this somewhat singular business can practically be recorded from the reports of Bruno's trial.

The trial was presided over by Mr. Justice Monkhouse, one of those who are jeered at as humourous judges, but who are generally much more serious than the serious judges, for their levity comes from a living impatience of professional solemnity; while the serious judge is really filled with frivolity, because he is filled with vanity. All the chief actors being of a worldly importance, the barristers were well balanced; the prosecutor for the Crown was Sir Walter Cowdray, a heavy but weighty advocate of the sort that knows how to seem English and trustworthy, and how to be rhetorical with reluctance. The prisoner was defended by Mr. Patrick Butler, K.C., who was mistaken for a mere *flâneur* by those who misunderstood the Irish character—and those who had not been examined by him. The medical evidence involved no contradictions, the doctor whom Seymour had summoned on the spot, agreeing with the eminent surgeon who had later examined the body. Aurora Rome had been stabbed with some sharp instrument such as a knife or dagger; some instrument, at least, of which the blade was short. The wound was just over the heart, and she had died instantly. When the first doctor saw her she could hardly have been dead for twenty minutes. Therefore when Father Brown found her she could hardly have been dead for three.

Some official detective evidence followed, chiefly concerned with the presence or absence of any proof of a struggle; the only suggestion of this was the tearing of the dress at the shoulder, and this did not seem to fit in particularly well with the direction and finality of the blow. When these details had been supplied, though not explained, the first of the important witnesses was called.

Sir Wilson Seymour gave evidence as he did everything else that he did at all—not only well, but perfectly. Though himself much more of a public man than the judge, he conveyed exactly the fine shade of self-effacement before the King's justice; and though everyone looked at him as they would at the Prime Minister or the Archbishop of

Canterbury, they could have said nothing of his part in it but that it was that of a private gentleman, with an accent on the noun. He was also refreshingly lucid, as he was on the committees. He had been calling on Miss Rome at the theatre; he had met Captain Cutler there; they had been joined for a short time by the accused, who had then returned to his own dressing-room; they had then been joined by a Roman Catholic priest, who asked for the deceased lady and said his name was Brown. Miss Rome had then gone just outside the theatre to the entrance of the passage, in order to point out to Captain Cutler a flower-shop at which he was to buy her some more flowers; and the witness had remained in the room, exchanging a few words with the priest. He had then distinctly heard the deceased, having sent the Captain on his errand, turn round laughing and run down the passage towards its other end, where was the prisoner's dressing-room. In idle curiosity as to the rapid movements of his friends, he had strolled out to the head of the passage himself and looked down it towards the prisoner's door. Did he see anything in the passage? Yes; he saw something in the passage.

Sir Walter Cowdray allowed an impressive interval, during which the witness looked down, and for all his usual composure seemed to have more than his usual pallor. Then the barrister said in a lower voice, which seemed at once sympathetic and creepy, "Did you see it distinctly?"

Sir Wilson Seymour, however moved, had his excellent brains in full working-order. "Very distinctly as regards its outline, but quite indistinctly—indeed not at all—as regards the details inside the outline. The passage is of such length that anyone in the middle of it appears quite black against the light at the other end." The witness lowered his steady eyes once more and added, "I had noticed the fact before, when Captain Cutler first entered it." There was another silence, and the judge leaned forward and made a note.

"Well," said Sir Walter patiently, "what was the outline like? Was it, for instance, like the figure of the murdered woman?"

"Not in the least," answered Seymour quietly.

"What did it look like to you?"

"It looked to me," replied the witness, "like a tall man."

Everyone in court kept his eyes riveted on his pen or his umbrella-handle or his book or his boots or whatever he happened to be looking at. They seemed to be holding their eyes away from the prisoner by main force; but they felt his figure in the dock, and they felt it as gigantic. Tall as Bruno was to the eye, he seemed to swell taller and taller when all eyes had been torn away from him.

Cowdray was resuming his seat with his solemn face, smoothing his black silk robes and white silk whiskers. Sir Wilson was leaving the witness-box, after a few final particulars to which there were many other witnesses, when the counsel for the defence sprang up and stopped him.

"I shall only detain you a moment," said Mr. Butler, who was a rustic-looking person with red eyebrows and an expression of partial slumber. "Will you tell his lordship how you knew it was a man?"

A faint, refined smile seemed to pass over Seymour's features. "I'm afraid it is the vulgar test of trousers," he said. "When I saw daylight between the long legs I was sure it was a man, after all."

Butler's sleepy eyes opened as suddenly as some silent explosion. "After all!" he repeated slowly. "So you did think first it was a woman?"

Seymour looked troubled for the first time. "It is hardly a point of fact," he said, "but if his lordship would like me to answer for my impression, of course I shall do so. There was something about the thing that was not exactly a woman and yet was not quite a man; somehow the curves were different. And it had something that looked like long hair."

"Thank you," said Mr. Butler, K.C., and sat down suddenly, as if he had got what he wanted.

Captain Cutler was a far less plausible and composed witness than Sir Wilson, but his account of the opening incidents was solidly the same. He described the return of Bruno to his dressing-room, the dispatching of himself to buy a bunch of lilies-of-the-valley, his return to the upper end of the passage, the thing he saw in the passage, his suspicion of Seymour, and his struggle with Bruno. But he could give little artistic assistance about the black figure that he and Seymour had seen. Asked about its outline, he said he was no art critic—with a somewhat too obvious sneer at Seymour. Asked if it was a man or a woman, he said it looked more like a beast—with a too obvious snarl at the prisoner. But the man was plainly shaken with sorrow and sincere anger, and Cowdray quickly excused him from confirming facts that were already fairly clear.

The defending counsel also was again brief in his cross-examination; although (as was his custom) even in being brief, he seemed to take a long time about it. "You used a rather remarkable expression," he said, looking at Cutler sleepily. "What do you mean by saying that it looked more like a beast than a man or a woman?"

Cutler seemed seriously agitated. "Perhaps I oughtn't to have said that," he said, "but when the brute has huge humped shoulders like a chimpanzee, and bristles sticking out of its head like a pig —"

Mr. Butler cut short his curious impatience in the middle. "Never mind whether its hair was like a pig's," he said, "was it like a woman's?"

"A woman's!" cried the soldier. "Great Scott, no!"

"The last witness said it was," commented the counsel, with unscrupulous swiftness. "And did the figure have any of those serpentine and semi-feminine curves to which eloquent allusion has been made? No? No feminine curves? The figure, if I understand you, was rather heavy and square than otherwise?"

"He may have been bending forward," said Cutler, in a hoarse and rather faint voice.

"Or again, he may not," said Mr. Butler, and sat down suddenly for the second time.

The third witness called by Sir Walter Cowdray was the little Catholic clergyman, so little compared with the others, that his head seemed hardly to come above the box, so that it was like cross-examining a child. But unfortunately Sir Walter had somehow got it into his head (mostly by some ramifications of his family's religion) that Father Brown was on the side of the prisoner, because the prisoner was wicked and foreign and even partly black. Therefore, he took Father Brown up sharply whenever that proud pontiff tried to explain anything; and told him to answer yes or no, and tell the plain facts without any jesuitry. When Father Brown began, in his simplicity, to say who he thought the man in the passage was, the barrister told him that he did not want his theories.

"A black shape was seen in the passage. And you say you saw the black shape. Well, what shape was it?"

Father Brown blinked as under rebuke; but he had long known the literal nature of obedience. "The shape," he said, "was short and thick, but had two sharp, black projections curved upwards on each side of the head or top, rather like horns, and —"

"Oh! the devil with horns, no doubt," ejaculated Cowdray, sitting down in triumphant jocularity. "It was the devil come to eat Protestants."

"No," said the priest dispassionately; "I know who it was."

Those in court had been wrought up to an irrational but real sense of some monstrosity. They had forgotten the figure in the dock and thought only of the figure in the passage. And the figure in the passage, described by three capable and respectable men who had all seen it, was a shifting nightmare: one called it a woman, and the other a beast, and the other a devil....

The judge was looking at Father Brown with level and piercing eyes. "You are a most extraordinary witness," he said, "but there is something about you that makes me think you are trying to tell the truth. Well, who was the man you saw in the passage?"

"He was myself," said Father Brown.

Butler, K.C., sprang to his feet in an extraordinary stillness, and said quite calmly, "Your lordship will allow me to cross-examine?" And then, without stopping, he shot at Brown the apparently disconnected question, "You have heard about this dagger; you know the experts say the crime was committed with a short blade?"

"A short blade," assented Brown, nodding solemnly like an owl, "but a very long hilt."

Before the audience could quite dismiss the idea that the priest had really seen himself doing murder with a short dagger with a long hilt (which seemed somehow to make it more horrible), he had himself hurried on to explain.

"I mean daggers aren't the only things with short blades. Spears have short blades. And spears catch at the end of the steel just like daggers, if they're that sort of fancy spear they had in theatres; like the spear poor old Parkinson killed his wife with, just when she'd sent for me to settle their family troubles—and I came just too late, God for-give me! But he died penitent—he just died of being penitent. He couldn't bear what he'd done."

The general impression in court was that the little priest, who was gabbling away, had literally gone mad in the box. But the judge still looked at him with bright and steady eyes of interest; and the counsel for the defence went on with his questions, unperturbed.

"If Parkinson did it with that pantomime spear," asked Butler, "he must have thrust from four yards away. How do you account for signs of struggle, like the dress dragged off the shoulder?" He had slipped into treating this mere witness as an expert; but no one noticed it now.

"The poor lady's dress was torn," said the witness, "because it was caught in a panel that slid to just behind her. She struggled to free herself, and as she did so Parkinson came out of the prisoner's room and lunged with the spear."

"A panel?" repeated the barrister in a curious voice.

"It was a looking-glass on the other side," explained Father Brown. "When I was in the dressing-room I noticed that some of them could probably be slid out into the passage."

There was another vast and unnatural silence, and this time it was the judge who spoke. "So you really mean that, when you looked down that passage, the man you saw was yourself—in a mirror?"

"Yes, my lord; that was what I was trying to say," said Brown, "but they asked me for the shape; and our hats have corners just like horns, and so I —"

The judge leaned forward, his old eyes yet more brilliant, and said in specially distinct tones, "Do you really mean to say that when Sir Wilson Seymour saw that wild what-you-call-him with curves and a woman's hair and a man's trousers, what he saw was Sir Wilson Seymour?"

"Yes, my lord," said Father Brown.

"And you mean to say that when Captain Cutler saw that chim-panzee with humped shoulders and hog's bristles, he simply saw himself?"

"Yes, my lord."

The judge leaned back in his chair with a luxuriance in which it was hard to separate the cynicism and the admiration. "And can you tell us why," he asked, "you should know your own figure in a looking-glass, when two such distinguished men don't?"

Father Brown blinked even more painfully than before; then he stammered, "Really, my lord, I don't know ... unless it's because I don't look at it so often."

THE MISTAKE OF THE MACHINE

Flambeau and his friend the priest were sitting in the Temple Gardens about sunset; and their neighbourhood or some such accidental influence had turned their talk to matters of legal process. From the problem of the licence in cross-examination, their talk strayed to Roman and mediæval torture, to the examining magistrate in France and the Third Degree in America.

"I've been reading," said Flambeau, "of this new psychometric method they talk about so much, especially in America. You know what I mean; they put a pulsometer on a man's wrist and judge by how his heart goes at the pronunciation of certain words. What do you think of it?"

"I think it very interesting," replied Father Brown; "it reminds me of that interesting idea in the Dark Ages that blood would flow from a corpse if the murderer touched it."

"Do you really mean," demanded his friend, "that you think the two methods equally valuable?"

"I think them equally valueless," replied Brown. "Blood flows, fast or slow, in dead folk or living, for so many more million reasons than we can ever know. Blood will have to flow very funnily; blood will have to flow up the Matterhorn, before I will take it as a sign that I am to shed it."

"The method," remarked the other, "has been guaranteed by some of the greatest American men of science."

"What sentimentalists men of science are!" exclaimed Father Brown, "and how such more sentimental must American men of science be! Who but a Yankee would think of proving anything from heart-throbs? Why, they must be as sentimental as a man who thinks a woman is in love with him if she blushes! That's a test from the circulation of the blood, discovered by the immortal Harvey; and a jolly rotten test, too."

"But surely," insisted Flambeau, "it might point pretty straight at something or other."

"There's a disadvantage in a stick pointing straight," answered the other. "What is it? Why, the other end of the stick always points the opposite way. It depends whether you get hold of the stick by the right end. I saw the thing done once and I've never believed in it since." And he proceeded to tell the story of his disillusionment:

It happened nearly twenty years before, when he was chaplain to his co-religionists in a prison in Chicago—where the Irish population displayed a capacity both for crime and penitence which kept him tolerably busy. The official second-in-command under the Governor was an ex-detective named Greywood Usher, a cadaverous, careful-spoken Yankee philosopher, occasionally varying a very rigid visage with an odd apologetic grimace. He liked Father Brown in a slightly patronising way; and Father Brown liked him, though he heartily disliked his theories. His theories were extremely complicated and were held with extreme simplicity.

One evening he had sent for the priest, who, according to his custom, took a seat in silence at a table piled and littered with papers, and waited. The official selected from the papers a scrap of newspaper cutting, which he handed across to the cleric, who read it gravely. It appeared to be an extract from one of the pinkest of American Society papers, and ran as follows:

"Society's brightest widower is once more on the Freak Dinner stunt.[1] All our exclusive citizens will recall the Perambulator Parade Dinner, in which Last-Trick Todd, at his palatial home at Pilgrim's Pond, caused so many of our prominent *débutantes* to look even younger than their years. Equally elegant and more miscellaneous and large-hearted in social outlook was Last-Trick's show the year previous, the popular Cannibal Crush Lunch, at which the confections handed round were sarcastically moulded in the forms of human arms and legs, and during which more than one of our gayest mental gymnasts was heard offering to eat his partner. The witticism which will inspire this evening is as yet in Mr. Todd's pretty reticent intellect, or locked in the jewelled bosoms of our city's gayest leaders; but there is talk of a pretty

---

[1] The "Freak Dinner", a costumed party with an outlandish theme, became a fad during the years preceding the Great War. The practice was denounced by Chesterton in his *Illustrated London News* essay of March 24, 1906 (*CW* 37:148–52).

parody of the simple manners and customs at the other end of Society's scale. This would be all the more telling, as hospitable Todd is entertaining in Lord Falconroy, the famous traveller, a true-blooded aristocrat fresh from England's oak-groves. Lord Falconroy's travels began before his ancient feudal title was resurrected; he was in the Republic in his youth, and fashion murmurs a sly reason for his return. Miss Etta Todd is one of our deep-souled New Yorkers and comes into an income of nearly twelve hundred million dollars."

"Well," asked Usher, "does that interest you?"

"Why, words rather fail me," answered Father Brown. "I cannot think at this moment of anything in this world that would interest me less. And, unless the just anger of the Republic is at last going to electrocute journalists for writing like that, I don't quite see why it should interest you either."

"Ah!" said Mr. Usher dryly, and handing across another scrap of newspaper. "Well, does *that* interest you?"

The Paragraph was headed "Savage Murder of a Warder. Convict Escapes," and ran: "Just before dawn this morning a shout for help was heard in the Convict Settlement at Sequah in this State. The authorities, hurrying in the direction of the cry, found the corpse of the warder who patrols the top of the north wall of the prison, the steepest and most difficult exit, for which one man has always been found sufficient. The unfortunate officer had, however, been hurled from the high wall, his brains beaten out as with a club; and his gun was missing. Further inquiries showed that one of the cells was empty; it had been occupied by a rather sullen ruffian giving his name as Oscar Rian. He was only temporarily detained for some comparatively trivial assault; but he gave everyone the impression of a man with a black past and a dangerous future. Finally, when daylight had fully revealed the scene of murder, it was found that he had written on the wall above the body a fragmentary sentence, apparently with a finger dipped in blood, 'This was self-defence, and he had the gun. I meant no harm to him or any man but one. I am keeping the bullet for Pilgrim's Pond—O.R.' A man must have used most fiendish treachery or most savage and amazing bodily daring to have stormed such a wall in spite of an armed man."

"Well, the literary style is somewhat improved," admitted the priest cheerfully, "but still I don't see what I can do for you. I should cut a poor figure, with my short legs, running about this State after an athletic assassin of that sort. I doubt whether anybody could find him. The convict settlement at Sequah is thirty miles from here; the country between is wild and tangled enough, and the country beyond, where he will surely have the sense to go, is a perfect no-man's land tumbling away to the prairies. He may be in any hole or up any tree."

"He isn't in any hole," said the governor; "he isn't up any tree."

"Why, how do you know?" asked Father Brown, blinking.

"Would you like to speak to him?" inquired Usher.

Father Brown opened his innocent eyes wide. "He is here?" he exclaimed. "Why, how did your men get hold of him?"

"I got hold of him myself," drawled the American, rising and lazily stretching his lanky legs before the fire. "I got hold of him with the crooked end of a walking-stick. Don't look so surprised. I really did. You know I sometimes take a turn in the country lanes outside this dismal place; well, I was walking early this evening up a steep lane with dark hedges and grey-looking ploughed fields on both sides; and a young moon was up and silvering the road. By the light of it I saw a man running across the field towards the road; running with his body bent and at a good mile-race trot. He appeared to be much exhausted; but when he came to the thick black hedge he went through it as if it were made of spiders' webs; or rather (for I heard the strong branches breaking and snapping like bayonets) as if he himself were made of stone. In the instant in which he appeared up against the moon, crossing the road, I slung my hooked cane at his legs, tripping him and bringing him down. Then I blew my whistle long and loud, and our fellows came running up to secure him."

"It would have been rather awkward," remarked Brown, "if you had found he was a popular athlete practising a mile race."

"He was not," said Usher grimly. "We soon found out who he was; but I had guessed it with the first glint of the moon on him."

"You thought it was the runaway convict," observed the priest simply, "because you had read in the newspaper cutting that morning that a convict had run away."

"I had somewhat better grounds," replied the governor coolly. "I pass over the first as too simple to be emphasised—I mean that fashionable athletes do not run across ploughed fields or scratch their eyes out in bramble hedges. Nor do they run all doubled up like a crouching dog. There were more decisive details to a fairly well-trained eye. The man was clad in coarse and ragged clothes, but they were something more than merely coarse and ragged. They were so ill-fitting as to be quite grotesque; even as he appeared in black outline against the moonrise, the coat-collar in which his head was buried made him look like a hunchback, and the long loose sleeves looked as if he had no hands. It at once occurred to me that he had somehow managed to change his convict clothes for some confederates' clothes which did not fit him. Second, there was a pretty stiff wind against which he was running; so that I must have seen the streaky look of blowing hair, if the hair had not been very short. Then I remembered that beyond these ploughed fields he was crossing lay Pilgrim's Pond, for which (you will remember) the convict was keeping his bullet; and I sent my walking-stick flying."

"A brilliant piece of rapid deduction," said Father Brown; "but had he got a gun?"

As Usher stopped abruptly in his walk the priest added apologetically, "I've been told a bullet is not half so useful without it."

"He had no gun," said the other gravely, "but that was doubtless due to some very natural mischance or change of plans. Probably the same policy that made him change the clothes made him drop the gun; he began to repent the coat he had left behind him in the blood of his victim."

"Well, that is possible enough," answered the priest.

"And it's hardly worth speculating on," said Usher, turning to some other papers, "for we know it's the man by this time."

His clerical friend asked faintly, "But how?" And Greywood Usher threw down the newspapers and took up the two press-cuttings again.

"Well, since you are so obstinate," he said, "let's begin at the beginning. You will notice that these two cuttings have only one thing in common, which is the mention of Pilgrim's Pond, the estate, as you know, of the millionaire Ireton Todd. You also know that he is a remarkable character; one of those that rose on stepping-stones—"

"Of our dead selves to higher things," assented his companion.[2] "Yes; I know that. Petroleum, I think."

"Anyhow," said Usher, "Last-Trick Todd counts for a great deal in this rum affair."

He stretched himself once more before the fire and continued talking in his expansive, radiantly explanatory style.

"To begin with, on the face of it, there is no mystery here at all. It is not mysterious, it is not even odd, that a jailbird should take his gun to Pilgrim's Pond. Our people aren't like the English, who will forgive a man for being rich if he throws away money on hospitals or horses. Last-Trick Todd has made himself big by his own considerable abilities; and there's no doubt that many of those on whom he has shown his abilities would like to show theirs on him with a shot-gun. Todd might easily get dropped by some man he'd never even heard of; some labourer he'd locked out, or some clerk in a business he'd busted. Last-Trick is a man of mental endowments and a high public character; but in this country the relations of employers and employed are considerably strained.

"That's how the whole thing looks supposing this Rian made for Pilgrim's Pond to kill Todd. So it looked to me, till another little discovery woke up what I have of the detective in me. When I had my prisoner safe, I picked up my cane again and strolled down the two or three turns of country road that brought me to one of the side entrances of Todd's grounds, the one nearest to the pool or lake after which the place is named. It was some two hours ago, about seven by this time; the moonlight was more luminous, and I could see the long white streaks of it lying on the mysterious mere with its grey, greasy, half-liquid shores in which they say our fathers used to make witches walk until they sank. I'd forgotten the exact tale; but you know the place I mean; it lies north of Todd's house towards the wilderness, and has two queer wrinkled trees, so dismal that they look more like huge

---

[2] Father Brown completes a phrase from Tennyson's "In Memoriam" (1850): "That men may rise on stepping-stones / Of their dead selves to higher things."

fungoids than decent foliage. As I stood peering at this misty pool, I fancied I saw the faint figure of a man moving from the house towards it, but it was all too dim and distant for one to be certain of the fact, and still less of the details. Besides, my attention was very sharply arrested by something much closer. I crouched behind the fence which ran not more than two hundred yards from one wing of the great mansion, and which was fortunately split in places, as if specially for the application of a cautious eye. A door had opened in the dark bulk of the left wing; and a figure appeared black against the illuminated interior—a muffled figure bending forward, evidently peering out into the night. It closed the door behind it, and I saw it was carrying a lantern, which threw a patch of imperfect light on the dress and figure of the wearer. It seemed to be the figure of a woman, wrapped up in a ragged cloak and evidently disguised to avoid notice; there was something very strange both about the rags and the furtiveness in a person coming out of those rooms lined with gold. She took cautiously the curved garden path which brought her within half a hundred yards of me; then she stood up for an instant on the terrace of turf that looks towards the slimy lake, and holding her flaming lantern above her head, she deliberately swung it three times to and fro as for a signal. As she swung it the second time a flicker of its light fell for a moment on her own face, a face that I knew. She was unnaturally pale, and her head was bundled in her borrowed plebeian shawl; but I am certain it was Etta Todd, the millionaire's daughter.

"She retraced her steps in equal secrecy and the door closed behind her again. I was about to climb the fence and follow, when I realised that the detective fever that had lured me into the adventure was rather undignified; and that in a more authoritative capacity I already held all the cards in my hand. I was just turning away, when a new noise broke on the night. A window was thrown up in one of the upper floors, but just round the corner of the house so that I could not see it; and a voice of terrible distinctness was heard shouting across the dark garden to know where Lord Falconroy was, for he was missing from every room in the house. There was no mistaking that voice. I have heard it on many a political platform or meeting of directors; it was Ireton Todd himself. Some of the others seemed to have gone to the lower windows or onto the steps, and were calling up to him that Falconroy had gone for a stroll down to the Pilgrim's Pond an hour before, and could not be traced since. Then Todd cried 'Mighty Murder!' and shut down the window violently; and I could hear him plunging down the stairs inside. Repossessing myself of my former and wiser purpose, I whipped out of the way of the general search that must follow; and returned here not much later than eight o'clock.

"I now ask you to recall that little Society paragraph which seemed to you so painfully lacking in interest. If the convict was not keeping the shot for Todd, as he evidently wasn't, it is most likely that he was keeping it for Lord Falconroy; and it looks as if he had delivered the goods. No more handy place to shoot a man than in the curious geological surroundings of that pool, where a body thrown down would sink through thick slime to a depth practically unknown. Let us suppose, then, that our friend with the cropped hair came to kill Falconroy and not Todd. But, as I have pointed out, there are many reasons why many people in America might want to kill Todd. There is no reason why anybody in America should want to kill an English lord newly landed, except for the one reason mentioned in the pink paper—that the lord is paying his attentions to the millionaire's daughter. Our crop-haired friend, despite his ill-fitting clothes, must be an aspiring lover.

"I know the notion will seem to you jarring and even comic; but that's because you are English. It sounds to you like saying the Archbishop of Canterbury's daughter will be married in St. George's, Hanover Square, to a crossing-sweeper on ticket-of-leave. You don't do justice to the climbing and aspiring power of our more remarkable citizens. You see a good-looking grey-haired man in evening dress with a sort of authority about him, you know he is a pillar of the State, and you fancy he had a father. You are in error. You do not realise that a comparatively few years ago he may have been in a tenement or (quite likely) in a jail. You don't allow for our national buoyancy and uplift. Many of our most influential citizens have not only risen recently, but risen comparatively late in life. Todd's daughter was fully eighteen when her father first made his pile; so there isn't really anything impossible in her having a hanger-on in low life; or even in her hanging on to him, as I think she must be doing, to judge by the lantern business. If so, the hand that held the lantern may not be unconnected with the hand that held the gun. This case, sir, will make a noise."

"Well," said the priest patiently, "and what did you do next?"

"I reckon you'll be shocked," replied Greywood Usher, "as I know you don't cotton to the march of science in these matters. I am given a good deal of discretion here, and perhaps take a little more than I'm given; and I thought it was an excellent opportunity to test that Psychometric Machine I told you about. Now, in my opinion that machine can't lie."

"No machine can lie," said Father Brown, "nor can it tell the truth."

"It did in this case, as I'll show you," went on Usher positively. "I sat the man in the ill-fitting clothes in a comfortable chair, and simply wrote words on a blackboard; and the machine simply recorded the variations of his pulse; and I simply observed his manner. The trick is to introduce some word connected with the supposed crime in a list of words connected with something quite different, yet a list in which it occurs quite naturally. Thus I wrote 'heron' and 'eagle' and 'owl,' and when I wrote 'falcon' he was tremendously agitated; and when I began to make an 'r' at the end of the word, that machine just bounded. Who else in this republic has any reason to jump at the name of a newly arrived Englishman like Falconroy except the man who's shot him? Isn't that better evidence than a lot of gabble from witnesses: the evidence of a reliable machine?"

"You always forget," observed his companion, "that the reliable machine always has to be worked by an unreliable machine."

"Why, what do you mean?" asked the detective.

"I mean Man," said Father Brown, "the most unreliable machine I know of. I don't want to be rude; and I don't think you will consider Man to be an offensive or inaccurate description of yourself. You say you observed his manner; but how do you know you observed it right? You say the words have to come in a natural way; but how do you know that you did it naturally? How do you know, if you come to that, that he did not observe your manner? Who is to prove that you were not tremendously agitated? There was no machine tied on to your pulse."

"I tell you," cried the American in the utmost excitement, "I was as cool as a cucumber."

"Criminals also can be as cool as cucumbers," said Brown, with a smile. "And almost as cool as you."

"Well, this one wasn't," said Usher, throwing the papers about. "Oh, you make me tired!"

"I'm sorry," said the other. "I only point out what seems a reasonable possibility. If you could tell by his manner when the word that might hang him had come, why shouldn't he tell from your manner that the word that might hang him was coming? I should ask for more than words myself before I hanged anybody."

Usher smote the table, and rose in a sort of angry triumph.

"And that," he cried, "is just what I'm going to give you. I tried the machine first just in order to test the thing in other ways afterwards and the machine, sir, is right."

He paused a moment and resumed with less excitement. "I rather want to insist, if it comes to that, that so far I had very little to go on except the scientific experiment. There was really nothing against the man at all. His clothes were ill-fitting, as I've said, but they were rather better, if anything, than those of the submerged class to which he evidently belonged. Moreover, under all the stains of his plunging through ploughed fields or bursting through dusty hedges, the man was comparatively clean. This might mean, of course, that he had only just broken prison; but it reminded me more of the desperate decency of the comparatively respectable poor. His demeanour was, I am bound to confess, quite in accordance with theirs. He was silent and dignified as they are; he seemed to have a big, but buried, grievance, as they do. He professed total ignorance of the crime and the whole question; and showed nothing but a sullen impatience for something sensible that might come to take him out of his meaningless scrape. He asked me more than once if he could telephone for a lawyer who had helped him a long time ago in a trade dispute, and in every sense acted as you would expect an innocent man to act. There was nothing against him in the world except that little finger on the dial that pointed to the change of his pulse.

"Then, sir, the machine was on its trial; and the machine was right. By the time I came with him out of the private room into the vestibule where all sorts of other people were awaiting examination, I think he had already more or less made up his mind to clear things up by something like a confession. He turned to me, and began to say in a low voice, 'Oh, I can't stick this any more. If you must know all about me——'

"At the same instant one of the poor women sitting on the long bench stood up, screaming aloud and pointing at him with her finger. I have never in my life heard anything more demoniacally distinct. Her lean finger seemed to pick him out as if it were a pea-shooter. Though the word was a mere howl, every syllable was as clear as a separate stroke on the clock.

"'Drugger Davis!' she shouted. 'They've got Drugger Davis!'

"Among the wretched women, mostly thieves and street-walkers, twenty faces were turned, gaping with glee and hate. If I had never heard the words, I should have known by the very shock upon his features that the so-called Oscar Rian had heard his real name. But I'm not quite so ignorant, you may be surprised to hear. Drugger Davis was one of the most terrible and depraved criminals that ever baffled our police. It is certain he had done murder more than once long before his last exploit with the warder. But he was never entirely fixed for it, curiously enough, because he did it in the same manner as those milder—or meaner—crimes for which he was fixed pretty often. He was a handsome, well-bred-looking brute, as he still is, to some extent; and he used mostly to go about with barmaids or shop-girls and do them out of their money. Very often, though, he went a good deal farther; and they were found drugged with cigarettes or chocolates and their whole property missing. Then came one case where the girl was found dead; but deliberation could not quite be proved, and, what was more practical still, the criminal could not be found. I heard a rumour of his having reappeared somewhere in the opposite character this time, lending money instead of borrowing it; but still to such poor widows as he might personally fascinate, and still with the same bad result for them. Well, there is your innocent man, and there is his innocent record. Ever since then four criminals and three warders have identified him and confirmed the story. Now, what have you got to say to my poor little machine after that? Hasn't the machine done for him? Or do you prefer to say that the woman and I have done for him?"

"As to what you've done for him," replied Father Brown, rising and shaking himself in a floppy way, "you've saved him from the electrical chair. I don't think they can kill Drugger Davis on that old vague story of the poison; and as for the convict who killed the warder, I suppose it's obvious that you haven't got him. Mr. Davis is innocent of that crime, at any rate."

"What do you mean?" demanded the other. "Why should he be innocent of that crime?"

"Why, bless us all!" cried the small man in one of his rare moments of animation, "why, because he's guilty of the other crimes! I don't know what you people are made of. You seem to think that all sins are kept together in a bag. You talk as if a miser on Monday were always a spendthrift on Tuesday. You tell me this man you have here spent weeks and months wheedling needy women out of small sums of money; that he used a drug at the best, and a poison at the worst; that he turned up afterwards as the lowest kind of moneylender, and cheated more poor people in the same patient and pacific style. Let it be granted—let us admit, for the sake of argument, that he did all this. If that is so, I will tell you what he didn't do. He didn't storm a spiked wall against a man with a loaded gun. He didn't write on the wall with his own hand, to say he had done it. He didn't stop to state that his justification was self-defence. He didn't explain that he had no quarrel with the poor warder. He didn't name the house of the rich man to which he was going with the gun. He didn't write in his own initials in a man's blood. Saints alive! Can't you see the whole character is different, in good and evil? Why, you don't seem to be like I am a bit. One would think you'd never had any vices of your own."

The amazed American had already parted his lips in protest when the door of his private and official room was hammered and rattled in an unceremonious way to which he was totally unaccustomed.

The door flew open. The moment before Greywood Usher had been coming to the conclusion that Father Brown might possibly be mad. The moment after he began to think he was mad himself. There burst and fell into his private room a man in the filthiest rags, with a greasy squash hat still askew on his head, and a shabby green shade shoved up from one of his eyes, both of which were glaring like a tiger's. The rest of his face was almost undiscoverable, being masked with a matted beard and whiskers through which the nose could barely thrust itself, and further buried in a squalid red scarf or handkerchief. Mr. Usher prided himself on having seen most of the roughest specimens in the State, but he thought he had never seen such a baboon dressed as a scarecrow as this. But, above all, he had never in all his placid scientific existence heard a man like that speak to him first.

"See here, old man Usher," shouted the being in the red handkerchief, "I'm getting tired. Don't you try any of your hide-and-seek on me; I don't get fooled any. Leave go of my guests, and I'll let up on the fancy clockwork. Keep him here for a split instant and you'll feel pretty mean. I reckon I'm not a man with no pull."

The eminent Usher was regarding the bellowing monster with an amazement which had dried up all other sentiments. The mere shock to his eyes had rendered his ears almost useless. At last he rang a bell with a hand of violence. While the bell was still strong and pealing, the voice of Father Brown fell soft but distinct.

"I have a suggestion to make," he said, "but it seems a little confusing. I don't know this gentleman—but—but I think I know him. Now, you know him—you know him quite well—but you don't know him—naturally. Sounds paradoxical, I know."

"I reckon the Cosmos is cracked," said Usher, and fell asprawl in his round office chair.

"Now, see here," vociferated the stranger, striking the table, but speaking in a voice that was all the more mysterious because it was comparatively mild and rational though still resounding. "I won't let you in. I want—"

"Who in hell are you?" yelled Usher, suddenly sitting up straight.

"I think the gentleman's name is Todd," said the priest.

Then he picked up the pink slip of newspaper.

"I fear you don't read the Society papers properly," he said, and began to read out in a monotonous voice, " 'Or locked in the jewelled bosoms of our city's gayest leaders; but there is talk of a pretty parody of the manners and customs of the other end of Society's scale.' There's been a big Slum Dinner up at Pilgrim's Pond tonight; and a man, one of the guests, disappeared. Mr. Ireton Todd is a good host, and has tracked him here, without even waiting to take off his fancy dress."

"What man do you mean?"

"I mean the man with the comically ill-fitting clothes you saw running across the ploughed field. Hadn't you better go and investigate him? He will be rather impatient to get back to his champagne, from which he ran away, in such a hurry, when the convict with the gun hove in sight."

"Do you seriously mean——" began the official.

"Why, look here, Mr. Usher," said Father Brown quietly, "you said the machine couldn't make a mistake; and in one sense it didn't. But the other machine did; the machine that worked it. You assumed that the man in rags jumped at the name of Lord Falconroy, because he was Lord Falconroy's murderer. He jumped at the name of Lord Falconroy because he *is* Lord Falconroy."

"Then why the blazes didn't he say so?" demanded the staring Usher.

"He felt his plight and recent panic were hardly patrician," replied the priest, "so he tried to keep the name back at first. But he was just going to tell it you, when" —and Father Brown looked down at boots— "when a woman found another name for him."

"But you can't be so mad as to say," said Greywood Usher, very white, "that Lord Falconroy was Drugger Davis."

The priest looked at him very earnestly but with a baffling and undecipherable face.

"I am not saying anything about it," he said. "I leave all the rest to you. Your pink paper says that the title was recently revived for him; but those papers are very unreliable. It says he was in the States in youth; but the whole story seems very strange. Davis and Falconroy are both pretty considerable cowards, but so are lots of other men. I would not hang a dog on my own opinion about this. But I think," he went on softly and reflectively, "I think you Americans are too modest. I think you idealise the English aristocracy—even in assuming it to be so aristocratic. You see a good-looking Englishman in evening-dress; you know he's in the House of Lords; and you fancy he has a father. You don't allow for our national buoyancy and uplift. Many of our most influential noblemen have not only risen recently, but—"

"Oh, stop it!" cited Greywood Usher, wringing one lean hand in impatience against a shade of irony in the other's face.

"Don't stay talking to this lunatic" cited Todd brutally. "Take me to my friend."

Next morning Father Brown appeared with the same demure expression, carrying yet another piece of pink newspaper.

"I'm afraid you neglect the fashionable press rather," he said, "but this cutting may interest you."

Usher read the headlines: "Last-Trick's Strayed Revellers: Mirthful Incident near Pilgrim's Pond." The paragraph went on, "A laughable occurrence took place outside Wilkinson's Motor Garage last night. A policeman on duty had his attention drawn by larrikins to a man in prison dress who was stepping with considerable coolness into the steering seat of a pretty high-toned Panhard; he was accompanied by a girl wrapped in a ragged shawl. On the police interfering, the young woman threw back the shawl, and all recognised Millionaire Todd's daughter, who had just come from the Slum Freak Dinner at the Pond, where all the choicest guests were in a similar *déshabillé*. She and the gentleman who had donned prison uniform were going for the customary joy-ride."

Under the pink slip Mr. Usher found a strip of a later paper, headed, "Astounding Escape of Millionaire's Daughter with Convict. She had Arranged Freak Dinner. Now Safe in —"

Mr. Greenwood Usher lifted his eyes, but Father Brown was gone.

THE HEAD OF CÆSAR

There is somewhere in Brompton or Kensington an interminable avenue of tall houses, rich but largely empty, that looks like a terrace of tombs. The very steps up to the dark front doors seem as steep as the sides of pyramids; and one would hesitate to knock at the door, lest it should be opened by a mummy. But a yet more depressing feature in the grey façade is its telescopic length and changeless continuity. The pilgrim walking down it begins to think he will never come to a break or a corner; but there is one exception—a very small one, but hailed by the pilgrim almost with a shout. There is a sort of mews between two of the tall mansions, a mere slit like the crack of a door by comparison with the street, but just large enough to permit a pigmy ale-house or eating-house, still allowed by the rich to their stable-servants, to stand in the angle. There is something cheery in its very dinginess and something free and elfin in its very insignificance. At the feet of those grey stone giants it looks like a lighted house of dwarfs.

Anyone passing the place during a certain autumn evening itself almost fairylike might have seen a hand pull aside the red half-blind which (along with some large white lettering) half hid the interior from the street, and a face peer out not unlike a rather innocent goblin's. It was, in fact, the face of one with the harmless human name of Brown, formerly priest of Cobhole in Essex, and now working in London. His friend Flambeau, a semi-official investigator, was sitting opposite him, making his last notes of a case he had cleared up in the neighbourhood. They were sitting at a small table, close up to the window, when the priest pulled the curtain back and looked out. He waited till a stranger in the street had passed the window, to let the curtain fall into its place again. Then his round eyes rolled to the large white lettering on the window above his head, and then strayed to the next table, at which sat only a navvy with beer and cheese, and a young girl with red hair and a glass of milk. Then (seeing his friend put away the pocket-book), he said softly:

"If you've got ten minutes, I wish you'd follow that man with the false nose."

Flambeau looked up in surprise; but the girl with the red hair also looked up, and with something that was stronger than astonishment. She was simply and even loosely dressed in light brown sacking stuff; but she was a lady, and even, on a second glance, a rather needlessly haughty one: "The man with the false nose!" repeated Flambeau. "Who's he?"

"I haven't a notion," answered Father Brown. "I want you to find out; I ask it as a favour. He went down there" —and he jerked his thumb over his shoulder in one of his undistinguished gestures— "and can't have passed three lamp-posts yet. I only want to know the direction."

Flambeau gazed at his friend for some time, with an expression between perplexity and amusement; and then, rising from the table, squeezed his huge form out of the little door of the dwarf tavern, and melted into the twilight.

Father Brown took a small book out of his pocket and began to read steadily; he betrayed no consciousness of the fact that the red-haired lady had left her own table and sat down opposite him. At last she leaned over and said in a low, strong voice, "Why do you say that? How do you know it's false?"

He lifted his rather heavy eyelids, which fluttered in considerable embarrassment. Then his dubious eye roamed again to the white lettering on the glass front of the public-house. The young woman's eyes followed his, and rested there also, but in pure puzzledom.

"No," said Father Brown, answering her thoughts. "It doesn't say 'Sela', like the thing in the psalms;[1] I read it like that myself when I was wool-gathering just now; it says 'Ales.' "

"Well?" inquired the staring young lady. "What does it matter what it says?"

---

[1] *Selah* is a Hebrew word of uncertain meaning found throughout the Psalms and in the Book of Habakkuk. It is thought to be a liturgical notation of some sort, perhaps indicating a pause for reflection.

His ruminating eye roved to the girl's light canvas sleeve, round the wrist of which ran a very slight thread of artistic pattern, just enough to distinguish it from a working dress of a common woman and make it more like the working dress of a lady art-student. He seemed to find much food for thought in this; but his reply was very slow and hesitant. "You see, madam," he said, "from outside the place looks—well, it is a perfectly decent place—but ladies like you don't—don't generally think so. They never go into such places from choice, except —"

"Well?" she repeated.

"Except an unfortunate few who don't go in to drink milk."

"You are a most singular person," said the young lady. "What is your object in all this?"

"Not to trouble you about it," he replied, very gently. "Only to arm myself with knowledge enough to help you, if ever you freely ask my help."

"But why should I need help?"

He continued his dreamy monologue. "You couldn't have come in to see *protégés*, humble friends, that sort of thing, or you'd have gone through into the parlour ... and you couldn't have gone in because you were ill, or you'd have spoken to the woman of the place, who's obviously respectable ... besides, you don't look ill in that way, but only unhappy.... This street is the only original long lane that has no turning; and the houses on both sides are shut up.... I could only suppose that you'd seen somebody coming whom you didn't want to meet; and found the public-house was the only shelter in this wilderness of stone.... I don't think I went beyond the licence of a stranger in glancing at the only man who passed immediately after.... And as I thought he looked like the wrong sort ... and you looked like the right sort.... I held myself ready to help if he annoyed you; that is all. As for my friend, he'll be back soon; and he certainly can't find out anything by stumping down a road like this.... I didn't think he could."

"Then why did you send him out?" she cried, leaning forward with yet warmer curiosity. She had the proud, impetuous face that goes with reddish colouring and a Roman nose, as it did in Marie Antoinette.

THE HEAD OF CÆSAR

He looked at her steadily for the first time, and said, "Because I hoped you would speak to me."

She looked back at him for some time with a heated face, in which there hung a red shadow of anger; then, despite her anxieties, humour broke out of her eyes and the corners of her mouth, and she answered almost grimly, "Well, if you're so keen on my conversation, perhaps you'll answer my question." After a pause she added, "I had the honour to ask you why you thought the man's nose was false."

"The wax always spots like that just a little in this weather," answered Father Brown with entire simplicity.

"But it's such a *crooked* nose," remonstrated the red-haired girl.

The priest smiled in his turn. "I don't say it's the sort of nose one would wear out of mere foppery," he admitted. "This man, I think, wears it because his real nose is so much nicer."

"But why?" she insisted.

"What is the nursery-rhyme?" observed Brown absent-mindedly. "There was a crooked man and he went a crooked mile... That man, I fancy, has gone a very crooked road by following his nose."

"Why, what's he done?" she demanded, rather shakily.

"I don't want to force your confidence by a hair," said Father Brown, very quietly. "But I think you could tell me more about that than I can tell you."

The girl sprang to her feet and stood quite quietly, but with clenched hands, like one about to stride away; then her hands loosened slowly, and she sat down again. "You are more of a mystery than all the others," she said desperately; "but I feel there might be a heart in your mystery."

"What we all dread most," said the priest in a low voice, "is a maze with *no* centre. That is why atheism is only a nightmare."

"I will tell you everything," said the red-haired girl doggedly, "except why I am telling you; and that I don't know."

She picked at the darned table-cloth and went on, "You look as if you knew what isn't snobbery as well as what is; and when I say that ours is a good old family, you'll understand it is a necessary part of the story; indeed, my chief danger is in my brother's high-and-dry notions, *noblesse oblige*, and all that. Well, my name is Christabel Carstairs; and my father was that Colonel Carstairs you've probably heard of, who made the famous Carstairs Collection of Roman coins. I could never describe my father to you; the nearest I can say is that he was very like a Roman coin himself. He was as handsome and as genuine and as valuable and as metallic and as out-of-date. He was prouder of his Collection than of his coat-of-arms—nobody could say more than that. His extraordinary character came out most in his will. He had two sons and one daughter. He quarrelled with one son, my brother Giles, and sent him to Australia on a small allowance. He then made a will leaving the Carstairs Collection, actually with a yet smaller allowance, to my brother Arthur. He meant it as a reward, as the highest honour he could offer, in acknowledgment of Arthur's loyalty and rectitude and the distinctions he had already gained in mathematics and economics at Cambridge. He left me practically all his pretty large fortune; and I am sure he meant it in contempt.

"Arthur, you may say, might well complain of this; but Arthur is my father over again. Though he had some differences with my father in early youth, no sooner had he taken over the Collection than he became like a pagan priest dedicated to a temple. He mixed up these Roman halfpence with the honour of the Carstairs family in the same stiff, idolatrous way as his father before him. He acted as if Roman money must be guarded by all the Roman virtues. He took no pleasures; he spent nothing on himself; he lived for the Collection. Often he would not trouble to dress for his simple meals; but pottered about among the corded brown-paper parcels (which no one else was allowed to touch) in an old brown dressing-gown. With its rope and tassel and his pale, thin, refined face, it made him look like an old ascetic monk. Every now and then, though, he would appear dressed like a decidedly fashionable gentleman; but that was only when he went up to the London sales or shops to make an addition to the Carstairs Collection.

"Now, if you've known any young people, you won't be shocked if I say that I got into rather a low frame of mind with all this; the frame of mind in which one begins to say that the Ancient Romans were all very well in their way. I'm not like my brother Arthur; I can't help enjoying enjoyment. I got a lot of romance and rubbish where I got my red hair, from the other side of the family. Poor Giles was the same; and I think the atmosphere of coins might count in excuse for him; though he really did wrong and nearly went to prison. But he didn't behave any worse than I did; as you shall hear.

"I come now to the silly part of the story. I think a man as clever as you can guess the sort of thing that would begin to relieve the monotony for an unruly girl of seventeen placed in such a position. But I am so rattled with more dreadful things that I can hardly read my own feelings; and don't know whether I despise it now as a flirtation or bear it as a broken heart. We lived then at a little seaside watering-place in South Wales, and a retired sea-captain living a few doors off had a son about five years older than myself, who had been a friend of Giles's before he went to the Colonies. His name does not affect my tale; but I tell you it was Philip Hawker because I am telling you everything. We used to go shrimping together, and said and thought we were in love with each other; at least he certainly said he was, and I certainly thought I was. If I tell you he had bronzed curly hair and a falconish sort of face, bronzed by the sea also, it's not for his sake, I assure you, but for the story; for it was the cause of a very curious coincidence.

"One summer afternoon, when I had promised to go shrimping along the sands with Philip, I was waiting rather impatiently in the front drawing-room, watching Arthur handle some packets of coins he had just purchased and slowly shunt them, one or two at a time, into his own dark study and museum which was at the back of the house. As soon as I heard the heavy door close on him finally I made a bolt for my shrimping-net and tam-o'-shanter, and was just going to slip out when I saw that my brother had left behind him one coin that lay gleaming on the long bench by the window. It was a bronze coin, and the colour, combined with the exact curve of the Roman nose and something in the very lift of the long, wiry neck, made the head of Cæsar on it the almost precise portrait of Philip Hawker. Then I suddenly remembered Giles telling Philip of a coin that was like him, and Philip wishing he had it. Perhaps you can fancy the wild, foolish thoughts with which my head went round; I felt as if I had had a gift from the fairies. It seemed to me that if I could only run away with this, and give it to Philip like a wild sort of wedding-ring, it would be a bond between us for ever; I felt a thousand such things at once. Then there yawned under me, like the pit, the enormous, awful notion of what I was doing; above all, the unbearable thought, which was like touching hot iron, of what Arthur would think of it. A Carstairs a thief; and a thief of the Carstairs treasure! I believe my brother could see me burned like a witch for such a thing. But then, the very thought of such fanatical cruelty heightened my old hatred of his dingy old antiquarian fussiness and my longing for the youth and liberty that called to me from the sea. Outside was strong sunlight with a wind; and a yellow head of some broom or gorse in the garden rapped against the glass of the window. I thought of that living and growing gold calling to me from all the heaths of the world—and then of that dead, dull gold and bronze and brass of my brother's growing dustier and dustier as life went by. Nature and the Carstairs Collection had come to grips at last.

"Nature is older than the Carstairs Collection. As I ran down the streets to the sea, the coin clenched tight in my fist, I felt all the Roman Empire on my back as well as the Carstairs pedigree. It was not only the old lion argent that was roaring in my ear, but all the eagles of the Cæsars seemed flapping and screaming in pursuit of me. And yet my heart rose higher and higher like a child's kite, until I came over the loose, dry sand-hills and to the flat wet sands, where Philip stood already up to his ankles in the shallow shining water, some hundred yards out to sea. There was a great red sunset; and the long stretch of low water, hardly rising over the ankle for half a mile, was like a lake of ruby flame. It was not till I had torn off my shoes and stockings and waded to where he stood, which was well away from the dry land, that I turned and looked round. We were quite alone in a circle of sea-water and wet sand; and I gave him the head of Cæsar.

"At the very instant I had a shock of fancy: that a man far away on the sand-hills was looking at me intently. I must have felt immediately after that it was a mere leap of unreasonable nerves; for the man was only a dark dot in the distance; and I could only just see that he was standing quite still and gazing, with his head a little on one side. There was no earthly logical evidence that he was looking at me; he might have been looking at a ship, or the sunset, or the seagulls, or at any of the people who still strayed here and there on the shore between us. Nevertheless, whatever my start sprang from was prophetic; for, as I gazed, he started walking briskly in a bee-line towards us across the wide wet sands. As he drew nearer and nearer I saw that he was dark and bearded, and that his eyes were marked with dark spectacles. He was dressed poorly but respectably in black, from the old black top hat on his head to the solid black boots on his feet. In spite of these he walked straight into the sea without a flash of hesitation, and came on at me with the steadiness of a travelling bullet.

"I can't tell you the sense of monstrosity and miracle I had when he thus silently burst the barrier between land and water. It was as if he had walked straight off a cliff and still marched steadily in mid-air. It was as if a house had flown up into the sky or a man's head had fallen off. He was only wetting his boots; but he seemed to be a demon disregarding a law of Nature. If he had hesitated an instant at the water's edge it would have been nothing. As it was, he seemed to look so much at me alone as not to notice the ocean. Philip was some yards away with his back to me, bending over his net. The stranger came on till he stood within two yards of me, the water washing halfway up to his knees. Then he said, with a clearly modulated and rather mincing articulation, 'Would it discommode you to contribute elsewhere a coin with a somewhat different superscription?'

"With one exception there was nothing definably abnormal about him. His tinted glasses were not really opaque, but of a blue kind common enough, nor were the eyes behind them shifty, but regarded me steadily. His dark beard was not really long or wild; but he looked rather hairy, because the beard began very high up in his face, just under the cheek-bones. His complexion was neither sallow nor livid, but on the contrary rather clear and youthful; yet this gave a pink-and-white wax look which somehow (I don't know why) rather increased the horror. The only oddity one could fix was that his nose, which was otherwise of a good shape, was just slightly turned sideways at the tip; as if when it was soft it had been tapped on one side with a toy hammer. The thing was hardly a deformity; yet I cannot tell you what a living nightmare it was to me. As he stood there in the sunset-stained water, he affected me as some hellish sea-monster just risen roaring out of a sea like blood. I don't know why a touch on the nose should affect my imagination so much. I think it seemed as if he could move his nose like a finger. And as if he had just that moment moved it.

"'Any little assistance,' he continued with the same queer, priggish accent, 'that may obviate the necessity of my communicating with the family.'

"Then it rushed over me that I was being blackmailed for the theft of the bronze piece; and all my merely superstitious fears and doubts were swallowed up in one overpowering practical question. How could he have found out? I had stolen the thing suddenly and on impulse; I was certainly alone; for I always made sure of being unobserved when I slipped out to see Philip in this way. I had not, to all appearance, been followed in the street; and if I had, they could not 'X-ray' the coin in my closed hand. The man standing on the sand-hills could no more have seen what I gave Philip than shoot a fly in one eye, like the man in the fairy-tale.[2]

"'Philip,' I cried helplessly, 'ask this man what he wants.'

"When Philip lifted his head at last from mending his net he looked rather red, as if sulky or ashamed; but it may have been only the exertion of stooping and the red evening light; I may have only had another of the morbid fancies that seemed to be dancing about me. He merely said gruffly to the man, 'You clear out of this.' And, motioning me to follow, set off wading shoreward without paying further attention to him. He stepped on to a stone breakwater that ran out from among the roots of the sand-hills, and so struck homeward; perhaps thinking our incubus would find it less easy to walk on such rough stones, green and slippery with seaweed, than we, who were young and used to it. But my persecutor walked as daintily as he talked; and he still followed me, picking his way and picking his phrases.

---

[2] A reference to a story in *Grimms' Fairy Tales* ("How Six Made Their Way in the World") in which a band of men with various superhuman skills—great strength, great speed, and so on—includes a marksman who can hit the left eye of a fly at a distance of two miles.

I heard his delicate, detestable voice appealing to me over my shoulder, until at last, when we had crested the sand-hills, Philip's patience (which was by no means so conspicuous on most occasions) seemed to snap. He turned suddenly, saying, 'Go back. I can't talk to you now.' And, as the man hovered and opened his mouth, Philip struck him a buffet on it that sent him flying from the top of the tallest sand-hill to the bottom. I saw him crawling out below, covered with sand.

"This stroke comforted me somehow, though it might well increase my peril; but Philip showed none of his usual elation at his own prowess. Though as affectionate as ever, he still seemed cast down; and before I could ask him anything fully, he parted with me at his own gate, with two remarks that struck me as strange. He said that, all things considered, I ought to put the coin back in the Collection; but that he himself would keep it 'for the present.' And then he added, quite suddenly and irrelevantly, 'You know Giles is back from Australia?'"

The door of the tavern opened and the gigantic shadow of the investigator Flambeau fell across the table. Father Brown presented him to the lady in his own slight, persuasive style of speech, mentioning his knowledge and sympathy in such cases; and almost without knowing, the girl was soon reiterating her story to two listeners. But Flambeau, as he bowed and sat down, handed the priest a small slip of paper. Brown accepted it with some surprise and read on it, "Cab to Wagga Wagga, 379, Mafeking Avenue, Putney." The girl was going on with her story.

"I went up the steep street to my own house with my head in a whirl; it had not begun to clear when I came to the doorstep, on which I found a milk-can—and the man with the twisted nose. The milk-can told me the servants were all out; for, of course, Arthur, browsing about in his brown dressing-gown in a brown study, would not hear or answer a bell. Thus there was no one to help me in the house, except my brother, whose help must be my ruin. In desperation I thrust two shillings into the horrid thing's hand, and told him to call again in a few days, when I had thought it out. He went off sulking, but more sheepishly than I had expected—perhaps he had been shaken by his fall—and I watched the star of sand splashed on his back receding down the road with a horrid vindictive pleasure. He turned a corner some six houses down.

"Then I let myself in, made myself some tea, and tried to think it out. I sat at the drawing-room window looking on to the garden, which still glowed with the last full evening light. But I was too distracted and dreamy to look at the lawns and flower-pots and flower-beds with any concentration. So I took the shock the more sharply because I'd seen it so slowly.

"The man or monster I'd sent away was standing quite still in the middle of the garden. Oh, we've all read a lot about pale-faced phantoms in the dark; but this was more dreadful than anything of that kind could ever be. Because, though he cast a long evening shadow, he still stood in warm sunlight. And because his face was not pale, but had that waxen bloom still upon it that belongs to a barber's dummy. He stood quite still, with his face towards me; and I can't tell you how horrid he looked among the tulips and all those tall, gaudy, almost hothouse-looking flowers. It looked as if we'd stuck up a wax-work instead of a statue in the centre of our garden.

"Yet almost the instant he saw me move in the window he turned and ran out of the garden by the back garden gate, which stood open and by which he had undoubtedly entered. This renewed timidity on his part was so different from the impudence with which he had walked into the sea, that I felt vaguely comforted. I fancied, perhaps, that he feared confronting Arthur more than I knew. Anyhow, I settled down at last, and had a quiet dinner alone (for it was against the rules to disturb Arthur when he was rearranging the museum), and, my thoughts a little released, fled to Philip and lost themselves, I suppose. Anyhow, I was looking blankly, but rather pleasantly than otherwise, at another window, uncurtained, but by this time black as a slate with the final night-fall. It seemed to me that something like a snail was on the outside of the window-pane. But when I stared harder, it was more like a man's thumb pressed on the pane; it had that curled look that a thumb has. With my fear and courage reawakened together, I rushed at the window and then recoiled with a strangled scream that any man but Arthur must have heard.

"For it was not a thumb; any more than it was a snail. It was the tip of a crooked nose, crushed against the glass; it looked white with the pressure; and the staring face and eyes behind it were at first invisible and afterwards grey like a ghost. I slammed the shutters together somehow, rushed up to my room, and locked myself in. But, even as I passed, I could almost swear I saw a second black window with something on it that was like a snail.

"It might be best to go to Arthur after all. If the thing was crawling close all around the house like a cat, it might have purposes worse even than blackmail. My brother might cast me out and curse me for ever; but he was a gentleman, and would defend me on the spot. After ten minutes' furious thinking, I went down, knocked at the door and then went in: to see the last and worst sight.

"My brother's chair was empty; and he was obviously out. But the man with the crooked nose was sitting waiting for his return, with his hat still insolently on his head, and actually reading one of my brother's books under my brother's lamp. His face was composed and occupied, but his nose-tip still had the air of being the most mobile part of his face, as if it had just turned from left to right like an elephant's proboscis. I had thought him poisonous enough while he was pursuing and watching me. But I think his unconsciousness of my presence was more frightful still.

"I think I screamed loud and long; but that doesn't matter. What I did next does matter: I gave him all the money I had, including a good deal in paper which, though it was mine, I dare say I had no right to touch. He went off at last, with hateful, tactful regrets all in long words; and I sat down, feeling ruined in every sense. And yet I was saved that very night by a pure accident. Arthur had gone off suddenly to London, as he so often did, for bargains; and returned, late but radiant, having nearly secured a treasure that was an added splendour even to the family Collection. He was so resplendent that I was almost emboldened to confess the abstraction of the lesser gem; but he bore down all other topics with his overpowering projects. Because the bargain might still miss fire any moment, he insisted on my packing at once and going up with him to lodgings he had already taken in Fulham, to be near the curio-shop in question. Thus, in spite of myself, I fled from my foe almost in the dead of night—but from Philip also. . . . My brother was often at the South Kensington Museum, and, in order to make some sort of secondary life for myself, I paid for a few lessons at the Art Schools. I was coming back from them this evening, when I saw the abomination of desolation walking alive down the long straight street and the rest is as this gentleman has said.

"I've got only one thing to say. I don't deserve to be helped; and I don't question or complain of my punishment; it is just, it ought to have happened. But I still question, with bursting brains, how it can have happened. Am I punished by miracle? or how *can* anyone but Philip and myself know I gave him a tiny coin in the middle of the sea?"

"It is an extraordinary problem," admitted Flambeau.

"Not so extraordinary as the answer," remarked Father Brown, rather gloomily. "Miss Carstairs, will you be at home if we call at your Fulham place in an hour and a half hence?"

The girl looked at him; and then rose and put her gloves on. "Yes," she said, "I'll be there"; and almost instantly left the place.

That night the detective and the priest were still talking of the matter as they drew near the Fulham house, a tenement strangely mean even for a temporary residence of the Carstairs family.

"Of course the superficial, on reflection," said Flambeau, "would think first of this Australian brother who's been in trouble before, who's come back so suddenly, and who's just the man to have shabby confederates. But I can't see how he can come into the thing by any process of thought, unless—"

"Well?" asked his companion patiently.

Flambeau lowered his voice. "Unless the girl's lover comes in too, and he would be the blacker villain. The Australian chap did know that Hawker wanted the coin. But I can't see how on earth he could know that Hawker had got it; unless Hawker signalled to him or his representative across the shore."

"That is true," assented the priest, with respect.

"Have you noted another thing?" went on Flambeau eagerly; "this Hawker hears his love insulted, but doesn't strike till *he's got to the soft sand-hills*, where he can be victor in a mere sham-fight. If he'd struck amid rocks and sea, he might have hurt his ally."

"That is true again," said Father Brown, nodding.

"And now, take it from the start. It lies between few people, but at least three. You want one person for suicide; two people for murder; but at least three people for blackmail."

"Why?" asked the priest softly.

"Well, obviously," cried his friend, "there must be one to be exposed; one to threaten exposure; and one at least whom exposure would horrify."

After a long ruminant pause, the priest said, "You miss a logical step. Three persons are needed as ideas. Only two are needed as agents."

"What can you mean?" asked the other.

"Why shouldn't a blackmailer," asked Brown, in a low voice, "threaten his victim with himself? Suppose a wife became a rigid teetotaller *in order* to frighten her husband into concealing *his* pub-frequenting, and then wrote him blackmailing letters in another hand, threatening to tell his wife! Why shouldn't it work? Suppose a father forbade a son to gamble, and then, following him in a good disguise, threatened the boy with his own sham paternal strictness! Suppose—but here we are, my friend."

"My God!" cited Flambeau; "you don't mean—"

An active figure ran down the steps of the house and showed under the golden lamplight the unmistakable head that resembled the Roman coin. "Miss Carstairs," said Hawker without ceremony, "wouldn't go in till you came."

"Well," observed Brown confidentially, "don't you think it's the best thing she can do to stop outside—with you to look after her? You see, I rather guess you have guessed it all yourself."

"Yes," said the young man, in an undertone, "I guessed on the sands and now I know; that was why I let him fall soft."

Taking a latchkey from the girl and the coin from Hawker, Flambeau let himself and his friend into the house, and passed into the outer parlour. It was empty of all occupants but one. The man whom Father Brown had seen pass the tavern was standing against the wall as if at bay; unchanged, save that he had taken off his black coat and was wearing a brown dressing-gown.

"We have come," said Father Brown politely, "to give back this coin to its owner." And he handed it to the man with the nose.

Flambeau's eyes rolled. "Is this man a coin-collector?" he asked.

"This man is Mr. Arthur Carstairs," said the priest positively, "and he is a coin-collector of a somewhat singular kind."

The man changed colour so horribly that the crooked nose stood out on his face like a separate and comic thing. He spoke, nevertheless, with a sort of despairing dignity. "You shall see, then," he said, "that I have not lost all the family qualities." And he turned suddenly and strode into an inner room, slamming the door.

"Stop him!" shouted Father Brown, bounding and half falling over a chair; and, after a wrench or two, Flambeau had the door open. But it was too late. In dead silence Flambeau strode across and telephoned for doctor and police.

An empty medicine bottle lay on the floor. Across the table the body of the man in the brown dressing-gown lay amid his burst and gaping brown-paper parcels; out of which poured and rolled, not Roman, but very modern English coins.

The priest held up the bronze head of Cæsar. "This," he said, "was all that was left of the Carstairs Collection."

After a silence he went on, with more than common gentleness, "It was a cruel will his wicked father made, and you see he did resent it a little. He hated the Roman money he had, and grew fonder of the real money denied him. He not only sold the Collection bit by bit, but sank bit by bit to the basest ways of making money—even to blackmailing his own family in a disguise. He blackmailed his brother from Australia for his little forgotten crime (that is why he took the cab to Wagga Wagga in Putney), he blackmailed his sister for the theft he alone could have noticed. And that, by the way, is why she had that supernatural guess when he was away on the sand-dunes. Mere figure and gait, however distant, are more likely to remind us of somebody than a well made-up face quite close."

There was another silence. "Well," growled the detective, "and so this great numismatist and coin-collector was nothing but a vulgar miser."

"Is there so great a difference?" asked Father Brown, in the same strange, indulgent tone. "What is there wrong about a miser that is not often as wrong about a collector? What is wrong, except ... thou shalt not make to thyself any graven image; thou shalt not bow down to them nor serve them, for I ... but we must go and see how the poor young people are getting on."

"I think," said Flambeau, "that, in spite of everything, they are probably getting on very well."

THE PURPLE WIG

Mr. Edward Nutt, the industrious editor of *The Daily Reformer*, sat at his desk, opening letters and marking proofs to the merry tune of a typewriter, worked by a vigorous young lady.

He was a stoutish, fair man, in his shirt-sleeves; his movements were resolute, his mouth firm and his tones final; but his round, rather babyish blue eyes had a bewildered and even wistful look that rather contradicted all this. Nor indeed was the expression altogether misleading. It might truly be said of him, as of many journalists in authority, that his most familiar emotion was one of continuous fear; fear of libel actions, fear of lost advertisements, fear of misprints, fear of the sack.

His life was a series of distracted compromises, between the proprietor of the paper (and of him), who was a senile soap-boiler with three ineradicable mistakes in his mind, and the very able staff he had collected to run the paper; some of whom were brilliant and experienced men and (what was even worse) sincere enthusiasts for the political policy of the paper.

A letter from one of these lay immediately before him; and rapid and resolute as he was, he seemed almost to hesitate before opening it. He took up a strip of proof instead, ran down it with a blue eye, and a blue pencil, altering the word "adultery" to the word "impropriety," and the word "Jew" to the word "Alien," rang a bell and sent it flying upstairs.

Then with a more thoughtful eye, he ripped open the letter from his more distinguished contributor, which bore a postmark of Devonshire, and ran as follows:

"DEAR NUTT,—As I see you're working Spooks and Dooks at the same time, what about an article on that rum business of the Eyres of Exmoor; or as the old women call it down here, the Devil's Ear of Eyre? The head of the family, you know, is the Duke of Exmoor; he is one of the few really stiff old Tory aristocrats left, a sound old crusted

tyrant it is quite in our line to make trouble about. And I think I'm
on the track of a story that will make trouble.

"Of course I don't believe in the old legend about James I; and as
for you, you don't believe in anything, not even in journalism. The
legend, you'll probably remember, was about the blackest business in
English history—the poisoning of Overbury by that witch's cat Frances
Howard, and the quite mysterious terror which forced the King to
pardon the murderers. There was a lot of alleged witchcraft mixed up
with it; and the story goes that a manservant listening at a keyhole
heard the truth in a talk between the King and Carr; and the bodily
ear with which he heard grew large and monstrous as by magic, so
awful was the secret. And though he had to be loaded with lands and
gold and made an ancestor of dukes, the elf-shaped ear is still recurrent in the family. Well, you don't believe in black magic; and if you
did, you couldn't use it for copy. If a miracle happened in your office,
you'd have to hush it up, now so many bishops are agnostics. But that
is not the point. The point is that there really *is* something queer
about Exmoor and his family; something quite natural, I dare say, but
quite abnormal. And the Ear is in it somehow, I fancy; either a symbol or a delusion or a disease or something. Another tradition says
that Cavaliers just after James I began to wear their hair long only to
cover the ear of the first Lord Exmoor. This also is no doubt fanciful.

"The reason I point it out to you is this: It seems to me that we
make a mistake in attacking aristocracy entirely for its champagne and
diamonds. Most men rather admire the nobs for having a good time,
but I think we surrender too much when we admit that aristocracy
has made even the aristocrats happy. I suggest a series of articles pointing out how dreary, how inhuman, how downright diabolist, is the
very smell and atmosphere of some of these great houses. There are
plenty of instances; but you couldn't begin with a better one than the
Ear of the Eyres. By the end of the week I think I can get you the
truth about it.—Yours ever, FRANCIS FINN."

Mr. Nutt reflected a moment, staring at his left boot; then he called
out in a strong, loud and entirely lifeless voice, in which every syllable
sounded alike, "Miss Barlow, take down a letter to Mr. Finn, please."

"DEAR FINN,—I think it would do; copy should reach us second post Saturday.—Yours, E. NUTT."

This elaborate epistle he articulated as if it were all one word; and Miss Barlow rattled it down as if it were all one word. Then he took up another strip of proof and a blue pencil, and altered the word "supernatural" to the word "marvellous," and the expression "shoot down" to the expression "repress."

In such happy, healthful activities did Mr. Nutt disport himself, until the ensuing Saturday found him at the same desk, dictating to the same typewriter, and using the same blue pencil on the first instalment of Mr. Finn's revelations. The opening was a sound piece of slashing invective about the evil secrets of princes, and despair in the high places of the earth. Though written violently, it was in excellent English; but the editor, as usual, had given to somebody else the task of breaking it up into sub-headings; which were of a spicier sort, as "Peeress and Poisons," and "The Eerie Ear," "The Eyres in their Eyrie," and so on through a hundred happy changes. Then followed the legend of the Ear, amplified from Finn's first letter, and then the substance of his later discoveries, as follows.

"I know it is the practice of journalists to put the end of the story at the beginning and call it a headline. I know that journalism largely consists in saying 'Lord Jones Dead' to people who never knew that Lord Jones was alive. Your present correspondent thinks that this, like many other journalistic customs, is bad journalism; and that The Daily Reformer has to set a better example in such things. He proposes to tell his story as it occurred, step by step. He will use the real names of the parties, who in most cases are ready to confirm his testimony. As for the headlines, the sensational proclamations—they will come at the end.

"I was walking along a public path that threads through a private Devonshire orchard and seems to point towards Devonshire cider, when I came suddenly upon just such a place as the path suggested. It was a long, low inn, consisting really of a cottage and two barns; thatched all over with the thatch that looks like brown and grey hair grown before history. But outside the door was a sign which called it the Blue Dragon; and under the sign was one of those long rustic tables that used to stand outside most of the free English inns, before teetotallers and brewers between them destroyed freedom. And at this table sat three gentlemen, who might have lived a hundred years ago.

"Now that I know them all better, there is no difficulty about disentangling the impressions; but just then they looked like three very solid ghosts. The dominant figure, both because he was bigger in all three dimensions, and because he sat centrally in the length of the table, facing me, was a tall, fat man dressed completely in black, with a rubicund, even apoplectic visage, but a rather bald and rather bothered brow. Looking at him again, more strictly, I could not exactly say what it was that gave me the sense of antiquity, except the antique cut of his white clerical necktie and the barred wrinkles across his brow.

"It was even less easy to fix the impression in the case of the man at the right end of the table, who, to say truth, was as commonplace a person as could be seen anywhere, with a round, brown-haired head and a round snub nose, but also clad in clerical black, of a stricter cut. It was only when I saw his broad curved hat lying on the table beside him that I realised why I connected him with anything ancient. He was a Roman Catholic priest.

"Perhaps the third man at the other end of the table, had really more to do with it than the rest, though he was both slighter in physical presence and more inconsiderate in his dress. His lank limbs were clad, I might also say clutched, in very tight grey sleeves and pantaloons; he had a long, sallow, aquiline face which seemed somehow all the more saturnine because his lanterns jaws were imprisoned in his collar and neckcloth more in the style of the old stock; and his hair (which ought to have been dark brown) was of an odd dim, russet colour which, in conjunction with his yellow face, looked rather purple than red. The unobtrusive yet unusual colour was all the more notable because his hair was almost unnaturally healthy and curling, and he wore it full. But, after all analysis, I incline to think that what gave me my first old-fashioned impression was simply a set of tall, old-fashioned wine-glasses, one or two lemons and two church-warden pipes. And also, perhaps, the old-world errand on which I had come.

"Being a hardened reporter, and it being apparently a public inn, I did not need to summon much of my impudence to sit down at the long table and order some cider. The big man in black seemed very learned, especially about local antiquities; the small man in black, though he talked much less, surprised me with a yet wider culture. So we got on very well together; but the third man, the old gentleman in the tight pantaloons, seemed rather distant and haughty, until I slid into the subject of the Duke of Exmoor and his ancestry.

"I thought the subject seemed to embarrass the other two a little; but it broke the spell of the third man's silence most successfully. Speaking with restraint and with the accent of a highly educated gentleman, and puffing at intervals at his long church-warden pipe, he proceeded to tell me some of the most horrible stories I have ever heard in my life: how one of the Eyres in the former ages had hanged his own father; and another had his wife scourged at the cart tail through the village; and another had set fire to a church full of children, and so on.

"Some of the tales, indeed, are not fit for public print; such as the story of the Scarlet Nuns, the abominable story of the Spotted Dog, or the thing that was done in the quarry. And all this red roll of impieties came from his thin, genteel lips rather primly than otherwise, as he sat sipping the wine out of his tall, thin glass.

"I could see that the big man opposite me was trying, if anything, to stop him; but he evidently held the old gentleman in considerable respect, and could not venture to do so at all abruptly. And the little priest at the other end of the table, though free from any such air of fear or embarrassment, looked steadily at the table, and seemed to listen to the recital with great pain—as well as he might.

"'You don't seem,' I said to the narrator, 'to be very fond of the Exmoor pedigree.'

"He looked at me a moment, his lips still prim, but whitening and tightening; then he deliberately broke his long pipe and glass on the table and stood up, the very picture of a perfect gentleman with the flaming temper of a fiend.

"'These gentlemen,' he said, 'will tell you whether I have cause to like it. The curse of the Eyres of old has lain heavy on this country, and many have suffered from it. They know there are none who have suffered from it as I have.' And with that he crushed a piece of the fallen glass under his heel, and strode away among the green twilight of the twinkling apple-trees.

"'That is an extraordinary old gentleman,' I said to the other two; 'do you happen to know what the Exmoor family has done to him? Who is he?'

"The big man in black was staring at me with the wild air of a baffled bull; he did not at first seem to take it in. Then he said at last, 'Don't you know who he is?'

"I reaffirmed my ignorance, and there was another silence; then the little priest said, still looking at the table, 'That is the Duke of Exmoor.'

"Then, before I could collect my scattered senses, he added equally quietly, but with an air of regularising things, 'My friend here is Doctor Mull, the Duke's librarian. My name is Brown.'

"'But,' I stammered, 'if that is the Duke, why does he damn all the old dukes like that?'

"'He seems really to believe,' answered the priest called Brown, 'that they have left a curse on him.' Then he added, with some irrelevance, 'That's why he wears a wig.'

"It was a few moments before his meaning dawned on me. 'You don't mean that fable about the fantastic ear?' I demanded. 'I've heard of it, of course, but surely it must be a superstitious yarn spun out of something much simpler. I've sometimes thought it was a wild version of one of those mutilation stories. They used to crop criminals' ears in the sixteenth century.'

"'I hardly think it was that,' answered the little man thoughtfully, 'but it is not outside ordinary science or natural law for a family to have some deformity frequently reappearing—such as one ear bigger than the other.'

"The big librarian had buried his big bald brow in his big red hands, like a man trying to think out his duty. 'No,' he groaned. 'You do the man a wrong after all. Understand, I've no reason to defend him, or even keep faith with him. He has been a tyrant to me as to everybody else. Don't fancy because you see him sitting simply here that he isn't a great lord in the worst sense of the word. He would fetch a man a mile to ring a bell a yard off—if it would summon another man three miles to fetch a matchbox three yards off. He must have a footman to carry his walking-stick; a body servant to hold up his opera-glasses —'

" 'But not a valet to brush his clothes,' cut in the priest, with a curious dryness, 'for the valet would want to brush his wig too.'

"The librarian turned to him, and seemed to forget my presence; he was strongly moved, and, I think, a little heated with wine. 'I don't know how you know it, Father Brown,' he said, 'but you are right. He lets the whole world do everything for him—except dress him. And that he insists on doing in a literal solitude like a desert. Anybody is kicked out of the house without a character who is so much as found near his dressing-room door.'

" 'He seems a pleasant old party,' I remarked.

" 'No,' replied Dr. Mull quite simply; 'and yet that is just what I mean by saying you are unjust to him after all. Gentlemen, the Duke does really feel the bitterness about the curse that he uttered just now. He does, with sincere shame and terror, hide under that purple wig something he thinks it would blast the sons of man to see. I know it is so; and I know it is not a mere natural disfigurement, like a criminal mutilation, or a hereditary disproportion in the features. I know it is worse than that; because a man told me who was present at a scene that no man could invent, where a stronger man than any of us tried to defy the secret, and was scared away from it.'

"I opened my mouth to speak, but Mull went on in oblivion of me, speaking out of the cavern of his hands. 'I don't mind telling you, Father, because it's really more defending the poor Duke than giving him away. Didn't you ever hear of the time when he very nearly lost all the estates?'

"The priest shook his head; and the librarian proceeded to tell the tale as he had heard it from his predecessor in the same post, who had been his patron and instructor, and whom he seemed to trust implicitly. Up to a certain point it was a common enough tale of the decline of a great family's fortunes; the tale of a family lawyer. This lawyer, however, had the sense to cheat honestly, if the expression explains itself. Instead of using funds he held in trust, he took advantage of the Duke's carelessness to put the family in a financial hole, in which it might be necessary for the Duke to let him hold them in reality.

"The lawyer's name was Isaac Green, but the Duke always called him Elisha; presumably in reference to the fact that he was quite bald, though certainly not more than thirty.[1] He had risen very rapidly, but from very dirty beginnings; being first a 'nark' or informer, and then a money-lender: but as solicitor to the Eyres he had the sense, as I say, to keep technically straight until he was ready to deal the final blow. The blow fell at dinner; and the old librarian said he should never forget the very look of the lamp-shades and the decanters, as the little lawyer, with a steady smile, proposed to the great landlord that they should halve the estates between them. The sequel certainly could not be overlooked; for the Duke, in dead silence, smashed a decanter on the man's bald head, as suddenly as I had seen him smash the glass that day in the orchard. It left a red triangular scar on the scalp, and the lawyer's eyes altered, but not his smile.

"He rose tottering to his feet, and struck back as such men do strike. 'I am glad of that,' he said, 'for now I can take the whole estate. The law will give it to me.'

"Exmoor, it seems, was white as ashes, but his eyes still blazed. 'The law will give it you,' he said; 'but you will not take it.... Why not? Why? because it would mean the crack of doom for me; and if you take it *I shall take off my wig....* Why, you pitiful plucked fowl, anyone can see your bare head. But no man shall see mine and live.'

"Well, you may say what you like and make it mean what you like. But Mull swears it is the solemn fact that the lawyer, after shaking his knotted fists in the air for an instant, simply ran from the room and never reappeared in the countryside. And since then Exmoor has been feared more for a warlock than even for a landlord and a magistrate.

"Now Dr. Mull told his story with rather wild theatrical gestures, and with a passion I think at least partisan. I was quite conscious of

[1] The Biblical prophet Elisha was mocked for his bald head in 2 Kings 2:23.

the possibility that the whole was the extravagance of an old braggart and gossip. But before I end this half of my discoveries, I think it due to Dr. Mull to record that my two first inquiries have confirmed his story. I learned from an old apothecary in the village that there was a bald man in evening dress, giving the name of Green, who came to him one night to have a three-cornered cut on his forehead plastered. And I learnt from the legal records and old newspapers that there was a lawsuit threatened, and at least begun, by one Green against the Duke of Exmoor."

Mr. Nutt, of *The Daily Reformer*, wrote some highly incongruous words across the top of the copy, made some highly mysterious marks down the side of it, and called to Miss Barlow in the same loud, monotonous voice, "Take down a letter to Mr. Finn."

"DEAR FINN,—Your copy will do, but I have had to headline it a bit; and our public would never stand a Romanist priest in the story— you must keep your eye on the suburbs. I've altered him to Mr. Brown, a Spiritualist. —Yours,
    "E. NUTT."

A day or two afterwards found the active and judicious editor examining, with blue eyes that seemed to grow rounder and rounder, the second instalment of Mr. Finn's tale of mysteries in high life. It began with the words:

"I have made an astounding discovery. I freely confess it is quite different from anything I expected to discover, and will give a much more practical shock to the public. I venture to say, without any vanity, that the words I now write will be read all over Europe, and certainly all over America and the Colonies. And yet I heard all I have to tell before I left this same little wooden table in this same little wood of apple-trees.

"I owe it all to the small priest Brown; he is an extraordinary man. The big librarian had left the table, perhaps ashamed of his long tongue, perhaps anxious about the storm in which his mysterious master had vanished: anyway, he betook himself heavily in the Duke's tracks through the trees. Father Brown had picked up one of the lemons and was eyeing it with an odd pleasure.

"'What a lovely colour a lemon is!' he said. 'There's one thing I don't like about the Duke's wig—the colour.'

"'I don't think I understand,' I answered.

"'I dare say he's got good reason to cover his ears, like King Midas,' went on the priest, with a cheerful simplicity which somehow seemed rather flippant under the circumstances. 'I can quite understand that it's nicer to cover them with hair than with brass plates or leather flaps. But if he wants to use hair, why doesn't he make it look like hair? There never was hair of that colour in this world. It looks more like a sunset-cloud coming through the wood. Why doesn't he conceal the family curse better, if he's really so ashamed of it? Shall I tell you? It's because he isn't ashamed of it. He's proud of it.'

"'It's an ugly wig to be proud of—and an ugly story,' I said.

"'Consider,' replied this curious little man, 'how you yourself really feel about such things. I don't suggest you're either more snobbish or more morbid than the rest of us: but don't you feel in a vague way that a genuine old family curse is rather a fine thing to have? Would you be ashamed, wouldn't you be a little proud, if the heir of the Glamis horror called you his friend; or if Byron's family had confided, to you only, the evil adventures of their race? Don't be too hard on the aristocrats themselves if their heads are as weak as ours would be, and they are snobs about their own sorrows.'

"'By Jove!' I cried; 'and that's true enough. My own mother's family had a banshee; and, now I come to think of it, it has comforted me in many a cold hour.'

"'And think,' he went on, 'of that stream of blood and poison that spurted from his thin lips the instant you so much as mentioned his ancestors. Why should he show every stranger over such a Chamber of Horrors unless he is proud of it? He doesn't conceal his wig, he doesn't conceal his blood, he doesn't conceal his family curse, he doesn't conceal the family crimes—*but*—'

"The little man's voice changed so suddenly, he shut his hand so sharply, and his eyes so rapidly grew rounder and brighter like a waking owl's, that it had all the abruptness of a small explosion on the table.

"'But,' he ended, '*he does really conceal his toilet.*'

"It somehow completed the thrill of my fanciful nerves that at that instant the Duke appeared again silently among the glimmering trees, with his soft foot and sunset-hued hair, coming round the corner of the house in company with his librarian. Before he came within ear-shot, Father Brown had added quite composedly, 'Why does he really hide the secret of what he does with the purple wig? Because it isn't the sort of secret we suppose.'

"The Duke came round the corner and resumed his seat at the head of the table with all his native dignity. The embarrassment of the librarian left him hovering on his hind legs, like a huge bear. The Duke addressed the priest with great seriousness. 'Father Brown,' he said, 'Doctor Mull informs me that you have come here to make a request. I no longer profess an observance of the religion of my fathers; but for their sakes and for the sake of the days when we met before, I am very willing to hear you. But I presume you would rather be heard in private.'

"Whatever I retain of the gentleman made me stand up. Whatever I have attained of the journalist made me stand still. Before this paralysis could pass, the priest had made a momentarily detaining motion. 'If,' he said, 'your Grace will permit me my real petition, or if I retain any right to advise you, I would urge that as many people as possible should be present. All over this country I have found hundreds, even of my own faith and flock, whose imaginations are poisoned by the spell which I implore you to break. I wish we could have all Devonshire here to see you do it.'

"'To see me do what?' asked the Duke, arching his eyebrows.

"'To see you take off your wig,' said Father Brown.

"The Duke's face did not move; but he looked at his petitioner with a glassy stare which was the most awful expression I have ever seen on a human face. I could see the librarian's great legs wavering under him like the shadows of stems in a pool; and I could not banish from my own brain the fancy that the trees all around us were filling softly in the silence with devils instead of birds.

"'I spare you,' said the Duke in a voice of inhuman pity. 'I refuse. If I gave you the faintest hint of the load of horror I have to bear alone, you would lie shrieking at these feet of mine and begging to know no more. I will spare you the hint. You shall not spell the first letter of what is written on the altar of the Unknown God.'

"'I know the Unknown God,' said the little priest, with an unconscious grandeur of certitude that stood up like a granite tower. 'I know his name; it is Satan. The true God was made flesh and dwelt among us. And I say to you, wherever you find men ruled merely by mystery, it is the mystery of iniquity. If the devil tells you something is too fearful to look at, look at it. If he says something is too terrible to hear, hear it. If you think some truth unbearable, bear it. I entreat your Grace to end this nightmare now and here at this table.'

"'If I did,' said the Duke in a low voice, 'you and all you believe, and all by which alone you live, would be the first to shrivel and perish. You would have an instant to know the great Nothing before you died.'

"'The Cross of Christ be between me and harm,' said Father Brown. 'Take off your wig.'

"I was leaning over the table in ungovernable excitement; in listening to this extraordinary duel half a thought had come into my head. 'Your Grace,' I cried, 'I call your bluff. Take off that wig or I will knock it off.'

"I suppose I can be prosecuted for assault, but I am very glad I did it. When he said, in the same voice of stone, 'I refuse,' I simply sprang on him. For three long instants he strained against me as if he had all hell to help him; but I forced back his head until the hairy cap fell off it. I admit that, whilst wrestling, I shut my eyes as it fell.

"I was awakened by a cry from Mull, who was also by this time at the Duke's side. His head and mine were both bending over the bald head of the wigless Duke. Then the silence was snapped by the librarian exclaiming, 'What can it mean? Why, the man had nothing to hide. His ears are just like everybody else's.'

"'Yes,' said Father Brown, 'that is what he had to hide.'

"The priest walked straight up to him; but strangely enough did not even glance at his ears. He stared with an almost comical seriousness at his bald forehead; and pointed to a three-cornered cicatrice, long healed, but still discernible. 'Mr. Green, I think,' he said politely, 'and he did get the whole estate after all.'

"And now let me tell the readers of *The Daily Reformer* what I think the most remarkable thing in the whole affair. This transformation-scene, which will seem to you as wild and purple as a Persian fairy-tale, has been (except for my technical assault) strictly legal and constitutional from its first beginnings. This man with the odd scar and the ordinary ears is not an impostor. Though (in one sense) he wears another man's wig and claims another man's ear, he has not stolen another man's coronet. He really is the one and only Duke of Exmoor. What happened was this. The old Duke really had a slight malformation of the ear, which really was more or less hereditary. He really was morbid about it; and it is likely enough that he did invoke it as a kind of curse in the violent scene (which undoubtedly happened) in which he struck Green with the decanter. But the contest ended very differently. Green pressed his claim and got the estates; the dispossessed nobleman shot himself and died without issue. After a decent interval the beautiful English Government revived the 'extinct' peerage of Exmoor, and bestowed it, as is usual, on the most important person, the person who had got the property.

"This man used the old feudal fables—probably, in his snobbish soul, really envied and admired them. So that thousands of poor English people trembled before a mysterious chieftain with an ancient destiny and a diadem of evil stars—when they are really trembling before a gutter-snipe who was a pettifogger and a pawnbroker not twelve years ago. I think it very typical of the real case against our aristocracy as it is, and as it will be till God sends us braver men."

Mr. Nutt put down the manuscript and called out with unusual sharpness, "Miss Barlow, please take down a letter to Mr. Finn:

"DEAR FINN,—You must be mad; we can't touch this. I wanted vampires and the bad old days and aristocracy hand-in-hand with superstition. They like that. But you must know the Exmoors would never forgive this. And what would our people say then, I should like to know! Why, Sir Simon is one of Exmoor's greatest pals; and it would ruin that cousin of the Eyres that's standing for us at Bradford. Besides, old Soap-Suds was sick enough at not getting his peerage last year; he'd sack me by wire if I lost him it with such lunacy as this. And what about Duffey? He's doing us some rattling articles on 'The Heel of the Norman.' And how can he write about Normans if the man's only a solicitor? Do be reasonable.—Yours,

"E. NUTT."

As Miss Barlow rattled away cheerfully, he crumpled up the copy and tossed it into the waste-paper basket; but not before he had, automatically and by mere force of habit, altered the word "God" to the word "circumstances."

THE PERISHING
OF THE PENDRAGONS

Father Brown was in no mood for adventures. He had lately fallen ill with over-work, and when he began to recover, his friend Flambeau had taken him on a cruise in a small yacht with Sir Cecil Fanshaw, a young Cornish squire and an enthusiast for Cornish coast scenery. But Brown was still rather weak; he was no very happy sailor; and though he was never of the sort that either grumbles or breaks down, his spirits did not rise above patience and civility. When the other two men praised the ragged violet sunset or the ragged volcanic crags, he agreed with them. When Flambeau pointed out a rock shaped like a dragon, he looked at it and thought it very like a dragon. When Fanshaw more excitedly indicated a rock that was like Merlin he looked at it, and signified assent. When Flambeau asked whether this rocky gate of the twisted river was not the gate of Fairyland, he said "Yes." He heard the most important things and the most trivial with the same tasteless absorption. He heard that the coast was death to all but careful seamen; he also heard that the ship's cat was asleep. He heard that Fanshaw couldn't find his cigar-holder anywhere; he also heard the pilot deliver the oracle "Both eyes bright, she's all right; one eye winks, down she sinks." He heard Flambeau say to Fanshaw that no doubt this meant the pilot must keep both eyes open and be spry. And he heard Fanshaw say to Flambeau that, oddly enough, it didn't mean this: it meant that while they saw two of the coast-lights, one near and the other distant, exactly side by side, they were in the right river-channel; but that if one light was hidden behind the other, they were going on the rocks. He heard Fanshaw add that his country was full of such quaint fables and idioms; it was the very home of romance; he even pitied this part of Cornwall against Devonshire, as a claimant to the laurels of Elizabethan seamanship. According to him there had been captains among these coves and islets compared with whom Drake was practically a landsman. He heard Flambeau laugh, and ask if, perhaps, the adventurous title of "Westward Ho!" only meant that all

Devonshire men wished they were living in Cornwall.[1] He heard
Fanshaw say there was no need to be silly; that not only had Cornish
captains been heroes, but that they were heroes still: that near that
very spot there was an old admiral, now retired, who was scarred by
thrilling voyages full of adventures; and who had in his youth found
the last group of eight Pacific Islands that was added to the chart of
the world. This Cecil Fanshaw was, in person, of the kind that commonly urges such crude but pleasing enthusiasms; a very young man,
light-haired, high-coloured, with an eager profile; with a boyish bra-
vado of spirits, but an almost girlish delicacy of tint and type. The big
shoulders, black brows and black mousquetaire swagger of Flambeau
were a great contrast.

All these trivialities Brown heard and saw; but heard them as a tired
man hears a tune in the railway wheels or saw them as a sick man sees
the pattern of his wall-paper. No one can calculate the turns of mood
in convalescence; but Father Brown's depression must have had a great
deal to do with his mere unfamiliarity with the sea. For as the river
mouth narrowed like the neck of a bottle, and the water grew calmer
and the air warmer and more earthy, he seemed to wake up and take
notice like a baby. They had reached that phase just after sunset when
air and water both look bright, but earth and all its growing things
look almost black by comparison. About this particular evening, however, there was something exceptional. It was one of those rare atmospheres in which a smoked glass slide seems to have been slid away
from between us and Nature; so that even dark colours on that day
look more gorgeous than bright colours on cloudier days. The trampled earth of the river-banks and the peaty stain in the pools did not
look drab but glowing umber, and the dark woods astir in the breeze
did not look, as usual, dim blue with mere depth or distance, but
more like wind-tumbled masses of some vivid violet blossom. This
magic clearness and intensity in the colours was further forced on
Brown's slowly reviving senses by something romantic and even secret
in the very form of the landscape.

[1] *Westward Ho!* (1855) is Charles Kingley's historical novel about the voyages of
Drake, which begins in a Devonshire setting.

The river was still well wide and deep enough for a pleasure boat so small as theirs; but the curves of the country-side suggested that it was closing in on either hand; the woods seemed to be making broken and flying attempts at bridge-building; as if the boat were passing from the romance of a valley to the romance of a hollow and so to the supreme romance of a tunnel. Beyond this mere look of things there was little for Brown's freshening fancy to feed on; he saw no human beings, except some gipsies trailing along the river bank, with faggots and osiers cut in the forest; and one sight no longer unconventional, but in such remote parts still uncommon: a dark-haired lady, bareheaded, and paddling her own canoe. If Father Brown ever attached any importance to either of these, he certainly forgot them at the next turn of the river, which brought in sight a singular object.

The water seemed to widen and split, being cloven by the dark wedge of a fish-shaped and wooded islet. With the rate at which they went, the islet seemed to swim towards them like a ship; a ship with a very high prow—or, to speak more strictly, a very high funnel. For at the extreme point nearest them stood up an odd-looking building, unlike anything they could remember or connect with any purpose. It was not specially high, but it was too high for its breadth to be called anything but a tower. Yet it appeared to be built entirely of wood, and that in a most unequal and eccentric way. Some of the planks and beams were of good, seasoned oak; some of such wood cut raw and recent; some again of white pinewood and a great deal more of the same sort of wood painted black with tar. These black beams were set crooked or criss-cross at all kinds of angles; giving the whole a most patchy and puzzling appearance. There were one or two windows, which appeared to be coloured and leaded in an old-fashioned but more elaborate style. The travellers looked at it with that paradoxical feeling we have when something reminds us of something, and yet we are certain it is something very different.

Father Brown, even when he was mystified, was clever in analysing his own mystification. And he found himself reflecting that the oddity seemed to consist in a particular shape cut out in an incongruous material; as if one saw a top-hat made of tin or a frock-coat cut out of tartan. He was sure he had seen timbers of different tints arranged like that somewhere, but never in such architectural proportions. The next moment a glimpse through the dark trees told him all he wanted to know; and he laughed. Through a gap in the foliage there appeared for a moment one of those old wooden houses, faced with black beams, which are still to be found here and there in England, but which most of us see imitated in some show called "Old London" or "Shakespeare's England." It was in view only long enough for the priest to see that, however old-fashioned, it was a comfortable and well-kept country-house, with flower beds in front of it. It had none of the piebald and crazy look of the tower that seemed made out of its refuse.

"What on earth's this?" said Flambeau, who was still staring at the tower.

Fanshaw's eyes were shining, and he spoke triumphantly. "Aha! you've not seen a place quite like this before, I fancy; that's why I've brought you here, my friend. Now you shall see whether I exaggerate about the mariners of Cornwall. This place belongs to Old Pendragon, whom we call the Admiral; though he retired before getting the rank. The spirit of Raleigh and Hawkins is a memory with the Devon folk; it's a modern fact with the Pendragons. If Queen Elizabeth were to rise from the grave and come up this river in a gilded barge, she would be received by the Admiral in a house exactly such as she was accustomed to, in every corner and casement, in every panel on the wall or plate on the table. And she would find an English Captain still talking fiercely of fresh lands to be found in little ships, as much as if she had dined with Drake."

"She'd find a rum sort of thing in the garden," said Father Brown, "which would not please her Renaissance eye. That Elizabethan domestic architecture is charming in its way; but it's against the very nature of it to break out into turrets."

"And yet," answered Fanshaw, "that's the most romantic and Elizabethan part of the business. It was built by the Pendragons in the very days of the Spanish wars; and though it's needed patching and even rebuilding for another reason, it's always been rebuilt in the old way. The story goes that the lady of Sir Peter Pendragon built it in this place and to this height, because from the top you can just see the corner where vessels turn into the river mouth; and she wished to be the first to see her husband's ship, as he sailed home from the Spanish Main."

"For what other reason," asked Father Brown, "do you mean that it has been rebuilt?"

"Oh, there's a strange story about that, too," said the young squire with relish. "You are really in a land of strange stories; King Arthur was here and Merlin and the fairies before him. The story goes that Sir Peter Pendragon, who (I fear) had some of the faults of the pirates as well as the virtues of the sailor, was bringing home three Spanish gentlemen in honourable captivity, intending to escort them to Elizabeth's court. But he was a man of flaming and tigerish temper; and coming to high words with one of them, he caught him by the throat and flung him, by accident or design, into the sea. A second Spaniard, who was the brother of the first, instantly drew his sword and flew at Pendragon, and after a short but furious combat in which both got three wounds in as many minutes, Pendragon drove his blade through the other's body and the second Spaniard was accounted for. As it happened the ship had already turned into the river mouth and was close to comparatively shallow water. The third Spaniard sprang over the side of the ship, struck out for the shore, and was soon near enough to it to stand up to his waist in water. And turning again to face the ship, and holding up both arms to Heaven like a prophet calling plagues upon a wicked city, he called out to Pendragon in a piercing and terrible voice, that he at least was yet living, that he would go on living, that he would live for ever; and that generation after generation the house of Pendragon should never see him or his, but should know by very certain signs that he and his vengeance were alive. With that he dived under the wave, and was either drowned or swam so long under water that no hair of his head was seen afterwards."

"There's that girl in the canoe again," said Flambeau irrelevantly, for good-looking young women would call him off any topic. "She seems bothered by the queer tower just as we were."

Indeed, the black-haired young lady was letting her canoe float slowly and silently past the strange islet; and was looking intently up at the strange tower, with a strong glow of curiosity on her oval and olive face.

"Never mind girls," said Fanshaw impatiently, "there are plenty of them in the world, but not many things like the Pendragon Tower. As you may easily suppose, plenty of superstitions and scandals have followed in the track of the Spaniard's curse; and no doubt, as you would put it, any accident happening to this Cornish family would be connected with it by rural credulity. But it is perfectly true that this tower has been burnt down two or three times; and the family can't be called lucky, for more than two, I think, of the Admiral's near kin have perished by shipwreck; and one at least, to my own knowledge, on practically the same spot where Sir Peter threw the Spaniard overboard."

"What a pity!" exclaimed Flambeau. "She's going."

"When did your friend the Admiral tell you this family history?" asked Father Brown, as the girl in the canoe paddled off, without showing the least intention of extending her interest from the tower to the yacht, which Fanshaw had already caused to lie alongside the island.

"Many years ago," replied Fanshaw; "he hasn't been to sea for some time now, though he is as keen on it as ever. I believe there's a family compact or something. Well, here's the landing-stage; let's come ashore and see the old boy."

They followed him on to the island just under the tower; and Father Brown, whether from the mere touch of dry land, or the interest of something on the other bank of the river (which he stared at very hard for some seconds), seemed singularly improved in briskness. They entered a wooded avenue between two fences of thin greyish wood, such as often enclose parks or gardens; and over the top of which the dark trees tossed to and fro like black and purple plumes upon the hearse of a giant. The tower, as they left it behind, looked all the quainter, because such entrances are usually flanked by two towers; and this one looked lop-sided. But for this, the avenue had the usual appearance of the entrance to a gentleman's grounds; and, being so curved that the house was now out of sight, somehow looked a much larger park than any plantation on such an island could really be. Father Brown was, perhaps, a little fanciful in his fatigue, but he almost thought the whole place must be growing larger, as things do in a nightmare. Anyhow, a mystical monotony was the only character of their march, until Fanshaw suddenly stopped, and pointed to something sticking out through the grey fence— something that looked at first rather like the imprisoned horn of some beast. Closer observation showed that it was a slightly curved blade of metal that shone faintly in the fading light.

Flambeau, who like all Frenchmen had been a soldier, bent over it and said in a startled voice, "Why, it's a sabre! I believe I know the sort; heavy and curved, but shorter than the cavalry; they used to have them in artillery and the —"

As he spoke the blade plucked itself out of the crack it had made and came down again with a more ponderous slash, splitting the fissiparous fence to the bottom, with a rending noise. Then it was pulled out again, flashed above the fence some feet farther along, and again split it halfway down with the first stroke; and after waggling a little to extricate itself (accompanied with curses in the darkness) split it down to the ground with a second. Then a kick of devilish energy sent the whole loosened square of thin wood flying into the pathway, and a great gap of dark coppice gaped in the paling.

Fanshaw peered into the dark opening, and uttered an exclamation of astonishment. "My dear Admiral!" he exclaimed, "do you— er—do you generally cut out a new front door whenever you wan't to go for a walk?"

The voice in the gloom swore again, and then broke into a jolly laugh. "No," it said; "I've really got to cut down this fence somehow; it's spoiling all the plants, and no one else here can do it. But I'll only carve another bit off the front door, and then come out and welcome you."

And sure enough, he heaved up his weapon once more, and, hacking twice, brought down another and similar strip of fence, making the opening about fourteen feet wide in all. Then through this larger forest gateway he came out into the evening light, with a chip of grey wood sticking to his sword-blade.

He momentarily fulfilled all Fanshaw's fable of an old piratical Admiral; though the details seemed afterwards to decompose into accidents. For instance, he wore an ordinary broad-brimmed hat as protection against the sun; but the front flap of it was turned up straight to the sky, and the two corners pulled down lower than the ears; so that it stood across his forehead in a crescent like the old cocked hat worn by Nelson. He wore an ordinary dark-blue jacket, with nothing special about the buttons, but the combination of it with white linen trousers somehow had a sailorish look. He was tall and loose, and walked with a sort of swagger, which was not a sailor's roll, and yet somehow suggested it. And he held in his hand a short sabre which was like a navy cutlass, but about twice as big. Under the bridge of the hat, his eagle face looked eager, all the more because it was not only clean-shaven, but without eyebrows. It seemed almost as if all the hair had come off his face from his thrusting it through a throng of elements. His eyes were prominent and piercing. His colour was curiously attractive, while partly tropical; it reminded one vaguely of a blood-orange. That is, that while it was ruddy and sanguine, there was a yellow in it that was in no way sickly, but seemed rather to glow like gold apples of the Hesperides. Father Brown thought he had never seen a figure so expressive of all the romances about the countries of the Sun.

When Fanshaw had presented his two friends to their host, he fell again into a tone of rallying the latter about his wreckage of the fence and his apparent rage of profanity. The Admiral pooh-poohed it at first as a piece of necessary but annoying garden work; but at length the ring of real energy came back into his laughter, and he cried with a mixture of impatience and good humour:

"Well, perhaps I do go at it a bit rabidly, and feel a kind of pleasure in smashing anything. So would you if your only pleasure was in cruising about to find some new Cannibal Islands, and you had to stick on this muddy little rockery in a sort of rustic pond. When I remember how I've cut down a mile and a half of green poisonous jungle with an old cutlass half as sharp as this; and then remember I must stop here and chop this matchwood, because of some confounded old bargain scribbled in a family Bible, why, I —"

He swung up the heavy steel again; and this time sundered the wall of wood from top to bottom at one stroke.

"I feel like that," he said laughing, but furiously flinging the sword some yards down the path, "and now let's go up to the house; you must have some dinner."

The semicircle of lawn in front of the house was varied by three circular garden beds, one of red tulips, a second of yellow tulips, and the third of some white waxen-looking blossoms that the visitors did not know and presumed to be exotic. A heavy, hairy and rather sullen-looking gardener was hanging up a heavy coil of garden hose. The corners of the expiring sunset which seemed to cling about the corners of the house gave glimpses here and there of the colours of remoter flower-beds; and in a treeless space on one side of the house opening upon the river stood a tall brass tripod on which was tilted a big brass telescope. Just outside the steps of the porch stood a little painted green garden table, as if someone had just had tea there. The entrance was flanked with two of those half-featured lumps of stone with holes for eyes that are said to be South Sea idols; and on the brown oak beam across the doorway were some confused carvings that looked almost as barbaric.

As they passed indoors, the little cleric hopped suddenly on to the table, and standing on it peered unaffectedly through his spectacles at the mouldings in the oak. Admiral Pendragon looked very much astonished, though not particularly annoyed; while Fanshaw was so amused with what looked like a performing pigmy on his little stand, that he could not control his laughter. But Father Brown was not likely to notice either the laughter or the astonishment.

He was gazing at three carved symbols, which, though very worn and obscure, seemed still to convey some sense to him. The first seemed to be the outline of some tower or other building, crowned with what looked like curly pointed ribbons. The second was clearer; an old Elizabethan galley with decorative waves beneath it, but interrupted in the middle by a curious jagged rock, which was either a fault in the wood or some conventional representation of the water coming in. The third represented the upper half of a human figure, ending in an escalloped line like the waves; the face was rubbed and featureless; and both arms were held very stiffly up in the air.

"Well," muttered Father Brown, blinking, "here is the legend of the Spaniard plain enough. Here he is holding up his arms and cursing in the sea; and here are the two curses: the wrecked ship and the burning of Pendragon Tower."

Pendragon shook his head with a kind of venerable amusement. "And how many other things might it not be?" he said. "Don't you know that that sort of half man, like a half lion or half stag, is quite common in heraldry? Might not that line through the ship be one of those *parti-per-pale* lines, *indented*, I think they call it? And though the third thing isn't so very heraldic, it would be more heraldic to suppose it a tower crowned with laurel than with fire; and it looks just as like it."

"But it seems rather odd," said Flambeau, "that it should exactly confirm the old legend."

"Ah," replied the sceptical traveller, "but you don't know how much of the old legend may have been made up from the old figures. Besides, it isn't the only old legend. Fanshaw, here, who is fond of such things, will tell you there are other versions of the tale, and much more horrible ones. One story credits my unfortunate ancestor with having had the Spaniard cut in two; and that will fit the pretty picture also. Another obligingly credits our family with the possession of a tower full of snakes and explains those little, wriggly things in that way. And a third theory supposes the crooked line on the ship to be a conventionalised thunderbolt; but that alone, if seriously examined, would show what a very little way these unhappy coincidences really go."

"Why, how do you mean?" asked Fanshaw.

"It so happens," replied his host coolly, "that there was no thunder and lightning at all in the two or three shipwrecks I know of in our family."

"Oh!" said Father Brown, and jumped down from the little table.

There was another silence in which they heard the continuous murmur of the river; then Fanshaw said, in a doubtful and perhaps disappointed tone, "Then you don't think there is anything in the tales of the tower in flames?"

"There are the tales, of course," said the Admiral, shrugging his shoulders, "and some of them, I don't deny, on evidence as decent as one ever gets for such things. Someone saw a blaze hereabout, don't you know, as he walked home through a wood; someone keeping sheep on the uplands inland thought he saw a flame hovering over Pendragon Tower. Well, a damp dab of mud like this confounded island seems the last place where one would think of fires."

"What is that fire over there?" asked Father Brown with a gentle suddenness pointing to the woods on the left river-bank. They were all thrown a little off their balance, and the more fanciful Fanshaw had even some difficulty in recovering his, as they saw a long, thin stream of blue smoke ascending silently into the end of the evening light.

Then Pendragon broke into a scornful laugh again. "Gipsies!" he said; "they've been camping about here for a week. Gentlemen, you want your dinner," and he turned as if to enter the house.

But the antiquarian superstition in Fanshaw was still quivering; and he said hastily, "But, Admiral, what's that hissing noise quite near the island? It's very like fire."

"It's more like what it is," said the Admiral laughing as he led the way; "it's only some canoe going by."

Almost as he spoke, the butler, a lean man in black, with very black hair and a very long, yellow face, appeared in the doorway and told him that dinner was served.

The dining-room was as nautical as the cabin of a ship; but its note was rather that of the modern than the Elizabethan captain. There were, indeed, three antiquated cutlasses in a trophy over the fireplace, and one brown sixteenth-century map, with Tritons and little ships dotted about a curly sea. But such things were less prominent on the white panelling than some cases of quaint coloured South American birds, very scientifically stuffed, fantastic shells from the Pacific, and several instruments so rude and queer in shape that savages might have used them either to kill their enemies or to cook them. But the alien colour culminated in the fact that, besides the butler, the Admiral's only servants were two negroes, somewhat quaintly clad in tight uniforms of yellow. The priest's instinctive trick of analysing his own impressions told him that the colour and the little neat coat-tails of these bipeds had suggested the word "Canary," and so by a mere pun connected them with Southward travel. Towards the end of the dinner they took their yellow clothes and black faces out of the room, leaving only the black clothes and yellow face of the butler.

"I'm rather sorry you take this so lightly," said Fanshaw to the host, "for the truth is I've brought these friends of mine with the idea of their helping you, as they know a good deal of these things. Don't you really believe in the family story at all?"

"I don't believe in anything," answered Pendragon very briskly, with a bright eye cocked at a red tropical bird. "I'm a man of science."

Rather to Flambeau's surprise, his clerical friend, who seemed to have entirely woke up, took up the digression and talked natural history with his host with a flow of words and much unexpected information, until the dessert and decanters were set down and the last of the servants vanished. Then he said, without altering his tone:

"Please don't think me impertinent, Admiral Pendragon. I don't ask for curiosity, but really for my guidance and your convenience. Have I made a bad shot if I guess you don't want these old things talked of before your butler?"

The Admiral lifted the hairless arches over his eyes and exclaimed, "Well, I don't know where you got it; but the truth is I can't stand the fellow, though I've no excuse for discharging a family servant. Fanshaw, with his fairy tales, would say my blood moved against men with that black, Spanish-looking hair."

Flambeau struck the table with his heavy fist. "By Jove!" he cried; "and so had that girl!"

"I hope it'll all end tonight," continued the Admiral, "when my nephew comes back safe from his ship. You looked surprised. You won't understand, I suppose, unless I tell you the story. You see, my father had two sons; I remained a bachelor, but my elder brother married, and had a son who became a sailor like all the rest of us, and will inherit the proper estate. Well, my father was a strange man; he somehow combined Fanshaw's superstition with a good deal of my scepticism; they were always fighting in him; and after my first voyages, he developed a notion which he thought somehow would settle finally whether the curse was truth or trash. If all the Pendragons sailed about anyhow, he thought there would be too much chance of natural catastrophes to prove anything. But if we went to sea one at a time in strict order of succession to the property, he thought it might show whether any connected fate followed the family as a family. It was a silly notion, I think, and I quarrelled with my father pretty heartily; for I was an ambitious man and was left to the last, coming, by succession, after my own nephew."

"And your father and brother," said the priest, very gently, "died at sea, I fear."

"Yes," groaned the Admiral; "by one of those brutal accidents on which are built all the lying mythologies of mankind, they were both shipwrecked. My father, coming up this coast out of the Atlantic, was washed up on these Cornish rocks. My brother's ship was sunk, no one knows where, on the voyage home from Tasmania. His body was never found. I tell you it was from perfectly natural mishap; lots of other people besides Pendragons were drowned; and both disasters are discussed in a normal way by navigators. But, of course, it set this forest of superstition on fire; and men saw the flaming tower everywhere. That's why I say it will be all right when Walter returns. The girl he's engaged to was coming today; but I was so afraid of some chance delay frightening her that I wired her not to come till she heard from me. But he's practically sure to be here some time tonight; and then it'll all end in smoke—tobacco smoke. We'll crack that old lie when we crack a bottle of this wine."

"Very good wine," said Father Brown, gravely lifting his glass, "but, as you see, a very bad wine-bibber. I most sincerely beg your pardon": for he had spilt a small spot of wine on the table-cloth. He drank and put down the glass with a composed face; but his hand had started at the exact moment when he became conscious of a face looking in through the garden window just behind the Admiral—the face of a woman, swarthy with Southern hair and eyes, and young, but like a mask of tragedy.

After a pause the priest spoke again in his mild manner. "Admiral," he said, "will you do me a favour? Let me, and my friends if they like, stop in that tower of yours just for tonight? Do you know that in my business you're an exorcist almost before anything else?"

Pendragon sprang to his feet and paced swiftly to and fro across the window, from which the face had instantly vanished. "I tell you there is nothing in it," he cried, with ringing violence. "There is one thing I know about this matter. You may call me an atheist. I am an atheist." Here he swung round and fixed Father Brown with a face of frightful concentration. "This business is perfectly natural. There is no curse in it at all."

Father Brown smiled. "In that case," he said, "there can't be any objection to my sleeping in your delightful summer-house."

"The idea is utterly ridiculous," replied the Admiral, beating a tattoo on the back of his chair.

"Please forgive me for everything," said Brown in his most sympathetic tone, "including spilling the wine. But it seems to me you are not quite so easy about the flaming tower as you try to be."

Admiral Pendragon sat down again as abruptly as he had risen; but he sat quite still, and when he spoke again it was in a lower voice. "You do it at your own peril," he said; "but wouldn't *you* be an atheist to keep sane in all this devilry?"

Some three hours afterwards Fanshaw, Flambeau and the priest were still dawdling about the garden in the dark; and it began to dawn on the other two that Father Brown had no intention of going to bed either in the tower or the house.

"I think the lawn wants weeding," said he dreamily. "If I could find a spud or something I'd do it myself."

They followed him, laughing and half remonstrating; but he replied with the utmost solemnity, explaining to them, in a maddening little sermon, that one can always find some small occupation that is helpful to others. He did not find a spud; but he found an old broom made of twigs, with which he began most energetically to brush the fallen leaves off the grass.

"Always some little thing to be done," he said with idiotic cheerfulness; as George Herbert says, 'Who sweeps an Admiral's garden in Cornwall as for Thy laws makes that and the action fine.' [2] And now," he added, suddenly slinging the broom away, "let's go and water the flowers."

[2] Father Brown makes a parody of two lines from "The Elixir", by the clergyman-poet George Herbert (1593–1633): "Who sweeps a room as for thy laws / Makes that and th' action fine."

With the same mixed emotions they watched him uncoil some considerable lengths of the large garden hose, saying with an air of wistful discrimination, "The red tulips before the yellow, I think. Look a bit dry, don't you think?"

He turned the little tap on the instrument, and the water shot out straight and solid as a long rod of steel.

"Look out, Samson," cried Flambeau; "why, you've cut off the tulip's head."

Father Brown stood ruefully contemplating the decapitated plant.

"Mine does seem to be a rather kill or cure sort of watering," he admitted, scratching his head. "I suppose it's a pity I didn't find the spud. You should have seen me with the spud! Talking of tools, you've got that swordstick, Flambeau, you always carry? That's right; and Sir Cecil could have that sword the Admiral threw away by the fence here. How grey everything looks!"

"The mist's rising from the river," said the staring Flambeau.

Almost as he spoke the huge figure of the hairy gardener appeared on a higher ridge of the trenched and terraced lawn, hailing them with a brandished rake and a horribly bellowing voice. "Put down that hose," he shouted; "put down that hose and go to your —"

"I am fearfully clumsy," replied the reverend gentleman weakly; "do you know, I upset some wine at dinner." He made a wavering half-turn of apology towards the gardener, with the hose still spouting in his hand. The gardener caught the cold crash of the water full in his face like the crash of a cannon-ball; staggered, slipped and went sprawling with his boots in the air.

"How very dreadful!" said Father Brown, looking round in a sort of wonder. "Why, I've hit a man!"

He stood with his head forward for a moment as if looking or listening; and then set off at a trot towards the tower, still trailing the hose behind him. The tower was quite close, but its outline was curiously dim.

"Your river mist," he said, "has a rum smell."

"By the Lord it has," cried Fanshaw, who was very white. "But you can't mean—"

"I mean," said Father Brown, "that one of the Admiral's scientific predictions is coming true tonight. This story is going to end in smoke."

As he spoke a most beautiful rose-red light seemed to burst into blossom like a gigantic rose; but accompanied with a crackling and rattling noise that was like the laughter of devils.

"My God! what is this?" cried Sir Cecil Fanshaw.

"The sign of the flaming tower," said Father Brown, and sent the driving water from his hose into the heart of' the red patch.

"Lucky we hadn't gone to bed!" ejaculated Fanshaw. "I suppose it can't spread to the house."

"You may remember," said the priest quietly, "that the wooden fence that might have carried it was cut away."

Flambeau turned electrified eyes upon his friend, but Fanshaw only said rather absently, "Well, nobody can be killed, anyhow."

"This is rather a curious kind of tower," observed Father Brown; "when it takes to killing people, it always kills people who are somewhere else."

At the same instant the monstrous figure of the gardener with the streaming beard stood again on the green ridge against the sky, waving others to come on; but now waving not a rake but a cutlass. Behind him came the two negroes, also with the old crooked cutlasses out of the trophy. But in the blood-red glare, with their black faces and yellow figures, they looked like devils carrying instruments of torture. In the dim garden behind them a distant voice was heard calling out brief directions. When the priest heard the voice, a terrible change came over his countenance.

But he remained composed; and never took his eye off the patch of flame which had begun by spreading, but now seemed to shrink a little as it hissed under the torch of the long silver spear of water. He kept his finger along the nozzle of the pipe to ensure the aim, and attended to no other business, knowing only by the noise and that semi-conscious corner of the eye, the exciting incidents that began to tumble themselves about the island garden. He gave two brief directions to his friends. One was, "Knock these fellows down somehow and tie them up, whoever they are; there's rope down by those faggots. They want to take away my nice hose." The other was, "As soon as you get a chance, call out to that canoeing girl; she's over on the bank with the gipsies. Ask her if they could get some buckets across and fill them from the river." Then he closed his mouth and continued to water the new red flower as ruthlessly as he had watered the red tulip.

He never turned his head to look at the strange fight that followed between the foes and friends of the mysterious fire. He almost felt the island shake when Flambeau collided with the huge gardener; he merely imagined how it would whirl round them as they wrestled. He heard the crashing fall; and his friend's gasp of triumph as he dashed on to the first negro; and the cries of both the blacks as Flambeau and Fanshaw bound them. Flambeau's enormous strength more than redressed the odds in the fight, especially as the fourth man still hovered near the house, only a shadow and a voice. He heard also the water broken by the paddles of a canoe; the girl's voice giving orders, the voices of gipsies answering and coming nearer, the plumping and sucking noise of empty buckets plunged into a full stream; and finally the sound of many feet around the fire. But all this was less to him than the fact that the red rent, which had lately once more increased, had once more slightly diminished.

Then came a cry that very nearly made him turn his head. Flambeau and Fanshaw, now reinforced by some of the gipsies, had rushed after the mysterious man by the house; and he heard from the other end of the garden the Frenchman's cry of horror and astonishment. It was echoed by a howl not to be called human, as the being broke from their hold and ran along the garden. Three times at least it raced round the whole island, in a way that was as horrible as the chase of a lunatic, both in the cries of the pursued and the ropes carried by the pursuers; but was more horrible still, because it somehow suggested one of the chasing games of children in a garden. Then, finding them closing in on every side, the figure sprang upon one of the higher river banks and disappeared with a splash into the dark and driving river.

"You can do no more, I fear," said Brown in a voice cold with pain. "He has been washed down to the rocks by now, where he has sent so many others. He knew the use of the family legend."

"Oh, don't talk in these parables," cried Flambeau impatiently. "Can't you put it simply in words of one syllable?"

"Yes," answered Brown, with his eye on the hose. "'Both eyes bright, she's all right; one eye blinks, down she sinks.'"

The fire hissed and shrieked more and more, like a strangled thing, as it grew narrower and narrower under the flood from the pipe and buckets, but Father Brown still kept his eye on it as he went on speaking:

"I thought of asking this young lady if it were morning yet, to look through that telescope at the river mouth and the river. She might have seen something to interest her: the sign of the ship, or Mr. Walter Pendragon coming home, and perhaps even the sign of the half-man, for though he is certainly safe by now, he may very well have waded ashore. He has been within a shave of another shipwreck; and would never have escaped it, if the lady hadn't had the sense to suspect the old Admiral's telegram and come down to watch him. Don't let's talk about the old Admiral. Don't let's talk about anything. It's enough to say that whenever this tower, with its pitch and resin-wood, really caught fire, the spark on the horizon always looked like the twin light to the coast lighthouse."

"And that," said Flambeau, "is how the father and brother died. The wicked uncle of the legends very nearly got his estate after all."

Father Brown did not answer; indeed, he did not speak again, save for civilities, till they were all safe round a cigar-box in the cabin of the yacht. He saw that the frustrated fire was extinguished; and then refused to linger, though he actually heard young Pendragon, escorted by an enthusiastic crowd, come tramping up the river bank; and might (had he been moved by romantic curiosities) have received the combined thanks of the man from the ship and the girl from the canoe. But his fatigue had fallen on him once more; and he only started once, when Flambeau abruptly told him he had dropped cigar-ash on his trousers.

"That's no cigar-ash," he said rather wearily. "That's from the fire, but you don't think so because you're all smoking cigars. That's just the way I got my first faint suspicion about the chart."

"Do you mean Pendragon's chart of his Pacific Islands?" asked Fanshaw.

"You thought it was a chart of the Pacific Islands," answered Brown. "Put a feather with a fossil and a bit of coral and everyone will think it's a specimen. Put the same feather with a ribbon and an artificial flower and everyone will think it's for a lady's hat. Put the same feather with an ink-bottle, a book, and a stack of writing-paper, and most men will swear they've seen a quill pen. So you saw that map among tropic birds and shells and thought it was a map of Pacific Islands. It was the map of this river."

"But how do you know?" asked Fanshaw.

"I saw the rock you thought was like a dragon, and the one like Merlin, and —"

"You seem to have noticed a lot as we came in," cried Fanshaw. "We thought you were rather abstracted."

"I was sea-sick," said Father Brown simply. "I felt simply horrible. But feeling horrible has nothing to do with not seeing things." And he closed his eyes.

"Do you think most men would have seen that?" asked Flambeau. He received no answer: Father Brown was asleep.

THE GOD OF THE GONGS

It was one of those chilly and empty afternoons in early winter, when the daylight is silver rather than gold and pewter rather than silver. If it was dreary in a hundred bleak offices and yawning drawing-rooms, it was drearier still along the edges of the flat Essex coast, where the monotony was the more inhuman for being broken at very long intervals by a lamp-post that looked less civilised than a tree, or a tree that looked more ugly than a lamp-post. A light fall of snow had half-melted into a few strips, also looking leaden rather than silver, when it had been fixed again by the seal of frost; no fresh snow had fallen, but a ribbon of the old snow ran along the very margin of the coast, so as to parallel the pale ribbon of the foam.

The line of the sea looked frozen in the very vividness of its violet-blue, like the vein of a frozen finger. For miles and miles, forward and back, there was no breathing soul, save two pedestrians, walking at a brisk pace, though one had much longer legs and took much longer strides than the other.

It did not seem a very appropriate place or time for a holiday, but Father Brown had few holidays, and had to take them when he could, and he always preferred, if possible, to take them in company with his old friend Flambeau, ex-criminal and ex-detective. The priest had had a fancy for visiting his old parish at Cobhole, and was going north-eastward along the coast.

After walking a mile or two farther, they found that the shore was beginning to be formally embanked, so as to form something like a parade; the ugly lamp-posts became less few and far between and more ornamental, though quite equally ugly. Half a mile farther on Father Brown was puzzled first by little labyrinths of flowerless flower-pots, covered with the low, flat, quiet-coloured plants that look less like a garden than a tessellated pavement, between weak curly paths studded with seats with curly backs. He faintly sniffed the atmosphere of a certain sort of seaside town that he did not specially care about, and, looking ahead along the parade by the sea, he saw something that put the matter beyond a doubt. In the grey distance the big bandstand of a watering-place stood up like a giant mushroom with six legs.

"I suppose," said Father Brown, turning up his coat-collar and drawing a woollen scarf rather closer round his neck, "that we are approaching a pleasure resort."

"I fear," answered Flambeau, "a pleasure resort to which few people just now have the pleasure of resorting. They try to revive these places in the winter, but it never succeeds except with Brighton and the old ones. This must be Seawood, I think—Lord Pooley's experiment; he had the Sicilian Singers down at Christmas, and there's talk about holding one of the great glove-fights here. But they'll have to chuck the rotten place into the sea; it's as dreary as a lost railway-carriage."

They had come under the big bandstand, and the priest was looking up at it with a curiosity that had something rather odd about it, his head a little on one side, like a bird's. It was the conventional, rather tawdry kind of erection for its purpose: a flattened dome or canopy, gilt here and there, and lifted on six slender pillars of painted wood, the whole being raised about five feet above the parade on a round wooden platform like a drum. But there was something fantastic about the snow combined with something artificial about the gold that haunted Flambeau as well as his friend with some association he could not capture, but which he knew was at once artistic and alien.

"I've got it," he said at last. "It's Japanese. It's like those fanciful Japanese prints, where the snow on the mountain looks like sugar, and the gilt on the pagodas is like gilt on gingerbread. It looks just like a little pagan temple."

"Yes," said Father Brown. "Let's have a look at the god." And with an agility hardly to be expected of him he hopped up onto the raised platform.

"Oh, very well," said Flambeau, laughing; and the next instant his own towering figure was visible on that quaint elevation.

Slight as was the difference of height, it gave in those level wastes a sense of seeing yet farther and farther across land and sea. Inland the little wintry gardens faded into a confused grey copse; beyond that, in the distance, were long low barns of a lonely farmhouse, and beyond that nothing but the long East Anglian plains. Seawards there was no sail or sign of life save a few seagulls; and even they looked like the last snowflakes, and seemed to float rather than fly.

Flambeau turned abruptly at an exclamation behind him. It seemed to come from lower down than might have been expected, and to be addressed to his heels rather than his head. He instantly held out his hand, but he could hardly help laughing at what he saw. For some reason or other the platform had given way under Father Brown, and the unfortunate little man had dropped through to the level of the parade. He was just tall enough, or short enough, for his head alone to stick out of the hole in the broken wood, looking like St. John the Baptist's head on a charger. The head wore a disconcerted expression, as did, perhaps, that of St. John the Baptist.

In a moment he began to laugh a little. "This wood must be rotten," said Flambeau. "Though it seems odd it should bear me, and you go through the weak place. Let me help you out."

But the little priest was looking rather curiously at the corners and edges of the wood alleged to be rotten, and there was a sort of trouble on his brow.

"Come along," cried Flambeau impatiently, still with his big brown hand extended. "Don't you want to get out?"

The priest was holding a splinter of the broken wood between his finger and thumb, and did not immediately reply. At last he said thoughtfully, "Want to get out? Why, no. I rather think I want to get in." And he dived into the darkness under the wooden floor so abruptly as to knock off his big curved clerical hat and leave it lying on the boards above, without any clerical head in it.

Flambeau looked once more inland and out to sea, and once more could see nothing but seas as wintry as the snows, and snows as level as the sea.

There came a scurrying noise behind him, and the little priest came scrambling out of the hole faster than he had fallen in. His face was no longer disconcerted, but rather resolute, and, perhaps only through the reflections of the snow, a trifle paler than usual.

"Well?" asked his tall friend. "Have you found the god of the temple?"

"No," answered Father Brown. "I have found what was sometimes more important. The Sacrifice."

"What the devil do you mean?" cried Flambeau, quite alarmed.

Father Brown did not answer. He was staring, with a knot in his forehead, at the landscape; and he suddenly pointed at it. "What's that house over there?" he asked.

Following his finger, Flambeau saw for the first time the corners of a building nearer than the farmhouse, but screened for the most part with a fringe of trees. It was not a large building, and stood well back from the shore; but a glint of ornament on it suggested that it was part of the same watering-place scheme of decoration as the bandstand, the little gardens, and the curly-backed iron seats.

Father Brown jumped off the bandstand, his friend following; and as they walked in the direction indicated the trees fell away to right and left, and they saw a small, rather flashy hotel, such as is common in resorts—the hotel of the Saloon Bar rather than the Bar Parlour. Almost the whole frontage was of gilt plaster and figured glass, and between that grey seascape and the grey, witch-like trees, its gimcrack quality had something spectral in its melancholy. They both felt vaguely that if any food or drink were offered at such a hostelry, it would be the paste-board ham and empty mug of the pantomime.

In this, however, they were not altogether confirmed. As they drew nearer and nearer to the place they saw in front of the buffet, which was apparently closed, one of the iron garden-chairs with curly backs that had adorned the gardens, but much longer, running almost the whole length of the frontage. Presumably, it was placed so that visitors might sit there and look at the sea, but one hardly expected to find anyone doing it in such weather.

Nevertheless, just in front of the extreme end of the iron seat stood a small round restaurant table, and on this stood a small bottle of chablis and a plate of almonds and raisins. Behind the table and on the seat sat a dark-haired young man, bare-headed, and gazing at the sea in a state of almost astonishing immobility.

But though he might have been a waxwork when they were within four yards of him, he jumped up like a jack-in-the-box when they came within three, and said in a deferential, though not undignified, manner, "Will you step inside, gentlemen? I have no staff at present, but I can get you anything simple myself."

"Much obliged," said Flambeau. "So you are the proprietor?"

"Yes," said the dark man, dropping back a little into his motionless manner. "My waiters are all Italians, you see, and I thought it only fair they should see their countryman beat the black, if he really can do it. You know the great fight between Malvoli and Nigger Ned is coming off, after all?"

"I'm afraid we can't wait to trouble your hospitality seriously," said Father Brown. "But my friend would be glad of a glass of sherry, I'm sure, to keep out the cold and drink success to the Latin champion."

Flambeau did not understand the sherry, but he did not object to it in the least. He could only say amiably, "Oh, thank you very much."

"Sherry, sir—certainly," said their host, turning to his hostel. "Excuse me if I detain you a few minutes. As I told you, I have no staff—" And he went towards the black windows of his shuttered and unlighted inn.

"Oh, it doesn't really matter," began Flambeau, but the man turned to reassure him.

"I have the keys," he said. "I could find my way in the dark."

"I didn't mean—" began Father Brown.

He was interrupted by a bellowing human voice that came out of the bowels of the uninhabited hotel. It thundered some foreign name loudly but inaudibly, and the hotel proprietor moved more sharply towards it than he had done for Flambeau's sherry. As instant evidence proved, the proprietor had told, then and after, nothing but the literal truth. But both Flambeau and Father Brown have often confessed that, in all their (often outrageous) adventures, nothing had so chilled their blood as that voice of an ogre, sounding suddenly out of a silent and empty inn.

"My cook!" cried the proprietor hastily. "I had forgotten my cook. He will be starting presently. Sherry, sir?"

And, sure enough, there appeared in the doorway a big white bulk with white cap and white apron, as befits a cook, but with the needless emphasis of a black face. Flambeau had often heard that negroes made good cooks. But somehow something in the contrast of colour and caste increased his surprise that the hotel proprietor should answer the call of the cook, and not the cook the call of the proprietor. But he reflected that head cooks are proverbially arrogant; and, besides, the host had come back with the sherry, and that was the great thing.

"I rather wonder," said Father Brown, "that there are so few people about the beach, when this big fight is coming on after all. We only met one man for miles."

The hotel proprietor shrugged his shoulders. "They come from the other end of the town, you see—from the station, three miles from here. They are only interested in the sport, and will stop in hotels for the night only. After all, it is hardly weather for basking on the shore."

"Or on the seat," said Flambeau, and pointed to the little table.

"I have to keep a lookout," said the man with the motionless face. He was a quiet, well-featured fellow, rather sallow; his dark clothes had nothing distinctive about them, except that his black necktie was worn rather high, like a stock, and secured by a gold pin with some grotesque head to it. Nor was there anything notable in the face, except something that was probably a mere nervous trick—a habit of opening one eye more narrowly than the other, giving the impression that the other was larger, or was, perhaps, artificial.

The silence that ensued was broken by their host saying quietly, "Whereabouts did you meet the one man on your march?"

"Curiously enough," answered the priest, "close by here—just by that bandstand."

Flambeau, who had sat on the long iron seat to finish his sherry, put it down and rose to his feet, staring at his friend in amazement. He opened his mouth to speak, and then shut it again.

"Curious," said the dark-haired man thoughtfully. "What was he like?"

"It was rather dark when I saw him," began Father Brown, "but he was—"

As has been said, the hotel-keeper can be proved to have told the precise truth. His phrase that the cook was starting presently was fulfilled to the letter, for the cook came out, pulling his gloves on, even as they spoke.

But he was a very different figure from the confused mass of white and black that had appeared for an instant in the doorway. He was buttoned and buckled up to his bursting eyeballs in the most brilliant fashion. A tall black hat was tilted on his broad black head— a hat of the sort that the French wit has compared to eight mirrors. But somehow the black man was like the black hat. He also was black, and yet his glossy skin flung back the light at eight angles or more. It is needless to say that he wore white spats and a white slip inside his waistcoat. The red flower stood up in his buttonhole aggressively, as if it had suddenly grown there. And in the way he carried his cane in one hand and his cigar in the other there was a certain attitude—an attitude we must always remember when we talk of racial prejudices: something innocent and insolent—the cake walk.

"Sometimes," said Flambeau, looking after him, "I'm not surprised that they lynch them."

"I am never surprised," said Father Brown, "at any work of hell. But as I was saying," he resumed, as the negro, still ostentatiously pulling on his yellow gloves, betook himself briskly towards the watering-place, a queer music-hall figure against that grey and frosty scene— "as I was saying, I couldn't describe the man very minutely, but he had a flourish and old-fashioned whiskers and moustachios, dark or dyed, as in the pictures of foreign financiers; round his neck was wrapped a long purple scarf that thrashed out in the wind as he walked. It was fixed at the throat rather in the way that nurses fix children's comforters with a safety-pin. Only this," added the priest, gazing placidly out to sea, "was not a safety-pin."

The man sitting on the long iron bench was also gazing placidly out to sea. Now he was once more in repose, Flambeau felt quite certain that one of his eyes was naturally larger than the other. Both were now well opened, and he could almost fancy the left eye grew larger as he gazed.

"It was a very long gold pin, and had the carved head of a monkey or some such thing," continued the cleric; "and it was fixed in a rather odd way—he wore pince-nez and a broad black ——"

The motionless man continued to gaze at the sea, and the eyes in his head might have belonged to two different men. Then he made a movement of blinding swiftness.

Father Brown had his back to him, and in that flash might have fallen dead on his face. Flambeau had no weapon, but his large brown hands were resting on the end of the long iron seat. His shoulders abruptly altered their shape, and he heaved the whole huge thing high over his head, like a headsman's axe about to fall. The mere height of the thing, as he held it vertical, looked like a long iron ladder by which he was inviting men to climb towards the stars. But the long shadow, in the level evening light, looked like a giant brandishing the Eiffel Tower. It was the shock of that shadow, before the shock of the iron crash, that made the stranger quail and dodge, and then dart into his inn, leaving the flat and shining dagger he had dropped exactly where it had fallen.

"We must get away from here instantly," cried Flambeau, flinging the huge seat away with furious indifference on the beach. He caught the little priest by the elbow and ran him down a grey perspective of barren back garden, at the end of which there was a closed back garden door. Flambeau bent over it an instant in violent silence, and then said, "The door is locked."

As he spoke a black feather from one of the ornamental firs fell, brushing the brim of his hat. It startled him more than the small and distant detonation that had come just before. Then came another distant detonation, and the door he was trying to open shook under the bullet buried in it. Flambeau's shoulders again filled out and altered suddenly. Three hinges and a lock burst at the same instant, and he went out into the empty path behind, carrying the great garden door with him, as Samson carried the gates of Gath.

Then he flung the garden door over the garden wall, just as a third shot picked up a spurt of snow and dust behind his heel. Without ceremony he snatched up the little priest, slung him astraddle on his shoulders, and went racing towards Seawood as fast as his long legs could carry him. It was not until nearly two miles farther on that he set his small companion down. It had hardly been a dignified escape, in spite of the classic model of Anchises, but Father Brown's face only wore a broad grin.[1]

"Well," said Flambeau, after an impatient silence, as they resumed their more conventional tramp through the streets on the edge of the town, where no outrage need be feared, "I don't know what all this means, but I take it I may trust my own eyes that you never met the man you have so accurately described."

"I did meet him in a way," Brown said, biting his finger rather nervously— "I did really. And it was too dark to see him properly, because it was under that bandstand affair. But I'm afraid I didn't describe him so very accurately, after all, for his pince-nez was broken under him, and the long gold pin wasn't stuck through his purple scarf, but through his heart."

"And I suppose," said the other, in a lower voice, "that glass-eyed guy had something to do with it."

"I had hoped he had only a little," answered Brown in a rather troubled voice, "and I may have been wrong in what I did. I acted on impulse. But I fear this business has deep roots and dark."

They walked on through some streets in silence. The yellow lamps were beginning to be lit in the cold blue twilight, and they were evidently approaching the more central parts of the town. Highly coloured bills announcing the glove-fight between Nigger Ned and Malvoli were slapped about the walls.

"Well," said Flambeau, "I never murdered anyone, even in my criminal days, but I can almost sympathise with anyone doing it in such a dreary place. Of all God-forsaken dustbins of Nature, I think the most heart-breaking are places like that bandstand, that were meant to be festive and are forlorn. I can fancy a morbid man feeling he must kill his rival in the solitude and irony of such a scene. I remember once taking a tramp in your glorious Surrey hills, thinking of nothing but gorse and skylarks, when I came out on a vast circle of land, and over me lifted a vast, voiceless structure, tier above tier of seats, as huge as

[1] In the *Aeneid*, Virgil's Trojan hero Aeneas carried away his aging father Anchises on his shoulders following the Greek victory.

a Roman amphitheatre and as empty as a new letter-rack. A bird sailed in heaven over it. It was the Grand Stand at Epsom. And I felt that no one would ever be happy there again."

"It's odd you should mention Epsom," said the priest. "Do you ever remember what was called the Sutton Mystery, because two suspected men—ice-cream men, I think—happened to live at Sutton? They were eventually released. A man was found strangled, it was said, on the downs round that part. As a fact, I know (from an Irish policeman who is a friend of mine) that he was found close up to the Epsom Grand Stand—in fact, only hidden by one of the lower doors being pushed back."

"That is queer," assented Flambeau. "But it rather confirms my view that such pleasure places look awfully lonely out of season, or the man wouldn't have been murdered there."

"I'm not so sure he—" began Brown, and stopped.

"Not so sure he was murdered?" queried his companion.

"Not so sure he was murdered out of the season," answered the little priest, with simplicity. "Don't you think there's something rather tricky about this solitude, Flambeau? Do you feel sure a wise murderer would always *want* the spot to be lonely? It's very, very seldom a man is *quite* alone. And, short of that, the more alone he is the more certain he is to be seen. No; I think there must be some other— Why, here we are at the Pavilion or Palace, or whatever they call it."

They had emerged on a small square, brilliantly lighted, of which the principal building was gay with gilding, gaudy with posters, and flanked with two giant photographs of Malvoli and Nigger Ned.

"Hallo!" cried Flambeau, in great surprise, as his clerical friend stumped straight up the broad steps. "I didn't know pugilism was your latest hobby. Are you going to see the fight?"

"I don't think there will be any fight," replied Father Brown.

They passed rapidly through ante-rooms and inner rooms; they passed through the hall of combat itself, raised, roped, and padded with innumerable seats and boxes, and still the cleric did not look round or pause till he came to a clerk at a desk outside a door marked "Committee." There he stopped and asked to see Lord Pooley.

The attendant observed that his lordship was very busy, as the fight was coming on soon, but Father Brown had a good-tempered tedium of reiteration for which the official mind is generally not prepared. In a few moments the rather baffled Flambeau found himself in the presence of a man who was still shouting directions to another man going out of the room. "Be careful, you know, about the ropes after the fourth— Well, and what do you want, I wonder!"

Lord Pooley was a gentleman, and, like most of the few remaining to our race, was worried—especially about money. He was half grey and half flaxen, and he had the eyes of fever and a high-bridged, frost-bitten nose.

"Only a word," said Father Brown. "I have come to prevent a man being killed."

Lord Pooley bounded off his chair, as if a spring had flung him from it. "I'm damned if I'll stand any more of this!" he cried. "You and your committees and parsons and petitions![2] Weren't there parsons in the old days, when they fought without gloves? Now they're fighting with the regulation gloves, and there's not the rag of a possibility of either of the boxers being killed."

"I didn't mean either of the boxers," said the little priest.

"Well, well, well!" said the nobleman, with a touch of frosty humour. "Who's going to be killed? The referee?"

"I don't know who's going to be killed," replied Father Brown, with a reflective stare. "If I did, I shouldn't have to spoil your pleasure. I could simply get him to escape. I never could see anything wrong about prize-fights. As it is, I must ask you to announce that the fight is off for the present."

"Anything else?" jeered the gentleman with feverish eyes. "And what do you say to the two thousand people who have come to see it?"

[2] Lord Pooley jumps to the conclusion that Father Brown is a pacifist in the mold of the Baptist clergyman F. B. Meyer, who in 1911 led a successful campaign to cancel the London prizefight between the black American heavyweight champion Jack Johnson and the white British champion Billy "Bombardier" Wells.

"I say there will be one thousand nine hundred and ninety-nine of them left alive when they have seen it," said Father Brown.

Lord Pooley looked at Flambeau. "Is your friend mad?" he asked.

"Far from it," was the reply.

"And look here," resumed Pooley in his restless way, "it's worse than that. A whole pack of Italians have turned up to back Malvoli—swarthy, savage fellows of some country, anyhow. You know what these Mediterranean races are like. If I send out word that it's off we shall have Malvoli storming in here at the head of a whole Corsican clan."

"My lord, it is a matter of life and death," said the priest. "Ring your bell. Give your message. And see whether it is Malvoli who answers."

The nobleman struck the bell on the table with an odd air of new curiosity. He said to the clerk who appeared almost instantly in the doorway, "I have a serious announcement to make to the audience shortly. Meanwhile, would you kindly tell the two champions that the fight will have to be put off."

The clerk stared for some seconds as if at a demon, and vanished.

"What authority have you for what you say?" asked Lord Pooley abruptly. "Whom did you consult?"

"I consulted a bandstand," said Father Brown, scratching his head. "But, no, I'm wrong; I consulted a book, too. I picked it up on a bookstall in London—very cheap, too."

He had taken out of his pocket a small, stout, leather-bound volume, and Flambeau, looking over his shoulder, could see that it was some book of old travels, and had a leaf turned down for reference.

"'The only form in which Voodoo—'" began Father Brown, reading aloud.

"In which what?" inquired his lordship.

"'In which Voodoo,'" repeated the reader, almost with relish, "'is widely organised outside Jamaica itself is in the from known as the Monkey, or the God of the Gongs, which is powerful in many parts of the two American continents, especially among half-breeds many of whom look exactly like white men. It differs from most other forms of devil-worship and human sacrifice in the fact that the blood is not shed formally on the altar, but by a sort of assassination among the crowd. The gongs beat with a deafening din as the doors of the shrine open and the monkey-god is revealed; almost the whole congregation rivet ecstatic eyes on him. But after—'"

The door of the room was flung open, and the fashionable negro stood framed in it, his eyeballs rolling, his silk hat still insolently tilted on his head. "Huh!" he cried, showing his apish teeth. "What this? Huh! Huh! You steal a coloured gentleman's prize—prize his already— yo' think yo' jes' save that white 'Talian trash —"

"The matter is only deferred," said the nobleman quietly. "I will be with you to explain in a minute or two."

"Who you to—" shouted Nigger Ned, beginning to storm.

"My name is Pooley," replied the other, with a creditable coolness. "I am the organising secretary, and I advise you just now to leave the room."

"Who is this fellow?" demanded the dark champion, pointing to the priest disdainfully.

"My name is Brown," was the reply. "And I advise you just now to leave the country."

The prize-fighter stood glaring for a few seconds, and then, rather to the surprise of Flambeau and the others, strode out, sending the door to with a crash behind him.

"Well," asked Father Brown, rubbing his dusty hair up, "what do you think of Leonardo da Vinci? A beautiful Italian head."

"Look here," said Lord Pooley, "I've taken a considerable responsibility on your bare word. I think you ought to tell me more about this."

"You are quite right, my lord," answered Brown. "And it won't take long to tell." He put the little leather book in his overcoat pocket. "I think we know all that this can tell us, but you shall look at it to see if I'm right. That negro who has just swaggered out is one of the most dangerous men on earth, for he has the brains of a European, with the instincts of a cannibal. He has turned what was clean, common-sense butchery among his fellow-barbarians into a very modern and scientific secret society of assassins. He doesn't know I know it, nor, for the matter of that, that I can't prove it."

There was a silence, and the little man went on:

"But if I want to murder somebody, will it really be the best plan to make sure I'm alone with him?"

Lord Pooley's eyes recovered their frosty twinkle as he looked at the little clergyman. He only said, "If you *want* to murder somebody, I should advise it."

Father Brown shook his head, like a murderer of much riper experience. "So Flambeau said," he replied, with a sigh. "But consider. The more a man feels lonely the less he can be sure he is alone. It must mean empty spaces round him, and they are just what make him obvious. Have you never seen one ploughman from the heights, or one shepherd from the valleys? Have you never walked along a cliff, and seen one man walking along the sands? Didn't you know when he'd killed a crab, and wouldn't you have known if it had been a creditor? No! No! No! For an intelligent murderer, such as you or I might be, it is an impossible plan to make sure that nobody is looking at you."

"But what other plan is there?"

"There is only one," said the priest. "To make sure that everybody is looking at something else. A man is throttled close by the big stand at Epsom. Anybody might have seen it done while the stand stood empty—any tramp under the hedges or motorist among the hills. But nobody would have seen it when the stand was crowded and the whole ring roaring, when the favourite was coming in first—or wasn't. The twisting of a neck-cloth, the thrusting of a body behind a door could be done in an instant—so long as it was *that* instant. It was the same, of course," he continued turning to Flambeau, "with that poor fellow under the bandstand. He was dropped through the hole (it wasn't an accidental hole) just at some very dramatic moment of the entertainment, when the bow of some great violinist or the voice of some great singer opened or came to its climax. And here, of course, when the knock-out blow came—it would not be the only one. That is the little trick Nigger Ned has adopted from his old God of Gongs."

"By the way, Malvoli—" Pooley began.

"Malvoli," said the priest, "has nothing to do with it. I dare say he has some Italians with him, but our amiable friends are not Italians.

They are octoroons and African half-bloods of various shades, but I
fear we English think all foreigners are much the same so long as they
are dark and dirty. Also," he added, with a smile, "I fear the English
decline to draw any fine distinction between the moral character produced by my religion and that which blooms out of Voodoo."

  The blaze of the spring season had burst upon Seawood, littering
its foreshore with families and bathing-machines, with nomadic
preachers and nigger minstrels, before the two friends saw it again,
and long before the storm of pursuit after the strange secret society
had died away. Almost on every hand the secret of their purpose
perished with them. The man of the hotel was found drifting dead
on the sea like so much seaweed; his right eye was closed in peace,
but his left eye was wide open, and glistened like glass in the moon.
Nigger Ned had been overtaken a mile or two away, and murdered
three policemen with his closed left hand. The remaining officer
was surprised—nay, pained—and the negro got away. But this was
enough to set all the English papers in a flame, and for a month or
two the main purpose of the British Empire was to prevent the
buck nigger (who was so in both senses) escaping by any English
port. Persons of a figure remotely reconcilable with his were sub-
jected to quite extraordinary inquisitions, made to scrub their faces
before going on board ship, as if each white complexion were made
up like a mask of grease-paint. Every negro in England was put
under special regulations and made to report himself; the outgoing
ships would no more have taken a nigger than a basilisk. For people
had found out how fearful and vast and silent was the force of the
savage secret society, and by the time Flambeau and Father Brown
were leaning on the parade parapet in April, the Black Man meant
in England almost what he once meant in Scotland.[3]

  "He must be still in England," observed Flambeau, "and horridly
well hidden, too. They must have found him at the ports if he had
only whitened his face."

[3] What the "Black Man" once meant in Scotland was the Devil. The name derives
from seventeenth-century rites of witchcraft in which the devil was represented by a
man dressed entirely in black.

"You see, he is really a clever man," said Father Brown apologetically. "And I'm sure he wouldn't whiten his face."

"Well, but what would he do?"

"I think," said Father Brown, "he would blacken his face."

Flambeau, leaning motionless on the parapet, laughed and said, "My dear fellow!"

Father Brown, also leaning motionless on the parapet, moved one finger for an instant into the direction of the soot-masked niggers singing on the sands.

THE SALAD OF COLONEL CRAY

Father Brown was walking home from Mass on a white weird morning when the mists were slowly lifting—one of those mornings when the very element of light appears as something mysterious and new. The scattered trees outlined themselves more and more out of the vapour, as if they were first drawn in grey chalk and then in charcoal. At yet more distant intervals appeared the houses upon the broken fringe of the suburb; their outlines became clearer and clearer until he recognised many in which he had chance acquaintances, and many more the names of whose owners he knew. But all the windows and doors were sealed; none of the people were of the sort that would be up at such a time, or still less on such an errand. But as he passed under the shadow of one handsome villa with verandas and wide ornate gardens, he heard a noise that made him almost involuntarily stop. It was the unmistakable noise of a pistol or carbine or some light firearm discharged; but it was not this that puzzled him most. The first full noise was immediately followed by a series of fainter noises—as he counted them, about six. He supposed it must be the echo; but the odd thing was that the echo was not in the least like the original sound. It was not like anything else that he could think of; the three things nearest to it seemed to be the noise made by siphons of soda-water, one of the many noises made by an animal, and the noise made by a person attempting to conceal laughter. None of which seemed to make much sense.

Father Brown was made of two men. There was a man of action, who was as modest as a primrose and as punctual as a clock; who went his small round of duties and never dreamed of altering it. There was also a man of reflection, who was much simpler but much stronger, who could not easily be stopped; whose thought was always (in the only intelligent sense of the words) free thought. He could not help, even unconsciously, asking himself all the questions that there were to be asked, and answering as many of them as he could; all that went on like his breathing or circulation. But he never consciously carried his actions outside the sphere of his own duty; and in this case the two attitudes were aptly tested. He was just about to resume his trudge in the twilight, telling himself it was no affair of his, but instinctively twisting and untwisting twenty theories about what the odd noises might mean. Then the grey sky-line brightened into silver, and in the broadening light he realised that he had been to the house which belonged to an Anglo-Indian Major named Putnam; and that the Major had a native cook from Malta who was of his communion. He also began to remember that pistol-shots are sometimes serious things; accompanied with consequences with which he was legitimately concerned. He turned back and went in at the garden gate, making for the front door.

Half-way down one side of the house stood out a projection like a very low shed; it was, as he afterwards discovered, a large dustbin. Round the corner of this came a figure, at first a mere shadow in the haze, apparently bending and peering about. Then, coming nearer, it solidified into a figure that was, indeed, rather unusually solid. Major Putnam was a bald-headed, bull-necked man, short and very broad, with one of those rather apoplectic faces that are produced by a prolonged attempt to combine the oriental climate with the occidental luxuries. But the face was a good-humoured one, and even now, though evidently puzzled and inquisitive, wore a kind of innocent grin. He had a large palm-leaf hat on the back of his head (suggesting a halo that was by no means appropriate to the face), but otherwise he was clad only in a very vivid suit of striped scarlet and yellow pyjamas; which, though glowing enough to behold, must have been, on a fresh morning, pretty chilly to wear. He had evidently come out of his house in a hurry; and the priest was not surprised when he called out without further ceremony, "Did you hear that noise?"

"Yes," answered Father Brown. "I thought I had better look in, in case anything was the matter."

The Major looked at him rather queerly with his good-humoured gooseberry eyes. "What do you think the noise was?" he asked.

"It sounded like a gun or something," replied the other, with some hesitation; "but it seemed to have a singular sort of echo."

The Major was still looking at him quietly, but with protruding eyes, when the front door was flung open, releasing a flood of gaslight on the face of the fading mist; and another figure in pyjamas sprang or tumbled out into the garden. The figure was much longer, leaner, and more athletic; the pyjamas, though equally tropical, were comparatively tasteful, being of white with a light lemon-yellow stripe. The man was haggard, but handsome, more sunburned than the other; he had an aquiline profile and rather deep-sunken eyes, and a slight air of oddity arising from the combination of coal-black hair with a much lighter moustache. All this Father Brown absorbed in detail more at leisure. For the moment he only saw one thing about the man: which was the revolver in his hand.

"Cray!" exclaimed the Major, staring at him, "did you fire that shot?"

"Yes, I did," retorted the black-haired gentleman hotly, "and so would you in my place. If you were chased everywhere by devils and nearly —"

The Major seemed to intervene rather hurriedly. "This is my friend Father Brown," he said. And then to Brown, "I don't know whether you've met Colonel Cray of the Royal Artillery."

"I have heard of him, of course," said the priest innocently. "Did you—did you hit anything?"

"I thought so," answered Cray with gravity.

"Did he —" asked Major Putnam in a lowered voice, "did he fall or cry out, or anything?"

Colonel Cray was regarding his host with a strange and steady stare. "I'll tell you exactly what he did," he said. "He sneezed."

Father Brown's hand went half-way to his head, with the gesture of a man remembering somebody's name. He knew now what it was that was neither soda-water nor the snorting of a dog.

"Well," ejaculated the staring Major, "I never heard before that a service revolver was a thing to be sneezed at."

"Nor I," said Father Brown faintly. "It's lucky you didn't turn your artillery on him, or you might have given him quite a bad cold." Then, after a bewildered pause, he said, "Was it a burglar?"

"Let us go inside,'" said Major Putnam, rather sharply, and led the way into his house.

The interior exhibited a paradox often to be marked in such morning hours: that the rooms seemed brighter than the sky outside; even after the Major had turned out the one gaslight in the front hall. Father Brown was surprised to see the whole dining-table set out as for a festive meal, with napkins in their rings, and wine-glasses of some six unnecessary shapes set beside every plate. It was common enough, at that time of the morning, to find the remains of a banquet overnight; but to find it freshly spread so early was unusual.

While he stood wavering in the hall Major Putnam rushed past him and sent a raging eye over the whole oblong of the tablecloth. At last he spoke, spluttering, "All the silver gone!" he gasped. "Fish-knives and forks gone. Old cruet-stand gone. Even the old silver cream-jug gone. And now, Father Brown, I am ready to answer your question of whether it was a burglar."

"They're simply a blind," said Cray stubbornly. "I know better than you why people persecute this house; I know better than you why —"

The Major patted him on the shoulder with a gesture almost peculiar to the soothing of a sick child, and said, "It was a burglar. Obviously it was a burglar."

"A burglar with a bad cold," observed Father Brown, "that might assist you to trace him in the neighbourhood."

The Major shook his head in a sombre manner. "He must be far beyond tracing now, I fear," he said.

Then, as the restless man with the revolver turned again towards the door into the garden, he added in a husky, confidential voice, "I doubt whether I should send for the police, for fear my friend here has been a little too free with his bullets, and got on the wrong side of the law. He's lived in very wild places; and, to be frank with you, I think he sometimes fancies things."

"I think you once told me," said Brown, "that he believes some Indian secret society is pursuing him."

Major Putnam nodded, but at the same time shrugged his shoulders. "I suppose we'd better follow him outside," he said. "I don't want any more—shall we say, sneezing?"

They passed out into the morning light, which was now even tinged with sunshine, and saw Colonel Cray's tall figure bent almost double, minutely examining the condition of gravel and grass. While the Major

strolled unobtrusively towards him, the priest took an equally indo-
lent turn, which took him round the next corner of the house to
within a yard or two of the projecting dustbin.

He stood regarding this dismal object for some minute and a half;
then he stepped towards it, lifted the lid, and put his head inside. Dust
and other discolouring matter shook upwards as he did so; but Father
Brown never observed his own appearance, whatever else he observed.
He remained thus for a measurable period, as if engaged in some
mysterious prayers. Then he came out again, with some ashes on his
hair, and walked unconcernedly away.

By the time he came round to the garden door again he found a
group there which seemed to roll away morbidities as the sunlight
had already rolled away the mists. It was in no way rationally reassur-
ing; it was simply broadly comic, like a cluster of Dickens's characters.
Major Putnam had managed to slip inside and plunge into a proper
shirt and trousers, with a crimson cummerbund, and a light square
jacket over all; thus normally set off, his red festive face seemed bursting with a commonplace cordiality. He was indeed emphatic, but then
he was talking to his cook—the swarthy son of Malta, whose lean,
yellow, and rather careworn face contrasted quaintly with his snow-
white cap and costume. The cook might well be careworn, for cookery was the Major's hobby. He was one of those amateurs who always
knows more than the professional. The only other person he even
admitted to be a judge of an omelette was his friend Cray—and as
Brown remembered this, he turned to look for the other officer. In
the new presence of daylight and people clothed and in their right
mind, the sight of him was rather a shock. The taller and more elegant
man was still in his night-garb, with tousled black hair, and now crawling about the garden on his hands and knees, still looking for traces of
the burglar; and now and again, to all appearance, striking the ground
with his hand in anger at not finding him. Seeing him thus quadru-
pedal in the grass, the priest raised his eyebrows rather sadly; and for
the first time guessed that "fancies things" might be an euphemism.

The third item in the group of the cook and the epicure was also
known to Father Brown; it was Audrey Watson, the Major's ward and
housekeeper; and at this moment, to judge by her apron, tucked-up

sleeves, and resolute manner, much more the housekeeper than the ward.

"It serves you right," she was saying, "I always told you not to have that old-fashioned cruet-stand."

"I prefer it," said Putnam, placably. "I'm old-fashioned myself; and the things keep together."

"And vanish together, as you see," she retorted. "Well, if you are not going to bother about the burglar, I shouldn't bother about the lunch. It's Sunday, and we can't send for vinegar and all that in the town; and you Indian gentlemen can't enjoy what you call a dinner without a lot of hot things. I wish to goodness now you hadn't asked Cousin Oliver to take me to the musical service. It isn't over till half-past twelve, and the Colonel has to leave by then. I don't believe you men can manage alone."

"Oh yes, we can, my dear," said the Major, looking at her very amiably. "Marco has all the sauces; and we've often done ourselves well in very rough places, as you might know by now. And it's time you had a treat, Audrey; you mustn't be a housekeeper every hour of the day; and I know you want to hear the music."

"I want to go to church," she said, with rather severe eyes.

She was one of those handsome women who will always be handsome, because the beauty is not in an air or a tint, but in the very structure of the head and features. But though she was not yet middle-aged and her auburn hair was of a Titianesque fullness in form and colour, there was a look in her mouth and around her eyes which suggested that some sorrows wasted her, as winds waste at last the edges of a Greek temple. For indeed the little domestic difficulty of which she was now speaking so decisively was rather comic than tragic. Father Brown gathered, from the course of the conversation, that Cray, the other *gourmet*, had to leave before the usual lunch-time; but that Putnam, his host, not to be done out of a final feast with an old crony, had arranged for a special *déjeuner* to be set out and consumed in the course of the morning, while Audrey and other graver persons were at morning service. She was going there under the escort of a relative and old friend of hers, Dr. Oliver Oman, who, though a scientific man of a somewhat bitter type, was enthusiastic for music, and would go even to church to get it. There was nothing in all this that could conceivably concern the tragedy in Miss Watson's face; and by a half conscious instinct, Father Brown turned again to the seeming lunatic grubbing about in the grass.

When he strolled across to him, the black, unbrushed head was lifted abruptly, as if in some surprise at his continued presence. And indeed, Father Brown, for reasons best known to himself, had lingered much longer than politeness required; or even, in the ordinary sense, permitted.

"Well!" cried Cray, with wild eyes. "I suppose you think I'm mad, like the rest?"

"I have considered the thesis," answered the little man composedly. "And I incline to think you are not."

"What do you mean?" snapped Cray quite savagely.

"Real madmen," explained Father Brown, "always encourage their own morbidity. They never strive against it. But you are trying to find traces of the burglar; even when there aren't any. You are struggling against it. You want what no madman ever wants."

"And what is that?"

"You want to be proved wrong," said Brown.

During the last words, Cray had sprung or staggered to his feet and was regarding the cleric with agitated eyes. "By hell, but that is a true word!" he cried. "They are all at me here that the fellow was only after the silver—as if I shouldn't be only too pleased to think so! *She's* been at me," and he tossed his tousled black head towards Audrey, but the other had no need of the direction, "she's been at me today about how cruel I was to shoot a poor harmless housebreaker, and how I have the devil in me against poor harmless natives. But I was a good-natured man once—as good-natured as Putnam."

After a pause he said, "Look here, I've never seen you before; but you shall judge of the whole story: Old Putnam and I were friends in the same mess; but, owing to some accidents on the Afghan border, I got my regiment much sooner than most men;[1] only we were both

---

[1] In some later editions, "I got my regiment" has been broadened to "I got my command."

invalided home for a bit. I was engaged to Audrey out there; and we all travelled back together. But on the journey back things happened. Curious things. The result of them was that Putnam wants it broken off, and even Audrey keeps it hanging on—and I know what they mean. I know what they think I am. So do you.

"Well, these are the facts: The last day we were in an Indian city, I asked Putnam if I could get some Trichinopoli cigars; he directed me to a little place opposite his lodgings. I have since found he was quite right; but 'opposite' is a dangerous word when one decent house stands opposite five or six squalid ones; and I must have mistaken the door. It opened with difficulty, and then only on darkness; but as I turned back, the door behind me sank back and settled into its place with a noise as of innumerable bolts. There was nothing to do but to walk forward; which I did through passage after passage, pitch-dark. Then I came to a flight of steps, and then to a blind door, secured by a latch of elaborate Eastern iron-work, which I could only trace by touch, but which I loosened at last. I came out again upon gloom, which was half turned into a greenish twilight by a multitude of small but steady lamps below. They showed merely the feet or fringes of some huge and empty architecture. Just in front of me was something that looked like a mountain. I confess I nearly fell on the great stone platform on which I had emerged, to realise that it was an idol. And, worst of all, an idol with its back to me.

"It was hardly half human, I guessed; to judge by the small squat head, and still more by a thing like a tail or extra limb turned up behind and pointing, like a loathsome large finger, at some symbol graven in the centre of the vast stone back. I had begun, in the dim light, to guess at the hieroglyphic, not without horror, when a more horrible thing happened. A door opened silently in the temple wall behind me and a man came out, with a brown face and a black coat. He had a carved smile on his face, of copper flesh and ivory teeth; but I think the most hateful thing about him was that he was in European dress. I was prepared, I think, for shrouded priests or naked fakirs. But this seemed to say that the devilry was over all the earth. As indeed I found it to be.

"'If you had only seen the Monkey's Feet,' he said, smiling steadily and without other preface, 'we should have been very gentle—you would only be tortured and die. If you had seen the Monkey's Face, still we should be very moderate, very tolerant—you would only be tortured and live. But as you have seen the Monkey's Tail, we must pronounce the worst sentence. Which is—Go Free.'

"When he said the words I heard the elaborate iron latch with which I had struggled automatically unlock itself; and then far down the dark passages I had passed I heard the heavy street-door shifting its own bolts backwards.

"'It is vain to ask for mercy; you must go free,' said the smiling man. 'Henceforth a hair shall slay you like a sword, and a breath shall bite you like an adder; weapons shall come against you out of nowhere; and you shall die many times.' And with that he was swallowed once more in the wall behind; and I went out into the street."

Cray paused; and Father Brown unaffectedly sat down on the lawn and began to pick daisies.

Then the soldier continued, "Putnam, of course, with his jolly common sense, pooh-poohed all my fears; and from that time dates his doubt of my mental balance. Well, I'll simply tell you, in the fewest words, the three things that have happened since; and you shall judge which of us is right.

"The first happened in an Indian village on the edge of the jungle, but hundreds of miles from the temple, or town, or type of tribes and customs where the curse had been put on me. I woke in black midnight, and lay thinking of nothing in particular, when I felt a faint tickling thing, like a thread or hair, trailed across my throat. I shrank back out of its way, and could not help thinking of the words in the temple. But when I got up and sought lights and a mirror, the line across my neck was a line of blood.

"The second happened in a lodging in Port Said, later, on our journey home together. It was a jumble of tavern and curiosity-shop; and though there was nothing there remotely suggesting the cult of the Monkey, it is, of course, possible that some of its images or talismans were in such a place. Its curse was there, anyhow. I woke again in the dark with a sensation that could not be put in colder or more literal words than that a breath bit like an adder. Existence was an agony of extinction; I dashed my head against walls until I dashed it against a window; and fell rather than jumped into the garden below. Putnam, poor fellow, who had called the other thing a chance scratch, was bound to take seriously the fact of finding me half insensible on the grass at dawn. But I fear it was my mental state he took seriously; and not my story.

"The third happened in Malta. We were in a fortress there; and as it happened our bedrooms overlooked the open sea, which almost came up to our window-sills, save for a flat white outer wall as bare as the sea. I woke up again; but it was not dark. There was a full moon, as I walked to the window; I could have seen a bird on the bare battlement, or a sail on the horizon. What I did see was a sort of stick or branch circling, self-supported in the empty sky. It flew straight in at my window and smashed the lamp beside the pillow I had just quitted. It was one of those queer-shaped war-clubs some Eastern tribes use. But it had come from no human hand."

Father Brown threw away a daisy-chain he was making, and rose with a wistful look. "Has Major Putnam," he asked, "got any Eastern curios, idols, weapons and so on, from which one might get a hint?"

"Plenty of those, though not much use, I fear," replied Cray; "but by all means come into his study."

As they entered they passed Miss Watson buttoning her gloves for church, and heard the voice of Putnam downstairs still giving a lecture on cookery to the cook. In the Major's study and den of curios they came suddenly on a third party, silk-hatted and dressed for the street, who was poring over an open book on the smoking-table—a book which he dropped rather guiltily, and turned.

Cray introduced him civilly enough, as Dr. Oman, but he showed such disfavour in his very face that Brown guessed the two men, whether Audrey knew it or not, were rivals. Nor was the priest wholly unsympathetic with the prejudice. Dr. Oman was a very well-dressed gentleman indeed; well-featured, though almost dark enough for an Asiatic. But Father Brown had to tell himself sharply that one should be in charity even with those who wax their pointed beards, who have small gloved hands, and who speak with perfectly modulated voices.

Cray seemed to find something specially irritating in the small prayer-book in Oman's dark-gloved hand. "I didn't know that was in your line," he said rather rudely.

Oman laughed mildly, but without offence. "This is more so, I know," he said, laying his hand on the big book he had dropped, "a dictionary of drugs and such things. But it's rather too large to take to church." Then he closed the larger book, and there seemed again the faintest touch of hurry and embarrassment.

"I suppose," said the priest, who seemed anxious to change the subject, "all these spears and things are from India?"

"From everywhere," answered the doctor. "Putnam is an old soldier, and has been in Mexico and Australia, and the Cannibal Islands for all I know."

"I hope it was not in the Cannibal Islands," said Brown, "that he learnt the art of cookery." And he ran his eye over the stew-pots or other strange utensils on the wall.

At this moment the jolly subject of their conversation thrust his laughing, lobsterish face into the room. "Come along, Cray," he cried. "Your lunch is just coming in. And the bells are ringing for those who want to go to church."

Cray slipped upstairs to change; Dr. Oman and Miss Watson betook themselves solemnly down the street, with a string of other church-goers; but Father Brown noticed that the doctor twice looked back and scrutinised the house; and even came back to the corner of the street to look at it again.

The priest looked puzzled. "*He* can't have been at the dustbin," he muttered. "Not in those clothes. Or was he there earlier today?"

Father Brown, touching other people, was as sensitive as a barometer; but today he seemed about as sensitive as a rhinoceros. By no social law, rigid or implied, could he be supposed to linger round the lunch of the Anglo-Indian friends; but he lingered, covering his position with torrents of amusing but quite needless conversation. He was the more puzzling because he did not seem to want any lunch. As one after another of the most exquisitely balanced kedgerees of curries, accompanied before with their appropriate vintages, were laid before the other two, he only repeated that it was one of his fast-days, and munched a piece of bread and sipped and then left untasted a tumbler of cold water. His talk however, was exuberant.

"I'll tell you what I'll do for you," he cried; "I'll mix you a salad! I can't eat it, but I'll mix it like an angel! You've got a lettuce there."

"Unfortunately it's the only thing we have got," answered the good-humoured Major. "You must remember that mustard, vinegar, oil, and so on vanished with the cruet and the burglar."

"I know," replied Brown, rather vaguely. "That's what I've always been afraid would happen. That's why I always carry a cruet-stand about with me. I'm so fond of salads."

And to the amazement of the two men he took a pepper-pot out of his waistcoat pocket and put it on the table.

"I wonder why the burglar wanted mustard, too," he went on, taking a mustard-pot from another pocket. "A mustard plaster, I suppose. And vinegar" —producing that condiment— "haven't I heard something about vinegar and brown paper? As for oil, which I think I put in my left—"

His garrulity was an instant arrested; for lifting his eyes, he saw what no one else saw—the black figure of Dr. Oman standing on the sunlit lawn and looking steadily into the room. Before he could quite recover himself, Cray had cloven in.

"You're an astounding card," he said, staring. "I shall come and hear your sermons if they're as amusing as your manners." His voice changed a little, and he leaned back in his chair.

"Oh, there are sermons in a cruet-stand, too," said Father Brown, quite gravely. "Have you heard of faith like a grain of mustard-seed; or charity that anoints with oil? And as for vinegar, can any soldiers forget solitary soldier, who, when the sun was darkened —"

Colonel Cray leaned forward a little and clutched the table-cloth.

Father Brown, who was making the salad, tipped two spoonfuls of the mustard into the tumbler of water beside him; stood up, and said in a new, loud and sudden voice— "Drink that!"

At the same moment the motionless doctor in the garden came running and bursting open a window, cried, "Am I wanted? Has he been poisoned?"

"Pretty near," said Brown, with the shadow of a smile; for the emetic had very suddenly taken effect. And Cray lay in a deck-chair, gasping as for life, but alive.

Major Putnam had sprung up, his purple face mottled. "A crime!" he cried hoarsely. "I will go for the police!"

The priest could hear him dragging down his palm-leaf hat from the peg and tumbling out the front door; he heard the garden gate slam. But he only stood looking at Cray; and after a silence said quietly:

"I shall not talk to you much; but I will tell you what you want to know. There is no curse on you. The Temple of the Monkey was either a coincidence or a part of the trick; the trick was the trick of a white man. There is only one weapon that will bring blood with that mere feathery touch: a razor held by a white man. There is one way of making a common room full of invisible overpowering poison: turning on the gas—the crime of a white man. And there is only one kind of club that can be thrown out of a window, turn in mid air and come back to the window next to it: the Australian boomerang. You'll see some of them in the Major's study."

With that he went outside and spoke for a moment to the doctor. The moment after, Audrey Watson came rushing into the house and fell on her knees beside Cray's chair. He could not hear what they said to each other; but their faces moved with amazement, not unhappiness. The doctor and the priest walked slowly towards the garden gate.

"I suppose the Major was in love with her, too," he said with a sigh; and when the other nodded observed, "You were very generous, doctor. You did a fine thing. But what made you suspect?"

"A very small thing," said Oman; "but it kept me restless in church till I came back to see that all was well. That book on his table was a work on poisons; and was put down open at the place where it stated that a certain Indian poison, though deadly and difficult to trace, was particularly easily reversible by the use of the commonest emetics. I suppose he read that at the last moment —"

"And remembered that there were emetics in the cruet-stand," said Father Brown. "Exactly. He threw the cruet in the dustbin, where I found it, along with other silver, for the sake of a burglary blind. But if you look at that pepper-pot I put on the table, you'll see a small hole. That's where Cray's bullet struck, shaking up the pepper and making the criminal sneeze."

There was a silence. Then Dr. Oman said grimly, "The Major is a long time looking for the police."

"Or the police in looking for the Major?" said the priest. "Well, good-bye."

THE STRANGE CRIME
OF JOHN BOULNOIS

Mr. Calhoun Kidd was a very young gentleman with a very old face, a face dried up with its own eagerness, framed in blue-black hair and a black butterfly tie. He was the emissary in England of the colossal American daily called *The Western Sun* — also humorously described as the "Rising Sunset." This was in allusion to a great journalistic declaration (attributed to Mr. Kidd himself) that "he guessed the sun would rise in the west yet if American citizens did a bit more hustling." Those, however, who mock American journalism from the standpoint of somewhat mellower traditions forget a certain paradox which partly redeems it. For while the journalism of the States permits a pantomimic vulgarity long past anything English, it also shows a real excitement about the most earnest mental problems, of which English papers are innocent, or rather incapable. The *Sun* was full of the most solemn matters treated in the most farcical way. William James figured there as well as "Weary Willie," [1] and pragmatists alternated with pugilists in the long procession of its portraits.

Thus, when a very unobtrusive Oxford man named John Boulnois wrote in a very unreadable review called *The Natural Philosophy Quarterly* a series of articles on alleged weak points in Darwinian evolution, it fluttered no corner of the English papers; though Boulnois's theory (which was that of a comparatively stationary universe visited occasionally by convulsions of change) had some rather faddy fashionableness at Oxford, and got so far as to be named "Catastrophism." But many American papers seized on the challenge as a great event; and the *Sun* threw the shadow of Mr. Boulnois quite gigantically across its pages. By the paradox already noted, articles of valuable intelligence and enthusiasm were presented with headlines apparently written by an illiterate maniac; headlines such as "Darwin Chews Dirt; Critic Boulnois Says He Jumps the Shocks" — or "Keep

[1] Weary Willy was a hobo character from *Illustrated Chips*, an American comic magazine of the day.

Catastrophic, Says Thinker Boulnois." And Mr. Calhoun Kidd, of *The Western Sun*, was bidden to take his butterfly tie and lugubrious visage down to the little house outside Oxford where Thinker Boulnois lived in happy ignorance of such a title.

That fated philosopher had consented, in a somewhat dazed manner, to receive the interviewer, and had named the hour of nine that evening. The last of a summer sunset clung about Cumnor and the low wooded hills; the romantic Yankee was both doubtful of his road and inquisitive about his surroundings; and, seeing the door of a genuine feudal old-country inn, The Champion Arms, standing open, he went in to make inquiries.

In the bar parlour he rang the bell, and had to wait some little time for a reply to it. The only other person present was a lean man with close red hair and loose horsey-looking clothes, who was drinking very bad whisky, but smoking a very good cigar. The whisky, of course, was the choice brand of The Champion Arms; the cigar he had probably brought with him from London. Nothing could be more different than this cynical *négligé* from the dapper dryness of the young American; but something in his pencil and open notebook, and perhaps in the expression of his alert blue eye, caused Kidd to guess, correctly, that he was a brother journalist.

"Could you do me the favour," asked Kidd, with the courtesy of his nation, "of directing me to the Grey Cottage, where Mr. Boulnois lives, as I understand?"

"It's a few yards down the road," said the red-haired man, removing his cigar; "I shall be passing it myself in a minute, but I'm going on to Pendragon Park to try and see the fun."

"What is Pendragon Park?" asked Calhoun Kidd.

"Sir Claude Champion's place — haven't you come down for that, too?" asked the other pressman, looking up. "You're a journalist, aren't you?"

"I have come to see Mr. Boulnois," said Kidd.

"I've come to see Mrs. Boulnois," replied the other. "But I shan't catch her at home." And he laughed rather unpleasantly.

"Are you interested in Catastrophism?" asked the wondering Yankee.

"I'm interested in catastrophes; and there are going to be some," replied his companion gloomily. "Mine's a filthy trade, and I never pretend it isn't."

With that he spat on the floor; yet somehow in the very act and instant one could realise that the man had been brought up as a gentleman.

The American pressman considered him with more attention. His face was pale and dissipated, with the promise of formidable passions yet to be loosed; but it was a clever and sensitive face; his clothes were coarse and careless, but he had a good seal ring on one of his long, thin fingers. His name, which came out in the course of talk, was James Dalroy; he was the son of a bankrupt Irish landlord, and attached to a pink paper which he heartily despised, called *Smart Society*, in the capacity of reporter and of something painfully like spy.

Smart Society, I regret to say, felt none of that interest in Boulnois on Darwin which was such a credit to the head and hearts of *The Western Sun*. Dalroy had come down, it seemed, to snuff up the scent of a scandal which might very well end in the Divorce Court, but which was at present hovering between Grey Cottage and Pendragon Park.

Sir Claude Champion was known to the readers of the *Western Sun* as well as Mr. Boulnois. So were the Pope and the Derby Winner; but the idea of their intimate acquaintanceship would have struck Kidd as equally incongruous. He had heard of (and written about, nay, falsely pretended to know) Sir Claude Champion, as "one of the brightest and wealthiest of England's Upper Ten"; as the great sportsman who raced yachts round the world; as the great traveller who wrote books about the Himalayas, as the politician who swept constituencies with a startling sort of Tory Democracy, and as the great dabbler in art, music, literature, and, above all, acting. Sir Claude was really rather magnificent in other than American eyes. There was something of the Renascence Prince about his omnivorous culture and restless publicity; he was not only a great amateur, but an ardent one. There was in him none of that antiquarian frivolity that we convey by the word "dilettante."

That faultless falcon profile with purple-black Italian eyes, which had been snap-shotted so often both for *Smart Society* and *The Western*

Sun, gave everyone the impression of a man eaten by ambition as by a fire, or even a disease. But though Kidd knew a great deal about Sir Claude—a great deal more, in fact, than there was to know—it would never have crossed his wildest dreams to connect so showy an aristocrat with the newly-unearthed founder of Catastrophism, or to guess that Sir Claude Champion and John Boulnois could be intimate friends. Such, according to Dalroy's account, was nevertheless the fact. The two had hunted in couples at school and college, and, though their social destinies had been very different (for Champion was a great landlord and almost a millionaire, while Boulnois was a poor scholar and, until just lately, an unknown one), they still kept in very close touch with each other. Indeed, Boulnois's cottage stood just outside the gates of Pendragon Park.

But whether the two men could be friends much longer was becoming a dark and ugly question. A year or two before, Boulnois had married a beautiful and not unsuccessful actress, to whom he was devoted in his own shy and ponderous style; and the proximity of the household to Champion's had given that flighty celebrity opportunities for behaving in a way that could not but cause painful and rather base excitement. Sir Claude had carried the arts of publicity to perfection; and he seemed to take a crazy pleasure in being equally ostentatious in an intrigue that could do him no sort of honour. Footmen from Pendragon were perpetually leaving bouquets for Mrs. Boulnois; carriages and motor-cars were perpetually calling at the cottage for Mrs. Boulnois; balls and masquerades perpetually filled the grounds in which the baronet paraded Mrs. Boulnois, like the Queen of Love and Beauty at a tournament. That very evening, marked by Mr. Kidd for the exposition of Catastrophism, had been marked by Sir Claude Champion for an open-air rendering of *Romeo and Juliet*, in which he was to play Romeo to a Juliet it was needless to name.

"I don't think it can go on without a smash," said the young man with red hair, getting up and shaking himself. "Old Boulnois may be squared —or he may be square. But if he's square he's thick — what you might call cubic. But I don't believe it's possible."

"He is a man of grand intellectual powers," said Calhoun Kidd, in a deep voice.

"Yes," answered Dalroy; "but even a man of grand intellectual powers can't be such a blighted fool as all that. Must you be going on? I
shall be following myself in a minute or two."

But Calhoun Kidd, having finished a milk and soda, betook himself smartly up the road towards the Grey Cottage, leaving his cynical
informant to his whisky and tobacco. The last of the daylight had
faded; the skies were of a dark green-grey like slate, studded here and
there with a star, but lighter on the left side of the sky, with the promise of a rising moon.

The Grey Cottage, which stood entrenched, as it were, in a square
of stiff, high thorn-hedges, was so close under the pines and palisades
of the Park that Kidd at first mistook it for the Park Lodge. Finding
the name on the narrow wooden gate, however, and seeing by his
watch that the hour of the "Thinker's" appointment had just struck,
he went in and knocked at the front door. Inside the garden hedge,
he could see that the house, though unpretentious enough, was larger
and more luxurious than it looked at first, and was quite a different
kind of place from a porter's lodge. A dog-kennel and a beehive stood
outside like symbols of old English country life; the moon was rising
behind a plantation of prosperous pear trees; the dog that came out of
the kennel was reverend-looking and reluctant to bark; and the plain,
elderly manservant who opened the door was brief but dignified.

"Mr. Boulnois asked me to offer his apologies, sir," he said, "but
he has been obliged to go out suddenly."

"But see here, I had an appointment," said the interviewer, with a
rising voice. "Do you know where he went to?"

"To Pendragon Park, sir," said the servant, rather sombrely, and
began to close the door.

Kidd started a little. "Did he go with Mrs. — with the rest of the
party?" he asked rather vaguely.

"No, sir," said the man shortly; "he stayed behind, and then went
out alone." And he shut the door, brutally, but with an air of duty not
done.

The American, that curious compound of impudence and sensi-
tiveness, was annoyed. He felt a strong desire to hustle them all along
a bit and teach them business habits; the hoary old dog and the grizzled,

heavy-faced old butler with his prehistoric shirt-front, and the drowsy old moon, and above all, the scatter-brained old philosopher who couldn't keep an appointment.

"If that's the way he goes on, he deserves to lose his wife's purest devotion," said Mr. Calhoun Kidd. "But perhaps he's gone over to make a row. In that case I reckon a man from *The Western Sun* will be on the spot."

And turning the corner by the open lodge-gates, he set off, stumping up the long avenue of black pine-woods that pointed in abrupt perspective towards the inner gardens of Pendragon Park. The trees were as black and orderly as plumes upon a hearse; there were still a few stars. He was a man with more literary than direct natural associations; the word "Ravenswood" came into his head repeatedly.[2] It was partly the raven colour of the pine-woods; but partly also an indescribable atmosphere almost described in Scott's great tragedy; the smell of something that died in the eighteenth century; the smell of dank gardens and broken urns, of wrongs that will never now be righted; of something that is none the less incurably sad because it is strangely unreal.

More than once, as he went up that trim, black road of tragic artifice, he stopped startled, thinking he heard steps in front of him. He could see nothing in front but the twin sombre walls of pine and the wedge of starlit sky above them. At first he thought he must have fancied it or been mocked by a mere echo of his own tramp. But as he went on he more and more inclined to conclude, with the remains of his reason, that there really were other feet upon the road. He thought hazily of ghosts; and was surprised how swiftly he could see the image of an appropriate and local ghost, one with a face as white as Pierrot's, but patched with black. The apex of the triangle of dark-blue sky was growing brighter and bluer, but he did not realise as yet that this was because he was coming nearer to the lights of the great house and garden. He only felt that the atmosphere was growing more intense; there was in the sadness more

---

[2] Mr. Kidd is brooding over Sir Walter Scott's historical novel of doom and love deceived, *The Bride of Lammermoor* (1819), and its hero, Edgar of Ravenswood.

violence and secrecy—more—he hesitated for the word, and then said it with a jerk of laughter—Catastrophism.

More pines, more pathway slid past him, and then he stood rooted as by a blast of magic. It is vain to say that he felt as if he had got into a dream; but this time he felt quite certain that he had got into a book. For we human beings are used to inappropriate things; we are accustomed to the clatter of the incongruous; it is a tune to which we can go to sleep. If one appropriate thing happens, it wakes us up like the pang of a perfect chord. Something happened such as would have happened in such a place in a forgotten tale.

Over the black pine-wood came flying and flashing in the moon a naked sword — such a slender and sparkling rapier as may have fought many an unjust duel in that ancient park. It fell on the pathway far in front of him and lay there glistening like a large needle. He ran like a hare and bent to look at it. Seen at closer quarters it had rather a showy look; the big red jewels in the hilt and guard were a little dubious. But there were other red drops upon the blade which were not dubious.

He looked round wildly in the direction from which the dazzling missile had come, and saw that at this point the sable façade of fir and pine was interrupted by a smaller road at right angles; which, when he turned it, brought him in full view of the long, lighted house, with a lake and fountains in front of it. Nevertheless, he did not look at this, having something more interesting to look at.

Above him, at the angle of the steep green bank of the terraced garden, was one of those small picturesque surprises common in the old landscape gardening; a kind of small round hill or dome of grass, like a giant mole-hill, ringed and crowned with three concentric fences of roses and having a sundial in the highest point in the centre. Kidd could see the finger of the dial stand up dark against the sky like the dorsal fin of a shark; and the vain moonlight clinging to that idle clock. But he saw something else clinging to it also, for one wild moment — the figure of a man.

Though he saw it there only for a moment, though it was outlandish and incredible in costume, being clad from neck to heel in tight crimson, with glints of gold, yet he knew in one flash of moonlight who it was. That white face flung up to heaven, clean-shaven and so unnaturally young, like Byron with a Roman nose, those black curls already grizzled — he had seen the thousand public portraits of Sir Claude Champion. The wild red figure reeled an instant against the sundial; the next it had rolled down the steep bank and lay at the American's feet, faintly moving one arm. A gaudy unnatural gold ornament on the arm suddenly reminded Kidd of *Romeo and Juliet*; of course, the tight crimson suit was part of the play. But there was a long red stain down the bank from which the man had rolled—that was no part of the play. He had been run through the body.

Mr. Calhoun Kidd shouted and shouted again. Once more he seemed to hear phantasmal footsteps, and started to find another figure already near him. He knew the figure, and yet it terrified him. The dissipated youth who had called himself Dalroy had a horribly quiet way with him; if Boulnois failed to keep appointments that had been made, Dalroy had a sinister air of keeping appointments that hadn't. The moonlight discoloured everything; against Dalroy's red hair his wan face looked not so much white as pale green.

All this morbid impressionism must be Kidd's excuse for having cried out, brutally and beyond all reason, "Did you do this, you devil?"

James Dalroy smiled his unpleasing smile; but before he could speak, the fallen figure made another movement of the arm, waving vaguely towards the place where the sword fell; then came a moan, and then it managed to speak.

"Boulnois ... Boulnois, I say ... Boulnois did it ... jealous of me ... he was jealous, he was, he was ..."

Kidd bent his head down to hear more, and just managed to catch the words:

"Boulnois ... with my own sword ... he threw it ..."

Again the falling hand waved towards the sword, and then fell rigid with a thud. In Kidd rose from its depths all that acrid humour that is the strange salt of the seriousness of his race.

"See here," he said sharply and with command, "you must fetch a doctor. This man's dead."

"And a priest, too, I suppose," said Dalroy in an undecipherable manner. "All these Champions are papists."

The American knelt down by the body, felt the heart, propped up the head, and used some last efforts at restoration; but before the other journalist reappeared, followed by a doctor and a priest, he was already prepared to assert they were too late.

"Were you too late also?" asked the doctor, a solid, prosperous-looking man, with conventional moustache and whiskers, but a lively eye, which darted over Kidd dubiously.

"In one sense," drawled the representative of the *Sun*. "I was too late to save the man, but I guess I was in time to hear something of importance. I heard the dead man denounce his assassin."

"And who was the assassin?" asked the doctor, drawing his eyebrows together.

"Boulnois," said Calhoun Kidd, and whistled softly.

The doctor stared at him gloomily with a reddening brow; but he did not contradict. Then the priest, a shorter figure in the background, said mildly, "I understood that Mr. Boulnois was not coming to Pendragon Park this evening."

"There again," said the Yankee grimly. "I may be in a position to give the old country a fact or two. Yes, *sir*, John Boulnois was going to stay in all this evening; he fixed up a real good appointment there with me. But John Boulnois changed his mind; John Boulnois left his home abruptly and all alone, and came over to this derned Park an hour or so ago. His butler told me so. I think we hold what the all-wise police call a clue — have you sent for them?"

"Yes," said the doctor. "But we haven't alarmed anyone else yet."

"Does Mrs. Boulnois know?" asked James Dalroy; and again Kidd was conscious of an irrational desire to hit him on his curling mouth.

"I have not told her," said the doctor gruffly. "But here come the police."

The little priest had stepped out into the main avenue, and now returned with the fallen sword, which looked ludicrously large and theatrical when attached to his dumpy figure, at once clerical and commonplace. "Just before the police come," he said apologetically, "has anyone got a light?"

The Yankee journalist took an electric torch from his pocket, and the priest held it close to the middle part of the blade, which he examined with blinking care. Then, without glancing at the point or pommel, he handed the long weapon to the doctor.

"I fear I'm no use here," he said, with a brief sigh. "I'll say good-night to you, gentlemen." And he walked away up the dark avenue toward the house, his hands clasped behind him and his big head bent in cogitation.

The rest of the group made increased haste towards the lodge-gates, where an inspector and two constables could already be seen in consultation with the lodge-keeper. But the little priest only walked slower and slower in the dim cloister of pine, and at last stopped dead, on the steps of the house. It was his silent way of acknowledging an equally silent approach; for there came towards him a presence that might have satisfied even Calhoun Kidd's demands for a lovely and aristocratic ghost. It was a young woman in silvery satins of a Renascence design; she had golden hair in two long shining ropes, and a face so startlingly pale between them that she might have been chryselephantine — made, that is, like some old Greek statues, out of ivory and gold. But her eyes were very bright, and her voice, though low, was confident.

"Father Brown?" she said.

"Mrs. Boulnois?" he replied gravely. Then he looked at her and immediately said, "I see you know about Sir Claude."

"How do you know I know?" she asked steadily.

He did not answer the question, but asked another, "Have you seen your husband?"

"My husband is at home," she said. "He has nothing to do with this." Again he did not answer; and the woman drew nearer to him, with a curiously intense expression on her face.

"Shall I tell you something more?" she said, with a rather fearful smile. "I don't think he did it, and *you* don't either."

Father Brown returned her gaze with a long, grave stare, and then nodded, yet more gravely.

"Father Brown," said the lady, "I am going to tell you all I know, but I want you to do me a favour first. Will you tell me *why* you haven't jumped to the conclusion of poor John's guilt, as all the rest have done? Don't mind what you say: I—I know about the gossip and the appearances that are against him."

Father Brown looked honestly embarrassed, and passed his hand across his forehead. "Two very little things," he said. "At least, one's very trivial and the other very vague. But such as they are, they don't fit in with Mr. Boulnois being the murderer."

He turned his blank round face up to the stars and continued absent-mindedly, "To take the vague idea first. I attach a good deal of importance to vague ideas. All those things that 'aren't evidence' are what convince me. I think a moral impossibility the biggest of all impossibilities. I know your husband only slightly, but I think this crime of his, as generally conceived, something very like a moral impossibility. Please do not think I mean that Boulnois could not be so wicked. Anybody can be wicked—as wicked as he chooses. We can direct our moral wills; but we can't generally change our instinctive tastes and ways of doing things. Boulnois might commit a murder, but not this murder. He would not snatch Romeo's sword from its romantic scabbard; or slay his foe on the sundial as on a kind of altar; or leave his body among the roses; or fling the sword away among the pines. If Boulnois killed anyone he'd do it quietly and heavily, as he'd do any other doubtful thing—take a tenth glass of port, or read a loose Greek poet. No, the romantic setting is not like Boulnois. It's more like Champion."

"Ah!" she said, and looked at him with eyes like diamonds.

"And the trivial thing was this," said Brown. "There were finger-prints on that sword; finger-prints can be detected quite a time after they are made if they're on some polished surface like glass or steel. These were on a polished surface. They were half-way down the blade of the sword. Whose prints they were I have no earthly clue; but why should anybody hold a sword half-way down? It was a long sword, but length is an advantage in lunging at an enemy. At least, at most enemies. At all enemies except one."

"Except one!" she repeated.

"There is only one enemy," said Father Brown, "whom it is easier to kill with a dagger than a sword."

"I know," said the woman. "Oneself."

There was a long silence, and then the priest said quietly but abruptly, "Am I right, then? Did Sir Claude kill himself?"

"Yes," she said, with a face like marble. "I saw him do it."

"He died," said Father Brown, "for love of you?"

An extraordinary expression flashed across her face, very different from pity, modesty, remorse, or anything her companion had expected: her voice became suddenly strong and full. "I don't believe," she said, "he ever cared about me a rap. He hated my husband."

"Why?" asked the other, and turned his round face from the sky to the lady.

"He hated my husband because . . . it is so strange I hardly know how to say it . . . because . . ."

"Yes?" said Brown patiently.

"Because my husband wouldn't hate him."

Father Brown only nodded, and seemed still to be listening; he differed from most detectives in fact and fiction in a small point — he never pretended not to understand when he understood perfectly well.

Mrs. Boulnois drew near once more with the same contained glow of certainty. "My husband," she said, "is a great man. Sir Claude Champion was not a great man: he was a celebrated and successful man. My husband has never been celebrated or successful; and it is the solemn truth that he has never dreamed of being so. He no more expects to be famous for thinking than for smoking cigars. On all that side he has a sort of splendid stupidity. He has never grown up. He still liked Champion exactly as he liked him at school; he admired him as he would admire a conjuring trick done at the dinner table. But he couldn't be got to conceive the notion of *envying* Champion. *And Champion wanted to be envied.* He went mad and killed himself for that."

"Yes," said Father Brown; "I think I begin to understand."

"Oh, don't you see?" she cried. "The whole picture is made for that — the place is planned for it. Champion put John in a little house at his very door, like a dependent — to make him *feel* a failure. He never felt it. He thinks no more about such things than — than an absent-minded lion. Champion would burst in on John's shabbiest hours or homeliest meals with some dazzling present or announcement or expedition that made it like the visit of Haroun Alraschid, and John would accept or refuse amiably, with one eye off, so to speak,

like one lazy schoolboy agreeing or disagreeing with another. After
five years of it John had not turned a hair; and Sir Claude Champion
was a monomaniac."

"And Haman began to tell them," said Father Brown, "of all the
things wherein the king had honoured him; and he said, 'All these
things profit me nothing while I see Mordecai the Jew sitting in the
gate.' " [3]

"The crisis came," Mrs. Boulnois continued, "when I persuaded
John to let me take down some of his speculations and send them to
a magazine. They began to attract attention, especially in America;
and one paper wanted to interview him. When Champion (who was
interviewed nearly every day) heard of this late little crumb of success
falling to his unconscious rival, the last link snapped that held back
his devilish hatred. Then he began to lay that insane siege to my own
love and honour which has been the talk of the shire. You will ask me
why I allowed such atrocious attentions. I answer that I could not
have declined them except by explaining to my husband, and there
are some things the soul cannot do, as the body cannot fly. Nobody
could have explained to my husband. Nobody could do it now. If you
said to him in so many words, 'Champion is stealing your wife,' he
would think the joke a little vulgar: that it could be anything but a
joke—that notion could find no crack in his great skull to get in by.
Well, John was to come and see us act this evening, but just as we
were starting he said he wouldn't; he had got an interesting book and
a cigar. I told this to Sir Claude, and it was his death-blow. The monomaniac suddenly saw despair. He stabbed himself, crying out like a
devil that Boulnois was slaying him; he lies there in the garden dead
of his own jealousy to produce jealousy; and John is to sitting in the
dining-room reading a book."

There was another silence, and then the little priest said, "There
is only one weak point, Mrs. Boulnois, in all your very vivid account.
Your husband is not sitting in the dining-room reading a book. That
American reporter told me he had been to your house, and your

---

[3] Father Brown quotes the Book of Esther, in which the Persian king's favorite,
Haman, becomes obsessed with Mordecai, a commoner who refuses to bow to him.

butler told him Mr. Boulnois had gone to Pendragon Park, after all."

Her bright eyes widened to an almost electric glare; and yet it seemed rather bewilderment than confusion or fear. "Why, what *can* you mean?" she cried. "All the servants were out of the house, seeing the theatricals. And we don't keep a butler, thank goodness!"

Father Brown started and spun half round like an absurd teetotum. "What, what?" he cried seeming galvanised into sudden life. "Look here — I say — can I make your husband hear if I go to the house?"

"Oh, the servants will be back by now," she said, wondering.

"Right, right!" rejoined the cleric energetically, and set off scuttling up the path towards the Park gates. He turned once to say, "Better get hold of that Yankee, or 'Crime of John Boulnois' will be all over the Republic in large letters."

"You don't understand," said Mrs. Boulnois. "He wouldn't mind. I don't think he imagines that America really is a place."

When Father Brown reached the house with the beehive and the drowsy dog, a small and neat maid-servant showed him into the dining-room, where Boulnois sat reading by a shaded lamp, exactly as his wife described him. A decanter of port and a wine-glass were at his elbow; and the instant the priest entered he noted the long ash stand out unbroken on his cigar.

"He has been here for half an hour, at least," thought Father Brown. In fact, he had the air of sitting where he had sat when his dinner was cleared away.

"Don't get up, Mr. Boulnois," said the priest, in his pleasant, prosaic way. "I shan't interrupt you a moment. I fear I break in on some of your scientific studies."

"No," said Boulnois. "I was reading 'The Bloody Thumb.' " He said it with neither frown nor smile, and his visitor was conscious of a certain deep and virile indifference in the man which his wife had called greatness. He laid down a gory yellow "shocker" without even feeling its incongruity enough to comment on it humorously. John Boulnois was a big, slow-moving man with a massive head, partly grey and partly bald, and blunt, burly features. He was in shabby and very old-fashioned evening dress, with a narrow triangular opening of shirt-front: he had assumed it that evening in his original purpose of going to see his wife act Juliet.

"I won't keep you long from 'The Bloody Thumb' or any other catastrophic affairs," said Father Brown, smiling. "I only came to ask you about the crime you committed this evening."

Boulnois looked at him steadily, but a red bar began to show across his broad brow; and he seemed like one discovering embarrassment for the first time.

"I know it was a strange crime," assented Brown, in a low voice. "Stranger than murder perhaps—to you. The little sins are sometimes harder to confess than the big ones—but that's why it's so important to confess them. Your crime is committed by every fashionable hostess six times a week: and yet you find it sticks to your tongue like a nameless atrocity."

"It makes one feel," said the philosopher slowly, "such a damned fool."

"I know," assented the other, "but one often has to choose between feeling a damned fool and being one."

"I can't analyse myself well," went on Boulnois, "but sitting in that chair with that story I was as happy as a schoolboy on a half-holiday. It was security, eternity — I can't convey it ... the cigars were within reach ... the matches were within reach ... the *Thumb* had four more appearances to ... it was not only a peace, but a plenitude. Then that bell rang, and I thought for one long mortal minute that I couldn't get out of that chair — literally, physically, muscularly couldn't. Then I did it like a man lifting the world, because I knew all the servants were out. I opened the front door, and there was a little man with his mouth open to speak and his notebook open to write in. I remembered the Yankee interviewer I had forgotten. His hair was parted in the middle, and I tell you that murder — "

"I understand," said Father Brown. "I've seen him."

"I didn't commit murder," continued the Catastrophist mildly, "but only perjury. I said I had gone across to Pendragon Park and shut the door in his face. That is my crime, Father Brown, and I don't know what penance you would inflict for it."

"I shan't inflict any penance," said the clerical gentleman, collecting his heavy hat and umbrella with an air of some amusement; "quite the contrary. I came here specially to let you off the little penance which would otherwise have followed your little offence."

"And what," asked Boulnois, smiling, "is the little penance I have so luckily been let off?"

"Being hanged," said Father Brown.

THE FAIRY TALE
OF FATHER BROWN

The picturesque city and state of Heiligwaldenstein was one of those toy kingdoms of which certain parts of the German Empire still consists. It had come under the Prussian hegemony quite late in history—hardly fifty years before the fine summer day when Flambeau and Father Brown found themselves sitting in its gardens and drinking its beer. There had been not a little of war and wild justice there within living memory, as will soon be shown. But in merely looking at it one could not dismiss that impression of childishness which is the most charming side of Germany — those little pantomime paternal monarchies in which a king seems as domestic as a cook. The German soldiers by the innumerable sentry-boxes looked strangely like German toys, and the clean-cut battlements of the castle, gilt by the sunshine, looked the more like the gilt gingerbread. For it was brilliant weather. The sky was as Prussian a blue as Potsdam itself could require, but it was yet more like that lavish and glowing use of the colour which a child extracts from a shilling paint-box. Even the grey-ribbed trees looked young, for the pointed buds on them were still pink, and in a pattern against the strong blue looked like innumerable childish figures.

Despite his prosaic appearance and generally practical walk of life, Father Brown was not without a certain streak of romance in his composition, though he generally kept his day-dreams to himself, as many children do. Amid the brisk, bright colours of such a day, and in the heraldic framework of such a town, he did feel rather as if he had entered a fairy tale. He took a childish pleasure, as a younger brother might, in the formidable sword-stick which Flambeau always flung as he walked, and which now stood upright beside his tall mug of Münich. Nay, in his sleepy irresponsibility he even found himself eyeing the knobbed and clumsy head of his own shabby umbrella, with some faint memories of the ogre's club in a coloured toy-book. But he never composed anything in the form of fiction, unless it be the tale that follows:

"I wonder," he said, "whether one would have real adventures in a place like this, if one put oneself in the way? It's a splendid back-scene for them, but I always have a kind of feeling that they would fight you with pasteboard sabres more than real, horrible swords."

"You are mistaken," said his friend. "In this place they not only fight with swords, but kill without swords. And there's worse than that."

"Why, what do you mean?" asked Father Brown.

"Why," replied the other, "I should say this was the only place in Europe where a man was ever shot without firearms."

"Do you mean a bow and arrow?" asked Brown in some wonder.

"I mean a bullet in the brain," replied Flambeau. "Don't you know the story of the late Prince of this place? It was one of the great police mysteries about twenty years ago. You remember, of course, that this place was forcibly annexed at the time of Bismarck's very earliest schemes of consolidation—forcibly, that is, but not at all easily.[1] The empire (or what wanted to be one) sent Prince Otto of Grossenmark to rule the place in the Imperial interests. We saw his portrait in the gallery there—a handsome old gentleman if he'd had any hair or eyebrows, and hadn't been wrinkled all over like a vulture; but he had things to harass him, as I'll explain in a minute. He was a soldier of distinguished skill and success, but he didn't have altogether an easy job with this little place. He was defeated in several battles by the celebrated Arnhold brothers—the three guerrilla patriots to whom Swinburne wrote a poem, you remember:

> 'Wolves with the hair of the ermine,
> Crows that are crowned and kings—
> These things be many as vermin,
> Yet Three shall abide these things.'[2]

[1] Flambeau refers to Prussia's Prince Otto von Bismarck (1815–1898), who early in his career coerced Austria and other neighboring states into a North German Federation that was to be led by Prussia.

[2] Flambeau appears to be quoting Charles Algernon Swinburne (1837–1909), but these four Swinburnesque lines are purely Chesterton's invention.

Or something of that kind. Indeed, it is by no means certain that the occupation would ever have been successful had not one of the three brothers, Paul, despicably, but very decisively declined to abide these things any longer, and, by surrendering all the secrets of the insurrection, ensured its overthrow and his own ultimate promotion to the post of chamberlain to Prince Otto. After this, Ludwig, the one genuine hero among Mr. Swinburne's heroes, was killed, sword in hand, in the capture of the city, and the third, Heinrich, who, though not a traitor, had always been tame and even timid compared with his active brothers, retired into something like a hermitage, became converted to a Christian quietism which was almost Quakerish, and never mixed with men except to give nearly all he had to the poor. They tell me that not long ago he could still be seen about the neighbourhood occasionally, a man in a black cloak, nearly blind, with very wild, white hair, but a face of astonishing softness."

"I know," said Father Brown. "I saw him once."

His friend looked at him in some surprise.

"I didn't know you'd been here before," he said. "Perhaps you know as much about it as I do. Anyhow, that's the story of the Arnholds, and he was the last survivor of them. Yes, and of all the men who played parts in that drama."

"You mean that the Prince, too, died long before?"

"Died," repeated Flambeau, "and that's about as much as we can say. You must understand that towards the end of his life he began to have those tricks of the nerves not uncommon with tyrants. He multiplied the ordinary daily and nightly guard round his castle till there seemed to be more sentry-boxes than houses in the town, and doubtful characters were shot without mercy. He lived almost entirely in a little room that was in the very centre of the enormous labyrinth of all the other rooms, and even in this he erected another sort of central cabin or cupboard, lined with steel, like a safe or a battleship. Some say that under the floor of this again was a secret hole in the earth, no more than large enough to hold him, so that, in his anxiety to avoid the grave, he was willing to go into a place pretty much like it. But he went further yet. The populace had been supposed to be disarmed ever since the suppression of the revolt, but Otto now insisted, as governments very seldom insist, on an absolute and literal disarmament. It was carried out with extraordinary thoroughness and severity, by very well-organised officials over a small and familiar area, and, so far as human strength and science can be absolutely certain of anything, Prince Otto was absolutely certain that nobody could introduce so much as a toy pistol into Heiligwaldenstein."

"Human science can never be quite certain of things like that," said Father Brown, still looking at the red budding of the branches over his head, "if only because of the difficulty about definition and connotation. What is a *weapon*? People have been murdered with the mildest domestic comforts; certainly with tea-kettles, probably with tea-cosies. On the other hand, if you showed an Ancient Briton a revolver, I doubt if he would know it was a weapon — until it was fired into him, of course. Perhaps somebody introduced a firearm so new that it didn't even look like a firearm. Perhaps it looked like a thimble or something. Was the bullet at all peculiar?"

"Not that I ever heard of," answered Flambeau; "but all my information is fragmentary, and only comes from my old friend Grimm. He was a very able detective in the German service, and he tried to arrest me; I arrested him instead, and we had many interesting chats. He was in charge here of the inquiry about Prince Otto, but I forgot to ask him anything about the bullet. According to Grimm, what happened was this." He paused a moment to drain the greater part of his dark lager at a draught, and then resumed:

"On the evening in question, it seems, the Prince was expected to appear in one of the outer rooms, because he had to receive certain visitors whom he really wished to meet. They were geological experts sent to investigate the old question of the alleged supply of gold from the rocks round here, upon which (as it was said) the small city-state had so long maintained its credit and been able to negotiate with its neighbours even under the ceaseless bombardment of bigger armies. Hitherto it had never been found by the most exacting inquiry which could — "

"Which could be quite certain of discovering a toy pistol," said Father Brown, with a smile. "But what about the brother who ratted? Hadn't he anything to tell the Prince?"

"He always asseverated that he did not know," replied Flambeau; "that this was the one secret his brothers had not told him. It is only right to say that it received some support from fragmentary words spoken by the great Ludwig in the hour of death, when he looked at Heinrich but pointed at Paul, and said, 'You have not told *him* ...' and was soon afterwards incapable of speech. Anyhow, the deputation of distinguished geologists and mineralogists from Paris and Berlin were there in the most magnificent and appropriate dress, for there are no men who like wearing their decorations so much as the men of science—as anybody knows who has ever been to a soirée of the Royal Society. It was a brilliant gathering, but very late, and gradually the Chamberlain — you saw his portrait, too: a man with black eyebrows, serious eyes, and a meaningless sort of smile underneath — the Chamberlain, I say, discovered there was everything there except the Prince himself. He searched all the outer *salons*; then, remembering the man's mad fits of fear, hurried to the inmost chamber. That also was empty, but the steel turret or cabin erected in the middle of it took some time to open. When it did open, it was empty, too. He went and looked into the hole in the ground, which seemed deeper and somehow all the more like a grave — this is his account, of course. And even as he did so he heard a burst of cries and tumult in the long rooms and corridors without.

"First it was a distant din and thrill of something unthinkable on the horizon of the crowd, even beyond the castle. Next it was a wordless clamour startlingly close, and loud enough to be distinct if each word had not killed the other. Next came words of a terrible clearness, coming nearer, and next one man, rushing into the room and telling the news as briefly as such news is told.

"Otto, Prince of Heiligwaldenstein and Grossenmark, was lying in the dews of the darkening twilight in the woods beyond the castle, with his arms flung out and his face flung up to the moon. The blood still pulsed from his shattered temple and jaw, but it was the only part of him that moved like a living thing. He was clad in his full white and yellow uniform, as to receive his guests within, except that the sash or scarf had been unbound and lay rather crumpled by his side. Before he could be lifted he was dead. But, dead or alive, he was a riddle — he who had always hidden in the inmost chamber out there in the wet woods, unarmed and alone."

"Who found his body?" asked Father Brown.

"Some girl attached to the Court named Hedwig von something or other," replied his friend, "who had been out in the wood picking wild flowers."

"Had she picked any?" asked the priest, staring rather vacantly at the veil of the branches above him.

"Yes," replied Flambeau. "I particularly remember that the Chamberlain, or old Grimm or somebody, said how horrible it was, when they came up at her call, to see a girl holding spring flowers and bending over that — that bloody collapse. However, the main point is that before help arrived he was dead, and the news, of course, had to be carried back to the castle. The consternation it created was something beyond even that natural in a Court at the fall of a potentate. The foreign visitors, especially the mining experts, were in the wildest doubt and excitement, as well as many important Prussian officials, and it soon began to be clear that the scheme for finding the treasure bulked much bigger in the business than people had supposed. Experts and officials had been promised great prizes or international advantages, and some even said that the Prince's secret apartments and strong military protection were due less to fear of the populace than to the pursuit of some private investigation of —"

"Had the flowers got long stalks?" asked Father Brown.

Flambeau stared at him. "What an odd person you are!" he said. "That's exactly what old Grimm said. He said the ugliest part of it, he thought—uglier than the blood and bullet—was that the flowers were quite short, plucked close under the head."

"Of course," said the priest, "when a grown up girl is *really* picking flowers, she picks them with plenty of stalk. If she just pulled their heads off, as a child does, it looks as if — "And he hesitated.

"Well?" inquired the other.

"Well, it looks rather as if she had snatched them nervously, to make an excuse for being there after — well, after she was there."

"I know what you're driving at," said Flambeau rather gloomily. "But that and every other suspicion breaks down on the one point — the want of a weapon. He could have been killed, as you say, with lots of other things — even with his own military sash; but we have to explain not how he was killed, but how he was shot. And the fact is we can't. They had the girl most ruthlessly searched, for, to tell the truth, she was a little suspect, though the niece and ward of the wicked old Chamberlain, Paul Arnhold. But she was very romantic, and was suspected of sympathy with the old revolutionary enthusiasm in her family. All the same, however romantic you are, you can't imagine a big bullet into a man's jaw or brain without using gun or pistol. And there was no pistol, though there were two pistol shots. I leave it to you, my friend."

"How do you know there were two shots?" asked the little priest.

"There was only one in his head," said his companion, "but there was another bullet-hole in the sash."

Father Brown's smooth brow became suddenly constricted. "Was the other bullet found?" he demanded.

Flambeau started a little. "I don't think I remember," he said.

"Hold on! Hold on! Hold on!" cried Brown, frowning more and more, with a quite unusual concentration of curiosity. "Don't think me rude. Let me think this out for a moment."

"All right," said Flambeau, laughing, and finished his beer. A slight breeze stirred the budding trees and blew up into the sky cloudlets of white and pink that seemed to make the sky bluer and the whole coloured scene more quaint. They might have been cherubs flying home to the casements of a sort of celestial nursery. The oldest tower of the castle, the Dragon Tower, stood up as grotesque as the ale-mug, but as homely. Only beyond the tower glimmered the wood in which the man had lain dead.

"What became of this Hedwig eventually?" asked the priest at last.

"She is married to General Schwartz," said Flambeau. "No doubt you've heard of his career, which was rather romantic. He had distinguished himself even before his exploits at Sadowa and

Gravelotte;[3] in fact, he rose from the ranks, which is very unusual even in the smallest of the German — "

Father Brown sat up suddenly.

"Rose from the ranks!" he cried, and made a mouth as if to whistle. "Well, well, what a queer story! What a queer way of killing a man; but I suppose it was the only one possible. But to think of hate so patient — "

"What do you mean?" demanded the other. "In what way did they kill the man?"

"They killed him with the sash," said Brown carefully; and then, as Flambeau protested, "Yes, yes, I know about the bullet. Perhaps I ought to say he died of having a sash. I know it doesn't sound like having a disease."

"I suppose," said Flambeau, "that you've got some notion in your head, but it won't easily get the bullet out of his. As I explained before, he *might* easily have been strangled. But he *was* shot. By whom? By what?"

"He was shot by his own orders," said the priest.

"You mean he committed suicide?"

"I didn't say by his own wish," replied Father Brown. "I said by his own orders."

"Well, anyhow, what is your theory?"

Father Brown laughed. "I am only on my holiday," he said. "I haven't got any theories. Only this place reminds me of fairy stories, and, if you like, I'll tell you a story."

The little pink clouds, that looked rather like sweetstuff, had floated up to crown the turrets of the gilt gingerbread castle, and the pink baby fingers of the budding trees seemed spreading and stretching to reach them; the blue sky began to take a bright violet of evening, when Father Brown suddenly spoke again:

"It was on a dismal night, with rain still dripping from the trees and dew already clustering, that Prince Otto of Grossenmark stepped hurriedly out of a side door of the castle and walked swiftly into the

---

[3] Sadowa and Gravelotte were the scenes of two decisive nineteenth-century Prussian military victories (over the Austrians in 1866 and the French in 1871).

wood. One of the innumerable sentries saluted him, but he did not notice it. He had no wish to be specially noticed himself. He was glad when the great trees, grey and already greasy with rain, swallowed him up like a swamp. He had deliberately chosen the least frequented side of his palace, but even that was more frequented than he liked. But there was no particular chance of officious or diplomatic pursuit, for his exit had been a sudden impulse. All the full-dressed diplomatists he left behind were unimportant. He had realised suddenly that he could do without them.

"His great passion was not the much nobler dread of death, but the strange desire of gold. For this legend of the gold he had left Grossenmark and invaded Heiligwaldenstein. For this and only this he had bought the traitor and butchered the hero, for this he had long questioned and cross-questioned the false Chamberlain, until he had come to the conclusion that, touching his ignorance, the renegade really told the truth. For this he had, somewhat reluctantly, paid and promised money on the chance of gaining the larger amount; and for this he had stolen out of his palace like a thief in the rain, for he had thought of another way to get the desire of his eyes, and to get it cheap.

"Away at the upper end of a rambling mountain path to which he was making his way, among the pillared rocks along the ridge that hangs above the town, stood the hermitage, hardly more than a cavern fenced with thorn, in which the third of the great brethren had long hidden himself from the world. He, thought Prince Otto, could have no real reason for refusing to give up the gold. He had known its place for years, and made no effort to find it, even before his new ascetic creed had cut him off from property or pleasures. True, he had been an enemy, but he now professed a duty of having no enemies. Some concession to his cause, some appeal to his principles, would probably get the mere money secret out of him. Otto was no coward, in spite of his network of military precautions, and, in any case, his avarice was stronger than his fears. Nor was there much cause for fear. Since he was certain there were no private arms in the whole principality, he was a hundred times more certain there were none in the Quaker's little hermitage on the hill, where he lived on herbs, with two old rustic servants, and with no other voice of man for year after year. Prince Otto looked down with something of a grim smile at the bright, square labyrinths of the lamp-lit city below him. For as far as the eye could see there ran the rifles of his friends, and not one pinch of powder for his enemies. Rifles ranked so close even to that mountain path that a cry from him would bring the soldiers rushing up the hill, to say nothing of the fact that the wood and ridge were patrolled at regular intervals; rifles so far away, in the dim woods, dwarfed by distance, beyond the river, that an enemy could not slink into the town by any détour. And round the palace rifles at the west door and the east door, at the north door and the south, and all along the four façades linking them. He was safe.

"It was all the more clear when he had crested the ridge, and found how naked was the nest of his old enemy. He found himself on a small platform of rock, broken abruptly by the three corners of precipice. Behind was the black cave, masked with green thorn, so low that it was hard to believe that a man could enter it. In front was the fall of the cliffs and the vast but cloudy vision of the valley. On the small rock platform stood an old bronze lectern or reading-stand, groaning under a great German Bible. The bronze or copper of it had grown green with the eating airs of that exalted place, and Otto had instantly the thought, 'Even if they had arms, they must be rusted by now.' Moonrise had already made a deathly dawn behind the crests and crags, and the rain had ceased.

"Behind the lectern, and looking across the valley, stood a very old man in a black robe that fell as straight as the cliffs around him, but whose white hair and weak voice seemed alike to waver in the wind. He was evidently reading some daily lesson as part of his religious exercises. 'They trust in their horses ...'

"'Sir,' said the Prince of Heiligwaldenstein, with quite unusual courtesy, 'I should like only one word with you.'

"'... and in their chariots,' went on the old man weakly, 'but we will trust in the name of the Lord of Hosts ...' His last words were inaudible, but he closed the book reverently and, being nearly blind, made a groping movement and gripped the reading-stand. Instantly his two servants slipped out of the low-browed cavern and supported him. They wore dull-black gowns like his own, but they had not the frosty silver on the hair, nor the frost-bitten refinement of the features. They were peasants, Croat or Magyar, with broad, blunt visages and blinking eyes. For the first time something troubled the Prince, but his courage and diplomatic sense stood firm.

"'I fear we have not met,' he said, 'since that awful cannonade in which your poor brother died.'

"'All my brothers died,' said the old man, still looking across the valley. Then, for one instant turning on Otto his drooping, delicate features, and the wintry hair that seemed to drip over his eyebrows like icicles, he added, 'You see, I am dead, too.'

"'I hope you'll understand,' said the Prince, controlling himself almost to a point of conciliation, 'that I do not come here to haunt you, as a mere ghost of those great quarrels. We will not talk about who was right or wrong in that, but at least there was one point on which we were never wrong, because you were always right. Whatever is to be said of the policy of your family, no one for one moment imagines that you were moved by the mere gold; you have proved yourself above the suspicion that — '

"The old man in the old black gown had hitherto continued to gaze at him with watery blue eyes and a sort of weak wisdom in his face. But when the word 'gold' was said he held out his hand as if in arrest of something, and turned away his face to the mountains.

"'He has spoken of gold,' he said. 'He has spoken of things not lawful. Let him cease to speak.'

"Otto had the vice of his Prussian type and tradition, which is to regard success not as an incident but as a quality. He conceived himself and his like as perpetually conquering peoples who were perpetually being conquered. Consequently, he was ill acquainted with the emotion of surprise, and ill prepared for the next movement, which startled and stiffened him. He had opened his mouth to answer the hermit, when the mouth was stopped and the voice strangled by a strong, soft gag suddenly twisted round his head like a tourniquet. It was fully forty seconds before he even realised that the two Hungarian servants had done it, and that they had done it with his own military scarf.

"The old man went again weakly to his great brazen-supported Bible, turned over the leaves, with a patience that had something horrible about it, till he came to the Epistle of St. James, and then began to read, 'The tongue is a little member, but — '

"Something in the very voice made the Prince turn suddenly and plunge down the mountain-path he had climbed. He was halfway towards the gardens of the palace before he even tried to tear the strangling scarf from his neck and jaws. He tried again and again, and it was impossible; the men who had knotted that gag knew the difference between what a man can do with his hands in front of him and what he can do with his hands behind his head. His legs were free to leap like an antelope on the mountains, his arms were free to use any gesture or wave any signal, but he could not speak. A dumb devil was in him.

"He had come close to the woods that walled in the castle before he had quite realised what his wordless state meant and was meant to mean. Once more he looked down grimly at the bright, square labyrinths of the lamp-lit city below him, and he smiled no more. He felt himself repeating the phrases of his former mood with a murderous irony. Far as the eye could see ran the rifles of his friends, every one of whom would shoot him dead if he could not answer the challenge. Rifles were so near that the wood and ridge could be patrolled at regular intervals; therefore, it was useless to hide in the wood till morning. Rifles were ranked so far away that an enemy could not slink into the town by any détour; therefore it was vain to return to the city by any remote course. A cry from him would bring his soldiers rushing up the hill. But from him no cry would come.

"The moon had risen in strengthening silver and the sky showed in stripes of bright, nocturnal blue between the black stripes of the pines about the castle. Flowers of some wide and feathery sort — for he had never noticed such things before — were at once made luminous and discoloured by the moonshine, and seemed indescribably fantastic as they clustered, as if crawling about the roots of the trees. Perhaps his reason had been suddenly unseated by the unnatural captivity he carried with him, but in that wood he felt something unfathomably German — the fairy tale. He knew with half his mind that he

was drawing near to the castle of an ogre — he had forgotten that he
was the ogre. He remembered asking his mother if bears lived in the
old park at home. He stooped to pick a flower, as if it were a charm
against enchantment. The stalk was stronger than he expected, and
broke with a slight snap. Carefully trying to place it in his scarf, he
heard the halloo, 'Who goes there?' Then he remembered the scarf
was not in its usual place.

"He tried to scream, and was silent. The second challenge came;
and then a shot that shrieked as it came and then was stilled suddenly
by impact. Otto of Grossenmark lay very peacefully among the fairy
trees, and would do no more harm either with gold or steel; only the
silver pencil of the moon would pick out and trace here and there the
intricate ornament of his uniform, or the old wrinkles on his brow.
May God have mercy on his soul.

"The sentry who had fired, according to the strict orders of the
garrison, naturally ran forward to find some trace of his quarry. He
was a private named Schwartz, since not unknown in his profession,
and what he found was a bald man in uniform, but with his face so
bandaged by a kind of mask made of his own military scarf that nothing but open, dead eyes could be seen, glittering stonily in the moon.
The bullet had gone through the gag into the jaw; that is why there
was a shot-hole in the scarf, but only one shot. Naturally, if not correctly, young Schwartz tore off the mysterious silken mask and cast it
on the grass; and then he saw whom he had slain.

"We cannot be certain of the next phase. But I incline to believe
that there was a fairy tale, after all, in that little wood, horrible as was
its occasion. Whether the young lady named Hedwig had any previous knowledge of the soldier she saved and eventually married, or
whether she came accidentally upon the accident and their intimacy
began that night, we shall probably never know. But we can know, I
fancy, that this Hedwig was a heroine, and deserved to marry a man
who became something of a hero. She did the bold and the wise
thing. She persuaded the sentry to go back to his post, in which place
there was nothing to connect him with the disaster; he was but one of
the most loyal and orderly of fifty such sentries within call. She remained
by the body and gave the alarm; and there was nothing to connect her

with the disaster either, since she had not got, and could not have, any firearms.

"Well," said Father Brown, rising cheerfully, "I hope they're happy."

"Where are you going?" asked his friend.

"I'm going to have another look at that portrait of the Chamberlain, the Arnhold who betrayed his brethren," answered the priest. "I wonder what part — I wonder if a man is less a traitor when he is twice a traitor?"

And he ruminated long before the portrait of a white-haired man with black eyebrows and a pink, painted sort of smile that seemed to contradict the black warning in the eyes.

THE DONNINGTON AFFAIR

1914

THE DONNINGTON AFFAIR

Part One

by Max Pemberton

The following statement of the Donnington affair has been written from the original notes by the Priest-in-charge of the Parish of Borrow-in-the-Vale.

John Barrington Cope came to Sussex from King's College, Cambridge, at a time when the aged vicar could no longer undertake single-handed even the pleasant duties of that rural charge.

He had been nearly two years at Borrow when the tragedy occurred. A man of considerable scholastic attainment, he appears immediately to have realised the magnitude of the mystery and to have set down, without loss of time, an orderly statement of the facts as they presented themselves to him.

The accepted lover of Evelyn Donnington's sister Harriet, he enjoyed the liberties of Borrow Close, and was almost daily at the house. It was at his suggestion that "another" was summoned from London to investigate a case which promised at an early moment to baffle alike the vigilance of the police and the curiosity of the public.

Mr. Cope's notes were written primarily for Father Brown's perusal. An amplification of them seems to be the swiftest method of putting the reading public in possession of the salient features of this amazing occurrence.

I

My name is John Barrington Cope, and I had been priest-in-charge of the parish of Borrow-in-the-Vale for twenty-one months.

I last saw Evelyn Donnington alive on Sunday evening at a quarter past ten o'clock. I had supped at Borrow Close as it has been my privilege to do almost every Sunday evening since I came to the parish. The fact that my fiancée, Harriet Donnington, was and is at Bath made no difference.

Sir Borrow Donnington has few friends. He is not a man who loves the society of other men, nor, for that matter, of women. It may be that I understand him a little better than his fellows. I am welcome at Borrow Close, and there is no other house which has a prior claim upon me.

I saw Evelyn Donnington alive and well at a quarter past ten on the evening of Sunday last, the 24th day of July. She came to the porch with me to tell me of a letter she had received from Harriet on the previous day, and there I said "good-night" to her.

The rectory stands perhaps a third part of a mile across the park, and is best reached by a bridle-path through what is known as Adam's Thicket. The way is dark and shut in by the magnificent beeches for which Borrow is famous. I saw no living thing as I returned to the rectory, nor heard any sound that was ominous.

Two hours later a footman from the Close awakened me to say that Evelyn was dead. "Murdered, sir!" he gasped, and without another word he ran on headlong towards the doctor's house.

I had fallen into a light sleep when this man's ring awakened me. There had been much trouble at Borrow Close since I came to the parish. The world is well acquainted with the nature of this, and knows much of the shame which has overtaken the Donnington family. Whatever sympathy it may have withheld from Sir Borrow Donnington himself, it has lavished freely upon his daughters.

To me Evelyn was already as a sister. I was to have married Harriet in September, though God knows what may be in store for us now.

Men deride omens, though often they are but the mind's logic waging a war upon our optimism. Though the affair of Southby Donnington would appear to have been settled by his conviction and imprisonment, I dreaded from the first that such could not be the end of it; and it was of Southby Donnington, Sir Borrow's only son, that I had been dreaming in my sleep when the footman awakened me.

What a sardonic chapter in the history of human nature! An only son—a wealthy father! Upon the one side a profligacy almost without parallel, upon the other side a parsimony stupendous in its ironic selfishness.

Southby Donnington was sent to Eton and to Trinity (Cambridge) as an Army candidate. A disgraceful affair at a gambling den in London, with a subsequent appearance at a police-court, finished his university career in his first term. He could not even pass the trivial examination now demanded for Sandhurst. He would suggest no other vocation. The man became a derelict in the dangerous seas of London's underworld. In vain his sisters pleaded with Sir Borrow. The baronet had finished with his son. A man of iron resolution which nothing could bend, he swore that Southby should never enter his house again. There followed the cataclysm.

We heard of the boy's arrest in London upon a charge of forgery. He was committed for trial, defended with what money his sisters could supply him, sent to the Old Bailey, convicted. The sentence was one of three years' penal servitude. We learned that he had been taken to Wormwood Scrubs, and nine months later that he was at Parkhurst.

It is no place here to dwell upon the secrets of the stricken house or of the aftermath of this terrible downfall.

Borrow Close is an old mansion lying between Ashdown Forest and Crowborough. It has always been remote from men and affairs, and there is no domain in the south of England so wonderful in its solitudes.

All about it is the forest. The very park is primeval woodland; here abounding in undergrowth so thick that the foot of man might never have been set therein; there characterised by marshy pools and groves where noonday is but a shimmer of reluctant light. Few were admitted to the house even in the days when Lady Donnington was its mistress. Since her death it has become mediæval in its isolation. The old baronet had nothing in common with his neighbours; his daughters were always afraid of him, and they go through life as it were on tiptoe, fearing that if they speak above a whisper they will awake the curiosity of the world beyond their gates.

It is true that Southby flouted the sanctities of this retreat, despite the baronet's displeasure. Parties of wild undergraduates made the "welkin ring" during the vacations; the story of Evelyn and Harriet's beauty was not unknown in the courts at Cambridge. Few of the boys, however, had the courage to persist, and I think that even Southby himself was astonished when Captain Willy Kennington appeared suddenly upon the scene as a suitor for Evelyn's hand, and was not to be repulsed even by Sir Borrow's savage discouragement.

Captain Kennington had met Evelyn at her aunt's house in Kensington some three months before the downfall. Her womanly gifts should have made an appeal to any man who became well acquainted with them, and I do not wonder that the young soldier surrendered to the spell.

Very simple in all her ideas, not a little afraid of the world, yet gifted with an imagination which years of solitary reading had stimulated, she seemed to be at once the woman and the child; wise above her years, yet afflicted by those ideals for which woman often pays so dearly. Fear of her father forbade that immediate acceptance of the soldier's advances which her heart dictated. She returned to Borrow Close, and was followed there shortly by the captain himself.

What was my astonishment to hear a few days later that Sir Borrow had refused all discussion of the matter, and in one of those violent paroxysms of temper, with which neither God nor man could reason, had ordered the captain from his house.

To give him his due, Southby played a man's part in this affair. He interceded warmly for his sister, returning from South Africa for that purpose. The scene between father and son is remembered at the Close as the culminating episode of an estrangement as discreditable to one as to the other. Passion dominated it, and set finality upon it. No word was spoken between these two men until the end.

Three months later Southby was a convict, and I remained the one man who visited the baronet in the days of his shame.

II

These are the events of sixteen months ago. I have already disclaimed any intention of dwelling upon the intimate days of sorrow which followed after. "The evil that men do lives after them," and while for the world the tragedy was but a nine days' wonder, it lay heavy upon the house of Borrow. No longer did the old baronet receive the visits of the few friends hitherto admitted to the Close. He shut the doors alike upon the old world and the new. His daughters saw no one but the servants and myself. In their turn, his neighbours shrank from him. Men had come to say that lust of gold drove Southby to the crime, and to believe that the boy was less guilty than the father.

The one man who stood by the stricken family was Captain Kennington, who owed so little to the baronet. Now, in the darkest hour, he came forward to demand Evelyn's hand anew. It went without saying that she would not accept him. A rare type of womanhood, the very fact that she loved was the barrier between them. Nothing, she felt, could ever blot out the shame of this happening, or minimise its consequences. The harvest of sin was not gathered in Parkhurst Prison, but here in the ancient house, where women reaped with sickles of tears.

My own relations to Harriet were, God be praised, but superficially affected by Southby's downfall. We had learned to know each other so well before the trouble came that it but set a seal upon our mutual sense of help and sacrifice, and although I knew that she would not marry me immediately, I left the future to lead us as it might. Sir Donnington himself now seemed to find in my society the sole consolation of his declining years. He did not go to church, but I visited them for worship early every Sunday morning, and was always at the Close to supper when in residence at the rectory.

So the months rolled on, and time, the healer, came to our aid. The bitterness of fear and doubt had passed down and given place to a brave attempt to face the future. We made many plans for Southby upon his release, and were determined to start him in a farm in South Africa if we could. Kennington went so far as to visit the prison and see the convict. His own father was one of the visiting inspectors, as it chanced, and so an advantage was permitted him.

He told us that he found Southby quite resigned to his fate, and he spoke of him as a man who was convinced that he had not committed a crime, but had been the victim of those who had betrayed him when they discovered that nothing was to be extorted from the baronet.

Parkhurst, it seems, is the gentleman's prison, and Southby was in aristocratic company there. I confess that the intimation was not without its saving humour, and permitted some reflection upon the permanence of those social aspirations which could afflict men even in a prison. Better, it appeared, to pick oakum with a lord than to earn an honest living among plebeians.[1]

Kennington spoke of cheerfulness and of content, but I remembered afterwards one phrase in his letter which should have struck me as significant. Prison makes strange bedfellows, and so far as man may have a confidant in captivity, Southby had found one in a man by the name of Mester.

"This fellow," said Kennington, "is the cheeriest soul possible. He has been well educated in France, where he fell upon evil times. Then he became chauffeur to an Austrian baron, entered a motor-car factory at Suresnes, turned his attention to flying at Issy, and finally was accused of a savage assault and an attempt to rob an old lady at Dover who was about to establish him in a motor-car business there."

Mester declared to the end that the crime was the work of others. He protested that he was the victim of circumstances, and that the clues upon which the police convicted him were false. Nevertheless, he was found guilty and sentenced to four years' penal servitude upon the day following Southby's conviction.

Between these men a strange friendship took root. Each believed himself wrongfully convicted; each could sympathise with the other. And just as Mester declared that he would bring the old baronet to his senses when he got out, so could Southby interest himself in Mester's story, and implore certain old colleagues on the Press to investigate it.

As we know, one great novelist has already busied himself with the affair, and is convinced of the man's innocence. Admittedly a person of no stable character and unquestionably the associate of thieves, there would yet seem to be a doubt whether the graver crime were committed, and quite a reasonable supposition that the police may have been in error.

[1] To "pick oakum"—a tedious chore for convicts of the time—means to pick old rope apart for the fiber.

Mester himself did not hesitate to affirm that if he were free for a month he would establish his innocence beyond all question. So convinced was he of this that he appears to have told Southby quite plainly that he would escape from Parkhurst if the opportunity presented itself.

I thought nothing of the matter at the time, and, indeed, the threat must be one often made by prisoners to whom crime has not become a habit and the cell a refuge. But I confess that astonishment was no word for it when, a few weeks later, upon opening my morning paper, I read that two men had escaped from Parkhurst, and, despite the efforts of the police, were still at large.

"Southby and Mester," I said to myself. I was not wrong, as you shall presently hear.

III

Here was an upset if you will, and one to send me running to the Close with the tidings. Sir Borrow himself I would not tell, dreading the effect of the news upon a mind so deranged; but Evelyn and Harriet heard me eagerly, and the former I began to suspect was already in possession of the story. This fact did not in the beginning impress me as it should have done. Some letter, I thought, must have come from Southby himself, and yet had I reflected upon it I would have perceived that such a thing was hardly possible under the circumstances.

The man had escaped but yesterday, and even had a letter been posted from the Isle of Wight or the mainland on the previous evening, it would not have reached Borrow Close at nine o'clock. Later on I discovered, quite accidentally, that Captain Kennington hinted at some such possibility in a letter received on the previous day, and whatever thoughts the discovery suggested, I kept them strictly to myself. The immediate thing was the excitement the news occasioned at the Close, and the momentous events which must follow upon it.

For my own part, I was early of the opinion that the fugitives would swiftly be overtaken, and that that would be the end of the matter.

Their escape, briefly narrated in the newspapers, had been admirably contrived. It appears that they scaled a high wall at a moment when a heavy mist drifted across the island from the mainland, that they then crossed an enclosure in which other prisoners were at work, climbed a second wall by the aid of a silk ladder, which they left behind them, and so made their way to the sea.

Authority believed that their flight was there cut short, and that they had not succeeded in reaching the mainland; but another account spoke of a mysterious motor-boat which had been seen recently off St. Catherine's Point, and, remembering Mester's acquaintance with the motor fraternity and its less desirable characters, the writer of the report seemed to be of the opinion that this might have some connexion with the matter. The latter, I must confess, occurred to me as a plausible deduction. These flying people are unusually clever. They possess a daring which is proved, and their resources are many. I detected now the meaning of Southby's friendship for this undesirable mechanic, and I saw that the men were pledged to make the attempt together. For the moment it looked as though they had succeeded.

It was a little before nine o'clock when I arrived at the Close, and not until after lunch that I left. As usual, Sir Borrow spent the morning about his gardens, and kept me some while with him speaking of this plant or that with which I was always familiar, but never naming the son who would succeed to this splendid inheritance. When he retired to his study at twelve o'clock, I took the girls aside and resumed a conversation so full of meaning for us all. Naturally, we asked each other many questions which we were unable to answer. Where would Southby go if he reached the mainland? Could he get money? Would he return to Borrow?

"If he comes here," said I, "he is lost! It will be the first place the police will watch!"

Harriet agreed with me in this. Yet where else could he go with any prospect of getting money, by which alone ultimate success could be assured?

We thought of many places, but of one with conviction. Sir Borrow's sister, the aged Lady Rosmar, then lived at Bath. She had been staunch to the boy as far as her means permitted, and might be still a friend to him in such an emergency as this. We decided that Harriet should go to Bath without loss of time, in case she could be of any assistance there. Evelyn and I, meanwhile, would watch and wait at Borrow. God knows what we hoped to do if the boy came there, yet I think we both prayed for his coming.

It seemed such an impossible thing that he could evade the hue and cry which must attend this flight. Yet if he did evade it, might not we take up his burden and start him in that new life wherein so much might be achieved if the lesson had been truly learned? Foolish the hope may have been, yet it came natural to those who had suffered so much, and over whom the prison gate was ever the emblem of a terrible sorrow. We believed that Southby would come, and in ten days' time our faith was justified. He was there at Borrow Close, the police upon his heels, his own father ignorant that the house harboured him. Of such dire things have I now to tell in the story that comes after.

IV

I have said that we supposed the house would be watched by the police, and in this we were not mistaken.

Frequently, in the few days immediately prior to Southby's return, I had seen strange men in the park, and more than once I had been stopped upon an idle pretence and questioned concerning Sir Borrow and his affairs. Such a subterfuge would have deceived no one, and, fortunately, I was able to deal with the men quite frankly.

"You are a police-officer," I said to one of them.

And he did not deny it.

"The lad's sure to come here, sir," was his answer, "and, if he does, we shall take him. There isn't a road within ten miles we are not watching."

We fell to other talk, and chiefly of the escape. Officially the police thought there had been some connivance on the part of the warders, but of this I naturally knew nothing.

"The young men had a lot of friends between them," the detective said, "and as for Lionel Mester, he knows half the crooks in Europe!"

I replied that in such a case the friends in question might be expected to shelter their comrades.

"And," said I, "it is idle to look for your men here. Surely you know of the relations between Sir Borrow and his son?"

He was much interested in this, and questioned me closely—a proceeding I did not resent under the circumstances. A few days later I was stopped in the park by an American lady and her daughter, who pretended to be much interested in the old place, and asked me if it were not possible to get permission to visit it. In these I recognised also the agents of the police, and I put them off with what excuses I could; not that it would have mattered at such a time, for Southby had not then returned. He was to come three days afterwards, at dead of night, and the two who were to know of his coming would have stood at nothing for his sake. They were his sister Evelyn and Wellman, the butler, who had loved Southby as his own son.

It was from Wellman himself that I had the news at nine o'clock on the following morning. He came carrying a pretended letter from Sir Borrow, and not until we were alone in my study, and the door shut behind us, did he dare to speak freely.

"Mr. Southby's home, sir," he said in a whisper. "He's in the priest's room." [2]

I feared to speak for a moment. Instantly I had visions of the hunted lad, fleeing from thicket to thicket of the forest he knew so well, and finally gaining that deep glen wherein is the subterranean entrance to the Close. That he had thought of it when none of us remembered! Of course, the police would know nothing of that. The very servants, save Wellman alone, are in ignorance of the existence of the passage, and locally it is believed that it perished long ago. Sir Borrow let them think so.

---

[2] Priests' rooms (or "priests' holes") were secret hiding spaces constructed in Catholic homes during the reign of Elizabeth I, when priests were considered enemy agents and harboring them was a crime.

It was one of his humours to have the place opened up by the engineers who came from London to sink his artesian well. He liked to go to and fro as he pleased, to catch his servants when they least expected him. And so he used the priest's room for the purpose, or did use it until the tragedy happened. Nothing afterwards interested him. The secret chamber remained unopened after Southby was convicted. The rest of us, I think, had almost forgotten its existence.

The chamber lies at the western end of the long gallery. There is an octagon tower there, with an ancient stone staircase cunningly built within its walls. To this you gain access from the gallery by opening a panel upon the right-hand side of the smaller chimney. The room lies at the foot of one flight of stairs, and is lighted from two narrow windows giving upon the battlements. These are filled by stained glass of the fourteenth century, and show former abbots of Borrow in alb and chasuble. The room itself is large and commodious, and has a fireplace and an alcove for the bed. Those who desire to go from it to the forest descend the staircase until they find themselves in the old crypt which dates from Saxon times. The subterranean passage leads from that to Adam's Thicket, where it enters an ancient well, long dried up, and now but a pit of grass and bramble. I did not doubt that Southby had gained the forest by a devious route and had made his way by one of those paths which no stranger would discover. And so he had gone straight to the priest's chamber, and thence to Evelyn's bedroom.

"He waked her about one this morning," said Wellman, who still appeared to be trembling with the excitement of the news. "They wouldn't let you know sooner, sir, for fear of the police. Miss Evelyn is dreadfully afraid that the squire will find out, and so I came to you at once. Lucky for us, it was only yesterday afternoon that Superintendent Matthews searched the Close from garret to cellar. He must have had wind that Mr. Southby was on the road."

I was astonished to hear this.

"Superintendent Matthews—yesterday!" I exclaimed. "Is it really possible, and Miss Evelyn told me nothing of it? But, of course, it may have been difficult to send. Does he know anything of the priest's hole, Wellman? Surely you don't fear that?"

He shook his head, being a man of uncommon caution.

"They know a great deal too much nowadays, sir—more's the pity. The question is, what are we to do with the young master, since Miss Evelyn is at her wits' end? She would be pleased to see you at the Close, indeed and she would. It's a hard task for a young lady, as you can well imagine, sir."

I agreed, and, putting on my hat, went over with him immediately. Our way lay through Adam's Thicket, and I confess that I suffered some alarm when a stranger appeared upon our path not a hundred paces from the ancient basin by which the passage is reached. He was a short, thick-set man, wearing a serge suit with black leather leggings and a peaked cap, and when he saw us he stopped abruptly for a moment, then turned his back upon us and pretended to light a cigarette while we passed.

"He is no policeman," I said to Wellman, when the stranger was out of hearing. The old servant agreed with me.

"But he might be an inquiry agent, sir. I've heard tell in London of the tricks they play with their clothes. Don't trust him too far."

"I am not going to trust him at all," said I. "The fellow looked to me as though he were a chauffeur."

"A bad lot, believe me, sir. There's been few honest men upon wheels since they robbed us of our horses. A man wants the nose of a setter to keep track of such as him. I wouldn't trust one of them with a silver-plated soup-ladle, upon my word I wouldn't."

I told him he was a laudator temporis acti,[3] but as that conveyed nothing to him we pushed on, and found Evelyn in the boudoir.

She was dreadfully agitated, but Sir Borrow being there, no word of the affair might pass between us. The baronet plainly thought that his daughter had become hysterical, and when I was alone with him he hinted that she must have had some news from that d—d scoundrel.

"Whatever it is," he added, "I don't want to hear of it or of him. It would be a great day for me if the fellow were six feet underground, and I hope to God he soon will be. That's the truth, Cope, and none

[3] Cope has quoted the *Ars Poetica* of the Roman poet Horace (65–68 B.C.): "*laudator temporis acti se puero*", literally, "a praiser of the time when he was a lad").

of your philosophy can change it. I have no longer a son; I am trying to forget that I ever had one."

I shrank from his anger, knowing well how little such a man would suffer a rebuke. Happily, he set out to drive into the town almost immediately, and Evelyn and I went at once to the priest's hole and interviewed Southby. He was in a sorry plight, I must say, his face and hands torn by the brambles of the thickets, his clothes splashed with mud, his beard unshaved, and his eyes bloodshot. I thought also a little delirious from want of food and exposure, and he talked incoherently of ships and the sea, of men who had betrayed him, and of others who were his friends. By-and-by, when he became calmer, he told me that the ignominy of prison affected him to such an extent that he would have gone mad if he had remained at Parkhurst.

"I couldn't have done it, Cope, by God I couldn't," he said. "You don't know what it means to a man who has lived as I have. I had to go or it would have been all up with me. If they take me I will shoot myself. That's an oath and I'll keep it."

"But," cried I, "whatever will you do, Southby? You must know that we cannot long protect you here."

He laughed defiantly, pushing the black hair from his forehead quite in the old way.

"Lionel will do it," he said. "I trust Lionel. He got me out; he'll see I don't get in again. You must know Lionel. He's a white man all through, and the prison that can hold him has got to be made. Why, it was his idea about the motor-boat—who else would have thought of it? —he and his friend at Hendon. They picked us up in the cove at high tide, and we were landed at Hayling Island before morning. I knew we should get through when Lionel undertook it."

"Then," exclaimed I, quite at hazard, "Captain Kennington knew nothing of it?"

His brow darkened at this. He looked at Evelyn curiously, and appeared afraid to speak out.

"No, I don't trust Kennington—not much. Mind what you're doing in that quarter, Evelyn. Kennington isn't thirty cents—you remember it."

She flashed out at this, a girl of spirit and a good heart.

"Do not say a word against Captain Kennington!" she cried. "He is the only friend you ever had who remained staunch to you. You should be grateful to him."

He still persisted, though with a weakening resolution.

"That may or may not be. It's my opinion he tried to give us away, and I shall stick to it. Now, get me a drink for heaven's sake. I am as dry as a camel."

She fetched him a brandy-and-soda, and he drank it eagerly. It was already a danger to pass to and from the long gallery, and I began to perceive the peril of the situation. Let the servants know and sooner or later the news would go to the village, and thence to the police. When we discussed it frankly between ourselves there seemed but one solution. Evelyn must be ill, and Harriet must be recalled from Bath to wait upon her. Meanwhile, Wellman must have a confidant, and none seemed better suited to the purpose than Turner, the head housemaid. Sooner or later this woman would discover us. We determined that it should be sooner, and, calling her to the conference, we put our fortunes into her hands. Good woman, she had a brother of her own, and Evelyn was beloved by them all.

We made our plans, and for the moment they were successful.

Harriet, unfortunately, could not return from Bath, her aunt being taken seriously ill and really requiring her assistance. Evelyn, however, feigned an indisposition very cleverly, and although it put me to some conscientious difficulty, I suffered myself to think of the greater good of that unhappy family and to acquiesce. Nevertheless, I understood that it was but a brief respite. The perils of the situation were manifest. Any day, any hour might discover us, and we began to go as those who feared their own shadows.

Perhaps my fears may have been responsible for a delusion, but there were moments when I thought that Sir Borrow suspected us. His manner became suddenly aggressive, and he questioned me more closely than he had done for a long time. Had I heard from that "d—d" son of his? Was Evelyn worrying about "the worthless scoundrel"? To all of which I responded with what wit I could, though God knows my position was difficult. Later on I discovered him in Evelyn's bedroom, and that very night, after dinner, he spoke of Kennington. Oddly enough, his opinion of that gallant soldier was exactly that of his son. He did not trust him, doubted his record, and stigmatised him most unjustly as a penniless adventurer. As to my knowledge the captain is in possession of an income of eight hundred pounds a year, I resented the slander, and did not fear to speak my mind. The result was a sharp quarrel, and the expression upon his part of a shabby apology, with which in any other circumstances I would have been far from satisfied. As it was, I had to bear with him, and to listen while he told me that, whatever happened, he would not have Kennington in the house again. Then he went off to his study, I to the priest's room to tell them of my suspicions.

Southby had always been afraid of his father. My news alarmed him, and he did not hesitate to affirm that the old man would deliver him up to the police should he be discovered at the Close. Evelyn herself appeared to be of the same opinion, and when we were alone she confessed the terror of her situation.

"Captain Kennington is coming here at the week-end," she said. I told her what Sir Borrow had said, and it did but alarm her the more. "Sometimes I wish I were dead," she declared.

And I, who knew how much that gentle soul had suffered, prayed to God that strength might be granted her.

The following night I was to meet Lionel Mester in the thicket, and to experience an apprehension more acute than any I had yet suffered in this woeful affair.

It was the Sabbath eve, and I was returning from the Close to the choir practice in our beautiful old parish church. A hundred yards from the well's head, where the secret entrance lies, I met again the short, thick-set man whom Wellman had declared to be a detective. This time he stopped, and begging me to step aside into the thicket, he introduced himself immediately.

"You'll have heard of me, sir—Lionel Mester, Mr. Southby's pal."

"Yes," I said, "I have heard of you. Why do you come to this dangerous place?"

"Because there's something Southby must know, and it can't come any other way. You see him every day, and can take this letter to him. I've been hanging about nearly a week trying to get it delivered.

Usually I don't trust devil dodgers[4]—not much. But you've got a decent mug on you, and I'm going to trust you. Take him this letter, and tell him, if he acts on it, it's all right and the wheels go round. Otherwise I do a double watch, and be d—d to it! Lord, I've been sleeping on stinging nettles for a week, and that's about enough of it! Tell Southby so, and you'll see no more of me."

He thrust a bulky letter into my hand, and was about to say more when we heard a sound of footsteps, and instantly he plunged into the undergrowth with the agility of a wild-cat. He was shod, I saw, in rubber-soled shoes, and carried a formidable stick; but the quickness of his movements was the surprising thing, and uttering but one word "police," he disappeared from my view. For my part, I thrust the letter into the inner pocket of my coat and at once regained the path. Fifty paces further on I passed Superintendent Matthews, and exchanged a good-night with him. He appeared to be in a hurry, and was going towards the Hall. But he did not stop to gossip with me, as he usually does, and for that I was grateful.

It will be understood that this unexpected turn perplexed me very much. I had expected that Lionel Mester would come to Borrow sooner or later, but now that he had come I perceived how considerable a danger he must be to us all. It was not to be hidden from me that I myself might be the victim of this unhappy family, and must answer to the law for the part that I had played. So much I was willing to do for a woman's sake, but now that discovery trod upon our heels, and all the shame and suffering of exposure hovered in the shadows about that ancient house, I confess that my courage almost failed me. The letter seemed a damning document which would convict me in any court. Yet I determined to deliver it, and that very night, about ten o'clock, I went up to the Hall and put it into Evelyn's hands. Upon my return an unknown man followed me through the thicket, and watched me enter the rectory. I believe that he was a police officer, though whether he were so or not mattered little since the letter was delivered.

---

[4] In the slang of the day, a "devil dodger" was a parson or preacher.

That night I slept but ill, fearing so many things, dreading the peril of a situation which had become almost intolerable. The next day was the Sabbath, given almost entirely to the schools and the church, and it was not until we sat down to supper at the Close that I got the news of Evelyn. She had given out that she was a little better, and would sit down with us. The few words we exchanged in the porch when I said "Good-night" to her were of some moment, though not unexpected.

"Southby is going tonight," she said.

I answered, "Thank God," for I knew that none of us could stand the strain of it much longer.

And so we parted, and I was never to see her alive again. So brave, so gentle she was, blessed among women truly, an offering to man's sin, a martyr for whom men's tears should fall. They heard a loud cry in the house a little before midnight. Sir Borrow was awake, and first upon the scene. They found her lying at the foot of the circular staircase which leads down from the long gallery to the secret room. Evidently there had been a struggle. A jagged bar of iron lay upon the stairs at her feet. The lamp she had carried was shattered; the very window in the angle of the octagon was broken, and the glass littered about. What was not a little remarkable was the discovery of nine pounds in gold wrapped in a yellow kid glove, the very shape and colour of the gloves always worn by Captain Kennington.

She was dressed in a long bedgown, I should tell you, and wore a dressing gown over it. The door of the secret chamber stood open, but no one was to be discerned within. Southby had fled the house. Sir Borrow and Wellman alone stooped to the assistance of the stricken woman.

She was quite dead, a terrible wound in the throat having deprived her of life almost instantaneously. Naturally the police were called upon the instant, and not a moment was lost by them. Beaters began to search every thicket of the forest round about; there were motors abroad upon every road. Yet nothing was discovered, not a shadow of a clue to be found. Even Captain Kennington could offer no suggestion. I discovered to my surprise that he had come

448   THE DONNINGTON AFFAIR

to Borrow on Saturday evening as he promised, but hearing Evelyn's story had gone to the town to sleep. The hue and cry waked him—to such a morn as few men are called upon to live.

And so here is this terrible crime committed, and no man to be brought to justice for it. God send us enlightenment that the guilty may be punished!

Part Two

by G. K. Chesterton

It was natural, of course, that we should think of calling in expert opinion on the tragedy; or, at least, something subtler than the passing policeman. But I could think of few people or none whom it would be useful to consult thus privately. I remembered an investigator who had taken some interest in Southby's original trouble; merely because I remembered the curious surname of Shrike; but report told me that he had since grown rich and retired, and was now yachting inaccessibly among the Pacific Islands.

My old friend Brown, the Roman priest at Cobhole, who had often given me good advice in small problems, had wired that he feared he could not come down, even for an hour. He merely added—what, I confess, I thought inconsequent—that the key might be found in the sentence that "Mester was the cheeriest soul possible."

Superintendent Matthews still carries weight with any considering person who has actually talked to him; but he is naturally in most cases officially reticent, and in some cases officially slow.

Sir Borrow seemed stricken rigid by this final tragedy; a thing pardonable enough in a very old man who, whatever his faults, had never had anything but tragedy upon tragedy out of his own blood and name.

Wellman can be trusted with anything up to the Crown jewels; but not with an idea. Harriet is far too good a woman to be a good detective. So I was left with my unsatisfied appetite for expert advice. I think the others shared it to some extent; I think we wished a man different from all of us would walk into the room, a man of the world outside us, a man of wider experience, a man of experience so wide—if it were possible—that he should know even one case that was like our own. Certainly none of us had the wildest suspicion of who the man would be.

I have explained that when poor Evelyn's body was found it was clad in a dressing-gown, as if she had been suddenly summoned from her room, and the door of the Priest's Room stood open. Acting on I know not what impulse, I had closed it to; and, so far as I know, it was not opened again till it was opened from within. I confess that for me that opening was terrible.

Sir Borrow, Wellman, and I were alone in the chamber of slaughter. At least we were alone till a total stranger strolled into the room, without even pulling the peaked cap off his head. He was a sturdy man, stained with travel, especially as regards his leggings, which were loaded with clay and slime of innumerable ditches. But he was entirely unconcerned, which is more than I was. For, despite his extra dirt and his extra impudence, I recognised him as the fugitive convict, Mester, whose letter I had so foolishly passed on to his fellow convict. He entered the room with his hands in his pockets, and whistling. Then the whistling ceased, and he said:

"You seem to have shut the door again. I suppose you know it's not easy to open again on this side."

Through the broken window which gave upon the garden I could see Superintendent Matthews standing passively among the shrubs, with his broad back to the house. I walked to the window, and also whistled, but in a far more practical spirit. And yet, I know not why I should call it practical, for the superintendent, who must have heard me, did not turn his head, nor so much as shift a shoulder.

"I shouldn't worry poor old Matthews," said the man in the peaked cap in a friendly tone, "he is one of the best men in the service, and he must be awfully tired. I expect I can answer nearly all the questions that he could." And he relighted a cigarette.

"Mr. Mester," I replied with some heat, "I was sending for the superintendent to arrest you!"

"Quite so," he answered, throwing his wax match out of the window. "Well, he won't!"

He was gazing at me with a grave stolidity. And yet I fancy that the gravity of his full face had less effect on me than the large, indifferent back of the policeman.

The man called Mester resumed.

"I mean that my position here may not be quite what you suppose. It's true enough I assisted the young fellow to escape; but I don't imagine you know why I did it. It is an old rule in our profession —"

Before he could finish I had uttered a cry.

"Stop!" I cried out. "Who is that behind the door?"

I could see, by the very movement of Mester's mouth, that he was just about to answer, "What door?" But before the lips could move he also was answered. And from behind the sealed door of the secret chamber came the noise of something that was alive, if it were not human, or was moving, if it were not alive.

"What is in the Priest's Room?" I cried, and looked round for something with which to break down the door. I had half lifted the piece of jagged iron bar for the purpose. And then the horrid part it had played in that night overwhelmed me, and I fell against the door and beat on it with feeble hands, only repeating, "What is in the Priest's Room?" It was the awful fact that a voice, obscure but human, answered from behind the closed door, "The Priest!"

The heavy door was opened very slowly, apparently pushed by a hand no stronger than my own. The same voice which had said "The Priest," said in rather simpler tones, "Whom else did you expect?" The door swung out slowly to the full compass of its hinges, and revealed the black silhouette of a stumpy, apologetic person, with a big hat and a bad umbrella. He was in every way a very unromantic and inappropriate person to be in the Priest's Room, save in the accidental detail of being a priest.

He walked straight up to me before I could cry, "You have come, after all!"

He shook my hand, and, before he dropped it, looked at me with a steady and singular expression, sad, and yet rather serious than sad. I can only say it was the face we wear at the funeral of one dear as a friend, not that we wear by the deathbed of any directly dear to us.

"I can at least congratulate *you*," said Father Brown.

I think I put my hand wildly through my hair. I am sure I answered:
"And what is there in this nightmare on which I can be congratulated?"

He answered me with the same solid face:
"On the innocence of the woman who will be your wife."

"No one," I cried indignantly, "has attempted to connect her with the matter."

He nodded gravely, as if in assent.

"That was the danger, doubtless," he said with a slight sigh, "but she's all right now, thank God. Isn't she?" And as if to give the last touch to the topsyturvydom, he turned to ask his question of the man in the peaked cap.

"Oh, she's safe enough!" said the man called Mester.

I cannot deny that there was suddenly lifted off my heart a load of doubt, which I had never known was there. But I was bound to pursue the problem.

"Do you mean, Father Brown," I asked, "that you know who was the guilty person?"

"In a sense, yes," he answered. "But you must remember that in a murder case the guiltiest person is not always the murderer."

"Well, the guiltiest person, then," I cried impatiently. "How are we to bring the guiltiest person to punishment?"

"The guiltiest person is punished," said Father Brown.

There was a long silence in the twilight turret, and my mind laboured with doubts that were too large for it. At last Mester said gruffly, but not without a kind of good-nature:

"I think you two reverend gentlemen had better go and have a talk somewhere. About Hades, say, or hassocks, or whatever you do talk about. I shall have to look into this by myself. My name is Stephen Shrike; you may have heard of me."

Even before such fancies had been swallowed up in my sudden fear at the movements in the secret room, I had faced the startling possibility that this escaped convict was really a detective. But I had not dreamed of his being so famous a one. The man who had been concerned for Southby, and since gained colossal prestige, had some claim in the case; and I followed Brown, who had already strolled down towards the entrance of the garden.

"The distinction between Hades and hassocks—" began Father Brown.

"Don't play the fool!" I said, roughly enough.

"Was not without some philosophical value," continued the little priest, with unruffled good temper. "Human troubles are mostly of two kinds. There is an accidental kind, that you can't see because they are so close you fall over as you do over a hassock. And there is the other kind of evil, the real kind. And that a man will go to seek however far off it is—down, down, into the lost abyss." And he unconsciously pointed his stumpy finger downward towards the grass, which was sprinkled with daisies.

"It was good of you to come, after all," I said; "but I wish I could make more sense of the things you say."

"Well," he replied patiently, "have you made sense of the one thing I did say before I came down?"

"Why, you made some wild statement," I replied, "that the key of the story was in Mester's being cheerful, but—why, bless my soul, and so it is the key, in a way!"

"Only the key, so far," said my companion, "but my first guess seems to have been right. It is not very common to find such sparkling gaiety in people undergoing penal servitude, especially when ruined on a false charge. And it seemed to me that Mester's optimism was a little overdone. I also suspected that his aviation, and all the rest of it, true or false, were simply meant to make Southby think the escape feasible. But if Mester was such a demon for escaping, why didn't he escape by himself? Why was he so anxious to lug along a young gentleman who does not seem to have been much use to him? As I was wondering, my eye fell on another sentence in your manuscript."

"What was that?" I asked.

He took out a scrap of paper on which there were some scribbles in pencil, and read out:

"'They then crossed an enclosure in which other prisoners were at work.'"

After another pause, he resumed:

"That, of course, was plain enough. What kind of convict prison is it where prisoners work without any warders overseeing or walking about? What sort of warders are they to allow two convicts to climb two walls and go off as if for a picnic? All that is plain. And the conclusion is plainer from many other sentences. 'It seemed such an impossible thing that he could evade the hue and cry that must attend this flight.' It would have been impossible if there *had* been any hue and cry. 'Evelyn and Harriet heard me eagerly, and the former, I began to suspect, was already in possession of the story.' How could she be in possession of it so early as that, unless the police cars and telephones helped to send word from Southby? Could the convicts catch a camel or an ostrich? And look at the motor-boat. Do motor-boats grow on trees? No, that's all simple. Not only was the companion in the escape a police detective, but the whole scheme of the escape was a police scheme, engineered by the highest authorities of the prison."

"But why?" I asked, staring. "And what has Southby to do with it?"

"Southby had nothing to do with it," he answered. "I believe he is now hiding in some ditch or wood in the sincere belief that he is a hunted fugitive. But they won't trouble him any more. He has done their work for them. He is innocent. It was essential that he should be innocent."

"Oh, I don't understand all this!" I cried impatiently.

"I don't understand half of this," said Father Brown. "There are all sorts of difficulties I will ask you about later. You knew the family. I only say that the sentence about cheerfulness *did* turn out to be a key-sentence, after all. Now, I want you to concentrate your attention on another key-sentence. 'We decided that Harriet should go to Bath without loss of time, in case she should be of any assistance there.' Note that this comes soon after your expression of surprise that someone should have communicated with Evelyn so early. Well, I suppose we none of us think the governor of the prison wired to her, 'Have connived at escape of your brother, Convict 99.' The message must have come in Southby's name, at any rate."

I ruminated, looking at the roll of the downs as it rose and repeated itself through every gap in the garden trees; then I said, "Kennington?"

My old friend looked at me for a moment with a look which, this time, I could not analyse.

"Captain Kennington's part in the business is unique in my experience," he said, "and I think we had better return to him later. It is enough that, by your own account, Southby did not give him his confidence."

I looked again at the glimpses of the downs, and they looked grander but greyer, as my companion went on, like one who can only put things in their proper order.

"I mean the argument here is close, but clear. If she had any secret message from her brother about his escaping, why shouldn't she have a message about where he was escaping to? Why should she send off her sister to Bath, when she might just as well have been told that her brother wasn't going there? Surely a young gentleman might more safely say, in a private letter, that he was going to Bath than that he was escaping from prison? Somebody or something must have influenced Southby to leave his destination uncertain. And who could influence Southby except the companion of his flight?"

"Who was acting for the police, on your theory."

"No. On his confession." After a sort of snorting silence, Brown said, with an emphasis I have never seen in him, throwing himself on a garden-seat: "I tell you this whole business of the two cities of refuge—this whole business of Harriet Donnington going to Bath—was a suggestion that came through Southby, but from Mester, or Shrike, or whatever his name is, and is the key of the police plot."

He had settled himself on a seat facing me, clasping his hands over the huge head of his umbrella in a more truculent manner than was typical of him. But an evening moon was brightening above the little plantation under which he sat, and when I saw his plain face again, I saw it was as mild as the moon.

"But why," I asked, "should they want such a plot?"

"To separate the sisters," he said. "That is the key."

I answered quickly, "The sisters could not really be separated."

"Yes, they could," said Father Brown, "quite simply, and that is why—" Here his simplicity failed, and he hesitated.

"That is why?" I insisted.

"That is why I can congratulate you," he said at last.

Silence sank again for a little, and I could not define the irritation with which I answered:

"Oh, I suppose you know all about it?"

"No, no, really!" he said, leaning forward as if to deny an accusation of injustice. "I am puzzled about the whole business. Why didn't the warders find it sooner? Why did they find it at all? Was it slipped in the lining? Or is the handwriting so bad as that? I know about the thing being gentlemanly; but surely they took his clothes! How could the message come? It *must* be the lining."

His face was turned up as honestly as a flat and floating fish, and I could say with corresponding mildness:

"I really do not know what you are talking about, you and your linings. But if you mean how could Southby get his message safely to his sister without the risks of interception, I should say there were no people more likely to do it successfully. The boy and girl were always great friends from childhood, and had, to my knowledge, one of those secret languages that children often have, which may easily have been turned afterwards into some sort of cypher. And now I come to think of it —"

The heavy-knobbed umbrella slipped from the seat and slammed on the gravel, and the priest stood upright.

"What an idiot I am!" he said. "Why, anybody might have thought of a cypher! That was a score for you, my friend. I suppose you know all about it now?"

I am certain he did not realise that he was repeating in sincerity what I had said in irony.

"No," I answered, with real seriousness; "I do not know all about it, but I think it quite possible that you do. Tell me the story."

"It is not a good story," he said, in a rather stony way — "at least, the good thing about it is that it is over. But first let me say what I least like saying—that you must be prepared for a different view of a character that you knew well. I have thought a good deal about a certain kind of intellectual English lady, especially when she is at once aristocratic and provincial. I think she is judged much too easily. Or, perhaps, I should say, judged much too hardly; since she is supposed to be incapable of mortal passions and temptations. Let her decline champagne at dinner, let her be beautiful and know what is meant by dignity in dress, let her read a great many books and talk about high ideals, and you all assume that she alone of her kind cannot covet or lie;[5] that her ideas are always simple, and her ideals always fulfilled. But, really and truly, my friend, by your account of it, the character was more mixed than that. Evelyn feigned an indisposition very cleverly. Assuming her to be blameless, I cannot see why she needed to feign anything. But, anyhow, it is scarcely one of the powers given to the saints. You 'began to suspect' that Evelyn already knew about the escape. Why didn't she *tell* you she already knew about it? You were astonished that Superintendent Matthews had called, and she had been silent about it; but you supposed it was difficult to send. Why should it be difficult to send? You seem to have been sent for whenever you were really wanted. No; I will try to speak of this woman as of one for whose soul I will pray, and whose true defence I shall never hear. But while there are living people whose honour is in cruel danger undeservedly, I simply refuse to start with the assumption that Evelyn Donnington could do no wrong."

The noble hills of Sussex looked as dreary as Yorkshire moors as he went on heavily, prodding the earth with his umbrella.

"The first facts in her defence, if she needed one, are that her father is a miser, that he has a violent temper combined with a rather Puritanic sort of family pride; and, above all, that she was afraid of him. Now, suppose she really wanted money, perhaps for a good purpose; or, again, perhaps not. She and her brother, you told me, had always had secret languages and plots; they are common among cowed and terrorised children. I firmly believe myself that she went a step further in some desperate strait, and that she was really and criminally responsible for the false document with which her brother seemed to be seeking financial help. We

[5] The phrase "she alone of her kind", has a long history and ultimately traces back to *Paschale Carmen* by the fifth-century Roman poet Caelius Sedulius: "Sola sine exemplo placuisti femina Christo." ("You alone, without exception among women, have been pleasing to Christ.")

know there is often a family resemblance in handwritings almost amounting to facsimile. I cannot see, therefore, why there should not be a similar family resemblance in the flaws by which experts detect a forgery. Anyhow, the brother had a bad record, which goes for a great deal more than it ought with the police; and he was sent to gaol. I think you will agree that he has a very good record now."

"You mean," I said, curiously thrilled by the very restraint of his expression, "that Southby suffered all that time rather than speak?"

"Rejoice not against me, Satan, mine enemy," said Father Brown, "for when I fall I shall arise.[6] This part of the story really is good."

After a silence he continued:

"When he was arrested, I am now almost certain, he had on him some letter or message from his sister. I hope and believe that it was some sort of penitent message. But whatever it was, it must have contained two things—some admission or allusion that made her own guilt clear, and some urgent request that her brother should come straight to her as soon as he was free to do so. Most important of all, it was not signed with a Christian name, but only 'Your unhappy sister.' "

"But, my good man," I cried, "you talk as if you had seen the letter!"

"I see it in its consequences," he answered. "The friendship with Mester, the quarrel with Kennington, the sister in Bath and the brother in the Priest's Room, came from that letter, and no other letter."

"The letter, however, was in cypher; and one very hard to follow, having been invented by children. Does that strike you as paradoxical? Don't you know that the hardest signs to read are arbitrary ones? And if two children agree that 'grunk' means bedtime and 'splosh' means Uncle William, it would take an expert much longer to learn this than to expose any system of substituted letters or numbers. Consequently, though the police found the paper, of course, it took them

---

[6] Father Brown's words echo the Old Testament's "Rejoice not against me: when I fall I shall arise" (Micah 7:8).

half-way through Southby's term to make head or tail of it. Then they knew that one of Southby's sisters was guilty, that he was innocent; and by this time they had the sense to see that he would never betray the truth. The rest, as I said, was simple and logical. The only other thing they could do was to take advantage of Southby being asked to go straight to his guilty correspondent. He was given every facility for escaping and communicating as quickly as possible, so long as the police could secure the separation of the sisters, by Mester getting the other one to Bath. Given that, the sister Southby went for must be the guilty one. And when, through those awful nights, the police gathered round you thick as wolves and still as ghosts—it was not for Southby they were waiting."

"But why did they wait for anyone?" I asked suddenly, after a silence. "If they were sure, why didn't they arrest?"

He nodded and sighed:

"Perhaps you're right. Perhaps it's best to take the Kennington case here. Well, of course, he knew all about it from the inside. You yourself noticed that he had privileges in that prison. It will grieve you, as a law-abiding person, to learn that he used his power to intercept what had been decided. A good deal can be done by missing appointments. A good deal more can be done by not missing people—vulgarly known as hitting them. He used every chance, right or wrong, to delay the arrest. One of the thousand small, desperate delays was 'feigning illness.' "

"Why did Southby call him a traitor?" I said suspiciously.

"On exceedingly good grounds," said my friend. "Suppose you had broken prison in all innocence, and your friend sent his car for you and it took you back there? Suppose your friend offered to get you away in his yacht, and it took the wrong course, till overtaken by a motor-boat? Suppose Southby was trying to get to Sussex, and Kennington always headed him off towards Cornwall or Ireland or Normandy, what would you expect Southby to call him?"

"Well," I said, "what would you call him?"

"Oh," said Father Brown, "I call him a hero."

I peered at his rather featureless face through the moony twilight; and then he suddenly rose and paced the path with the impatience of a schoolboy.

"If I could put pen to paper, I would write the best adventure story ever written about this. Was there ever such a situation? Southby was kicked backwards and forwards, as unconscious as a football, between two very able and vigorous men, one of whom wanted to make the footprints point towards the guilty sister, while the other wanted to twist the feet away at every turn. And Southby thought the friend of his house was his enemy, and the destroyer of his house his friend. The two that knew must fight in silence, for Mester could not speak without warning Southby, and Kennington could not speak without denouncing Evelyn. It is clear from Southby's words, about false friends and the sea, that Kennington eventually kidnapped Southby in a yacht, but lord knows in how many tangled woods, or river islands, or lanes leading nowhere, the same fight was fought; the fugitive and detective trying to keep the trail, the traitor and true lover trying to confuse it. When Mester won, and his men gathered round this house, the captain could do no more than come here and offer his help, but Evelyn would not open the door to him."

"But why not?"

"Because she had the fine side of fear as well as the bad side," said Father Brown. "'Not a little afraid of life' you said, with great penetration. She was afraid to go to prison; but, to her honour, she was afraid to get married, too. It is a type produced by all this refinement. My friend, I want to tell you and all your modern world a secret. You will never get to the good in people till you have been through the bad in them."

After a moment he added that we ought to be returning to the house, and walked yet more briskly in that direction.

"Of course," he remarked, as he did so, "the packet of banknotes you took through to Southby was only to help him away and spare him Evelyn's arrest. Mester's not a bad fellow for a 'tec. But she realised her danger, and was trying to get into the Priest's Room."

I was still brooding on the queer case of Kennington.

"Was not the glove found?" I asked.

"Was not the window broken?" he asked in return. "A man's glove twisted properly and loaded with nine pounds in gold, and probably a letter as well, will break most windows if it is slung by a man who has been a bowler. Of course, there was a note. And, of course, the note was imprudent. It left money for escape, and left the proofs of what she was escaping from."

"And then what happened to her?" I asked dully.

"Something of what happened to you," he said. "You also found the secret door difficult to open from outside. You also caught up that crooked curtain-rod or window-bar to beat on it. You also saw the door opening slowly from within. But you did not see what she saw."

"And what did she see?" I said at last.

"She saw the man she had wronged most," said Father Brown.

"Do you mean Southby?"

"No," he said, "Southby has shown heroic virtue, and he is happy. The man she wronged most was a man who had never had, or tried to have, more than one virtue—a kind of acrid justice. And she had made him unjust all his life—made him pamper the wicked woman and ruin the righteous man. You told me in your notes that he often hid in the Priest's Room, to discover who was faithful or unfaithful. This time he came out holding a sword left in that room in the days when men hunted my religion. He found the letter, but, of course, he destroyed it after he had done—what he did. Yes, old friend, I can feel the horror on your face without seeing it. But, indeed, you modern people do not know how many kinds of men there are in the world. I am not talking of approval, but of sympathy—the sort of sympathy I give to Evelyn Donnington. Have you *no* sympathy with cold, barbaric justice, or with the awful appeasements of such an intellectual appetite? Have you *no* sympathy with the Brutus who killed his friend? Have you *no* sympathy with the monarch who killed his son? Have you *no* sympathy with Virginius, who killed —.[7] But I think we must go in now."

We mounted the stairs in silence, but my surging soul expected some scene surpassing all the scenes of that tower. And in a sense I

[7] Father Brown alludes to three ancient stories often retold in modern literature: the Roman Marcus Brutus was the prime assassin of Julius Cæsar after Cæsar had appointed him Prætor; in the Persion legend, King Rustum unwittingly fought and killed his own son, Sohrab; in early Roman history, a centurion named Virginius killed his daughter rather than see her enslaved and debauched.

had it. The room was empty, save for Wellman, who stood behind an empty chair as impassively as if there had been a thousand guests.

"They have sent for Dr. Browning, sir," he said in colourless tones.

"What do you mean?" I cried. "There was no question about the death?"

"No, sir," he said, with a slight cough; "Dr. Browning required another doctor to be sent from Chichester, and they took Sir Borrow away." [8]

---

[8] According to the Madhouse Act of 1828, the one requirement for committing a person to an asylum was for two doctors to issue a medical certificate.

The text of this book has been set in Bembo by Beljan, Ltd., Dexter, Michigan. Printed on Glatfelter Spring Grove Offset, B-18 text stock by Thomson-Shore, Inc., Dexter, Michigan. Bound by Thomson-Shore, Inc. The cover and jacket design are by Darlene Lawless O'Rourke of Loyola Graphics, San Bruno, California.